WORTHY OF THIS GREAT CITY

A NOVEL

MIKE MILLER

PROLOGUE

"Everybody thinks God is on their side." Ruth put her coffee cup down on its heavy white restaurant saucer very deliberately, watching herself. Then she sent me this look full of drama, her huge blue eyes wary but defiant.

I'm a journalist, I should explain, and I knew this woman just well enough to be immediately dismissive. But she was very intense, now I noticed; waiting for me like it mattered. That was interesting. Here I'd always considered Ruth one of those breezy, satiric women proficient at deflecting curiosity.

Only I didn't need it and I didn't really care. Frankly there were things I never wanted to hear from her. We'd met by accident at one of those ubiquitous Center City cafes that's all calculated simplicity: quinoa salads, homemade soups, cranberry muffins, that kind of crap. It was lunch hour and the place was loud with competing conversations in those well-educated downtown voices, the entire scene as fundamentally deceptive as casual business attire. You could practically feel the pervasive atmosphere of unacknowledged cynicism on your skin, the deodorized vinegar emanating from all those dissatisfied young professionals amazed to have already acquired such long yet mysteriously undistinguished pasts.

So, Ruth Askew, running into me in those exceptionally ordinary surroundings, flat imprisoned me in unwanted intimacy in order to entrust me with a revelation of startling profundity and enormous human significance, effectively summoning me into history, granting me an unprecedented experience that would surely transform my life - or anyway something along those lines. Because she'd been all too impatiently awaiting a sign from Heaven and was toying with the idea that God had delivered me to her for use as disciple and authoritative witness. They're always looking for witnesses.

In all modesty, this type of situation isn't exactly unusual for me. I have this reputation for being brutally honest, so insecure types are constantly trying to impress me. I'm their living touchstone, a merciless judge that people frantic for confirmation can't resist. They need me; they can't keep away. Just as I'm reciprocally unable to resist exploiting my fatal magnetism, generally to express contempt but sometimes not.

That particular afternoon I'd been in a fairly perverse mood to start with, plus any opportunity to deny that insatiable, manipulative ego was delicious. Or maybe there was something a little too disquieting about her attitude. Whatever, my response was immediate and satisfying: I sat back on a vaguely admiring but indifferent little smile and stared blankly into the middle distance, allowing the moment to dissipate into that stale ambience of premium coffee and wasted lives, which is why this little scene is going nowhere.

To continue: before that summer I never considered Ruth worthy of much attention, although highly original and shrewd and determined, which isn't the same thing as consequential or talented but only a decent simulacrum.

She's a tall, fair, raw- boned woman of thirty-odd, Irish in her bones and not pretty but rather gaunt, with an aggressive but loose and uncoordinated physical presence, an unspecified oddness that gives you second thoughts. (You'll note I'm not about to be discreet in the name of neutrality because that's just digging the lie deeper and I'm through with all that.) I figured her performance that afternoon, to the extent I thought it through at all, either a preamble to an unwanted revelation about her marriage, or more probably rationalization for sharing some nasty piece of secondhand political gossip. But then the truth was hardly imaginable to the strictly sane.

She'd been prattling on, a little desperate.

"No one should simply expect to see good old Saint Peter welcoming them with this huge loving smile and throwing open the pearly gates because it's you! And then presumably all your dead relatives finally appreciate you and grovel. No one for one second questions their basic goodness or imagines they might have everything backwards." That with increased emphasis, in fact actually pleading because clearly, I wasn't seeing how intriguing and insightful she was and offering the required encouragement.

I mean, who pays attention to that kind of shit anyway, mere justification for something profitable and concrete? Ideas, and abstract ideas at that, never imply anything important anymore. Why pay attention to them? It's not like there was some portent of crucial real-world consequences in her moralistic maundering, some numinous harbinger of disaster arising like fog from her self-serving conclusions. Great thinkers don't sweat out their seminal philosophies in wishful suburban isolation;

3

genuine epiphanies are not inspired by inadequacy and neediness.

A noise of traffic outside our corner window, and an angled view of grungy sidewalk along a narrow side street of trendy storefronts illumined by thick afternoon sun: a strangely intimate scene at once self-important and impossibly spent in that way cities have. One random bar of light cut across our table, reminding us of the outside heat, adding to the general confusion.

That disjointed lunch in that pretentious location perfectly encapsulates my relationship with Ruth, which was and still is a lunchtime acquaintance at best. It naturally follows that much of the critical action recounted here occurred during exactly this sort of innocuous activity, right in front of the whole world but invisibly. We overlook how commonplace places do produce extraordinary drama, sometimes even for someone you know. Also, much of what supposedly happened never really happened at all, despite what you've heard rumored or even concluded to your own satisfaction. That's my main point. Another important point is that nothing would be any different now if I had listened and flattered her before kindly deflating her daydream that afternoon. She wouldn't have listened for long. Ultimately my dismissed opportunity meant nothing because all the vital processes were already well underway, the outcome inevitable one way or the other. I think you'll have to agree with me there.

Ruth was a moderately successful morning radio personality and the wife of a very popular politician, therefore an experienced professional practiced at public behavior. And she certainly didn't appear imbalanced or anything. She was more like a little girl clutching a magical secret or a million-dollar lottery ticket: all suppressed glee and opportunistic scheming.

That swift glance up for my reaction! That almost imperceptible flush! Ignorantly incarnating such magnificent, such perfect irony! Those months before she walked onto a literal stage, outdoors on a cloudy country night, alone against the virtuous horde. And despite all this vaunted modesty I suspect that during this period Ruth wasn't so much obeying God as striking out on her own, testing Him the way toddlers test their parents.

"That kind of moral complacency makes me sick to my stomach. To my soul." Expounding all this unsolicited nonsense to a mere professional acquaintance, what's more a reporter. Plus listen, whatever anyone says about themselves, you can safely assume the exact opposite is true

"Maybe that's just a little bit broad," I said. "Maybe not everyone on the planet thinks that way. I know I don't."

"Absolutely everyone on earth, because no one can tolerate seeing themselves in the wrong. And that matters more than anything."

But even Ruth could tell I meant it. Apparently, I wasn't the predestined confidante after all, nor this not her appointed hour. I remember she laughed, but probably she was secretly relieved, probably she did know better in some remote, rational corner of her mind. What she actually wanted was to hoard her alleged wisdom, to gloat over it deep in a cave in a mountain in the wilderness. But you see, forces were already building.

She was giving me this annoyed laughing exasperation while eying me surreptitiously, maybe suspecting the real irritation beneath the companionable patter, certainly furious with me for acting like a self-involved asshole. Although I am a self-involved asshole so what did she expect? Then she faced me full on with a kind of pugnacious, coy defiance - the automatic, intellectualized flirting of her kind. "You see it's just simple survival or evolution. Nature decrees the things we need to do, so naturally doing them defines what's right. It's like Noah being moral because he's the survivor, not the other way around." She had her chin on her fist, a reflective pose. "Anyway, I'm finding it fascinating, I'm thinking more and more about false righteousness. I've been absolutely obsessed with this stuff."

That pale face somehow too exposed: prominent arched nose, narrow lips, brutally vulnerable gaze. A peasant's face with thick dirty-blond hair flying every which way as though excited for its own reasons.

What can you do with people like that? I mean, where would you even start? They've gotten hold of something that feels true to them, which means power, so they're done listening.

And they get really intense.

"Well, it's interesting, I'll give you that." I said. "I'd enjoy talking about your ideas someday when we can make time." I threw her another falsely admiring little smile and fled.

My name is Constantine Manos. As a writer, I specialize in politics, which obviously includes issues of character, but until recently I never thought too much about how the personal dictates the political. The culture insists on assigning political ideas a misplaced dignity, as if these theories are just out there floating around, pure abstract concepts, when the fact is everyone's politics are about self-image and justification. What you feel decrees what you let yourself think; ideas themselves are powerless.

Physically I'm a small, trim man with too much wiry hair, a gigantic salt-and-pepper halo, a veritable Einstein corona. I'm third generation Greek-American on both sides, I was born in Chicago on Bicentennial day, and I've lived in or around Phil-a- *delf*-ya my entire adult life, yet I'm often mistaken for a tourist and not infrequently for a foreigner. It's been happening since college; I guess I'm just doomed to present as a stranger. These days I exaggerate the quirk, imitating the stereotypical visitor from abroad because it's effective both as an investigative technique and as a way to handle rage, including my own. I drop into a suitably quizzical posture and peer up into people so that they think me rudely inquisitive, or overly skeptical, or humble to the point of being legitimately liable to mockery if also endearing and comically brilliant. At public functions, someone invariably imitates me this way, as a presumptuous sparrow hopping along a city sidewalk. I appreciate the recognition and so far, I manage to tolerate the condescension, but it hurts.

Some part of this ineffable foreignness is simple physiognomy: I naturally appear saturnine, and people mutter that I glare, clearly an un-American activity. They really mean I don't take the proper steps to negate the negativity, don't smirk optimistically at every occasion. They always confuse honesty with aggression.

But I think the vital difference between myself and the typical Philadelphian is my exoneration from the unique local guilt. This is very real and not what you think, not that compensating blue-collar bravado of the stoops you get in all big American cities. This is a great chasm, a sharp disconnect that comes from having too much glorious past right in your face and knowing you've let everything go to hell in some unforgivable manner nobody ever really explains. Except that somehow this city has become a discredited nonentity deteriorating in a wasteland between two largely obsolete rivers.

Unlike Boston, where they still cling to their pretensions. The problem here is that what's supposed to matter to us, all those values we've been instructed to wholeheartedly endorse like reason and rule of law, just don't claim our attention right this very minute. But they lurk, these ideological ancestors, behind our busy little lives, disenchanted and watchful. They wag their finger, and their stink leaches out to saturate the gray air of our learned town with something oily and gritty and censorious that urges us to remember while there's still time. That's our characteristic smell.

That's the closest I can come to describing it. Only remember I'm protected from all this self-disgust to a pretty decent extent; being the servant of plain truth I automatically reject unrealistic expectations, they just promote hypocrisy.

Philadelphia's facade is a muted gray-brown as opposed to bright red brick or skyscraper silver; we bear the dull coloration of a side pigeon. Our modest elevations and well-spaced parks speak of ancient forethought and somewhat ameliorate the stench, so although it's true we're an unusually dirty city in various ways, beneath the grime we remain naturally vibrant, twinkling along beside our gray rivers, winking out of mica- flecked fieldstone. We blush with roseate sandstone, we flaunt a complexion of creamy, veined marble.

Now in speaking of the city I mean the *polis*, the living community and political body combined and inseparable. It's still a kindly thing, too, despite the current roaming viciousness. Popular outrage is tempered here, and sometimes we can still hear each other well enough to disagree without condemning.

That's only my Philadelphia, of course, not anyone else's, and naturally it's symbolic and revelatory, a straightforward self- portrait, and you can make of it what you want. It's real and it's highly relevant. And don't go denigrating me because you're the self-important habitué of some asshole dive in Port Richmond who gets to say what real Philadelphia is, because you're just exposing your own ignorance. Also, don't remind me about that other violent, desperate city. I've written about it, which arguably I don't have the right to do. But this is a different kind of report, concerning my own world and carrying a more ordinary kind of importance.

There are some other things I want to explain up front. To begin with, this book is a reinterpretation of fairly recent local events. I wrote it because I find the official version inadequate. Not inaccurate, mind you, so much as critically incomplete. I don't have any new facts so this is not a new theory but more of a correction of emphasis, an attempt to turn the tide. It reads pretty much like a straightforward recounting, but that's deceptive: this is my own creation, an arrangement with numerous additions in the way of personal histories and pertinent observations and naturally my own biased deductions to help you put things in perspective. You can't tell the truth without resorting to some degree of trickery.

Despite having an overall strategy, I wanted to write in the immediate, unfiltered voice I use to myself. So obviously, I'm not terribly concerned about Hemingway's weather or how there's too much exposition or anything that panders rather than serves, because first this is a report, an examination of a series of compelling flashbacks, and there's a lot that has to be explained before things speed up and there isn't time. And second, where's that jazz edge that stays ahead of you and leads you to the truth? I'd hoped to present something clumsy and troublesome with lame language that actually speaks, not just another of the honored walking dead, another obedient child maybe elegant enough to make your brain ache, maybe disguised with some trendy media shit or street jargon but with no real voice because indisputably deceased.

Lame is good – I sing of lame, glorious lame! I claim liberty from smooth editing and cosmetics and strategic marketing. No, give me free, fluid text! It's a revolution, isn't it? Let's unearth the bare bones of it, discover and vanquish the assumptions. Except I kept getting dragged back into the infinitely demanding past and I've shown myself for a coward; I'm ashamed by how traditional this has turned out because I'm suffocating. We all are. Suff-o-*ca*-tion. Instead I've been obsessed with how this little defense of the disappointing truth will be received by the city and naturally by Ruth in particular. How I have to get everything right.

Again, why I'm doing this: I intend to finally refute the crazy conspiracy shit being spread by our needy, brain-dead citizenry, all that cowardly electronic flocking, that irresponsible hubris. Probably not you, then, because who reads the opposition's argument, right? But touted by some clearly responsible citizens, people directly involved who chose to tolerate the mumblings, thereby permitting so much outrageous opportunism to take root. It's becoming canon; pretty soon schoolchildren will be repeating it to my face. Another reason I wanted to keep this immediate was so I could be careless and let in insights I didn't have myself. I wanted to be absolutely fair. I've said it and said it: ultimately, we're all completely, inescapably blind; we don't just overlook a few points or perspectives, we always miss everything.

Of course, all these theories and suspicions exist because there's plentiful room for speculation; there was so much going on concurrently, all stupid if not illegal and often both, with so many indications pointing in different directions that finally people thought it more intelligent to doubt the obvious. When sheer noise carries validity the only possible response is to shout even louder to more people, to force reason on the barbarians to the extent that's ever possible. I'm reasonably terrified that the world's running away from me, with even the basic categories of fact versus fiction organized by popular whim. Which actual apocalypse is not only widely acknowledged but actually approved by people who should know better but have gotten themselves confused. And yes, I know how clichéd this is but it happens to matter to me.

Some additional points:

The fact that I'm describing known events does not make this an interactive project. Don't email me your brilliant personal theories, political or otherwise, even if you know someone involved. I'm not interested in promoting your shirttail aspirations. Seriously.

As this is not a new investigation it's also not a whodunit, so obviously don't expect any bombshell revelations - or lascivious details for that matter, all you literary voyeurs out there. Any information I have I acquired while responsibly pursuing my profession.

11

Now, when I describe this work as a "reinterpretation," I mean that it's the only correct interpretation, the truth, and I use the word "truth" in neither an objective nor relative sense, but simply to signify what we all understand when we say something isn't a lie. Such an understanding, presented with simplicity and elegance if I may be so presumptuous, is able to stand on its own without benefit of theory. What sickens me, if I haven't yet made this clear, is today's evolving entitlement to democratically determined truth.

As to the specific events under discussion, unlike some other commentators I have an informed opinion: you'll see that I had a decent amount of access. But even so I remain utterly ignorant about so much that undoubtedly matters. To take the most glaring example, I had no entrée into the heart of the Askew marriage: the smell of shit in the bathroom, the despair of boredom - or the ongoing ecstasy, for that matter. All that urgent information is still folded up in their conjugal memory, packed away in some bottom dresser drawer. Maybe they got home and screamed profanity while holding satanic rituals; I wouldn't know. As to some others described here, of course I speculate: probably I've created illegitimate characters who don't exist in reality, except they exist now, don't they? You see, even today I have more questions than most people, because most people have bought into one of the current municipal myths, but at least I have the central facts straight, and I'll give you this much: I do agree contend that there was an "it," meaning a single series of causes and effects, with no significant coincidences.

Finally, as to me, you can forget any of the obvious tabloid suspicions about me being gay or obsessed or vengeful. Please realize that I can almost certainly outthink you, even regarding myself. And another thing: I consider the truth a gift that everyone should just graciously accept. Everything I share here I give lovingly and with respect.

Of necessity, I skim some hoary old issues in philosophy but I refuse to openly engage; it's relevant but you're basically on your own. I've lost patience with all the learned pundits and their belligerent, self-defeating worldview, the one where we've reached the limits of conceptual thought, cleverly enlightened ourselves out of our own minds and into an endless whimpering compromise with no further possibility of real movement, not even a rumor of joyful anarchy to vitalize the depressed present. Except that's what always does happen, everything wallowing in despair until some disobedient idea lands in an undiscovered corner, random quantum jitters to put an end to the apparent end of philosophy, one compelling thought to disturb the complacent pseudo-religions and redirect all that gleeful academic venom. You know it's got to happen eventually. Or anyway I know it.

Ruth thought she'd found the answer. Still does, for all she's gone coy now, concealing the grandiosity. She's essentially uneducated, of course, but she managed to bestow a thoroughly enjoyable fillip to the towering zeitgeist, to those dedicated professional thinkers and their clever reasoning against life. Visualizing herself on some cloud-wrapped mountaintop, some unique edge high above all us pedestrian sheep.

And the beauty, the confounding slipperiness of it! That by the very logic of the argument she didn't even have to be right! So what if her thesis was wrong, therefore it remained perfectly valid! The most ingenious defense possible, this indissoluble theory extracted from ill-defined notions of virtue and truth. Precise definitions weren't worth bothering about for the Ruth who operated, so she often claimed, on instinct and grace, delivering breathless revelations to the adoring masses.

"You have to break through the wall you never knew was there." Very eager and excited, with a metaphoric encouraging hand on my shoulder. And I suppose when people are in this state, happy to explain the universe to you, the best you can wish for them is a spectacular failure. A very sharp recollection even now: a dozen rows of folding chairs blocking a city sidewalk, a contradictory ambience combining funereal solemnity and official celebration, with a familiar face painted huge on a city wall, transmuted into an artifact.

If you're from the Philadelphia area you undoubtedly know the basics and are reasonably familiar with our local politicos and our mafia relicts and the more recent City Hall scandals. Looking at it prosaically, which is to say assuming money carries final authority, the plot revolves around the endlessly contested question of development along the Delaware waterfront at Penn's Landing. Maybe that's something to do with history and destiny: centuries ago our first settlers huddled in caves above that same riverbank, warming themselves on the seemingly infinite potential.

Ruth, who started it all with one lunatic outburst and kept right on spouting more illogical crap, ultimately talked too freely about everything except herself. That's a strange reversal for an age mesmerized by the personal yet terrified of profundity. As it happened I had the advantage of an affectionate acquaintance with Councilman-At-Large Thom Askew, and when I offered to do a profile of his wife, secretly a risky if purportedly inadvertent expose, he

14

was cautious but amenable, while of course she was nothing short of ecstatic. So during those months she was an occasional theme through my life, and I sacrificed a few days recording her practiced spiel. This character who envisioned herself a figure of great genius and extraordinary courage, who walked like Joan of Arc. Blithely inserting universal dictums into inappropriate conversations, haphazard shards of philosophy gleaned from the great books and reassembled into a grotesque whole without benefit of formal argument. Scorning reason not as impossible but as pedestrian, as a dull, archaic methodology.

Therefore joyfully embracing her own lack of erudition: "What people consider a good education leaches any originality right out of you. It's literally teaching you what not to think, narrowing your possibilities. It bullies."

I figured this for academic envy. "You've read Foucault?" "Some."

Then there was the confusion over politics, the partisan rush to interpret what happened as evidencing some extremist political position when in fact this was only incidentally the case; in fact the whole political thing was largely unimportant and none of it's going the way you think anyway. The real issues were much more fundamental and everyone sensed that. We were only surprised because Ruth was obviously an enlightened woman.

Now about what finally did happen.

First, understand the Philadelphia Folk Festival as a forthright exercise in Liberal musical theatre as much as a celebration of peoples and their endurance and joys. Taking place, as might be expected, in an aesthetically pure venue, typically under a blazing sun on drying August fields embraced by unremarkable trees, and featuring lots of suburbanites absolutely behaving themselves.

When there came Ruth Askew, taking that venerable stage to address that staunchly progressive audience. Standing rigid there, thin and broad-shouldered, a pale, unfathomable giantess on the twin Jumbotron screens.

That night was odd from the start. Behind the bright box of the stage those generic trees formed a black stockade against a threatening universe, and endless tattered, shit-colored clouds streamed past a gibbous yellow moon with exceptional speed. A shitting sky but no one really noticed.

I suspect Ruth walked out onto that stage in a rage of frustrated arrogance. For one endless minute she simply stood behind the microphone and stared out at us, the thousand dark humps under blankets, the bouncing neon glow sticks, the luminous haze at the line of food concessions, the smokers tapping off ash by the Porta Potties, and the awkward, restless shadows moving up and down the roped-off aisles or carefully stepping over the confusion of tarps and blankets.

Then she spat at us.

CHAPTER ONE

Earlier that day, I lay in the shade with only my bare toes exposed to the vicious sun, part of a modest audience similarly disposed beneath the modest fringe of trees surrounding the field. Light fell down through the foliage, thick victorious beams that described powerful angles in their descent inside the usual breathtaking green cathedral. Around me the grass was withered and compressed into a flattened mat over ground still saturated from the previous night's thunderstorms; everything smelled of baking wet earth, sunscreen, and greasy event food. I don't remember any intrusive insects or even visible birds except for a couple of extremely distant hawks, dull specks in the otherwise empty sky.

Another respectable scattering of spectators occupied the baking field, most sprawled directly in front of the small Camp Stage, true fans eagerly upright despite the merciless heat. So just as expected, one of those perfectly innocent afternoons you buy with the ticket, monotonous while deeply nourishing, readily absorbed through the whole skin like childhood summers.

I didn't know about the witches yet, but they were out in force. Yeah, it's a silly description but I don't know how else to capture the awful effect of those damn women.

So they were witches who'd been summoned by a highly demanding assembly of affluent suburbanites, people accustomed to commanding natural forces. And while arguably these were all benevolent females who only meant well, with witches you never know how it's going to turn out.

Every August for more than a decade I've headed out to Schwenksville for this dependable throwback party. And not precisely to enjoy the music, because although it commands my absolute respect I find it too intense for everyday entertainment. It's a kind of church music, an unashamed church of humanity: pure sound, plaintive and honest, twanging and rambunctious, dulcimer gentle. Fitting, then, for this late-summer pagan rite in honor of righteousness, and I immerse myself in it to perform a spiritual cleansing of sorts, processing across the fields from one rustic venue to another, affirming a succession of bluegrass pickers and ballad wailers and theatrical tellers of old tales. And it's a mildly uncomfortable ritual in another sense, but that's because of the mostly undamaged people, the one's who wholeheartedly enjoy everything and applaud too often. As with anything religious, there are incredibly subversive undercurrents longing to manifest, easy to exploit by those portending witches. Two of them performed that day, one with such tragic skill and clarity it unintentionally aroused huge amounts of self-loathing and subsequently resentment, at least in me. The second inspired a joy vigorous enough to move the plot. And the third exerted an indirect but equally damning influence courtesy of her own celebrity, her mere idea inciting a shaming nostalgia. In fact, it was dangerously stupid to speak her name aloud. All three arrived wearing absolute certainty.

This current festival setting, the Old Pool Farm, is perfectly suited to the occasion. There are wide fields to accommodate the generous crowds, a nicely crisp and sparkly creek, and the requisite gates and groves, all at a situation remote enough to evoke a wholly separate culture despite easy proximity to the city. Although that's not difficult, because even today you only have to poke your nose outside the nearer suburbs to spot a rusty silo on some decrepit farm with another of those filthy black-and-white, diarrhea-spewing dairy cows leaning against a sagging wire fence, its pelvis practically poking through its muddy hide. Peeling paint and hay bales directly across the road from another mushrooming pretentious development, a slum of dull, identical cheapjack townhouses. So despite the fervent country claptrap the festival is essentially a metropolitan scene, drawing a sophisticated crowd, and therefore in one sense condescending, an insult.

Murmurs of anticipation brought me up on my elbows to discover Hannah Lynch already onstage, a typically modest entrance. I sat up and paid attention, catching sight of her inside an amiable circle of probable musicians, a glimpse of her face and one thin shoulder between competent-looking backs in cowboy or cotton work shirts, all of them endlessly conversing there in surprisingly gentle voices.

Until finally they broke apart and here she came gliding towards the front of the tiny platform, moving within a reputation so illustrious it made her physical presence unlikely and you had to struggle for it. A tiny bird of a woman, an elderly, fragile sparrow with fine gray hair and hazel eyes and translucent skin, nodding to us and smiling nicely with small unremarkable teeth while seating herself on a wooden folding chair. She was dressed like good people, like a decent Christian farmwife in a faded print skirt and cotton blouse of mixed pastels, pink and beige and blue. Only with dangling silver jewelry to be noticed, since after all she was a major star.

With this one unshakable article of faith: that her famously quavering soprano was entirely unrelated to her own ordinary self, more of an imposition or a trust, an undeserved gift from God that in no way merited personal praise. So, she has stated. And accordingly, she exuded genuine empathy with all of us waiting out there for her, straining forward to better capture the spirit and stamina investing each word. A curve of laughter lit her face, and there was grief there too, but nothing to diminish that serene spirit.

Beside me Crystal, blatantly artificial trendoid in that audience of cosmopolitan pseudo-naturals, for once had the good sense to keep her mouth shut. Crystal, please note, was present only because she suspected this event mattered to me and meant to chain herself to it in my memory. She was an unashamed criminal, and really sweet, and I admired her.

Lynch sat there looking at us and hugging her guitar, once giving it a surreptitious pat like a favorite pet before launching into one of those unexpectedly piercing old songs, a rather shocking rush of raw bitterness and despair - nothing silvered there - railing rather than mourning yet cleanly tragic because without any confusion of entitlement or excuse, in fact totally untainted by melodrama, an expression of rightful fury to upend your sensibilities and make you cringe inside your pampered, complacent soul.

And onward, commanding that summer hour with a repertoire of futile longing, black misery, true love, unalloyed injustice, and journeying away as only the truly dispossessed can journey. How inadequate we were by comparison, what undeserved good fortune to be sitting there vicariously sharing the infinite human endurance of those former generations, thus beatified now. Sharing a deep pride in our good taste and our faultless fundamental values.

And that's how this festival always goes for me: a fusion of rapture and fleeting realization, of purging and rebirth I suppose. We avid celebrants being served by true vicars, unassuming conduits of grace because essentially craftspeople evincing the unquestioning self-respect of their kind, therefore automatically accepting us as equals and worthy of their respect, refusing to cater. That's how Lynch and her ilk deliver their deadly blows, how they incite our reckless, self-destructive impulses.

Because the problem is, nothing is enough and never can be, not in any case. And in addition to that, this particular event carries an impossible burden of triumphant civil rights baggage. A weight of expectation, purest gold and just as heavy, presses down on those fields like an approaching storm, flattening the trees, placing an unbearable strain on our moral muscles, making even the most authentic and engaged participant stagger for reasons most often never identified.

You see there's no battle here anymore, a situation as frustrating as it is pathetic. I mean, what's so pitiable as striving mightily to wage a war already won, or achieve a moral victory already popularly embraced? Like you're on some lone and dangerous crusade instead of enjoying a mere reenactment, an amusement park ride. As if any real social hazard or physical extremity ever threatened most of these initiates. As if they could face the real front line today. Come to that, what in the world ever sprang from this placid piece of Pennsylvania countryside anyway, or even its nearby metropolis, so far from the bloody front lines of decades past? What justifies this hallowed ambience? Everyone knows the real struggle was over in another state, in the deep South or New York or California, all that televised passion and pain. Yet here's a similar legacy, an undeserved renown.

Seriously, you have to consider this heritage of the sixties, that era of righteousness and innocence and victory, you have to ponder the connection to the contemporary lives and events I'm describing here. Resurrect that intoxicating scent of possibility. Realize how strong it is, what it can do. Watch any old news film and it's literally like viewing creatures from another planet, those young people are so alien, their gestures and expressions so certain and strident, an entire new world in their angry, accusatory eyes. What can any of that mean in this age of spent possibility?

So today the Folk Fest is largely a masturbatory farce of self-congratulation, courtesy of this pushy, upscale audience basking in its accustomed sunshine, displaying that forceful amiability that means money, smiling too brightly over bare freckled shoulders. Uniformly pale people displaying their ease on this bucolic faux battlefield, all aggressively self-aware. And meanwhile a barely perceptible, slightly demented energy flutters along at grass level, an intrepid narcissism bent on having a significant experience and more than a little desperate to measure up to itself.

I'm as progressive as anyone, I secretly gloat over my superiority, so for me all this underlying energy eventually manifests as low-grade irritation, and the fact that bad temper is implicitly verboten at this event only makes it that much worse. And then here comes Lynch to further emphasize everyone's obvious unworthiness and what can you do but silently seethe with frustrated moral ambition. This is the one Folk Fest constant I always dismiss until it's too late and I'm climbing aboard one of the yellow school buses that shuttle people in from the parking fields, listening to all the boisterous but balanced chatter. Probably a deliberate amnesia, because as I say, for me it's a religious event.

So by later that Saturday afternoon I was largely disgusted with myself and as you can imagine, wonderful company. Once again stretched out on my back but this time my whole body obstinately exposed to the brutal heat, and while I had a bucket hat shielding my face I'd raised my knees to better facilitate the burn penetrating my jeans. I reached my left hand out past the edge of Crystal's spongy blue blanket, feeling for the heart of the earth deep underneath the dispirited vegetation, Edna Millay style. There we greeted the second witch, and for an interlude of spontaneous revelry the whole phony carnival dissolved, wiping away our precious fictions to reveal the one face behind the infinitely varied masks. Rather commonplace moments to underline the supertext, a brief but blessed release from introspective angst, an intoxicated dance that anyway began wholeheartedly but inevitably dwindled into posturing before ultimately discarding us back into isolated, shattered pieces of humanity scattered over a sunlit field.

We were in front of the main stage, the Martin Guitar Stage, a venue that backs into some tame leftover woods. The smaller Tank Stage was to my right, with behind it a private area for performers, and to my left the equally small Craft Stage. Further left was all the familiar festival retail, folkie variety, striped tents selling hippie throwback goods like handcrafted ceramics, carved wooden bowls, tie-dye skirts, hand-strung glass beads, and bad art. In between the main and Craft Stages a tiny dirt path paralleled a shallow creek of sparkling mica and soft mud; both disappeared into the dim coolness of the Dulcimer Grove, a rather precious habitat of jugglers and magicians and others of that Renaissance Faire ilk, a determinedly magical place more or less reserved to scantily clad or frankly naked children, their cheeks painted with stars and moons in indigo and crimson. Either they're truly mesmerized by these archaic amusements or they're convinced they should be by the adults and the daycare atmosphere, because they all sit there expending fierce concentration on colored sand and sparkly fairy dust, their little pink tongues extended in effort. I mean, all the world is fake, even the kids. Around them circles a protective hillside of slender trees roped together by string hammocks in bright primary colors, a haphazard effect of beggars' rags pegged out to dry.

If you follow that same path straight on you come out on field with more dry grass, more distant trees, and another vacant horizon. On the right is the Camp Stage, site of Lynch's morning concert; on the left an unremarkable gate gives onto the campers' settlement, one of those ephemeral constructions of funky tent- and-RV fantasies, castles and pyramids and suburban estates complete with lawn furniture and barbeques and anything else you need for rustic comfort. The affable professional performers come here after the regular shows to sit and drink and play their music well into the summer nights, just for these special stalwarts. Notice how everyone's personal effects are carefully positioned to define private family spaces but without absolutely excluding the requisite hobnobbing community, because that would repudiate the spirit of the thing.

And anywhere you care to look there are all these exceptionally pleasant people, a seasonal confluence of the enlightened: middle-aged, nattily-bearded men with thick hairy ankles showing beneath those long gauzy skirts; visibly well- educated younger couples falling all over each other in reassuring mutual recognition; friendly teens aglow with their own laudable social spirit or familiarity with meaningful music or both; and grimy toddlers in T-shirts and shimmering plastic haloes with their baby curls shining and their fingers to their mouths and their tiny feet covered with dirt. Skimpy tank tops and glittery backpacks, idiosyncratic witches cones and sombreros and straw cowboy hats covered in button collections, pale muscled calves and freckled backs red with sun and damp with perspiration.

All these regulation types navigate cordially across the fields, buying and eating and exercising their approval, until later in the afternoon when the heat is truly intolerable and it's a matter of claiming a place for the folding chairs and coolers and settling in for the afternoon concert. When for a couple of hours all these enervated devotees create for themselves an enormous patchwork quilt of blankets and tarps, an American prayer rug rolled out beneath the glare.

I among them, hiding under my hat, squinting up from under the brim, intending not so much to watch the performances as to absorb them from a neutral distance. Meanwhile I was relishing the sense of Crystal beside me, resentful at having to endure all this legitimate music.

When here came a second celebrated woman into this extraordinary and disorganized day, an ineffably cosmopolitan presence in a white silk shirt that billowed out over notably slim hips and tight black jeans tucked into cowboy boots. The costume only emphasized the unmistakable sophistication in the sharp angle of her jaw and the sleek black bob swinging at her shoulder. That taut body edged itself onto the stage and into our attention, anticipation suffusing her narrow face, her whole person radiating the intrinsically cool self-content of a magician about to pull off the big illusion and astonish us all.

Lifting fiddle and bow, lowering them to call a comment offstage, bringing them back up to her pointed chin experimentally while a guitarist, drummer, and another violinist fooled with getting into position, and around me an expectant rustle shook off the afternoon lethargy, and once again I sat up and wiped the sweat and sunscreen from my forehead.

She leaned forward a fraction to acknowledge us.

"Hello all you very special people." Now decisively raising her instrument. "Three jigs."

Well, you know that kind of tritely manipulative music, but then her exceptional skill, that energy climbing into a frenzy, the first notes reaching us with the adolescent enthusiasm of uncurling spring leaves. Music so familiar and yet astonishingly fresh, something behind the insistence of it transcending its own rather sentimental imagining. Passages as fleet but powerful as pure energy, and you'd actually have to defend against the physical impact but why would you bother to fight off such delirious joy?

They have a reserved seating section in front of the main stage, a modest pen containing rows of wooden folding chairs surrounded by a fence of deliberately rickety palings. It was largely unpopulated for the afternoon performance. A dirt lane about ten feet wide separated this area from the field of common folk. Crystal and I were up front, right near the dusty edge of this path, and close to us, in the lane itself and with one tiny hand firmly grasping the enclosure fence, stood a fairy-slim blonde girl of five or six. Just as I fully noticed her she launched into the familiar steps of an Irish jig, lifting first one exquisite bare foot and then the other into tentative arcs, curving each arm alternately above her head. From her shoulders a pastel summer dress floated out in the shape of a loose triangle, and her movements caused her hair to caress her perfect little back.

With the increasing confidence of the music her delicate feet, fragile pale-pink petals, rose and crossed each other in an assured sequence that bespoke formal lessons, and meanwhile her eyes never lifted from her toes and her pallid face was tense in concentration. Only once did she manage a quick glance up to a middle-aged scholarly type, probably her father, who nodded mild encouragement but displayed, I thought, some slight annoyance. Now complex annotations around the tune turned tight elegant spirals; it was all self-interest now, you understand, nothing to do with us but instead its own internal voyage. In the path the child reworked her steps, her frown expressing frustration with her own limited expertise.

When suddenly appeared two barefoot, competent-looking women in their early thirties skipping down the lane, then widely twirling, then skipping again, their hands clasped and arms outstretched to form a traveling arrow. Both flaunting gauzy pastel skirts and silvery tank tops that exposed perspiring firm flesh, both draped with multiple glittering strands of Mardi Gras beads flashing purple and green and mauve. They acknowledged the blond child with an upward swing of their joined hands high over her head, a bridal arch speeding by on either side. It made her giggle but move closer to the fence.

The fiddler was bending practically in half over her bow and the second fiddler not being any slouch either, their hands and arms pushing towards the absolute limits of muscular possibility, straining against themselves to maintain their momentum.

Then four ethereally lithe teenage girls forming two pairs, and they were in regulation T-shirts and shorts except all bore silvery translucent wings that flapped at their slim shoulders; they went whirling around and around each other and simultaneously forward, delightful gyroscopes with their feet stomping hard on the infectious strain yet for all that maintaining the ludicrously disinterested expressions of runway models.

Promptly followed by a young couple charging along in an outright polka, aggressive but a tiny bit shamefaced, too: he was slim and wore a neatly-trimmed dark beard; she was sturdy and short with a pixie haircut and a refined air, like an educator. The little dancer flattened herself against the fence but continued a rhythmic bopping, presenting no less enchanting an image. And she was proved wise, because here came the same young couple back again, being the kind of people who need to underline the obvious. Passing midway an approaching male pair, seeming now a little more obliged than inspired, their muscular calves flashing below their khaki kilts: one was broad in the shoulders and chest with a thin ass and spindly legs; his partner was entirely slim, remarkably tall, and balding. Presenting the impression although little of the force of a strong wind, they nevertheless managed to turn the little dancer halfway round, her moist mouth open in wonder. She paused there, staring after them.

Now the dancing was everywhere. I stood up to confirm a modest sea of erratically bobbing heads at every side but especially to the right, past the Tank Stage: enlightened middlebrows and emotionally stranded hippies and likeable healthy teens and self-disciplined mandolin players and confident cultural elitists and miscellaneous commonsensical types engaged in a nearly impromptu production number, for one bright second emerged from behind the mask of individualism, openly expressing one joyously creative soul.

Well, we were dancing out in the field as well, all of us to some extent, the more exhibitionist characters gyrating on their bright blue tarps and lifting their hands in the air, and some efficient types illegally occupying the marked-off aisles, prancing with impudent liberty up and back. Patrons excessively enthusiastic or self-consciously hesitant but almost everyone involving themselves in the music. I was dancing too, not to make a spectacle of myself or anything but feeling myself a part of the gala. And about then I realized it was already ending because that's how these things always go.

Frenzied vibrations, faster than you could believe, and we listeners attended first with our ears and then with our bodies, stilling them now, desperate to capture every last second until inevitably all of it was swiftly and immaculately recalled into one compact point of silence and we found ourselves abandoned to our accustomed exile, returned to the pretense of our separate selves.

She played two more sets, we in her audience dutifully imitating our initial enthusiasm, grateful for the continuing reprieve. I've said it before: reality moves so fast anymore, we've all become experts at polite deceit. Folk Fest protocol is to kick everyone out around six, sweep the grounds, then ticket everyone back in for the evening concert. You wait in a cattle shoot, at least if you're fairly close to the gate, or anywhere nearby if you're not, until finally the loudspeakers blare a Sousa march and you grab your chairs and blankets and coolers and run like hell to beat the other folkies to a premium patch of grass. Therefore, it's prudent to leave early enough to ensure you're at the front of the return pack, and that afternoon, as usual, the knowledgeable attendees ignored the high, unrelenting sun, ignored even the name performer just introducing himself, and started unobtrusively filtering out.

I was making my own preliminary moves when I recognized Ruth off to the right, by herself and slightly beyond the audience proper. She was rather elaborately brushing grass off her shirt, and her hair was drifting into her face as usual; her entire aspect projected excruciating self-consciousness. It was the intricate performance of a woman uncoordinated at life yet used to being watched. She was in a lacy peasant blouse that didn't suit her big-boned frame - it was lavender, too, which didn't help - and loose black jeans over black cowboy boots. Her attention shifted to getting the blouse centered correctly; when finally she noticed me, that man standing perfectly still and staring at her, I waved a hand over my head in greeting. I have no idea why I didn't just avoid her. She assumed an automatic grin but then recognized me back and her smile turned beaming, and with it she transformed herself into a reasonably attractive woman, an odd but intriguing combination of big straight white teeth, thick dirty-blond hair, low forehead, pale freckles, and a long, arched nose that enlivened her profile with an aquiline swiftness.

Behind me Crystal was standing with our blanket gathered up in a big, baby blue synthetic wad; we watched Ruth maneuver through the half-seated, half-moving spectators, visibly enduring our inspection. When she got closer you noticed the deep frown lines between her brows and realized how much older she was than you'd assumed from the juvenile posturing.

A forthright greeting to Crystal and a frankly offered hand, all fraught with the deep disdain of the intelligent, accomplished woman encountering the undeserved self-esteem of the merely lovely. To which assault Crystal responded with her typical flaccid grip and a near shrug, an implied refusal to expend any more of her precious personal energy on uninteresting shit. Ruth turned away from us, towards the stage, where an athletic- looking but otherwise unassuming man of about forty in a tired cowboy hat was inaudibly explaining a song. That duty done, she faced us again.

"This is all new to me. It's wonderful! That dancing." She opened her arms wide to encompass the stage, the field, and the discreetly dispersing audience. "Very Caucasian." Well. The cowboy strummed an acoustic guitar, meanwhile calmly examining his surroundings for concealed gunslingers. And naturally I remembered our lunch but that was months ago, so surely whatever she was babbling about then was probably old news and anyway too vague to reference or be embarrassed over now.

She was brushing at her jeans for no discernable reason. "Did I tell you about Leticia Rowan?"

Just typical. What about Leticia Rowan? How aggravating when I hadn't seen Ruth for months! I knew Rowan was the night's closing act. Meanwhile my brain was automatically playing familiar media images backed by the old uplifting refrains: that bold soprano keening from the Capitol steps, debunking the myth of American justice; the slim, avid girl of the famous photograph where she's perched on a stool in a Greenwich Village coffee house, radiant with the novel excitement of causing real change. Set on living a validated life, perfectly exemplifying those decisive, glorious years, that age of energy and faith. Today still socially engaged, as you would expect, and while no longer that wondrous sylph just as lovely in the clean bone beneath the motherly padding. But most often appearing during those public broadcasting fund-raisers, programs aimed at prosperous boomers eager to relive a spurious past.

"I'm introducing her tonight." "The hell you are." It was such a stupid lie, not even remotely sustainable. Especially outrageous when you considered Ruth's musical identity: her morning drive-time show featured one of those feel-good formats: generic soft rock interspersed with headlines, traffic, celebrity gossip, and a few carefully screened listener calls. Media hypocrisy providing a safe harbor for the harried immature listener, carefully friendly and slick and sympathetic and definitely never politically or socially oriented when that might mean causing offense. Also never mind that Gene Shay, comfortably stout folkie radio program host from a very different station, legendary teller of truly horrendous jokes, always introduced the performers here, world without end, amen. Come on.

"Right, you know everything. I forgot. And you're never wrong." I suppose that was an ostensibly genial poke at my renowned erudition. I happen to think if someone asks you a question they should have the courtesy to listen to the answer.

"I'm speaking after Gene." Gene! And she was looking repulsively self-satisfied. "I asked Leticia Rowan if I could say a few words and she agreed, for some strange reason." Now slipping into her professional mode, that rather arch blend of certainty and faux intimacy delivered with an indelible Lina Lamont slur: *cay*-unt um-*an*-jin. Fingering the silver holy medals at her throat, a crucifix and two others piled up together on a single delicate silver chain: Jude of the impossible and the Virgin Mary.

And she laughed at my horrified expression and launched into what I assume was a fairly mendacious account of a reception for Women in the Media at the lovely old Bellevue, where at that sort of event there's a rigid social hierarchy: the unfed proletariat leaning forward from chairs up on the mezzanine to watch on monitors, and the elite dining at tables down on the ballroom floor. Ruth skipped over who was speaking on what and cut straight to dessert for the privileged few, she naturally among them being her gracious public self, wandering around being affable and networking with vibrant women in suits too bright for an office and intelligent men with refined, open faces, clearly expensive slacks and jackets, and beautifully cut hair.

And there was Leticia Rowan already in town and seated comfortably in a corner behind a tortured centerpiece of bamboo and tiny orange orchids, casually chatting with a couple of intimates. So Ruth went up and offered another of those frank handshakes. "I'm truly awed." Basically insinuating herself into the party, making it clear who was honoring whom.

Then went prattling on in her practiced glib fashion about youthful idealism and her own fictitious activist past, seasoning it with ingenuous regret over her current disengaged state to smooth along the manipulation. Although this with a woman surely inured to dubious approaches? There's something unconvincing about this I haven't the time to investigate but the result must hinge on Ruth's accumulating nervous tension, the months if not years behind the coming explosion. That kind of stress sets you performing impulsive actions, forcing unaccountable outcomes.

In retrospect I think Ruth once again mistook a fortuitous encounter for the hand of destiny and just barged ahead. Either that, or else she fell victim to that common desire to cleave to what one professes to despise.

I was dumbfounded. "Why?"

"Oh, envy I guess. I wanted to be part of it." Charmingly stated, her forehead furrowed in recollection. And what was I supposed to say to any of it?

Behind us the cowboy mooed through a mild dirge, disrupting nothing; around us the field was nearly empty, abandoned to the insistent sun. And Ruth was standing before me explaining too much and nothing at all, once again too intense, setting off all sorts of warning bells.

Crystal lifted a pastel spaghetti strap from a pink shoulder and raised her impudent big gray eyes, looking at Ruth with that innocent expression women use to express contempt. Her private opinion of Ruth: "Nobody has to be seen looking like that."

Crystal was another communications major and model manqué hoping to become, of all things, a personality. That ubiquitous blond hair, the pleasant features of no special distinction just slightly out of proportion: another responsibly raised, college-educated harpy bereft of individuality because nature abhors individuality. Instead she emanates sex, it's in her bones and baby face, her short upper lip and outrageous ambition. Don't expect her to evolve, because she'll never be other than she is right now. Fortunately she's immune to jealous criticism, not being that kind of stupid nor shy to succeed. She held some kind of entry-level management job at the Center City Holiday Inn Express, an occupation that never seemed to seriously impact her real life. Crystal is her birth name.

"Thom here?" I asked.

Ruth's husband, a frequent guest on her program as either political insider or amiable comic foil, was a local celebrity in his own right, a Philadelphia familiar, a compendium of agreeable ugliness, frightening intelligence, crooked teeth in a moist marshmallow grin, Ivy League polish, loud patterned shirts, genuine charm, horrible posture, an unrepentant gift for outrageous flattery, and an impudent, cutting wit. Outsiders considered him the epitome of Main Line class.

"He's in Harrisburg." Acknowledging my disquiet, looking amused for my benefit, but her eyes were shading into wariness. She pushed that uncontrollable hair from her damp forehead. "I'm running around loose today." And she gave me a minor, tight smile, raised a few fingers in a little goodbye salute, and strode purposefully towards the gate.

"Hunh!" Crystal said for both of us.

Festival security is handled by costumed volunteers: polite, energetic young people impersonating funky pirates or medieval wizards or just nameless creatures of purely idiosyncratic design. This clean-cut constabulary was now shepherding we stragglers to the main gate with cordial efficiency, their intricate hats, adorned with oversized badges of authority, visibly bobbing over the heads of the crowd. The cowboy singer had vanished.

I stood there in the empty afternoon glare, again hunting around for a rational line of thought but failing to find one. Finally, today, I have an insight: my being there that afternoon helped determine the event.

I navigated us out of the grounds and smuggled us under the rope to a decent spot not too far back in the queue; none of the polite people already there objected. Crystal was perking up now she could catch the scent of approaching evening, her posture opening up to opportunity, her eyes brightly observant. I ducked back under the ropes to get a couple of Cokes from a vending machine and together we waited out the forced restorative lull, letting the afternoon settle down around us, watching the families in lawn chairs eating their dinners, relaxing in public. At length the loudspeakers sounded and we all pushed forward through the gates and launched into the usual painfully hilarious sprint. I got us fairly far up front on the center aisle and bent over gratefully, hands to knees, while from the corner of my blurred vision I saw Crystal plop herself down with her mildly victimized face.

Faint applause, which had to be for the traditional bagpipe welcome; a moment later I could hear the piper myself, and then came Gene Shay with his terrible jokes. By twilight we were enduring a young bluegrass quartet of some nascent merit but an unfortunate air of artsy superiority. Then an enjoyable mambo interlude evoking romantic images out of fifties movies, and by full darkness the Jumbotron screens displayed a close-up of a frail, dedicated Canadian singer-songwriter, another of those admirable females. Insidious damp was seeping through my jeans and sweatshirt, chilling my ass. Disembodied light-sticks moved at random, children giggled, and the kindly scent of marijuana wafted by in sporadic gusts.

Crystal and I outlasted the Canadian over strawberry smoothies doctored with vodka while around us the night coalesced into a blackness that seemed physical and bulky, something you could push aside like drapes. Then there was that huge yellowed moon illuminating the speeding brown clouds, making the entire universe feel unusually sentient. Gene Shay was back with even more of those horrendous jokes, to be replaced by a middle-aged dignitary in a blazer over jeans, quietly defiant.

"We are the light of truth, the truth the capitalists and the banks and the conglomerates want forgotten. But we're still here, still burning bright through the darkness." He actually said that, sure of the personal politics of these many music lovers, all these people who could afford to share his opinion. Declaiming thus in an understated but confident bass, Main Line meets simple country boy to produce unfaltering self-respect. Positions shuffled onstage and there was Gene Shay back, leaning sideways into the standing mike to signal brevity.

"And now let's talk about one particular brilliant candle shining through the darkness, brighter than almost any other, one of the iconic voices of an era of civil renaissance: the inimitable Leticia Rowan." Grinning back offstage as if to a good friend, as maybe she was. "And just to underline how special this really is, we have an additional guest, because Philly's very own Ruth Askew is going to provide us a more personal introduction."

There was a kind of group shrug but nothing worrisome.

A further positional dance, the screens displaying indistinct blobs and random emptiness, and finally there was Ruth behind the microphone. We observed her taking us in: waving lights skittering over dull shapes, anticipatory shifting and murmurs, a few people in motion pausing on their way somewhere to see if it was worth the wait. Magnified, she looked brutally plain, with noticeable lines around her mouth and those disproportionately large, disturbingly vulnerable blue eyes.

And she just stood there, absolutely rigid, until we all paid complete attention. I think she was overwhelmed by pure contempt, that it confounded her ability to speak, so instead she spat at us

When everyone instinctively recoiled, as you can imagine, but now she was past her initial paralysis. More, she was beyond pretense, out in the wild ether, and you could almost see the crazy. We instinctively coalesced into a tight defensive silence.

"That's for all you virtue thieves." She'd struck this theatrical posture of aggressive confidence, all very square and speaking directly down to us. "But unfortunately for you, we've reached the end of righteousness. Not in this electronic age. No more fleeing consequences and calling yourself good. Time itself is nothing but our continual separating away from the primordial dead nothingness of absolute truth and rightness."

It's almost over, but I hope you see how excruciating it was. I'm sorry to have to assault your sensibilities with this shit but we were all squirming in unforgivable embarrassment and you should understand.

And to be fair, is your religion less silly? Isn't every great religion or even philosophy as impossibly childish? And here's something else: she was handing us a diagram of her own psyche and circumstances, issuing a perfectly clear warning that went ignored simply because it was way too obvious. Because this is, after all, a story about stupidity where everything is fucking clear if you just pay attention.

Ruth put a hand to the mike, still keeping that confident posture.

"This is the next great evolutionary leap. We will claim the future responsibly, and we will become more like God."

Just at that moment, the words flown, the energy abating, I could sense her dawning comprehension of the enormity of her situation. She looked to her side – for something, someone? And then she sent a little nod out to us, to the compact, alert darkness.

"Then to the elements be free, and fare thou well!"

That's Prospero, retiring his magic and releasing the slave- spirit Ariel at the end of *The Tempest*.

But Ruth stayed out there, holding that same strong, taut pose until a calm Gene Shay was suddenly present and gently thanking her from the stage, sending us a tolerant nod while herding her aside. And there at last was the great Leticia Rowan herself, that vast, benign goddess in a golden caftan, smiling an unrestrained country smile, exuding inexhaustible strength and kindness. Clearly decent people, both of them.

Ruth was barely visible now, but I saw her turn to take a final glance back at us, her face for one moment revealed to the giant screens, then as abruptly absent. Terrified of course, because terror is her resting state, and still insolent, and definitely smug.

CHAPTER TWO

I touched his shoulder in greeting, receiving something just short of a grin in reply along with that familiar, ironic lift of one eyebrow. Thom was reclining in his usual comfortable slump, his chair tilted back so far it almost hit the railing. I thought he looked marginally defensive but that wasn't so unusual.

"Good Morning. I note that the hour has come and that a quorum of this Council is present." This recited in the reedy and entirely disinterested tones of Council President Harry Ciccarelli and as usual incorrect, in that it was ten-thirty Thursday morning and the appointed hour was ten. "Our invocation today, at the invitation of Councilwoman Margery Haskell, is going to be given by the Reverend Michael Harrow from the First Baptist Church of Philadelphia. I ask that all members and visitors please rise."

We stood, our shoulders almost touching over the rail, but Thom turned in even closer and adopted the ludicrously secretive expression that always accompanied his patented pseudo- confidential whisper, a tone that perversely emphasized his already penetrating voice. "So here comes the Press, greedily rubbing its hands together." Demonstrating this gesture discreetly but with happy gusto.

41

He was wearing a yellow and green striped shirt that seemed to vibrate it was so painful to view, along with an unremarkable but clearly expensive gray suit and navy knit tie. Then he raised a fist to conceal that tangled marshmallow grin; way too often Thom behaved like Mrs. Askew's miraculous mid-life baby, that brilliant only child.

The Reverend Harrow, clearly a narrow, dry stick from childhood, was settling into his temporary prominence at the front of the chamber, frowning intently at the rich ceiling for inspiration during a very long moment of earnest meditation before loudly launching into his instructions to the Lord. "Jesus! Guide our hearts and minds this day so that we will not fail in our mission. Lead us along your path of mercy and understanding."

"Exactly right," I said.

"Allow us to partake of your compassionate judgment and understanding; let us reach out to one another in tolerance and a spirit of true cooperation for the benefit of this great city. In the name of Jesus Christ our Lord, Amen."

"We thank the Reverend for his invocation. Council will be at ease." All sitting within the bosom of the local legislative process, where despite unhappy reality a genuine reverence for something or other mysteriously resides, lending a reluctant dignity to the excessive architectural details, the rusty elegance and intimate proportions. Some proper circumspect tension, an implicit gravity mirrored in the purposeful stance of the participants, outright demanding consideration: that particular self-conscious and proudly virtuous air, that rather stagy sense of drama common to churches and courtrooms and some elementary schools. Council was the city's apex of the expression, the ultimate iteration, because here it was only about representing, about the joy and unfathomable power and grave responsibility of representing. An awareness somewhat mitigated by cheap posturing but truly any contamination was minimal. Representing! To symbolize, to speak for the multitudes, to carry public intention into the dimly twinkling, wonderfully malleable future.

An attitude suited to the immediate venue but much less appropriate once outside Council doors, because this particular modest yet elegant room was secreted, pearl-like, within the stomach of a preposterous monster, a veritable sentient castle, an excretion of history, the gross but magnificent erection of a hungry, ambitious, rampantly dishonorable age.

All cities favor particular tints, red brick or stylized primary colors, slick granite or Mediterranean pastels. Painting a portrait of Philadelphia requires a palette reflective of our refined and storied but equally crude past. Start with a grainy, muted charcoal outline, add a generous, nearly translucent wash of rust for our old brick rowhouses, then a thicker pink for the gentler blush of sandstone. You'll need a moderate touch of rich cocoa for brownstone, and generous amounts of cream and golden ocher for marble stoops and fractured, columned facades. (I may be repeating myself here, or almost; I tend to do that but I bear repeating.) Coruscating silver-gray fieldstone, difficult to capture! Plus infinitely varied greens for ginkgoes and sycamores, lush milkweed in abandoned lots, and ivy spilling out of Society Hill flower boxes. Rich purple for paulownia trees like soft flower candelabras along the rail lines, bursts of bright pink for mimosa, and clear blue for the chicory breaking through along the sidewalks, all those inner-city blessings people are trained to disparage or at least ignore. Then finish it off with the common contemporary glaze of glass and steel and the requisite regimented greenery.

But our sky, whether washed clean or hunkered beneath folds of trite cloud, remains essentially white, its pale glare outlining our rather pathetic but growing cluster of skyscrapers. Ultimately an empty canvas, a fearful purity in opaque, mysterious mother-of-pearl, a consistently lustrous, bleached, celestial white. Now visualize City Hall (meaning this 19th Century version of course, the Broad Street behemoth as opposed to that serene Colonial structure in the historic district) as a literal piece of that pale sky brought down to sidewalk level, consolidated by some unchecked hubris into an impossible pile of pale masonry, a stupendous fortress with its central courtyard the unavoidable crossroads of this city, a thoroughfare familiar to upstanding suburbanites with politely damning expressions, the disturbing urban poor, cubicle dwellers and retail workers rushing off to run a quick errand at lunch, tourists frowning up at the tower and snapping photographs in front of the flowerbeds, politicos, police, journalists - all that unremarkable flotsam going about their intensely self-important lives, an uninspiring stream flowing determinedly through this Second Empire monolith.

The building is a bully determined to squat in everyone's way no matter where they think they're going. It lurks, I swear; you're walking along and suddenly look up to find that tower tilting directly above you, Penn himself keeping his purposeful eye on you although never bothering to justify his interest or anything else. You turn a modern granite corner whole blocks away, thinking it a distant memory, and there it is again sprawling across a stretch of arty little side streets much nearer than it has any possible business being. A shimmering gray- white stone artifact of Philadelphia past, that once serious, even urgent city, the tallest masonry building in the world covering an entire square city block with its incredible mass, its supporting walls over twenty feet thick. Picture that: castle walls! Ornate to the point of obscenity, encompassing infinite examples of arcane sculpted symbols, veined marble cool to the touch, cantilevered stairways, unexpected entrances, sudden stops, and unrelieved damp. Bland linoleum squares sound at every footfall: you will be heard here, for better or worse. Water drips haphazardly onto piles of official documents stacked on the floors of half-empty offices. Hallways wander like something out of a horror movie mansion, endless corridors going off to nowhere. Elaborate mosaics and friezes occupy recessed spaces, deliberately situated so as be almost never viewed.

Generous nestling chambers of unabashed self-indulgence wait prudently concealed behind heavy carved doors, all leather sofas on Oriental rugs; you glimpse oil paintings belonging to some judge or patronage appointee in an outer office before his regulation tight-skirted, officious administrative assistant shuts the door in your face. Endless dim hallways ripe with the ubiquitous stench of urine echo to immoderate voices and magnify the sporadic scurrying of tired city personnel. Impatient potential jurors wait on wooden chairs lining walls painted an institutional beige, sheriffs escort uninspiring defendants to and from courtrooms, and avid, underpaid ADAs pass and nod and occasionally confer with equally harried, slightly sleazy defense attorneys. Every now and then a city aristocrat, a councilperson or ranking member of the mayor's administration comes whisking around a corner like a forgotten promise only to abruptly retreat and retrench behind the security posts and bailiffs and general intimidating paraphernalia of the elected elite.

Atop it all, supremely incongruous, stands bland Billy Penn, that stout, reformed delinquent, twenty-seven tons of immortalized Quaker equability. Unmistakable against the pallid sky, poised directly over Lawyerland with one hand pointing, perhaps, to his home estate at Pennsbury, or maybe to the Shakamaxon site of his peace treaty with the Lenni-Lenape, or maybe, as occasionally posited, to a certain whorehouse in Chinatown.

City Council meets on the fourth floor, secured behind black wrought iron gates displaying the immensity and imposing design you'd expect to find protecting a crusader fortress or a Hollywood mogul's estate, except that Council's are purportedly always open. Then on through etched-glass double saloon doors into Room 400, into a confined but elegant interior not unlike the inside of a tarnished antique jewelry box, gilded and lined in red, its inside lid an ornate coffered ceiling studded with marvelous hexagonal light fixtures.

Plain wooden visitor chairs line a rail of polished brass; small desks crafted from elaborately configured wood and intricate metalwork angle in close to each other out on the floor, each with its small microphone and padded leather chair. The carpet shrieks for attention with a blood-red pattern over vibrant crimson, although it's been years since we've had literal fisticuffs up here. Walls are covered in alternate sections of pale gray marble and blue-green panels of painted cloth, preparation for murals that never happened. And up front there's the President's chair, a virtual throne of marble and Tiffany glass and mother-of-pearl, properly flanked by the city and American flags, reminders of democratic grandiosity, an implied threat. So much ostentation, yet the chamber retains an undeserved nobility, demanding veneration for the democratic process despite the dubious record of this particular room and its serenely unreformed occupants.

Be rude enough to stare a little harder and you notice the brown burn marks on the light shades, the tarnished spots on the rail, the overall encroaching dinginess.

This was the first regular session following Council's frankly outrageous three-month summer break, and everything material in the room remained embalmed in the torpor of late summer, but I wasn't much surprised to find most of the visitor chairs filled with unusually alert faces.

Many of them belonging to self-respecting citizens present for legitimate purposes: small businessmen, educators dripping with certainty, parents on some mission with those firm parental jaws. Experienced functionaries from hospitals or high schools or whatever overbearing institution, that unimaginative company of serious thin men in everyday suits and overweight women in polyester slacks a tad too short. An elderly Asian gentleman sat to my right, berry-faced and pleased with everything, while a clutch of self-conscious, overdressed teenagers held the seats immediately to my left.

Usually those smaller groups up to something specific, the ones with the family holiday glow about them, drift in early for a round of official handshakes and introductions by the relevant councilperson's aide.

Otherwise it's generally quiet at first, just a few familiar faces with laptops. And then as ten o'clock moves on towards ten-thirty, and some self-satisfied activist is placing a small reminder gift on everyone's desk, and aides are delivering manila envelopes, and coffee mugs are being positioned just so, then during those few anticipatory minutes the murmurs swell into genuine noise and members magically manifest behind their desks as if they'd been there all along.

That particular day offered another bit of novel excitement, sufficient to momentarily eclipse even the fascinating matter of Thom's public demeanor. An unlikely figure came pushing himself down my row, hands to the rail, absorbing everyone's astonished attention just as the session was at last opening. A pathetic and brutal cliché, obscenely gross; he finally settled himself two chairs from me, his embarrassingly uncontained personal girth overflowing the seat, loose and visibly perspiring. All this overt pathology virtually sucked the air out of the immediate atmosphere; you breathed instead the enormous resentment seeping out of his pores.

This guy was still a kid, in his early twenties at most, sitting there as if scolded with his eyes straight ahead, holding himself perfectly still, flabby hands folded together atop the mountain of his lap. Naturally a pitiable spectacle until gradually you registered the accumulated aggression at the core, and then the thoughtfulness, as of someone carefully considering a multitude of unpleasant scenarios, all of it adding up to a serious potential for violence. When suddenly you decided to take him seriously and sat back to distance yourself. He was wearing a simple navy sports jacket and had thick dark hair long enough to rub against his collar combed straight back from a clear enough forehead. His surface persona evinced bored obedience and also some disgust, but primarily a simple determination to get through the morning.

This was Vinnie Scarpone, or as he preferred Vinnie the Shoe for various nasty but I understand mostly fictitious reasons. I recognized him from news video and newspaper photos from about a year ago dealing with a court case not relevant here. Vinnie was the needy minor appendage of a mob relict, just someone's unfortunate nephew. An automatic glance around told me the boy was probably on his own, so maybe on some personal, legitimate business. "At this time, the Chair recognizes Councilwoman Margery Haskell, who will present a resolution declaring September American Heart Association Month. Will Mrs. Kovacs and her companions please join Councilwoman Haskell at the podium."

Margery rose, expanding upward with her whole forceful soul, fully occupying even that miniscule moment in the spotlight. Reddish-brown hair cropped close to a round skull, a glowing halo of scintillating embers capturing the light; large gold hoops brushing her cocoa complexion. A person invariably adorned in something square, typically a suit in a darker shade; Margery's not exactly overweight but muscular and sturdy, a type you'd associate with a policewoman or someone in the military, straight up and down. She does nothing to hide it. That day it was a charcoal suit with tasteful gold jewelry. Those virtual uniforms are probably a complex defense against envy or attack, because for all the proud determination there's something damaged and still hurting about Margery, something fundamentally at odds with the highly intelligent, capable woman she presents. It's in those mildly belligerent postures, that chronically suspicious soul, the pugnacious expression in her slightly protuberant eyes. Well, overall she's remarkable if intimidating, and highly insightful although in my opinion a little paranoid. And an unthinking progressive, one of those unquestioning types who know what it means to do right by the people and woe to you if you're of the opposition because here's a woman all too inclined to speak decisively as a matter of policy, without reference to any other point of view. On some level she equates Republicans with the Holocaust. A generous woman, generally willing to help you help yourself if you're sufficiently serious and intelligent and disciplined but the hell with you if you're not because she draws a hard line on where your responsibility begins. She mentors from a judicious distance, issuing insights from her comfortable seat on God's lap. Margery holds a doctorate in something like organizational psychology of government management but training hasn't mitigated some elemental need, and when she does revert there's that always a slight shock where you realize she's been operating under a separate agenda all along.

The teenagers were getting to their feet, blessedly unaware of any larger considerations, not giving a damn about Thom if they even knew who he was. But glancing around I caught kindly concern in the wide, pitted countenance of David Cevallos, and from Jack Murphy greedy curiosity behind a shabby charade of compassion. Murphy was a lanky individual with thinning grayish hair and a good smile, and he had some laudable charity work to his credit, but if you saw him across a room you'd instinctively shout: "Snake!" As for Jimmy Spivak, that small, square bulldog, he alternated between peering over at us in sharp, preternatural suspicion and this equally hilarious imitation of political acuity, hand on fist, eyes straight ahead. I saw him feel my notice and immediately frown down at his desk, turning something over.

In a back row and so closer to me, the oleaginous Donny Mealy was as usual maintaining a virtual court, even in this severely regimented space. Or that was the impression he gave, and meant to give, lounging there with his legs arrogantly extended, repeatedly running his hand through that lustrous head of sable hair in an automatic tic. I was certain he, too, had been staring at us, but when I looked over he dropped his hand and proceeded to examine his manicure with absorption and apparently some small puzzlement. Sparing a quick glance over to where his nearest neighbor, old Wilmer van Zandt, was half dozing, and then back to those fascinating hands.

Councilwoman June Dupre was accompanying Margery and her guests to the podium, presenting her usual anxious appearance: her classic golden-brown bob borne like an uncomfortable accessory, her silk suit impaired by an habitual depressed slouch, her makeup modest but still noticeable. Everything worried June, but perhaps that was inevitable for a woman of her accomplishments, her exquisite taste and remarkable erudition. Such gifts distinguish a natural leader and therefore imply a duty to lead. I figured she was doing okay for a neighborhood schlep, an ambitious daughter of the crass lower middle.

Thom was rather speculatively studying our young monster neighbor, fist over grin, while Vinnie himself seemed to be observing nothing whatsoever but simply physically existing. I caught Thom's eye and he shrugged back my own bemusement.

"I see that the Councilwoman is being joined by Councilwoman Dupre and Councilman James Spivak." Thus prompted, Spivak rose and joined his colleagues.

"Publicity happens," I said.

Fist and grin. "I feel like I've finally arrived. My existence has been validated."

Beth Ann Green, Harry's longtime Chief Clerk and nothing more intimate so far as I know, was seated in front of a laptop at a plain table against the wall off to the right side of the podium, a comfortable, efficient vision in purple and black with shocking pink plastic nails, her jet black hair pinned into a tight bun. For once Harry himself seemed to be fully alert and deeply pondering, sucking in his weasel cheeks, his head back so that his heavy eyelids appeared open and aware. Action might be required, his expression seemed to say, but it would be imprudent to plot precipitously. Throwbacks, both of them, their days past for all they refused to acknowledge that fact, hanging on like limpets. When it comes to those two I'm describing a scene that wasn't really there and hadn't been for many years. But the long established municipal racial and ethnic power shift to today's contemporary venality is irrelevant for my current purposes, while Harry and his ilk, for some mysterious reason, remain pertinent.

And Harry was a survival for sure, having managed to enjoy forty-odd years of ghost payrolls, blatant influence pedaling, and ex officio sexual indiscretions while consistently maintaining not only his prominence but also his unique sense of personal honor. It was everyone else's ethics that mutated, bowing under the pressure of an increasingly indiscriminate tolerance, until Harry eventually harvested respect even from his former enemies.

I caught the distantly polite smile of someone's aide edging past me, his contemptuous shoulder to those virgin visitors who were present only because of their personal concern for Thom, identifying a bit too closely with a minor celebrity in kindly or vicious fashion and much too involved with their own emotions to appreciate the acute, primitive fascination beneath all the routine process, the trace of something a little dangerous patiently waiting. But it was affecting some of the other visitors, the sporadic but regular enough spectators and participants, the ones with those neighborhood faces you always think you should recognize. In fact I'm sure everyone familiar with that room displayed a vaguely distracted air that morning. And all this suspense because Thom Askew was as integral to the municipal scene as City Hall itself, as much a political fixture. This universally admired personage who had for Christ's sake always been honest about his sins, who instinctively shunned the dark.

A volatile but entertaining political presence right out of Penn, where he adroitly avoided posing as a scholar despite obvious academic brilliance, flaunting instead his talent as a compact and devious tight end. Openly, innocently cunning, you understand? A proud and amused iconoclast, an erudite and dangerous public wit eager to exploit anything unacceptably hypocritical or tediously pretentious or even marginally dense. Master of an almost miraculous ability to stroke the establishment even while tweaking it, and that was the real secret behind his value as a public commodity, behind so much of his exceptional social success: that ability to be an inoffensive although blatant climber, facilely at home anywhere with anyone, although as a saving grace attracted to the humble as much as to the elite. For Philadelphians he was forever the pattern of a perfect gentleman despite the open calculation and assumed spontaneity and famished ego and rampant vanity because such deficiencies just never mattered, his faults seemed to us weirdly admirable. And somehow his unremarkable sandy hair and irregular features only added to his appeal, making anything regularly pretty appear plastic and, ironically enough, false.

So an accommodating legend, making us all proud of ourselves, the wonder pet of the limitlessly indulgent local media, a constant ideal of our friends' parents. Also an erstwhile flagrant womanizer, but all that predated the Ruth era; afterwards it was all romantic knightly devotion and never so much as a whiff of rumor to the contrary, two posers guarding each other's backs without at all realizing it, assuming themselves in love.

Well, ultimately you had to take him into account just to do business in this city, so immense was the hold he had over our worshipping souls. Moving inviolate among responsible politicos who measured their success largely by how grievously they could curtail the aims of this impudent golden boy and so attain some slight degree of equality with him, their ingratiating enemy who somehow found time to know the names of every nearby falafel or Chinese food or fruit salad vendor and was invariably delighted to sample their wares with all due, outrageous trepidation. Although for his own lunch he preferred a quiet corner booth in a convenient gastropub if with friends, but otherwise a deli sandwich or salad to devour voraciously in his office, without tasting it.

"Thank you, Mister President. A resolution declaring September American Heart Association Month. Whereas," Margery read, and stepped back so that the three of them could take the rest of it in turns, Harry meanwhile looking down from his perch directly over the podium like a Greek god observing the goings-on at Troy.

I contemplated them, these three well-known figures gathered at the front of the room. Spivak bored me. June saddened me. And Margery made me angry.

I saw movement and caught van Zandt coming fully awake, rheumy gray eyes reorienting; he snorted and then smiled without embarrassment. Just fully returned to action after some kind of medical crisis over the summer, clearly frail, now more than ever he absolved himself from life with senile recalcitrance, upholding inexplicable prejudices in a very *screw you* kind of way: "I don't know why, but that just happens to be what I think." And then that saccharine smile; it was as if he'd become modern. Meanwhile his body, untouched by this anomalous spirit, had degenerated into a rather stately hollow hulk crowned with notably thick white hair, a veritable caricature of a statesman with narrow, observant eyes, concave porcelain cheeks, and the necessary generous hooked nose to bestow a fitting Roman profile even in repose. He was one of our few Republicans, visibly seeping down into local history. Consider him the symbol of a fading generation, a compendium of its trite, familiar moral and physical options; so far as I knew he'd never evinced any unexpected or original insight or behavior from vigorous youth through to current decrepitude. These days you addressed him with labored courtesy while surreptitiously checking that his fly was zipped.

55

"Resolved further, that an engrossed copy of this resolution be presented to the students of Northeast High School in appreciation of their dedicated efforts to increase awareness of this insidious disease and how to go about preventing it.

"Bee-*you*-ti-ful," Harry said. And then Mrs. Kovacs spoke, and then the students spoke individually, and sometime after that it was Councilman Murphy at the podium, to be joined there by David Cevallos and several additional upstanding citizens. "A resolution recognizing the excellent efforts of Philadelphia's Table to redistribute uneaten food to the needy."

It's always this exciting. From behind me I picked up the aroma of a menthol cough drop; Thom was thoughtfully twirling an unopened package of those toxic-orange peanut-butter-and- cheese crackers. Harry forged ahead to Communications, the Sergeant-at-Arms was requested to deliver the messages to the Chief Clerk. The mayor, it developed, had signed various bills, was forwarding to Council a recommendation of the City Planning Commission, and was transmitting ordinances for consideration regarding open-air cafes and lead-based paint coating on jewelry.

"The next order of business is the introduction of bills and resolutions." That one traveling the room, everyone taking a turn or passing: recreation field maintenance, congratulations to some charter school, amendments to varied titles of the City Code, resolutions duly seconded and resolved, and bills forwarded to the appropriate committee.

That initial tension was dissipating under the massage of routine.

Mr. Spivak: "An ordinance to amend the Philadelphia Zoning Maps by changing the zoning designations in certain areas of land located within an area bounded by Columbus Avenue, Locust Street, and Vine Street."

A gentle susurration: nothing dramatic, just a barely perceptible communal intake of breath prior to the commencement of a process that, once set in motion, might eventually require thought or risk or even prove significant unlikely as that was, all things considered. And not even today; today was about officially confirming issues already settled elsewhere.

This fascinating matter referencing Penn's Landing, that highly-contested stretch of real estate bordering the steely and businesslike Delaware River. The scene, a century after the glad arrival of Mr. Penn, of a flourishing commercial port giving access to the most successful city in America, later gradually reduced to the abandoned terminus of a 20th-century slum. And currently - what? The tantalizing appendage of a stretch of landmark urban redevelopment, an underutilized although hardly neglected public gathering place? Without question the centerpiece of a truly wonderful series of financial fiascos.

A site weirdly cursed despite the moderate popularity of the current facilities: the Great Plaza amphitheatre and the World Sculpture Garden and the ships and the Seaport Museum and the rest of it, all integral to our every municipal holiday, all barely nice enough and moderately utilized but never quite enough to revitalize the Landing in any satisfactory fashion, isolated as it was on the other side of I-95, insistently decomposing amidst a swirl of frustration and scandal. Every now and then there came another grand plan, generally from some out-of-town investor with an exciting proposal and no local expertise, these projects invariably doomed for who knows what stubborn underlying reasons. But we determinedly rise again to our self-imposed challenge, neurotically deaf to experience, and meantime the surrounding areas developed the way they wanted, by fitful yet successful inches.

Now here was our novice mayor's bill, and what this mayor wanted was a slots parlor, yet another casino on the Delaware but this one right downtown, easily accessible to the public transit crowd. He'd made his agenda more than clear, citing among other things the benefits to minority employment and revitalization spurred by a genuine destination attraction, the factual bases for his statements remaining obscure, and anyway the whole mess was so politically divisive it was being ignored by almost everyone outside the administration whenever possible for as long as possible. This all concerned one of two gaming licenses awarded Philadelphia and initially intended for South Philly, except that plan was blocked by this new mayor with his downtown plan. So then the license was supposed to be an old department store building right on Market Street, but community activists and the owners objected, the developers were fined for failing to submit designs and financials, two new backers appeared and disappeared, and Council attempted to halt development altogether through zoning control, overriding the mayor's veto and voting to put the issue straight on the ballot until the State Supreme Court nixed that idea. So ultimately the Gaming Control Board revoked the license, and now here it was up for grabs all over again.

"The bill will be referred to the appropriate committee." So we leaned back and stood down and everything droned along just as if nothing had happened, if in fact it had.

"What do you think?"

Eyebrows shooting way up, the better to sight along a familiar road. He shrugged. "My faith instructs me to believe in miracles." In truth Thom was a preacher's kid and took his faith seriously even while mocking the faithful, an intellectual embarrassed by simple believers. "The next order of business is reports from committees." Bills on Appropriations considered and returned to Council with favorable recommendations. Rules suspended to allow an immediate first reading. The bills just read placed on today's First Reading Calendar. "The next order of business being a consideration of the Calendar; I note the bill just reported from committee with a suspension of the rules deemed to have had a first reading, it will be placed on our Second Reading and Final Passage Calendar for our next Council session." The high school contingent openly stirred in its chairs, anxious to make this a proud memory. Thom was leaning over the cartoon page of a battered copy of Newsweek. Somewhere there was the click and flash of a camera.

I looked round again. Mealy was laughing silently at something with his immediate intimates. June appeared frozen into a fastidious curve, both hands flat on her desk, head lowered. She might have been praying; I wouldn't put it past her.

I sighed and leaned directly over to Thom. "Well, how are you, anyway?"

"Second reading - rules - suspended - Consent agenda to consider the following bills - all in favor - anyone objecting to a bill on the Consent Agenda may object."

The Chief Clerk read out the bills in the necessary excruciating detail, keeping her tone calm but brisk to demonstrate her professionalism. When so instructed, proceeding to read the roll. "Aye on all bills." "I'm quite well, actually. And yourself, Con? Still trying to be a real boy?" Looking shrewd out loud, angry but delighted with himself. Thom can be a total prick.

On to the regular Second Calendar and Final Passage Calendar. "This bill having been read on two different days, the question now is shall the bill pass finally." The roll droned round again. "The ayes are seventeen; the nays are zero."

"Are there speeches on the part of the minority?" There are not; the Republications are holding their peace for the time being. "Are there speeches on the part of the majority?"

There was one. "The Chair recognizes Councilman Cevallos."

"Thank you, Mister President." Now here was a solemn presence, dignified and trustworthy; we rather impatiently watched him delve into his own balanced psyche, garnering the required words of wisdom, meanwhile arranging himself in his chair and letting his practiced orator's eye measure us against his message. I know David well enough to know he's an artist in his soul, and that means he essentially evades my judgment. Once a dedicated educator, he's practiced at this kind of painful public introspection. Crystal is creeped out by him for reasons she refuses to examine, but I suspect she senses his unfavorable judgment, like God's. I do think David holds her in mild contempt and I resent his appropriating my prerogative. He's hardly attractive but even grotesque, his features coarse and asymmetrical, but he carries himself with a suave, old-fashioned Latin courtesy, and spends extravagantly on his elegant wardrobe.

"I would like to take this opportunity to say a few words regarding the bill introduced this morning by Councilman Spivak regarding a zoning adjustment in the area alongside the river." His magnified voice traveled the room, David himself following closely to monitor our reception. He has a beautiful speaking voice with a melodious cadence that floats out to seduce you. "All of us here understand the very serious considerations involved; we're talking about the first steps to bringing gambling to Penn's Landing, traditionally a family venue."

I could see he was going to have to be very severe with us despite his obvious distress at the necessity.

"I would remind Council that this legislation is inappropriate in that we all understand the Planning Commission has yet to complete their hearings on proposals regarding what's going to happen at that site. In addition, the Gaming Control Board has yet to approve any such proposal. Two separate issues."

"Well." Uttered as if he'd just that moment thought it through, putting one thick palm flat on his desk the better to gesture with the loose hand: a middle-aged, crude Hispanic tough dressed for church. Inspiring Thom to chew his knuckle and Margery to look irritated and June to consciously project intelligence with a puckered forehead and narrowed eyes and Harry to pretend to extreme boredom. "I have myself been out there on the sidewalks during much of this whole past year, I have been in the high school auditoriums and firehouses and in corporate conference rooms, putting together community forums, talking to experts, meeting with the Delaware River Waterfront Corporation."

"And out of all this invaluable input we have carefully established principles for the development of this area, and these principles or guidelines are about what the people of this city actually want to see in that location. So you see these guidelines have to be, absolutely must be honored and fully incorporated into whatever ultimate design we support."

Kindly if ponderously expounded as if to intelligent children, with the deliberate certainty of an arithmetical conclusion that left no room for question or confusion. Or possibly he was clarifying something for his own benefit and didn't get the universal insult.

"So we will consider this bill in Committee as is proper." This was stated sternly, no doubt reflecting his experience of this particular legislative body. "But I - and now also some of my colleagues on the Committee - we will not be rushed to judgment, and the mayor of this city and those who support his declared preferences in this matter need to recognize that this is a highly complex affair, that there is much to say against this particular bill, and that's not even considering the fact that it's clearly, it seems to me, too early to bring this bill."

Then he stopped short and stared straight at me, and everyone was staring at me in a kind of shock. I looked wildly down at myself to see if I was on fire or bleeding, then back at David. What?

It was Vinnie they were staring at. Vinnie two seats over from me and halfway on his feet, how could I have missed seeing his monumental torso tilted far forward and his tiny features constricted into a frightening grimace? At first I thought he was having some kind of attack but then he was up and moving rapidly, a sloppy avalanche rolling right past me.

He was through the gate and on the floor by the time I adjusted my facts again: it was old van Zandt who was sick, that's what was happening. Those ancient features showing a rather mild contortion of still attention, his spine rigid and pressed hard against the back of his chair, and Vinnie was heading straight towards him, and everyone's attention was bouncing between the two of them.

With a kind of natural inevitability, as if he'd been patiently awaiting our notice, van Zandt went lax, slumping down and to the side. And Vinnie stopped dead, staring at the old man's bulk and furiously engage his brain. Then he reversed course and made decisively for the exit. I turned back to find Margery hovering uselessly as Thom and David moved aside chairs; they took hold of an Zandt, Thom at his shoulders and David holding his legs, and laid him flat on the garish carpet. Two stolid guards were motioning everyone back but those at the scene remained close, tethered by a combination of concern and fascination and jealous opportunism.

I slipped out to the hallway in time to glimpse Vinnie vanish into a truncated corridor, so I followed along the mottled blue and gray linoleum, past all the glass cases displaying civic- minded art. He was on his phone, standing tight to a wall covered in amber tiles so luminous and intricate they pleaded to be housed in a museum. So I walked on a prudent distance, affecting a brisk, purposive stride, a reporter carrying the news. On past someone's dark portrait hanging above a long wooden table, on to a window looking out to yet another symbolic frieze. At

63

which point I backtracked to discover the side recess vacant.

Shit. Decaying Wilmer van Zandt of all conventionally venial people. I stood in place and flapped my hands to think.

My colleagues were out in the hall to note my return with questioning faces, but I shrugged. Of course everybody there had noted Vinnie's aborted approach, including my opposite from our tabloid daily who was eyeing me curiously. People were drifting around talking excitedly to each other or their phones; somebody jostled me cutting across to the Caucus Room. But this was no ongoing drama, and soon enough members and aides started moving off to their respective offices here or a floor above, Thom sending me a parting nod. A stern female marshaled the impressed students and other exhilarated visitors down towards the elevators. I saw Margery and Mealy with their heads together, he babbling, her with her lips pressed tight. David stood staring inside himself; June hugged her own slim frame, shivering in repressed horror and compassion. I heard sirens, but there are always sirens around City Hall just as there's always some degree of melodrama.

At Jefferson a practiced spokesperson said basically nothing so I went home to catch exclusive video of the shattered wife being escorted in through a parking garage, slept, and at dawn watched a well-endowed morning newsreader in a low-cut cocktail dress turn to address her handsome if aging colleague. "I telephoned the hospital this morning and they informed me that they suspect Councilman van Zandt suffered a massive stroke. He was eighty-one years old and suffered from various health issues." That was it, no substantial biography let alone any expression of public sorrow, nothing to inspire significant city veneration.

So what if Vinnie Scarpone noticed an old man in trouble? Except I knew better, plus there was the sudden about-face and phone call and his being there in the first place monitoring that fragile, irresponsible husk, which was almost certainly what he was doing there. Well, it wasn't like any of this was extraordinary; it was probably just more of the usual sordid crap. And in that disgusted appraisal I was absolutely correct. It's just that I always underestimate stupidity even though I know it rules the world.

CHAPTER THREE

"I see the river." Sophie at fifteen was able to converse intelligently some of the time; I found her companionable but reserved. Maybe that's for the best, maybe you don't want to know too much about your adolescent daughter but no danger there, she kept her own counsel. Even as a small child she seemed a complete, self-contained individual. I advocated for her name for sheer love of wisdom and naturally to reflect her heritage, and now there are Sophias all over the place and her brilliant, unique father is considered just another undistinguished sheep. It makes me crazy. Fortunately teenagers are great conformists so she perversely considers her name a kind of social confirmation.

She was giving me a minor lip pout over the usual determination; she doesn't love concept games but she's intensely competitive. When I looked at her she turned to stare out at the traffic on the expressway, which was moving decently for a change.

"And I repeat, how do you know?"

For much of her early childhood Sophie and her mother lived in Biloxi, but she's a very eastern type despite occasional lapses into a kind of resentful passivity; she has a sharp if quiet mind and an instinctive preference for reality, so I never thought Mississippi a compatible locale for her, however reputedly cosmopolitan these days. The air is too insidiously soft, the atmosphere implicitly devious. The one time I visited her there I found her a round little ball of a child, brown and complacent, sitting on the beach of that beautiful, placid gulf. Grasping her little yellow plastic spade with both chubby hands, happily digging for nothing. I pulled her up into my arms and lifted her above my head. "Sophie, look! Look around! Everything is alive, the sky is alive! Even the ocean is alive!" She burst out bawling, her baby feet kicking out at my face, the tears cutting runnels into her sandy cheeks.

Anyway I was meanly delighted when a second divorce sent her mother running back to her parents' protection. It's easy enough to denigrate conceited, ambitious suburbia, but even the protective enclave of Doylestown, Pennsylvania has a rudimentary attachment to the living earth: winters that are truly bitter and traumatic, foolishly ambitious autumns, summers with that exquisite gray perfume of hose water evaporating off cement. And then you can always run down the tacky Jersey shore if you miss the ocean. I'm more comfortable having Sophie in this environment.

I had an apartment near Washington Square, right off Pine Street in a renovated corner building, four large old rooms with thick walls and decent light. There was a liquor store on the opposite corner with a homeless alcoholic to decorate its window; a pair of local cops bought him new sneakers every so often as a reward for being where he was supposed to be, which warmed the heart.

My furniture was comfortably contemporary, soft neutral fabrics and uncomplicated lines flattered by the best carpets I could afford, brilliant islands of soft garnet and cream on a dark polished sea – I'm the kind of asshole who insists you take your shoes off. I had some decent paintings displayed on plain off- white walls because I happen to be into pure beauty. This surprises people, which is interesting given my reputation for unvarnished truth and how everyone accepts that truth is beauty, which it is if you can take it. When people comment on my taste, not even bothering to hide their astonishment that I'm not some sort of bitter puritan or indifferent slob, I explain that I'm a journalist and therefore beauty is my business. And then they look ashamed because they secretly consider me physically ugly but think I don't know. There'd once been a men's shop on the ground floor; Mason's Haberdashery was engraved in the marble lintel over the entrance. I notice it occasionally, and wonder about that era, the strictures and expectations reflected in gentlemanly hat and vest and spats. The gulf between then and today is impossibly wide: it's important to remember that it isn't true that things change, the truth is that everything changes together. No one can ever adequately resurrect the past because there's no stable place to stand while doing it.

Now there's a Realtor in that space, and twice every day I passed a display of miniscule photographs of desirable properties pinned up against a dun-colored board. When Sophie was with me we'd stop and analyze listings, comparing their amenities. Tending towards modesty, we rejected and sometimes outright mocked the spa bathrooms and gourmet kitchens required these days. Being acutely conscious of the situation in the wider world, we felt ourselves almost too fortunate already. I constantly worried about Sophie succumbing to cultural slavery, adopting somebody else's cheap dreams. Her mother's, for instance. I desperately wanted her to remain free in mind and taste and soul, but how likely is that?

Barring her birthday list suggestions on music and books and so on I can barely guess at her actual preferences. I don't want to fool myself about that ignorance, either. She's reticent on the big stuff and expresses no particular aspirations or passions to me, but I think she's waiting for something. A signal from the universe, I guess. I hear there are teens who confide in their fathers but as I've explained, I'm a scary guy, so it doesn't matter what I do, or how many long hours of her infancy I held her endlessly at my chest as if I could literally nurse her.

That summer her visible taste was trending towards tackiness, glitz and shine during daytime even at school, reflecting the new exhibitionism, the rejection of all that old weighty shame. On the whole I approve of that liberty despite the problematic lack of moral center. Why not? When you think about it, who's to say what's appropriate when?

I've adopted only one specific goal with Sophie: to inoculate her against the myth of the street, the lie of romantic rebellion and the progressive underclass. To force her to think critically about all that trendy shit, about the ludicrous stupidity of suburban coeds in designer prison garb. Teach her to discriminate without, you know, letting her revert into some kind of conventional, stupid robot.

So anyway I can't really tell how Sophie's assessing her new femininity or her encroaching adulthood. Her gaze doesn't exactly disguise impudence, but it isn't entirely innocuous, either. And she's developed a disturbing habit of denigrating everyone else against the impossible standard of her utterly faultless future self. One September Monday we headed out early to get her back up to school, the car filled with the happy aromas of coffee and sunscreen. It was the kind of perfect morning people take for granted.

Ruth's chirpy pseudo-reasonable radio voice, gamely attempting to clarify another instance of rash illogic, making an additional passenger, her virtual presence mingling into the general confusion of heat and sun and traffic.

"People used to be able to accept their own cruelty because it was about necessity so it wasn't even recognized as cruel. You have to be able to afford empathy. I mean, morality is basically about discovering what's successful for the family or tribe or whatever and that's what defines virtue."

The mechanical whine of a laughing female caller, possibly appreciative or maybe derisive; I never caught the main thread of it. Sophie was studying the view with her arm resting against the window, visibly thinking like crazy.

"No, well, you have this situation where underdeveloped nations are supposed to play by contemporary moral rules, our rules. Look at environmental policies, for example. Countries that aren't even industrialized yet. And individual people, too, of course, pushing ahead too fast."

This naïve shit had been polluting the airwaves since the Folk Fest: unfiltered statements, nonchalant eruptions of chaos into a previously inoffensive breakfast program. Her frustrated energy responding to the opportunity while it lasted, interspersing banal outbursts of inappropriate passion between soft pop hits and traffic updates, ostensibly in response to listener calls or Internet comments. According to one caller with a gruff male voice, reasonable and amused, Ruth proving herself one of those new Republicans who want their government strong abroad but compassionate at home.

"I'm everything. Everything so nothing specific." She made it a joke but blurted it, pushing it away; she was always a blurter and a political coward; I mean, I'd be ashamed too if I had identify with the willfully backward. Plus party affiliations are visceral these days, you have to be careful not to associate yourself with the wrong people.

"The signs tell me it's the river." Sophie said, hopeful but with practiced petulance clearly in reserve.

There'd been one extremely damning editorial in the local tabloid: they were known for pun headlines so that was a given. Print coverage was otherwise vague and inadequate. Then of course there was an orgasmic eruption of social media vitriol, briefly spent. But everyone was waiting for the rest of it, that other shoe to fall, some proper public or corporate response of deserved consequence, but the respective parties were keeping mum. And probably a decent segment of her public thought her a little deranged but still sympathized. Meanwhile those who imagined her an ally relished having someone voice their own irrational frustrations; she acquired new partisans, covert conservatives hugged themselves in private delight. The problem was, it was all so amorphous.

Of course the majority of her listeners weren't all that young or politically active or prone to violence or otherwise likely to command significant influence, so in that sense Ruth was basically screaming into the infinite silence of space. More pertinently, neither the station nor her sponsors objected, but that was temporary; the situation there was complicated and currently in flux, a proper response merely on hold. But we'll consider that business catastrophe shortly.

Needless to say, no public uprising of devoted adherents, no intelligent commendation, no thanks for the enlightenment.

"Now we're instantaneously seeing the consequences of every action and it's paralyzing us. You know what I think? I think soon they'll be proving how plants feel pain and emotion and then what'll the vegetarians eat?"

"How do you know what the signs say?"

Massive sigh. Sophie was dressed for school in a lacy white shirt with a baby blue tank under it, jeans, and ankle boots that brought her up to my height. Like me she's compact and square, but while I'm dark she's completely pale, so neutral a beige it seems designed, with bright round eyes under pale lashes, straight dirty-blond hair, and a heavy jaw terminating in a blunt chin. Although she's stubborn she's elusive about it, hesitant to articulate her ideas but adept at getting her way, and she's rarely where you think either physically or emotionally. When she decides to hold her ground she's unshakable, refusing to concede defeat even in the face of plainly contrary facts. Fully inhabiting her naturally pugnacious features, sticking out that unfortunately prominent chin.

I was trailing a black SUV, with to my left the twinkling Schuylkill, placid this morning under a few straggling wisps of lambent fog; to my right scrub trees and brush climbing straight up a ridge gouged orange in broad raw swaths, evidence of a recent downpour. Summers those ridges unexpectedly trap the heat over the water, preventing any refreshing river breeze. It was just after seven but it was already sweltering, the fresh sun glaring off cars and guardrails. I spotted a lone kayak out on the water, brilliant blue slicing cleanly through pellucid gray. This river cuts to the west of Center City, providing tap water that leaves a sticky residue in your toothbrush glass, and it can run shallow even around the lower reaches, being more of a recreational type of waterway as opposed to the more impressive and businesslike Delaware drawing our natural border to the east. Although I've seen the Schuylkill flood, too, and it's pretty damn impressive.

"I tend myself to think in terms of original sin, but I don't think it's always necessary to drag in religion." "Did you hear that? Did you hear that incense-marinated rosary-fondling holy-medal-kissing self-elected candidate for sainthood?"

I used to be your typical ambitious, self-satisfied scholarship undergrad, transient resident in a professionally landscaped, upscale township a few minutes outside Philadelphia. Looking out my dorm window at scenery primped to the epitome of good taste: carefully designed red-gold autumn foliage, springs decked out with pastel shrubbery and blossoming fruit trees, and in December extravagant Christmas decorations gilding the college gothic and precious faux-Colonial shops. It utterly delighted me, essentially penniless urbanite by history and inclination, just because it was so spurious and entitled and successful. Of course I secretly desired that life even while I rightly and loudly disparaged it.

But I loved the city itself from the first moment I strayed into Philadelphia, and I include the ubiquitous, disregarded natural city: the explosions of feathery pink mimosas, the irrepressible Trees of Heaven, the Queen Anne's Lace and delicate, tiny fleabane blossoms like miniature daisies, the tall yellow or purple clover. The stray neighborhoods with decrepit back fences cloaked in sweet-smelling honeysuckle and blue chicory pushing through along the sidewalk. No one else seemed to care for these humble urban delights, but I found them enchanting. The gardeners for my building were Hispanic, so of course I sporadically exploited them to convince myself I was a member of the proletariat. Their accommodating macho selves intimidated the hell out of me. "That's an amazing azalea." Inspiring this older guy with a thin, golden face and distant eyes to stand back proudly from what truly was a glorious hedge. "Over half a century old," he'd say, or something similar about whatever I happened to point to, reluctant to accept personal praise. This was compulsive behavior on my part; I was humiliated for these men.

The surrounding neighborhood formed a closed circle of disciplined self-approbation, of right prevailing and the teary- eyed faith of the fortunate. I recall the whole complacent town as a special American species of church devoted to an ideology of deserved success, and you know how you instinctively feel reverent when you enter a place of worship even if, like me, you're not religious.

Senior year I was living with my second college girlfriend Naomi, an ash blond, small and curvy, best described as essentially average, a woman who pretended to listen. We unwittingly drifted into a relationship of mutual convenience with nothing demanding or ecstatic about it. She was a bland caramel custard, diligent in bed like all girls are who have read up on the subject, but at that time I accepted our coupling as a natural progression. I'd just about determined to follow the academic track, of course planning to pass the torch to my own students. In retrospect this decision reflects an astonishing gullibility: critically questing after greater erudition while automatically adopting the given methodology, handing down the same shit. Incredible, when you think about it.

So far as the God question I think I was pretty average for my generation, a holiday worshipper brought up to consider the whole issue less than imperative, my parents refusing to offer prejudicial guidance or approval, demoting the fate of my eternal soul to something I could decide for myself one day, so enough said. Not that I had any nascent religious inklings, but I had no natural antipathy, either, merely disinterest. I'm not one of those tiresome atheists who use their position like a weapon, like those frightened science devotees who forget it's just a process that has nothing to do with safe, superior conclusions. My preferred practice is to employ truth in the purest sense, never in service to any underlying philosophy, even my own. Like Socrates I argue in order to expose error.

There was one ordinary enough early evening right after New Year's in our efficiency with the particle board furniture and gallery posters, the rumpled day bed and the coffee table piled with textbooks and notebooks with doodles and the local news playing on television. Naomi was sitting with her feet tucked under her in our one armchair, just watching me, and I was curled into the bed, absolutely rigid, sweating out a continuing abdominal pain, waiting and observing as it escalated into the kind of situation you know will radically alter your personal history.

There followed a lot of efficient movement without much input from me, occupied as I was with resignation and vomiting, and then I was lying on a gurney in pre-op, freezing to death, and hovering above me was an apparent doctor of about my own age, cheerful and chubby-faced and reassuring. I was thinking I'd get to see the inside of the operating theatre because I wasn't even sleepy when another physician moved into my view, an older man with a triumphant grin and a surgical mask loose around his neck who said everything had gone perfectly.

Talk about stupefying. It was absolute physical comprehension, the irrefutable flat fact of death with nothing muddled or dream-like or painful about it, no physical or mental presence or sense of continuation because there was no me to experience it, because for a discreet interval I'd been cleanly cut out of time.

I stared out a window giving onto a series of rooftop terraces with untidy planters and hopping sparrows, conceding what was anyway my fundamental suspicion. What flummoxed me, what I still find bewildering is why everyone who undergoes general anesthesia doesn't immediately concede this experience, this fact of nonexistence. "It's not like you have anything to offer." Naomi was sitting across the dinette table from me, a patchwork pillow tight against her stomach. I vividly remember that pillow. This was over a month after my appendicitis surgery, so a couple of weeks into our final semester and February bleak. I remember being mildly surprised by her bluntness but not by her attack or her message. Nuzzling her cushion, that bland hair over the royal purple and deep green material, a curtain for her round little face. And then she reverted to passivity, insisting I understand.

I was disgusted as much as anything, it was so contemptible and plain unfair, the entire pathetic show of assumed bravery and self-importance. I never even questioned her certainty so on some level I must have anticipated this kind of easy treachery.

Lifting that stubborn chin - so like Sophie's - but not to assert any religious or ethical prohibition, merely to reiterate her own decision. I know how this sounds but I was genuinely repelled and insulted. Anyway, I just waited.

"Well, I'm sorry since I realize you're not in favor of marriage."

I sat back against the bolster and tried to think. I certainly wasn't about to argue her point; she was familiar with my opinion of monogamy, and in fact we had an explicit agreement in place. But marriage was hardly a necessity, merely responsible paternal behavior. Surely that didn't require pretending to tolerate this woman now attempting to capture the affection and support of someone she'd just intellectually and emotionally violated.

I said, "I'm in favor of a short-term marriage."

That's how you can begin and end a marriage in one irreversible instant. Obviously I conceded more than was merited, but I guess I had my reasons: childhood fantasies lingering in my psyche to trip me up. At that moment we became the mortal enemies we are today, although we remain spuriously affectionate for Sophie's sake and because anything less would be too easy.

"Language. Symbols signifying river." "How do you know there even are words?" "Dad, are you really going to keep this up?"

One of those callers that make you cringe for all mankind, obviously reading from his list of statistics proving something of unappreciated import, why didn't everyone just admit it, stumbling a bit but oh so patronizing, sure of his unique insight into everything. The kind of guy who leaves comments to Internet articles.

Ruth simply ignored his argument. "Facts, you know. A fact by definition is a piece of the past, something that's considered true because it's done with. Only scared little people cling to facts." I exist within a contradiction, as all honest, intelligent men must these days, accepting that reality itself and all the appurtenances of truth including science, logic, and language are inextricably involved with the human mind, but at the same time viscerally convinced of an invariant, objective truth, a discoverable external reality indifferent to the human body or will. What's more refusing to embrace some game-ending, painstakingly clever compromise, some demeaning if reasonable way to worm out. My esteemed namesake, in one of his more famous poems, urges Antony to demonstrate dignity in defeat, to act in a manner worthy of the great city of Alexandria, his own municipal goddess. Philadelphia might not be as mighty a deity but I find it sufficiently demanding, and I can humbly admit my failure to resolve this one essential dilemma without cravenly refuting the possibility.

"Moral evolution is about realizing that something's right but not doing it and vice versa. Take abortion: it's wrong but it's very often the right wrong." That's Ruth's wishful redeemed Catholicism, flippant over yet another paltry, easily resolved human dilemma. "That's freedom; that's the future. Just don't be cheap, don't use some slanted, pseudo-scientific lie. Be honest for a change"

Of course she wasn't always this irrational or provocative; maybe that finally would have brought the deserved reprisals. She was smart enough to laugh at herself and go harmless for a couple of days between outrageous episodes. This is a compendium. You get the idea.

Some middle-aged woman's voice, strident with that South Philly vulgarity that keeps you anxious: "Ruth I love that you stand up for regular people."

"It's a lot of what I struggle to do. I do try hard, all the time. That's where all the real courage is and the real virtue, in getting up every single morning and going to the lousy job and feeding the family and being involved in the vital continuance of decent life. Genuinely nice women in their sixties putting on their earrings and eye shadow and getting the train every morning to go do their best. I'm in love with them, absolutely in love with them! I'm just a lucky egotist with these undeserved gifts of time and opportunity. But I try to remember how humility means appreciating the equal greatness of everyone, because everyone is equally great."

Humility lessons from Ruth.

I mean, okay, as I've said I too question the instinctive adoration of the revolutionary outsider; identification with the next wave is only prudent because those people truly are coming to annihilate your precious status quo, they're God if anything is. But nothing justifies going around glorifying the complacent, bigoted masses, lauding mere passive, unquestioning cows and sheep for their sheer animal stamina. I studied philosophy in grad school, anxious to place my own inchoate ideas in context. I needed to know more about where the notables stood, and I especially wanted to understand all those romantic and cool but totally confounding isms of the recent continentals. Silly pretensions notwithstanding, my desire was profound, even desperate. I'd never gone further than some introductory undergraduate courses when suddenly I realized I was going to graduate and never acquire any further knowledge forever. I wanted to isolate the unadorned truth and build some kind of ethics based on that still center. And so in a truly egregious error of judgment, encouraged by a greedy academic system and eagerly misidentifying my morbidly self-involved curiosity as an aptitude for scholarship, I determined to turn myself into a professional thinker-teacher-scribe.

To be fair, I would have made a decent, even excellent teacher, but I had no interest whatsoever in scholarship. Therefore the system rejected me.

Naomi and I moved into a tiny, toddler-dominated apartment in West Philly, close to my new slum-encircled but properly ivy-clad campus. It was a decent existence, a life of academic challenge with my remarkably self-possessed, observant baby daughter whom I immediately and completely adored, who taught me that even a minor deviation from conventional beauty, a too-short nose and naked round eyes of no outstanding shade, can inspire infinite absorption. Who proved the ability of mere humans to create life, although I still find it unbelievable.

I cheated on my marriage but I don't want to make too much of this; for one thing, my memories of this period are confused. I kind of believed in it; I thought I could be someone else from long ago, so I tried it out and it was a mistake. Naomi tried being hurt but gave it up when she grasped my revulsion. Her heart wasn't in it any more than mine; evenings she was diligently pursuing an MBA, developing this shark's smile to complement her middle-class avarice, getting even more self- disciplined. Picking out her next husband, it turned out.

Meanwhile at my university I experienced the inevitable vicious, clichéd pettiness, the endless watchful departmental jealousies that seemed at first blush admirable. Didn't that prove how much all this theorizing mattered to the initiates, mattered essentially and intimately and not just in a narrow professional sense but to their whole lives and values and worldviews? Like an idiot I sat at those cramped seminar tables feeling proud of myself, although even back then I realized most philosophy is basically crap. Look at Kant and Hume; it's just simplistic shit wrapped up in dense layers of jargon. Validity is determined by timing and credentials, that's all there is to it. Value's all in the packaging, otherwise no one will notice except to mock.

Those openly shabby, overheated, companionable but endlessly suspicious proving grounds of we stressed contestants, the entire clever, hip, narrow-minded ethos of that subtle arena, the notice boards with yellowed cartoons and faculty profiles, the torn orange vinyl on the lounge sofas, the classrooms with scarred wooden tables pushed together, the huge whiteboards crisscrossed with scrawled, recondite abbreviations differentiating postmodernism from structuralism from deconstruction: Foucault and Habermas and of course Derrida breaking apart those hidden oppositions, searching within and only within but never just fucking turning around. So much intense, urgent argument and analysis dedicated to describing an already circumscribed human prison, plus of course that ongoing defense of brilliant but eternally misunderstood Nietzsche. Styrofoam cups set next to laptops carefully recording every precious syllable of some shrewd middle-aged professor's exploratory word games, those little testing pokes at your cultural prowess and intellectual potential while you stared at the spotless soles of his heavy work boots propped oh so casually on a desk drawer. Faithful predictions of the return of socialism permeated those days despite that great dream's apparent demise, as did a courageous refusal to retreat from implacable atheism even in the face of overwhelming victory.

Look, I'm being unfair here if not outright lying. I understood the importance and supreme difficulty of all that work, I saw the literal enlightenment, the practical comprehension following in its wake. Not the work I wanted to do, although I couldn't admit that then, but admirable.

But still.

I adored it even as I wrestled with my complicit cowardice, despising myself. Not because I disagreed, precisely, although occasionally I did, but because there was clearly no use for any argument or discussion but merely for further exacting clarification. All of us carrying out an endless autopsy of human thought.

I suffered for my increasingly clouded future and often enough for my fellow students. That pervading stench of intellectual desperation was easy to confuse with normal graduate student angst, but I can recall a Husserl seminar that devolved into three full hours spent gleefully shredding a friend of mine, a decent man who'd missed a paper deadline because he was unwell, and who was unwell because he'd submitted himself to some university medical experiments to cover his tuition. In retrospect I think I escaped that kind of treatment because nobody there ever took me seriously. Well, and because I was coward enough to keep my head down. On another stupefying afternoon as I was watching the light climb down from the tall, sealed windows - rumored legacy of a jumper - and ignoring a discussion of I think Kitty McKinnon, this rather troubled-looking older woman raised her hand. "But isn't it self-contradictory? I mean, you can't actually give someone rights or freedoms; they have to be invested."

Hesitation all around while awaiting word from on high; it came in a mild enough tone with only a cursory glance up. "And unfortunately that ability is stifled by those protecting the status quo."

And of course that stern, unanimous agreement rising from the pierced and leather-clad guys on the floor by the back wall, from the career track scholars lounging at the table with thoughtful, approving nods, from the oft-petted TA with a dismissive if polite shrug.

They were all majestically tolerant, those experts, even more than their compatriots in the other humanities departments; they were masters of thorough political theory, eager delineators of the limits of human knowledge, geniuses of refutation, intolerant only of their analytic colleagues down the hall, those ignoramuses so bogged down in the deluded past they still sought certainty in matter and the material self and went nattering on about logic and consciousness and especially language. Imagine!

The level of inter-departmental animosity was enough to make you shudder to your least dendrite and hold tightly to the pitiful shreds of your academic optimism. Those educators who knew for an absolute fact how philosophy was over. And it's true that there hasn't been any real philosophy done for decades, but that's because no one's had the requisite balls. Momentously, the department cut down on admissions to the program, limiting intake to future scholars, no more mere dabblers in this business of higher thought. Even in retrospect, even taking my considerable resentment into account, it was pretty much an incestuous, self-perpetuating shithole.

All of this leaving me somewhere near the elevators, pretending to read the notices on the corkboards in order to protect myself against some passing professor's derisive interrogation.

Inside my mind, inside the car, I considered my child, the soft, colorless flesh encasing the developing woman. "Do you suppose we'll ever stumble across a really new idea? A new way of looking at everything? That someday, maybe thousands of years from today, we'll look back and be dumbfounded by how blind we were?"

This naturally disgusted her; she ignored me and went back to staring out her window. Being a teenager, Sophie's genuinely disturbed by the notion of a world that doesn't adhere to sensible rules and explanations inscribed somewhere official like D.C. or Heaven. Anything less would constitute an incomprehensible betrayal, which is precisely why I continue to torture her like this.

"Especially poetry, don't you think?" Ruth said. "Where words run ahead of the present, leaving grammar and logic behind and leaping straight into the future, feeling out the truth for reason to follow. Music, too, of course; music even more so." No doubt I escaped a life of scrounging for crumbs in adjunct hell. Okay, it wasn't as obvious back then: the rot in the tired, over-inflated humanities business. But it was there: the growing caution, the sense that an expected future was receding, that something radical and utterly unfair was afoot and all those properly annotated research papers were to no avail. Surely they sensed the approaching collapse up on that tense, shabby floor. "Listen," Ruth said. "The unheard people are the past that creates us. You can't ignore them without losing your way."

After my aborted stab at academia I trashed two precious years of my youth pursuing a meaningless career in financial services, breaking even but gaining nothing, living an excruciating cubicle existence where I literally struggled to survive another empty, exhausting day, wishing my life away in hourly increments, watching the good guys filter out and the creeps advance. But I knew I was lucky to have benefits and a chance, however slim, for an actual career, what with the Great Recession already on the horizon, so I numbly endured the my sense of inadequacy and the women's fake office voices until one afternoon I was running another superfluous report in order to export another irrelevant spreadsheet when I passed some inevitable tipping point.

I went to law school.

CHAPTER FOUR

At the station the fallout from Ruth's formal debut as a prophet, while obviously pending, hung in temporary suspension, just another troubling reality set aside until some responsible executive found time to make an informed decision. Meanwhile the business lingered in a tension of imminent crisis. You might think it was still 2008, economic recovery seemed so distant, a looming Sisyphean mountaintop insisting on staying in the story. When inevitably even more troubling news filtered down, those in supposed authority proved mysteriously unable to provide any real information regarding exactly what to expect or how soon. And then another round of remedial measures was adopted, and so on.

By that determinative Folk Fest summer WPHA had downsized to offices in a Broad Street renovation on the Avenue of the Arts, Philadelphia's music street. How happily appropriate! The broadcast studio itself, like many of its ilk, was deliberately neutral, a slick utilitarian space with very few decorative features and virtually no personal paraphernalia. A large corkboard over the console held a single sheet torn from a pocket notepad pinned way up in one corner as if intimidated, and a framed poster of the nighttime Philadelphia skyline covered much of one wall.

That photograph, taken from the Camden side of the Delaware, was an unoriginal composition meant to imply metropolitan glamour, with lighted skyscrapers and river and bridge and the station logo in blue superimposed over the reality like a neon bar sign. One of those expensive, unoriginal ad agency designs, it generated the excitement of an inspirational poster at the dentist's office if you saw it at all, and Ruth was vaguely ashamed of it.

Another poster, this one an unframed cardboard placard not quite two feet square, leant against the wall at one end of the curved countertop so that you couldn't help but see it from everywhere. This one, clearly a professional product, was nonetheless proudly juvenile and outrageously glitzy, with silver letters on a shiny azure field, the overall effect a cross between a kindergarten project and the cover of a gaudy paperback on an airport rack. Wide block capitals instructed you to REACH FOR THE STARS. Behind these words various improbable heavenly bodies evoked fifties sci-fi comic books featuring extraterrestrial sex. More silver letters running along the lower border explained that ATTITUDE EQUALS ALTITUDE.

Ruth briefly but openly admired her reflection in the glass over the city skyline photo, pushing her thick hair up into a knot, raising her chin to view her profile. She swiveled back round and stared at the more prominent poster, sighed to be noticed, and slumped her shoulders in huge mock resignation.

Out in the booth Bob Levine, her producer, almost grinned and almost shrugged but actually did neither because Rick Stanley, their latest Program Director, was standing behind him, leaning on the back of his chair, and the outdated, amateur initiative represented by that placard was Stanley's bright idea, brought in by him as a kind of bona fide, a demonstration of readiness from the expert expected to organize the station's traditional, comfortable chaos because no one could afford to be casual anymore just as no one could afford an untrained management team. All this reinforcing the suspicion of something seriously amiss, allowing more doubt to pile up in the corners of everyone's psyche. Those suspicions currently focused on the upper echelons since we all read the papers; pretty much everyone recognized this silly new concept, this whole weirdly anachronistic philosophy as insulting and a personal threat. So a truly remarkable display of deceitful policy, and a hellish introduction for Stanley, coming in toting this predestined failure. But how could he in the first place? I mean! Fiscal success based on spiritual perfection! "You're the company! It's all up to you! It's all your fault!" All those tired old exhortations plus a motivational motto under every signature line! And yet management encouraged this discredited shit with unflagging optimism, seemed even to be relying on it with a terrifyingly innocent unanimity, and the PHA employees suffering under the ridiculous scheme eventually turned fatalistic or chronically anxious or simply left.

To further aggravate Ruth, all this crap was passably tolerable to Bob, her sidekick, her supposed good buddy. Because Bob, despite his comfortable music industry persona of scruffy beard and saggy clean jeans and occasional denim vest, was never anybody's idealist to begin with let alone any kind of commercial martyr but ultimately just another sardonic realist with a family to support, another born cubby-dweller pretending to some kind of mellow authenticity. Whereas Ruth either didn't understand about consequences or else genuinely craved the rush she got from pushing corporate boundaries. Childishly twirling in her chair, radiating danger signals, one palm flat on the slick surface of some unidentifiable composite with its top layer already peeling up at the corner. This was earlier in the year, when the latest company crisis was still new and the underhanded spiritual regulations first seriously in effect. She sat on display inside that plain box with its one wide window to the booth, not unlike a reptile on exhibit at the zoo, expressing that kind of disinterest and universal contempt. The studio held a sleek console with neon-colored sliders, a standard phone, a deluxe curved black keyboard, monitors, black foam-capped mikes on swing arms, and a gray- and-black marbleized plastic pencil holder containing two obviously inexpensive pens from sponsors and a used emery board. She had her two constant security blankets: a yellow legal pad jammed with various ignored memos and notes, and a mug with that blue skyline logo and the call letters in bold crimson. She tended to carry one or both around the office with her for something to do, the mug generally half full of congealed coffee that she drank anyway.

There were generally three chairs, two at the guest side of the curving counter, just standard ergonomic office chairs upholstered in an inoffensive charcoal tweed. The carpeting was an industrial mulberry, and rough beige-and-tan fabric in a check pattern padded the walls. In sum, a business unit just short of sterile, imagined without consideration for anything whimsical or extraneous or creative like music or conversation.

So foreign not only to its purpose but also to the vaunted

PHA culture, the familiar image of the venerable station boasting a seminal authority that predated even the Bandstand days, commanding a survivor's respect and a valid if indirect claim to courage and glory, something vague having to do with desegregation and sexual liberation if you could trace it all out, something once boldly avant-garde in an unapologetically entrepreneurial way. The product of the first post-WWII teen afternoon mainstreaming of increasingly whitewashed rock 'n roll and the Stroll in your neighbor's basement and Saturday nights at a South Philly mixer for the whole family, toddlers to Grandma. Even from its beginnings handicapped by a reputation for being something of an amateur show, a family concern; today it shouted that proud appellation from billboards along I-76, additionally reminding everyone how the only independent station in the Delaware Valley was still here and thriving, no matter that people thought it commercial and lame.

The late, often adulated Joe Merriwether accomplished that first leap into the youth market practically before there were official teenagers. Joe being one of those curmudgeonly local business legends that keeps everyone chortling indulgently, fond but embarrassed, a throwback to a cruder industry era, a man capable of creating both amazing progress and deep resentment. Tell a Joe story to get your latent racial or sexual venom out there in all genuine innocence. Or if in kindlier mood, a story about Joe on a rowhouse stoop, answering a fan's complaint letter with a knock on the door and a bouquet of zinnias out of his own garden, old-fashioned mauves and pinks, stems dripping into newspaper. Those were the days; that was a better generation.

Always an unconcerned bigot, he nonetheless had the sagacity to leave his private preconceptions out of business. His shrewdness allowed him to grasp the profit possibility in the relentless beat of reality and oblivion combined, a joyous shout perfectly matched to the post-war era of expansion and restlessness, integration and rebellion: Little Richard and Buddy Holly steamrolling over Frankie Laine and Patti Page. So I suspect Joe, high on unexpected success and the optimism of the decade, complacently expected to program the background music for the second half of the century; he certainly gave it a convincing try, only more changes kept flooding in, undermining his efforts, and his entire adulterated enterprise was soon enough drowning in an overcrowded cutthroat market, an exploding, frightening kind of scene: anti-everything and then into serious drugs. And anyway Joe was a businessman first, not really a visionary or an idealist or even that much of a music lover.

Thus during the late sixties PHA gently mutated into a pap of generic, digestible soft covers and movie theme instrumentals for sentimental suburban mommies and daddies. Until eventually even that strategic corner fell subject to competitive pressure, the whole scene morphing to capture the new wave of young parents, sudden traditionalists seeking a safe family harbor. And again Joe displayed that insane spark of genius, that characteristic ability to risk literally everything on his own instinctive understanding of the market. He embraced a second roots revolution, except not really, marketing cleaned-up R&B via endlessly loving, immaculately cool DJs espousing a highly civilized spin on authenticity, the smooth jazz just then arising with The Sound Of Philadelphia, looking to wean an established audience from the familiarity of commiserative or uplifting pop.

What a spectacular, soul-satisfying catastrophe! The financial equivalent of an artist's wet dream, an anarchist's heaven: the slate wiped totally clean. Joe said it himself: "I made a mistake, but you know, it was honorable. It was a heartfelt mistake." This with the heartbroken outsized expression of an abandoned teddy bear. "Heartfelt." Thumping his fist against his barrel chest.

At that point, this being a year or so after I came to the area, Joe ceded control of the business to his son George, a slightly more refined and better-educated version of his dad, a boy who'd been brought up rich but turned out modestly intelligent, energetic, and socially adept. Like his father, George was a little too inclined to trust his own instincts, particularly regarding women, not that that matters here. Essentially cautious, he remained detached from the ruthless business of radio, preferring to exercise control from a remote executive distance. So George carefully reviewed his options and wisely retreated to a Top 40 format with a heavy disco emphasis, adhering to popular versions of the same safe strategy clear through the seventies and eighties, cultivating a solid stable of familiar DJs. Keeping his cool, never anxiously rushing to overtake the zeitgeist or beat the competition.

And basically that's how it went, packaged and saccharine, until the collapse of civilization into electronic media chaos, and of course you openly welcomed the future but everyone knew it was only the beginning and soon enough you'd be left behind. The forced enthusiasm disguised a deep sense of cosmic betrayal. Conceding his ignorance of a radically evolving industry without at all relinquishing his firm business school faith, George invited in the first of a series of outside experts. Upheaval signals opportunity, they explained, pasting that Chinese proverb over the new home page and effecting substantial cutbacks, and it more or less worked out because at that point the economy was still playing by the rules.

At the instigation of these experts PHA's already unthreatening format disintegrated into a full-out barrage of happiness, an unabashedly feel-good stationality continually refined through online audience participation: all your favorite songs plus the unembarrassed thrift of that canned music overnight. And eventually, of course, there was Ruth, such a quintessential Philadelphia personality returned from Florida of all foreign locales, clever but still obviously nice and level- headed and open-minded just like us.

Now through all of those transformations PHA held tight to its sense of tradition, operating as a family firm in every sense of the term, employing at one time or another practically everyone's nephew or second cousin until it would take a skilled genealogist to trace out the generations of remote relationships, never mind all the established crony cliques straight out of college. Everyone telling the identical old anecdotes, speaking a singular cant of silly incidents and former employees and summer company picnics; there was this tired swagger betraying the eternal chip on the company shoulder. George kept an actual company photo album.

Meanwhile the physical plant migrated from its dilapidated West Philadelphia birthplace to a glossy office tower out on City Line, then up to a business park in a better suburb convenient to two major malls, and now back into the city, into this trim renovation near the gracious old Academy of Music and the sprawling Kimmel Center and a whole enthusiastic host of various smaller venues and theatres with across the street the Walk of Fame, a sidewalk of inlaid tributes to the local greats: Marian Anderson and Leon Redbone, Dick Clark of course and Frankie Avalon, Jim Croce and Jerry Blavat, the Geater with the Heater. All of them. There to recover from the latest electronic wounds, home to reclaim the populace with the lure of the local, of tradition. So PHA sat on that dedicated thoroughfare and apparently committed itself to its own destruction, continuing to democratize the industry into nothing more than a platform for listener requests, another streaming service. Energetically hurrying the technological obliteration of all obstructive intervening media, your music right there in your ears right now.

Settling in to this new, modest existence, when abruptly new rumors of instability manifested in their entirety one day like an unexpected delivery of furniture, massive and unavoidable but eventually accepted as everyday fixtures. These more recent concerns were rarely discussed but were instead automatically classified as both broad and remote, national if not global, utterly separate from ratings or advertisers or anything else manageable. But wasn't that long over now? Occasionally someone repeated a bankruptcy rumor, whatever that meant. Well, you could stop your equally terrified supervisor for a little exploratory chat, have him actively listen but then shrug or even smile in professed unconcern. And because any open skepticism was even then decried as essentially immoral, resentment and a protective numbness continued to flourish.

Personnel adjustments were discreet and respectful, everything handled so competently it was arguably not even a matter of exigency but maybe just a small, necessary correction for the errors and excesses of long-term mismanagement. No one denied that history of informal management anymore; now it was the obvious culprit and happily it was being corrected. Initial terminations were limited to Sales and Promotion, nothing much more than a minor reshuffling on the cubicle level with very few serious shifts higher up the organizational chart. Very inconvenient emotionally, of course, with the unfortunates piling their family photos and assorted comic toys into those shameful cardboard cartons, but at least they had time for that, it wasn't like they were being escorted directly off the premises and their souvenir mugs confiscated for general use. That was later.

A spate of retraining clarified the situation: improvement was inevitable once each employee learned to communicate effectively, maintain an accurate schedule, and bring passion and commitment to the job every single day and blah blah blah straight out of the managerial bullshit industry, despicable spiel signifying nothing except that it was mostly the employees' fault. And so there were mandatory team games coached by self- declared experts, training sessions designed to make everyone easily replaceable, and supervised table discussions leading to predetermined conclusions. Meanwhile the on-air talent was separately schooled in the usual textbook platitudes: work with Sales, it's good for both of you. There's enormous unrealized value in effective contesting. Don't neglect forward promotion. Really punch those call letters! Keep that typical listener in mind, know her like your best friend, give her a name, know her secret desires, talk right to her because that's what comes across.

While you sat around a conference table exchanging psychobabble flash cards, indulging in conference room antics to repel catastrophe, being existentially humiliated by wishful crap that eroded the final remnants of your respect for your superiors and the world at large. But that first team of consultants was let go early and reputedly unpaid, so maybe somebody senior retained a particle of common sense.

Yet throughout this miserable transition Ruth was consistently rising in the Arbitron books, hers the name those individual diarists most often remembered, the favored personality hogging all the likeability. Meanwhile efficiently traveling that inevitable psychological progression from gratitude to entitlement. And she acquired more of a loyal following under those clouded stars than she'd managed to attract during her whole previous decade in the industry. Maybe thanks to the stress, the way it inspired her need for dramatic possibility and lent her voice this slight frisson of desperate empathy.

In short, she was important. She was being discussed behind doors with brass nameplates well before her August debacle.

"I need to touch base with her in the morning," her listeners said, and they kept saying it even when her uncensored ramblings turned more extreme and condescending. "She centers me," they explained with glorious illogic. People required her opinion in order to form their own. God knows she was diligently keeping that typical listener in mind, speaking to that overweight middle-aged woman with bleached hair trudging off to the cubicle or hospital or classroom or counter, longing only for dinner and some television and a chance to be herself.

And of course there was something fatally synergistic in the way listener devotion fed on and simultaneously encouraged Ruth's diva behavior. Not that she ever lost her professional balance on air, more that she'd always tended toward emotional misbehavior, often disgorging too much irrelevant erudition with too little prodding, boorishly insistent. Or holding onto an argument well after it was over with that unsettling intensity, or rushing in to propound a definitive, snarky opinion without forethought and then having to explain away her rather mean indiscretions in honest surprise, plunging into these laughing, baroque explanations. But all that was sporadic and reasonably controlled. That very spring she personally negotiated a respectable salary bump with George, although arguably that wasn't difficult.

Theoretically remaining madly in love with her career path, or anyway cherishing her power: "You know how Plato says about when modes of music change, the fundamental laws of the state change too? Well, in the end music is about morality." Finding affirmation even in the most prosaic listener feedback, the Facebook comments, the intimate sidewalk confidences and devotee tweets. For Ruth it was all predestined: how else explain the marvelous ease with which she'd attained this ideal platform out on the cutting edge?

Except it wasn't, and what's more like her audience Ruth preferred the sentimental; she had no taste for exploratory, mind- freeing jazz, for the demands of classical or for unregulated hard rock and rap. It was purely intellectual approval that found her expounding on the power and cultural significance of it all, hands flying and face alight, dropping names while secretly envisioning herself a character out of an MGM musical when it wasn't Amazing Grace. She had Bon Jovi and the swinging Sinatra on her phone, Elton John and Billy Joel and hits from Coldplay and U2 and Pink but not their complete albums. Such commonplace tastes, all those anthems: that's the word. When did we start thinking in terms of anthems, earworms for the clinically depressed?

Granted music mattered to her, really mattered, infiltrating her bloodstream with confounding intentions and facts, making it virtually impossible to sort out the self-aggrandizing from the reality, the actual from the carefully reconstructed history. "I remain a dedicated feminist." Mysteriously conveying a past of hairy underarms and floppy breasts and no make-up, possibly back during the sixties. "I carried my sign and I still do." But press her for specifics and she got vague and overcomplicated. "Oh, back when I was a kid, you know. When politicking was about sitting on the floor in a storefront headquarters, making endless phone calls, you know? Favorable or unfavorable or leave me alone." With that practiced comical sideways glance, "My God how those ward leaders could lie!"

This was on JFK one bright afternoon, the glare bouncing down from the office towers and Ruth striding head down as usual, hands deep in her pockets. She paused abruptly so I could catch up, forcing an irritated stream of pedestrians to part and flow around us. "Although even back when I was an unquestioning Democrat I had qualms about Liberalism: the automatic arrogance and the prerogative to make fun of people like they were ignorant and didn't matter because obviously the future was on our side."

Moving ahead again slowly. "I'm ashamed I never spoke up, if you want to know the truth."

Whatever Ruth's larger ambitions – I'm guessing syndication and television what with her basing her life on Ruby Keeler dancing on a giant typewriter – they lingered untested although never formally abandoned either, merely put on hold in favor of her intoxicating new status as half a celebrity couple. Or perhaps she was secretly more comfortable playing pap and the marriage excused that tacit renunciation, temporarily protecting her from any risky career moves. What I know is, she outright confiscated Thom: looking out triumphantly through his eyes, incorporating his preferences in beer and books. And not gradually as most married couples do but from the start, even mimicking his gentle mockery, his expressive raised brow. I'm not exaggerating here, and I felt her overnight transformation egregious and disturbing.

We found seats on one of the stone benches in front of the Comcast plaza, part of a lunchtime crowd relishing the sunshine. Ruth absently checked her phone for about the fourth time in the past hour; she was still intent on rearranging the emotional events of her youth and I was pretending I cared.

"You know, I always saw things from the position of the responsible party, I automatically thought of myself as the one who had to pay the price." Turning to look me in the face, eyes too wide and sincere, pushing back a clump of damp hair, checking out my reaction.

We met like this only a few times but I was already tired of having to study that tense, self-involved profile, playing the farce of brilliant subject and admiring biographer. For one thing, it all sounded a bit stale and rehearsed. Never once did she convince me of her ultimate excellence, although God knows that was her intention and I allowed her ample opportunity. She remained a phony on the lookout for shortcuts and glory.

"Anyway politics is just impossible anymore. It's so vicious, it makes me physically ill." We walked down from 21st Street and around onto Market Street, past one of those gaps between huge commercial buildings where habitués gather at tiny outdoor tables, clerical staff aping sophistication. There was this metal sculpture there: outsize, elongated nude family figures, two parents lifting their children above their heads and presumably above their own limitations with every muscle of their perfect young bodies. On eastward past where there's this gigantic mural of a vulva hovering over a hotel.

Ruth's success in radio was entirely due to her own natural talent; she had the determination required to dominate those precious morning hours, that one remaining refuge of personality and music combined. And she had the proper guise, this persona that allowed her to be the woman she pretended to be in real life, always appropriately amiable, original, gossipy, caring, grave, and informed. All that supported by genuine intelligence, expertise, and professionalism, and until recently a beneficial ability to focus on the local or individual and ignore anything even vaguely controversial.

"Right before Thanksgiving. Wasn't that fucking nice?" An afternoon that found Ruth striding in from lunch

100

to confront an atmosphere as thick as gelatin, everyone numbly minding their own business. "I was getting coffee and Leslie came in and told me what was happening." Leslie being a massively overweight, nicely sensible young woman from News and Public Affairs given to bright, stylish outfits and serious religion; she handled update breaks and hosted an intelligent Sunday morning interview program.

"They went by department, asking groups back to the small conference room. Leslie, Ruth, and some restless, avid others soft-voiced there in the kitchen, counting up the known casualties: six from Marketing and Promotions, six from Sales, five support people. Jeff the IT guy who Leslie said set up the television on 9/11. Glen from News who started out as an undergrad intern with old Joe himself, that teenager in the photo album painting the walls of some other new office. Energetic, incisive Brian, a natural leader who'd brought in two of his college friends. So many complex fraternal networks and in-law bonds cut without consideration, twenty-three members of the self-proclaimed family business deciding to seek other opportunities. Everything handled so expertly, too, with nothing of the destructive hysteria of those ancient individual terminations for cause, with no humane interval for communal grief.

"Which is to say, I realize it was perfectly ethical, in fact ethically required. But it was just so fucked up anyway."

When in came the next host of designated saviors, degreed executives all, trained management professionals utterly unfamiliar with the industry. First Jenny Hare, General Sales Manager reputedly out of Wharton, a tiny, chic woman of fifty- odd with sleekly coifed, prematurely white hair, classic silk suits, and proper unobtrusive heels. Ruth discovered her sitting behind the bare desk of a newly vacated office and stopped short, hand on the opened door, to offer a gracious welcome.

"I know it can be a bit confusing, but I'm excellent at answering questions if you have any."

"Thanks, I'll keep that in mind." Bestowing a superior's dismissive smile and gazing back down at her desk.

Hunh.

As her first public act, Jenny called an informal meeting for all staff and management out on the larger cubby floor, comically climbing up on a desk for visibility and holding up her right hand. "I am making a pledge to you. There will be transparency. There will be accountability." Taking her time to face them nearly one by one."

"She impressed me as incredibly competent and intelligent." Ruth said, leaving the door open to collaboration if not friendship. But Jenny, it developed, shared her inside jokes and insightful intimacies exclusively with the new Program Director, Rick Stanley. With whom, it was known, she shared a corporate history that unfortunately culminated in both of them blameless but at large, flotsam of a submerged advertising agency in a Baltimore suburb. Office spouses, then, examining everyone from their guarded joint viewpoint, conferring together privately often right there in the corridor or else with a cheery head poked round a door. Jenny politely commandeered Sara, George's middle-aged, ginger-haired personal assistant, a prudent, middle-aged suck-up.

"So they're constantly effing flaunting their crappy Lean Six Sigma jargon in front of the poor common people like no one's ever heard of it before and this worries no one?"

Consider Stanley a slightly superior version of every competently raised and adequately educated professional manager with collared knit shirt neatly tucked into khakis, only marginally more observant and determined than the common specimen. He had a surprisingly sharp gray-blue gaze that came at you from an angle, below or from the side, but you rarely remembered meeting it straight on, and any hint of personality tended to retreat behind a friendly, cooperative facade. A face both intelligent and passionate, with a thin nose, narrow mouth, and high cheekbones over concave cheeks; his features countered his studied normality with something austere that put one in mind of Cardinal Richelieu or an elite surgeon. He was quite tall, over six feet, and probably in his late forties, with close-cropped gray-blond hair. There was a watchfulness about him, a kind of avidity or tenseness that made you cautious and kept him from being genuinely attractive.

As expected, Ruth was invited to a private audience and aircheck in Stanley's new front office, an accommodation second only to George's vulgar decorator suite and certainly much grander than Jenny's deliberately modest space. Ruth knocked, pushed in the door, and stopped in surprise at the threshold. Paused there, torn between laughter and disbelief.

Thus they were lost in the stars. Two larger examples of those garish inspirational posters, the first Ruth ever encountered, were propped against the front of an immense dining table of a desk of some extremely dark, almost

103

black wood. Stars drawn with precision on an intricate flow chart were sketched out in blue marker across the whiteboard covering almost all of one narrow wall. More placards, the smaller versions that would later migrate out to cubicles and conference rooms, were stacked on a central glass coffee table, and even more were displayed singly on various shelves so that the visitor could better experience the overall effect of rocket ships rising on effusions of orange cartoon flames, five-pointed suns resembling children's gold stars, cratered but demurely smiling moons, and comets trailing silvery tails, all of it metallic and shimmering, expertly packaged, and hopelessly childish.

Ruth toured the premises deliberately, pausing before each poster, reading the imperatives printed across those unlikely heavens. Finally, again in her own good time, she took the chair opposite her new boss and, sitting, presented him with an expression combining overt incredulity with minor parental disappointment. More of the same crap, simplified and better packaged. He nodded in comprehension, this apparently intelligent human who'd for some reason inserted himself into their presence hugging this adolescent excrescence to his chest when he must have known better? "I expect some skepticism. That's fine." That consistent amiability, that characteristic watchful tilt, while at the same time he made small encouraging gestures, urging her closer.

So they leaned in towards each other over his broad desk like a pair of conspirators and set about reviewing her morning's broadcast, Ruth and this outsider who was surely tasked with determining her fate. He had a small framed photo of a respectable blond wife standing with her arms encircling two amorphous teenage daughters. "I'm very impressed, you know," Stanley said. "You have an extremely strong base. Well, you know that." A wave of one wrist. "Two times Major Market Personality of the Year finalist. I gather that's quite an accomplishment."

"It is," she said.

So onward with that same variety of dubious companionability, their two heads uncomfortably near while they played back her everyday intimate pleasantries, her polished formatics and laughing chatter with Bob and Leslie, her smooth liner readings and natural resets. Ruth's on-air persona was always approachable, even slightly vulnerable although never enough to undermine her ability to represent homecoming and security.

That initial review session went quite smoothly and Stanley had very few comments for her, none of them precisely critical. "You're surprising good with politics, keeping it neutral, but try to tone down the sarcasm." Really, that was all! But he'd just arrived; give him time. And then, "Sometimes you seem to be talking down or possibly even expressing contempt for your listeners." A palm to forestall protest. "I know that's not your intent."

"My God no!" That was unexpected and upsetting. "The opposite, in fact!" When? That couldn't be true. What was he hearing?

But afterwards there was no easy dismissal; instead Stanley leaned back into a corner of his executive's chair and observed her for a few long seconds, as if making up his mind. Finally he reached forward and patted the top of the stack of glitzy paperbacks still confined in a block of shrink wrap. They were upside-down; she saw a photo of a bland young man with a wide salesman's smile on the back cover with some bolded encouraging platitudes.

"You get this idea?" Those piercing, shielded eyes angling in to her again, evaluating her response. "It's all about taking responsibility." And shifting his tight little butt in his chair he sat forward again, suddenly almost eager. "PHA has always been an informally managed company, but these remain difficult times everywhere and that's why there has to be professional management, people with skills that transfer whether it's to chemicals or automobiles or broadcasting. Employees for their part have to meet a new standard of professionalism. Everyone at this station will be held accountable for their attitude. Attitude is the key. Everyone working here is going to bring optimism and energy to every job."

Ruth thought about that one, vaguely insulted by the general thrust, the accusatory note. It was so familiar, yet so troubling. There was slight of hand there somewhere. She blurted the first response that came to mind.

"That's not Christian."

He started in surprise, frowned, then recovered his supervisor's face. "Well, I consider myself a Christian and I don't feel that way."

A week or so in the new management team appropriated an empty barrack of a space down on the building's basement level, spacious enough to accommodate all the executives and staff on metal folding chairs around collapsible tables. It made for a deceptively casual and unthreatening ambience, like a church supper. In filed the support women from the neighborhoods, plump and nervous, and the entry-level types, all bouncy excitement, eager to properly integrate themselves. Such shiny young people with their clean minds and teeth and backgrounds, smiling around with cautious energy; identical products of irrelevant education, cursing the global economy.

Finally in came the management team itself, a pleased, chatty group given to lewd jokes, orthodox religious beliefs, and reverently right-wing politics. All of them apparently believing in this stuff like it was the American constitution, or at least setting an example. Even George was there, in among the common people to signal his commitment.

Stanley positioned himself at the front of the room, his feet slightly apart on the beige linoleum, repressing a slight embarrassment. He had one of those easels with a big pad of cheap blank paper. Taking a black marker he printed TAKE OFF! across the first pristine page with broad, dynamic strokes.

"What do I mean by that? I mean that it's time to leave the

safety of the familiar, tired methods behind." He stepped back so everyone could better view this principle, his eyes assessing audience acceptance. The letters unfortunately slanted downwards.

Turning over that page and writing on a fresh one, more strong downward strokes from a marker that squeaked: ATTITUDE DETERMINES OUTCOME! This time misjudging on size, having to squish in the final word. Everyone inferior to him in the company was enjoying this evidence of fallibility.

"Science tells us this. Philosophers have made this identical statement from ancient times. Psychologists insist on this same basic truth. We each define our own circumstances; this isn't just words – we do literally create our own worlds. Your success is the result of the attitude you bring into this office every single day, your commitment, your confidence, your optimism, your belief in our mission statement, and ultimately your belief in yourself."

"Jesus fucking Christ." Ruth was seated in an intentionally diverse group comprising two promotions people, the full-time receptionist, an apparently content Jenny, and Sara the personal assistant who was exhibiting more enthusiasm than the total handful of executives combined.

Supportive, patient glances from the group. "You have to give it a chance," Sara said.

"If I were a cartoon, there would have been steam coming out of my ears. The incomprehensible stupidity. The blatant, manipulative misuse of the concept!"

"Surely you've heard this kind of spiel before?"

"Well yeah, of course, but theoretically, not like a personal accusation. I mean, you can't imagine how barefaced offensive it was, like we were stupid little children who couldn't handle our own lives." Here are two random Ruth anecdotes dating from this same period, the month or so preceding the Folk Fest fiasco.

One: "I would wake up just before dawn physically terrified, knowing how in the end I'd be nothing but bones. It must have been out of a recurring dream, seeing my own skull and like skeleton pieces. I could sort of remember that image. Stark truth. Your kind of truth."

Two: "I was at my desk (she had a third of a fairly large office) kind of daydreaming, staring at the light coming through the blinds, and I had a vision, for want of a better term. Suddenly I was staring at this dog, this pit bull with that squat body they have, but it was glaring up at me from an angle so it was all prominent head and jaw and these incredible fangs. It was the essence of rage. I knew it symbolized just pure rage and I immediately recognized it as my own soul."

REFLECT THE STARLIGHT!

Stanley managed to inscribe this third dictum with reasonable tidiness, then broadened and deepened the exclamation point, really digging into the cheap paper. "Nobody shines alone. When we try to outshine others we always end up harming ourselves. But when we help others to do their best work we support our own success. That means no one ever has to be afraid, there's no need to hide your questions or mistakes when there's no competition." This drew a little snickering from the office guys, but they promptly pulled themselves back into reality and expressed their agreement with identical nods of fair consideration.

"Three principles. We'll be having more training sessions, and you're going to find them intense. Or I hope so, anyway. You'll be asked to examine your behavior. You'll learn techniques for dealing with each other and you'll learn to structure your time. And at the end of every workday, before you leave this office, each of you will email your supervisor examples of how you've enacted each of these three principles that day. You will briefly assess your mood, your level of interest and enthusiasm and whether or not it was all it should have been: distracted or bored or otherwise not fully present and focused on your job. You will note what steps you intend to employ in the future to correct your frame of mind."

"It's just like remolding." Ruth exclaimed. "Confess to your local cadre."

But the station was officially taking the recovery approach, and you were expected to buy into the narrative just as though you'd knocked on the therapist's door in happy synchronicity.

Back in the relative haven of her own space, Ruth placed a fresh mug of coffee atop a pile of outdated anonymous crap decorated with yellow sticky notes and marginalia and doodles before hurriedly perusing the latest typical Sara email: *Our exciting new era opens! Stand by for more information on how to put* REACH FOR THE STARS *into practice!*

Impulsively emailing Bob Levine, her occasionally supportive fake sidekick: *Thank God this crap has such incredible entertainment value!* Sending this out in relief even though, knowing Bob, she didn't anticipate more than a brief "Ha!" of acknowledgment.

I'm glad you find me amusing, Ruth. However I think you need to be more careful with your email. I'm sure we don't want to make an issue of this.

"My stomach dropped."

Sara, not you too! With shaking fingers, as if not utterly demoralized, as if she'd intended to reply to the wretched toady. *But you should understand that my objections are very real. Clearly my personal beliefs should under no circumstances interfere with my work. And clearly, vice versa?"*

Which exchange lingered in tense abeyance a full anxious month before eventuating in an unscheduled invitation to Stanley's office, where Ruth discovered both Sara and Valerie Zhang from Human Resources, a deceptively compliant young woman, not that that mattered. Which ominous assemblage signified an official warning, the initiation of a formal policy.

In lieu of thinking, Ruth offered in mitigation: "Well, my father's dying." This was true. Officialdom exchanged glances, allowing her some moments of silence to sit there opposite Stanley in his fantasy kingdom, Ruth maintaining the demeanor of a vaguely amused equal while he quietly watched her from deep back in his chair.

Finally speaking quite reasonably, anxious to address her valid concerns. "I understand that you might not agree with this program. Which is fine, as I told you before. But it's not to anyone's advantage to undermine a company effort."

And then, as if suddenly deciding to confer a special, deserved trust, he permitted himself a salesman's confidential smile and leaned in towards her. "We think this is a valuable concept for those who maybe aren't as sophisticated as you or I, who haven't been taught to examine their own attitudes and their impact on others or who've never really had to take responsibility for their own lives."

Ruth drew back instinctively, her contempt wonderfully justified.

"I understand responsibility," she said.

CHAPTER FIVE

Crystal was twisting her torso like an excited little girl, a clump of hair drifting into her wine glass. I set down my drink, captured those drunken strands, and ostentatiously ran my fingers down their length. She gave an indelicate snort, tipsy but unintentionally adorable, dissolving any potential censure. Then her head jerked up and she eyes widened.

"Holy shit! Look who's here." A supposedly discreet nod towards a circumspect corner group, barely visible past another convivial party being shepherded to a booth. We were at a moderately upscale venue given over for the evening to a children's charity event with local celebrities acting as servers: politicians, news media, sports figures, all that sort of professional personality.

Where Crystal was doing me proud despite some mildly borderline behavior, delicious in an obviously expensive but suitably ladylike blue silk thing that folded over itself like origami. And I was in a mellow mood anyway from the fine wine and excellent food and the satisfaction of observing my betters supporting a worthy cause.

Luigi's is relaxed and not really exorbitant; casual by calculation, you know? But even so the familiar South

Philly strategy was a genuine reflection of Luigi himself: hardly one of today's elite celebrity chefs but an established neighborhood luminary, an egregious, unabashed exhibitionist who surely would have suffocated in a more formal environment. His venerable Catherine Street restaurant exuded a comfortable reliability, an air of acquired tradition with nothing further to prove. Of course it was pasted over with the requisite photos of Luigi himself beaming next to Sinatra and Rizzo, Wilt Chamberlain and Joe Frazier, Daryl Hall and Patti LaBelle, Ed Rendell from when he was mayor and a hundred other such cherished or notorious figures, dozens of them covering the walls of the entry lounge so right away you knew exactly where you were, as was fitting. It was very natural but still just a front: Luigi's was only pretending to be itself. What you missed was how the décor took clever advantage of an arrogant relaxed attitude to cover recent financial constraints, implying a kind of reactionary disintegration where an honored tear or gouge was more precious than anything flashy and new. The place virtually flaunted its lack of pretension: woods were highly polished but cracked and creaking, deep windowsills concealed grungy corners, tasseled tie-backs confined heavy rose-colored drapery with visible shiny patches, and banquettes upholstered in striped fabric showed insignificant stains. Which said, the table linens were uniformly pristine, the glassware sparkled.

"Can I interest you in coffee or dessert?" The mayor of the great city of Philadelphia, that true prince of thieves and our server for the evening, materialized beside our table wearing a waiter's apron over his dinner jacket and offered a menu sheet printed for the occasion. Our mayor is small

113

and extremely quiet- spoken, which lends him a false authority.

"Right there!" Crystal continued, not meaning to ignore His Honor but simply unable to switch herself off her particular track in time. I looked, wondering who could claim such rapt attention in a room positively swarming with regional icons.

"Ah, you've noticed the heartwarming family party in the corner." Thom paused behind Crystal's chair on the way to or from one of his own tables. He was identically clad in traditional waiter's garb; beside our mayor, twin servitors prudently shielding an indiscreet sovereign.

Maybe there'd been confusion over the date? It was certainly an appropriate restaurant but this sure as hell wasn't Manetti's kind of crowd. There he was though, Jimmy Manetti, keeping well out of the excitement back in a shaded recess, a kind of raised side chapel containing only the one large round table where he attended to his companions, ignoring all the fund- raising commotion, the polite autograph requests and the phones capturing all the false intimacy and laughing adoration.

We all considered Manetti for a minute or two until eventually even Crystal grew bored with watching nothing and turned back around. The mayor went to fetch our coffee, and Thom resumed his own duties. So I leaned back as far as courtesy permitted and took my turn at openly staring although without any particular expectations. Once I thought about it why shouldn't he be here? Probably he came in twice a week.

In addition to being remotely situated, the Manetti table was partially screened by a pedestal holding a four-foot oriental vase containing that height again in entwined dahlias and roses, full-blown romantic blossoms reminiscent of cabbage roses on old-fashioned wallpaper. Even so I could view a broad section of the enclave, Manetti appropriately seated with his back to the wall. Even at that distance I could see him exuding that scripted mellow refinement, a clichéd facade of silvered hair and tasteful enough tailoring and practiced, avuncular twinkle. Everyone watches too many movies; nobody knows how to be real anymore. Apart from that polished veneer it requires a compendium of negatives to deliver an accurate description: Manetti was neither tall nor short nor overweight nor thin nor really handsome nor physically repellant nor especially charismatic. Sitting still, he drifted into the safety of a tired nullity; you'd ignore him on the train. That night, in that room packed with personalities, he was visible only because everyone was looking around so much.

Next to him, short, plump fingers neatly folded atop the pale pink damask tablecloth and sitting well back in her chair, Tina Manetti surveyed the surrounding commotion through tiny golden eyes. A bitter matron, a woman deceitfully well preserved by the everlasting formaldehyde of infinite resentment, but with the perfect oval countenance of the impetuous former child- beauty and wheedling flirt. She was stuffed into a dress of gold and brown brocade, an upholstered boudoir chair of a dress ornamented with great, soft throw-pillow breasts, and wore her hair twisted into a round knot studded with jeweled clips, purple and green gleaming against the black. A magnificently unaware character with a mouth at once unpleasantly down-turned and sweet, an innocent air of hesitation, and an exquisite patrician nose she tended to wrinkle in universal distaste.

Another man sat directly opposite Manetti, his back to me; he was of average size and had the taut neck and wide shoulders of obsessive athleticism, pale brown coloring, and a good blue suit. A businessman of some ilk, probably, and destined to remain secondary to someone or other forever.

No real surprise Vinnie Scarpone was there too, although I admit I started when I saw him. He was in a light tan suit with the jacket hanging open and looked much more comfortable in this Bella Vista locale than he had at City Council. He was openly gawking at the minor celebrities.

There were two more women there, but neither made much of an impact on me. One was young: from what I could tell in her early twenties if that, with lots of thick brown hair to her shoulders, perfectly acceptable if not actually pretty features, and the relaxed, unimpressed air of a close relative. There was something constrained about the modest cut of her dark green dress and the way she behaved, but there wasn't much modest about her otherwise, quite the opposite: she exuded a vulgar familiarity you knew would really come out when she was off with her peers.

The third and final female seemed about a decade older but a good half-century more sophisticated, reserved and self- confident; a very pale blond with glasses, an intelligent face, and no chin. She was clad in a conventional black silk suit and an unpretentious necklace of tiny rubies or garnets.

Then I noted something interesting: while these women were ostensibly busy eating and conversing, all three were secretly consumed with something or someone on the opposite side of the main room, past me to my left. Their heads kept popping up, their eyes briefly focusing. I turned to follow their line of sight, expecting to spot some A-list Hollywood type fortuitously in town for this event, but couldn't identify anyone exceptionally notable. Finally I spotted a door just inside a narrow hall to the restrooms with a sign taped to it, the outline of a hand in royal blue marker with under it the words: *SEE THE FUTURE!*

My God.

Up on his private stage, Manetti was making some general comments and receiving the proper wifely response, the others putting in a polite word or two as appropriate. Outside and down from this secluded platform I identified the exquisite Lane Baylor seated with her husband. Lane was a successful plastic surgeon, her husband Tim an attorney and the mayor's close friend, political supporter, and chief fundraiser. Together they made an admirable power couple on the municipal scene, ineluctably connecting themselves and the administration to various meritorious forms of civic endeavor. At that particular moment they were studiously and rather hilariously avoiding so much as one covert glance towards Manetti's table. I turned back to Crystal and found her frowning thoughtfully at the palm reader's closet.

So we were both glancing towards this magic portal when it opened and a young woman exited wearing an abashed but irrepressible grin; inside I caught a glimpse of another girl, dangerously underweight with unflattering, oily black hair and a purple sequined shawl around her bare

117

shoulders. She was gathering up her cards from a table jammed into a closet under a shelf with linens piled on it, this miniscule space illuminated by a single hanging light bulb draped with a filmy red scarf. Almost immediately another gullible female approached and hesitantly peeped inside.

"Why don't you go have your fortune told?" I suggested it because I'm a compassionate person, intending no denigration. When Crystal was slightly inebriated, as then, her features mysteriously reverted to childhood innocence and you could almost see the secret, slightly pudgy way she looked waking up in the morning, before the hair and make-up and desperate ambition. A common element was that pleasing, prattling frankness that betrays total self-ignorance.

Thom was back, hovering debonairly over an elderly couple immediately to our left. Both were white haired; he had that long-boned, slim elegance age doesn't much diminish, well complemented by a navy blazer bearing some kind of gold insignia; she was smaller, plump, and happy to be there, very dressed up in a cream-colored lace blouse with pinkish pearls at her ears and throat, and she was beaming up at Thom because everyone does.

The husband was fingering a bottle, and I realized he'd brought his own supply of brand name French dressing with him. As I watched he lifted his salad plate and very carefully tipped the excess back into the bottle. Following which exacting task he joined the ongoing conversation, speaking with a pleased expression and the shy intimacy of a man coaxed into divulging his most outlandish sexual fantasies. I strained to hear.

118

"I'm not the best gardener myself, mind you, but I know the history and location of every planting on my property."

"How marvelous!" Which was only Thom's usual enthusiasm, and you have to understand that he was convinced that he meant it, that he found everyone ultimately fascinating.

"Gardening is my greatest pleasure in life." This innocent marital affront, it developed, was untrue, because some months later, the pleasant-seeming wife dead of a stroke, this gentleman decided to depart his Barbados hotel room through a twentieth- floor window. They are for real, this Main Line type with their gentle little waves good-by. "All *righty*-roo." "Yes in-*dee*-dee."

Ruth came through from the kitchen, the basic black pants and white apron of the celebrity waitstaff emphasizing her paleness, affording her a sort of false elegance. I watched her weave her way extravagantly and I suspect unnecessarily through the appreciative tables bearing a loaded tray out in front of her like a suburban grandmother presenting the Thanksgiving turkey. She was so lost in concentration she brushed behind Crystal's chair without recognizing me.

Once up at Manetti's refuge she extracted a folding stand from some corner, settled her tray on it, relaxed her shoulders with a grin and started distributing plates, chatting with professional ease over the orders. Tina Manetti and the two younger women were happily attentive, buying into the patter, leaning forward on their elbows with all of them talking at once while at the same time aware of the men indulgently listening. All of them, even Ruth, also performing for these men.

Following which busy minutes, with everything settled and satisfied, Ruth breezily, unbelievably commandeered an extra chair from a lower table and inserted herself into the private party of Jimmy Manetti, famously reticent mob boss of a criminal organization at war against increased obsolescence.

"He dared me," she explained. "Joking, but still." Everything I knew about Manetti was common knowledge;

I've never expended the energy necessary to differentiate these unimaginative career thugs although I have colleagues who specialize in this stuff, get totally absorbed in it and covertly love the cleansing violence, even admire the whole mythical code of honor. Anyway, as I understood it Manetti was connected to three separate, prominent dynasties who between them split apart this region in the seventies. Reputedly a made man from that same period, these days found him a relatively unscathed survivor courtesy of his enormous self-control, his ability to avoid impulsive violence or overweening narcissism or undue ambition. He was a cautious bore, and it served him well.

And initially he was severely undervalued for this extraordinary patience and emotional restraint; he was never dynamic enough to attract notice, never really promising or threatening. So while still a fairly young man he found himself relegated to what was then the sad backwater of Atlantic City, a traditional Philly territory he managed with routine efficiency while building up a number of private businesses along the Jersey shore.

Competently toeing the line, pushing back on the ambitious Blacks and Russians and Asians and Mexicans inexorably encircling his terrain with their fresh takes on carnage and terrorism, their efficiency and contempt for boundaries. Manetti moved with the herd, concentrating on microcaps, health insurance, telephone cards, all those lucrative but relatively placid opportunities, although when required his problems disappeared without undue public outcry. He displayed equally solid judgment in his personal life, avoiding melodrama, marrying young and remaining wed, certainly without fidelity but also without scandal, never dishonoring his wife and family. So essentially an unimaginative drudge, as uninteresting and greedy and childishly spiteful as evil itself, but just intelligent enough to recognize his own limitations.

Then legalized gambling gained traction in Atlantic City and Manetti's luck was in big time, the casinos and unions and politicians of that damply disintegrating resort town showering him with sudden respect. He curtailed the endless ambitions of New York by vicious preemptive right, raking in the spoils until he was unexpectedly removed or promoted to a Philadelphia struggling to recover from an era of unprecedented bloodshed, tasked with curbing the egotism of an immature heir apparent, a brutal jerk much too eager to reign. Maybe that was lucky, considering AC these days. The idea was, Manetti would act as senior partner, mentor, and control, but somehow this didn't pan out as hoped, the kid slaughtered some people and went to jail, and Manetti carried on solo. Sitting quietly in a South Philly restaurant, being catered to.

"I'm going," Crystal announced, recapturing my attention. "Hunh?"

"I'm going to ask about us." On which threat she stood and draped the gold chain of her shiny little evening bag over her shoulder, assumed her public face, wheeled on a high-heeled sandal without incident and marched herself towards the door of enlightenment, which was closed. So she stood along the wall and looked back at me with a triumphant little smile.

Ruth was leaning on her fist and heeding Tina Manetti. I imagined that worthy freely scattering scorn upon the heads of the assembled local celebrities, and certainly the tight dismissive gestures directed towards anyone foolish enough not to be Mrs. Manetti herself or at least a close family member supported that supposition. Thom was closer to me, speaking mildly to someone I didn't know; I saw him send an indulgent smile towards his wife that I interpreted as a public show of unconcern.

Crystal had vanished. To reappear twenty minutes later totally pissed off, scraping out her chair and clearly holding me to blame me for whatever.

"Do you think people are jealous of me?" she demanded. "Because I happen to think I'm a pretty good judge of people and I think most people like me, including any women with short dark hair I can think of." Ignoring her cold coffee and swallowing down the final inch of wine in her glass, then looking round for a waiter. Someone, not the mayor, came and cleared our table.

"I mean it's so silly, like I'd buy this shit." Crystal almost never swears; she was struggling to contain tears of disappointment. "I mean, special purifying crystals to remove the strong negative influence from my unbalanced charkas, which is what's preventing my true happiness!"

"At this kind of function?" I was actually a little surprised. "Apparently I'm going to always have just enough money but never a lot. I'll never be rich. Plus I'm blocked from following my heart, so even though I'm definitely going to marry and have more than one child my heart will never be satisfied." She put her hands down flat on the table. "I think I want to go home right now. If you don't mind." The tears were winning out, glimmering brightly in those narrowed eyes.

"Nobody else came out crying. Maybe there is something wrong with your chakras." Ruth and Manetti were having a serious conversation; she'd moved over next to him, which was possible because the full female Manetti contingent was waiting outside the magic door, the younger two self-consciously laughing despite Mrs. Manetti shushing them so they wouldn't anger the spirits. Ruth continued to gaze steadily at Manetti; as I watched she started to speak to her own fingers, splayed out on the tablecloth, nodding a tiny bit and very solemn, and I realized she was at least a little drunk.

Manetti, though, seemed to be treating her with something akin to Thom's inexplicable leniency, bestowing delicate, encouraging smiles at reasonable intervals. "Up close he's darker, more gray than silver, and his skin looks darker. It's like he's made out of some dull metal. But his mouth is soft, the way he purses it in that prissy way, you know? Once I thought he was going to pat my hand but I think my expression stopped him. I'm not much for being patronized." Vinnie and the man in the blue suit were still at the table but concentrating on coffee and dessert, conspicuously ignoring their boss's conversation.

"I appreciate that you're honest. It's refreshing," Manetti sat back in his chair to better approve of her, all personal geniality.

"You should have seen him." (Although I pretty much had.) "Automatically assuming I was flattered and respected his opinion." Perhaps correctly interpreting his gently exploratory conversation as broadly insulting.

"Yes, I hope so." Smiling across at him from that cautious yet willing posture over the empty coffee cups and tiramisu crumbs and dirty flatware. Ruth was immediately comfortable accepting his flattery, not because she believed it but because meaningless flattery was a regular part of her public life. "But please don't misunderstand me; everyone seems to misunderstand me." Certainly it was tedious having to explain all this yet again. Adding to that discomfort her survival instinct was kicking in, warning her against revealing any additional profound secret of the universe since it would only fall on infertile ground, leaving her depleted. And God knows she knew more secrets.

"I wanted to explain that thinking you're virtuous is a kind of dodge or defense. Well, a lie, because you're as much wrong as right and you need to act responsibly and with respect."

Blanching a bit, halting to stare at the delicate centerpiece candle, a tiny flame in a low white glass nestled in pale pink rosebuds. "But even so that doesn't mean there's no right and wrong." Then with an impudent grin: "Personally I believe in the law the way I believe in breathing."

He was examining her from some remote place then, certainly without any false affection, but he responded with a shrug and brush of the arm that set his gray silk suit shimmering. "Oh, the law, there I agree with you wholeheartedly, more than you realize. No one should disrespect the law because they have some excuse about how life wasn't fair to them. As if they can do what they want with no consequences."

This trite idea expressed with easy contempt but genuine venom. "You look at some people in this city." Well, that was certainly a fortuitous suggestion given the circumstances; Manetti and Ruth both involuntarily glanced towards the chief executive, then leaning against the maitre d's podium and flirting with an impossibly thin hostess. "It used to be you had shame, but now everybody's proud to be a piece of shit."

"Yes, I think you may be right." Lightly, with a little laugh.

"Now your husband, he's one of the rare civilized people in this room. He epitomizes true civilization. That's right, isn't it? I'll tell you something in confidence: I think he's someone who makes the right decisions."

Ruth rose ass first in the manner of a retreating wild creature facing a serpent: a bird or a fawn, backing herself across the table without shifting her fixed, bland gaze. "Oh my gosh, you make me forget that I'm supposed to be working here!" Luckily Tina Manetti was just returning, and Manetti's purposeful energy reverted back to smooth gentility.

"I mean, can you imagine how outrageous and insulting! Just stupid! Only what did he mean, specifically? Do you think he meant something specific? I should have found out; it could have been important. Fuck, I should have encouraged him."

"For God's sake, he was just shitting you for his own amusement," I said. I still think that, too. "Or not even that. Stop being such a damn drama queen."

125

She quieted down. "Yeah, probably."

But then she basically fled to the kitchen, diving into that barrage of heat and noise and urgency only to immediately reappear strolling oh so casuallybackintothe main dining room, wiping her hands on her apron, glancing around. Thom was still chatting with the upper crust, observing everything sharply and so far as I could tell still utterly unfazed. Crystal and I were by then halfway to the foyer. Up front, I turned for a brief word with the mayor and saw Ruth poke her head into the psychic's lair, then enter and shut the door after herself.

This is what she discovered: She was a good person. She would have a long life with no major health problems, but there was some concern about the health an elderly member of the family. She was meant to have one marriage and more than one child. No? Well, it was supposed to happen. Also, someone was jealous of her, an older woman with short hair? She should be cautious because this person was very powerful. And her greatest fear in life was the fear of success. This fear is what stops her from doing what she secretly knows is her purpose in life. (Ruth prattled that twisted, flattering line obliviously, but I recognized it and marveled that such manipulative crap could reach even a Mandela.) And unfortunately her chakras were out of alignment, but this could be corrected with special crystals, available for a reasonable sum. This was important because she was in a time of turmoil and there would be great changes in her life.

CHAPTER SIX

The dedicated spokesman for the Delaware River Waterfront Corporation was understandably upset and not at all concerned with hiding it; he was standing halfway down the center aisle behind the tiny table that held his laptop, staring fixedly ahead at the screen with his hands on his hips. Not a very prepossessing stance for such an oversized, doughy individual, and his sweaty, middle-aged jowls and tiny pout did nothing to minimize the overall impression of petulance bridging on tears.

The slide currently projected to the room featured a list of names and percentages superimposed over a view of the Delaware waterfront, the lovely blue span of the Ben Franklin Bridge looming in the foreground, the river itself sparkling attractively in the sun, the unfortunate smudge of Camden still over there on the other side.

"As you can plainly see," the DRWC man insisted, plowing on without bothering to regain his composure, possibly even commencing a masochistic descent into civic martyrdom. "These forums resulted in a short list of explicit guidelines that are important not only to the individual community groups, but are in our opinion vital to the development of the Landing and obviously of the city itself."

A representative of PennDesign, the primary mover behind this valiant effort, stood resigned and contained beside his uneasy colleague. This second person was compact and younger, perhaps in his early forties, with an athletic build to him, pale eyes behind beige plastic glasses, and normal brown hair in a severe cut. He seemed a trifle uneasy in his inexpensive business suit. Superficially he seemed a combination of nerd and high school football coach, what with the aggressive way he projected intelligent assurance, his measured eagerness for the fight, but he kept shifting from foot to foot and occasionally stroked his own thigh, clearing feeling out of his depth.

It was a completely understandable nervousness, surrounded as these two were by a plainly unsympathetic if not actually hostile audience, all those chairs along the front and middle rows, a tight crescent of perhaps a hundred seats facing the Commission members filling that modestly appointed conference room with Chamber of Commerce types and local investors and out-of-state developers, gray and avid or else youthful and overeager, too many of them exhibiting that particular air of curt certainty that comes from adequately managing other people's vital concerns. Heads tilted in an impatient imitation of interest, feet restlessly jiggling, brows furrowed with bored distaste, the majority of them maintaining an unconscious protective distance from we less involved or damnably uninformed press and civilian spectators occupying the back rows.

At this point the PennDesign man took over the presentation, not much of an improvement; although introduced as a successful academician he had an unpleasantly intimate voice, that football coach inappropriately complimenting a player's physical perfection. Probably stress emphasized the trait: this business mattered to him, emotionally.

"These guidelines, as you can see, underline a requirement that any plan for the area constitute a genuine improvement to the city and to the waterfront itself, which is to say, not just more of the same but a type of development uniquely suited to the environment." Then a proper professor's pause to allow the class to fully visualize this dream.

Here's an interesting thing: these two had some real leverage but either didn't know it or didn't know what to do with it. I mean they practically begged to be exploited.

"The next slide we've all seen before ad infinitum and it remains an absolute imperative: the Landing must be connected to the city, which means we have to solve two separate problems. First there's the difficulty of access across I-95. Second, public walkways are required to tie together the entire waterfront into a commercial and recreational whole that stretches beyond the immediate Landing area north and south to the adjoining neighborhoods." And another of those tiny strategic breaks. Not that anyone was actively listening; ultimately this was only a formality, a ritual in the holy name of transparency.

"Naturally the whole project must be both affordable and sustainable." With calculated emphasis to make sure the message penetrated the general haze. "And finally, the public must be included in every step of the process." This with undiminished enthusiasm, which considered from one angle was pretty pathetic but from another demonstrated a sort of gallant faith on his part and indeed on the part of all these gentlemen and ladies present, highly competent professionals consenting to this totally bullshit public process because at some level they believed it crucial to something else absolutely essential.

"This overlay is only intended to protect the site while a master vision is decided on and carried out; however it's clear that many of the provisions proposed today both undermine the natural environment and hinder public access to the area." Pointed out in regret, but also with a suppressed fury that momentarily shortened his words and caused him to lift both hands sharply, as if he were rehearsing martial arts in his bedroom. "Needless to say, the effect on the environment needs further study, and the zoning provisions must be amended to prohibit any new encumbrances in the waterfront setback zone that would further limit public access."

And with a slight flurry he turned it back over to his larger colleague, who obediently jumped back in with barely a preparatory breath but then, catching himself up, commenced speaking in that same slow, repressive sing-song, that cadence of exceptional frustration and patience. "More-*ov*-er, be-cause as we *all* know *per*fectly well, *no* casino project has been *authorized* for this site by the Gaming Control Board in *Harrisburg*, and *no* such project is *included* in the *ov*-erlay, it's the *opinion* of the DRWC Board that *zoning* changes to permit *surface* parking in the t*em*-por-a-ry plan should be *denied* and that *any* such *casino* project eventually included in the *master* vision be *re*-quired to *com*-plete a garage *facility* sim-ul-*tan*-e- ous with its *o*-pening."

And those concluding remarks were directed, as everyone knew, at our mayor, so fervent and vocal in his support of that shiny riverfront casino, promoting that option as most likely to advance his overall agenda and therefore the public good. Knew too that His Honor was vehemently opposed to the competing entertainment and business complex proposal, tentatively known as the Columbus project, a vision of gleaming condominiums, better restaurants, a multiplex, upscale shopping, museums, and improvements to the marina. Of course, Columbus also violated all these DRWC community and environmental guidelines. The Philadelphia City Planning Commission is located in a renovated building on Arch Street, a significant sort of distance from the more impressive Center City office towers on Market Street and JFK above Broad, those slick newer constructions that house our major legal and financial concerns. We were far from everything, really, with the conference room's windows giving onto a neighboring wall of similar windows with voyeuristic views of potted plants and some vague human smudges, plus one guy facing us for a half hour or so but looking down like he was taking a leak. Next to that, a steep drop into the granite canyon separating two older, grungy cement blocks fundamentally identical to the one we were in. So it's not an especially impressive venue: I've frequented enough offices with truly spectacular vistas of this entire city, its rivers and the jets coming in, wonderful compensatory views hoarded by the elite. Here we had built-in pecan-finish sideboards filled with plastic forks and paper napkins, and gray industrial carpeting with indentations where someone had moved a conference table out of the way.

The Commission itself is a sprawling civic conglomeration combining ex officio members of the current administration – the Finance, Commerce, and Managing Directors – with additional mayoral appointees handling the roles of attorney, architect, urban planner, community representative, and so on. So it was interesting that despite the City Hall affiliations they were definitely leaning towards Columbus, which preference they optimistically assumed would substantially influence the Gaming

Control Board once that hearing got underway. Not to bore you. "So in sum what we propose is a comprehensive

renovation reaching far south and north of the Penn's Landing area, with multiple access points, each one anchored by a destination enterprise. The whole will be linked together with a nature trail for pedestrians as well as a shuttle loop."

This particular session was another of those disjointed affairs where foregone conclusions are promulgated basically as a civic defense, to permit subsequent events to proceed roughshod over competing and sometimes even technically overriding authorities. Never mind all the players who don't directly figure into my narrative: the responsible State Representative, one Jonathan Michaels (D.); the Delaware River Port Authority, which deals with extensions of public transit along the waterfront; the varied and uniformly vociferous community groups; the relevant and equally clamorous labor unions. All those staunch forces that combine to prevent everything.

I was trying to get a better grasp of this issue in part because Thom had succeeded to Wilmer van Zandt's position as Chair of Council's Standing Committee on Commerce and Economic Development - *the* committee, you understand. In addition to Thom it consisted of June Dupre, replacing Thom as Vice Chair; Margery Haskell; Jack Murphy, that reptilian Councilman-At-Large and one of the mayor's most ardent supporters in all things; Kevin Sullivan, a bland, upstanding man from the equally bland and self-respecting Greater Northeast, present not by popular mandate but because the City Charter insists on nominal minority representation; and David Cevallos, significantly a partner with PennDesign in the creation of the development guidelines about to be impolitely ignored by the financial powers that be. The final committee member, Donny Mealy, also held the informal but traditional right of veto granted every Councilperson on legislation directly affecting his district. Not coincidentally this same roster, plus two additional and here irrelevant members, comprised the Committee on Appropriations, because clearly nothing was going to happen barring the inclusion of some hefty municipal funding.

As for the separate issue of that zoning request presented to Council, it had been procedurally directed as was proper, first with the required notice of a public hearing to collect testimony concerning what was already common knowledge except where it was rank speculation, with that promptly followed by a meeting of the Committee on Rules also open to the public, and that in turn immediately followed by an announcement from Rules that further examination of the matter would continue in private.

This typical stratagem, which can be euphemistically described as maybe not precisely in accordance with the spirit of the City Charter, somehow failed to focus serious public attention on this latest incarnation of both the riverfront and casino issues, and while it was obvious to everyone which way the dominant winds were blowing I couldn't guess whether or not they were strong enough to force along any real results. Then the mystery, if you can call it that, surrounding van Zandt kept me sufficiently intrigued, anyway enough to go poking around, an eye out for some hint of criminal activity in the usual run of legitimized corruption. There was that and maybe how Manetti had toyed with Ruth if he actually had, but that was probably just his dull humor.

As a result I wasted some time clarifying stuff I knew wouldn't matter because everyone's real motivation went deeper and accordingly their stated positions were virtually intractable and unrelated to any actual events.

Now I need to explain that Councilwoman June Dupre and I share an entirely fictitious romantic past and an extremely improbable future together. It's a benign charade. While June is in some ways dependably vulnerable, she's also intelligent and dedicated and when it suits her can be informative. Plus I always feel a little guilty about her, or annoyed with her, or both: she exudes such a high level of anxiety; she makes everyone in her vicinity hyperventilate. And I'm amenable to a little innocent flirtation, so when she said we could meet out at her riding lesson, come admire me, I thought what the hell, it's little enough to pay.

Not that she was likely to have any really valuable information to spill, being a fervent supporter of Columbus, the presumptive victor. I figured if anything fishy was going on it was probably on the casino side. The odd thing is, today it seems like June was a central figure in all this when she wasn't. I think that's mostly her opportunism and her wistful imagination, but the fact is she's squeezed herself in.

This stable was situated right on the Schuylkill, just outside the city limits up River Road and not far north of Manayunk, that trendy reborn canal town still clinging to its close-knit, defensive neighborhood ethos - hard-bitten, hard- drinking, all about beer and church and tough pride.

So a pleasant enough locale for a Saturday digression. There's a serious bike culture out that way, with the river trail running parallel to the river that comes straight out from Center City and continues north until ultimately losing itself amid the lovely celadon fields and log recreations of Valley Forge, there among the delicate, unconcerned deer. I like the trail, everyone does; you're in constant danger of being run down by a uniformed rider in one of those streamlined, cleanly beautiful teams that pass you in a colorful blur, a living Neiman print. Whole families sway along on bicycles built for six, ridiculously athletic elderly men smile from contraptions designed to operate feet over heads, and young parents tow toddlers in netted, brightly-colored tents. Determined, overweight novices struggle along unaware of the protocols so neglecting to shout the requisite "On your left," and instead desperately pinging their tinny bells.

There's an unexpected amount of woodland out there, magically sandwiched in between the city proper and the major suburbs as if the dimensions went whimsical and inserted a good chunk of Kentucky between a couple of grungy industrial parks. The countryside inexplicably unfolds in front you, pure backwater trash in some parts, mirroring the worst of the Jersey Pine Barrens, but here and there enclosing purely romantic remnants of delicate, deteriorating Victorian edifices. In another era fashionable refugees from the sweltering city traveled out on the new railway to rent a horse and carriage, spend the day boating, or go wading in those striped bathing suits.

Today there are obstinate river rat communities along the bank, sometimes in doublewides but more recently occupying newer, pricey vacation constructions, their motorboats up on the sparse grass among the strutting geese. This even though these banks are closely flanked by the commuter and Conrail lines, and the highway is right there, too, never mind that the area floods on a fairly regular basis. The Septa rails continue on alongside the river, past the crumbling, anonymous stone foundations and the gritty shells of old factories that once exploited the river and canal, some renovated now into loft apartments, square brick edifices still decorated with ancient, barely legible painted advertisements, mercantile ghosts. Some of the truck garages of abandoned structures further upriver have been co-opted by sculling teams from the Main Line colleges and high schools, skeletal tiered racks of delicate long craft parked in weedy lots with students crawling about in all weathers. But many of the older buildings have vanished in the wake of yet more townhouse or office complexes, that pale, unoriginal new blight spreading inexorably over the ridges that shelter the water.

The Schuylkill itself, so different from the broader, businesslike Delaware, widens and shallows out between occasional minor dams; often the water is so low you can plainly see the trash-strewn bottom, and fishermen wade nearly halfway across. It's an area of shameful neglect; after every hard rain some of the trees nearest the water are left leaning low, stripped to their naked roots, until ultimately they topple in and vanish downriver. Now in some spots only mud and scant scrub separate the water from the Regional Rail tracks, a constant reminder that the generally placid Schuylkill is after all a river that after strong storms presents as a thick torrent of pure swirling energy the color of rich cocoa, a sludge of rushing debris. But in full flood presenting an entirely foreign, flat landscape that betrays no hint of the lost contours beneath, an eerie reformation.

I've come up here to an impossible cobalt October sky perfectly reflecting flame-hued leaves in luminous water, a preposterously beautiful scene like the photograph from a jigsaw puzzle box. Sometimes, too, in the evenings if the light is exactly right, the charcoal outlines of trees and brush across the river detach themselves and hover in a third-dimensional middle distance like an enchanted floating island. Or in late summer the trees and shrubs are so covered in vines they look like mysterious ghost topiary.

Well, the driveway up to June's appointed stable was all calculated bucolic serenity, unregulated honeysuckle vines still blossoming fragrantly in the hedges, wetness flattening the yellowing grass, twin riding ovals with freshly painted rails, and the sky a sheer film of white over the lightest pale blue, a final watercolor wash before the incomparable ultramarine of October.

At the long barn the persistent September heat intensified the good, vibrant scents of manure and beast and earth, the overall sheltered silence emphasizing the unearthly call of bullfrogs from a ditch choked with evil green algae. Dogs of varied sizes and mixed parentage were padding around inquisitively, and a huge yellow cat was stretched atop one of several standard redwood picnic

137

tables, enjoying what sun filtered through a stand of enormous oaks and pines, watching the leaves dance. Beyond the cleared yard fronting the barn the ground was carpeted with dried pine needles; there were small flowerbeds around some of the trees with plantings of familiar things like pansies and marigolds.

Not a fancy place, or even an especially prosperous one, or so I concluded from the patched blacktop on the drive and the shabby if punctilious condition of the barn. That building, its white paint scabbed and grimy, sat well above the river; you could just catch a glimpse of water down through the shallow woods, a thin, luminescent silver-gray flash. Several of those tall electrical structures like miniature Eiffel Towers rose scattered across the grounds, defacing the purity, and a substantial white house was barely visible at a little distance, lower than the barn and sheltered in a young grove.

But what you first noticed were the numerous teenage girls. The place was absolutely overrun with female adolescents, all of them dressed in unflattering jeans and muddy, scuffed paddock boots, and all of them reeking of casual competence mixed with a little compassionate contempt. They were variously occupied, some leading horses out of the shaded depths of the barn, others just inside the doors tacking up, two of them helping a handful of chatting, slender women in notably clean breeches up onto their respective mounts. Someone had cut a step into the stump of an enormous tree, a sycamore or an oak, and this fixture served as a rustic mounting block. Everyone seemed very nice.

But June wasn't among the group at the barn, and I was directed back along the drive. I followed the next class down, walking behind the slow parade of riders guiding their mounts at a clumsy walk, one at least almost stumbling at every other step which seemed to be the rider's fault. We reached the riding rings a quarter mile along, one to each side of the road, one occupied and one free.

My entourage filed into the vacant oval while I crossed to the opposite side and joined a couple of people sitting on the grass to observe the action. This ring contained maybe six or seven adult women pulled to a ragged halt around the rail while their instructor, another lithe, well-muscled teen, hectored them over some intricacy of horsemanship they apparently weren't quite grasping. She strode over the stony surface, adjusting the bars on jumps not three feet high, pausing once to stamp out her cigarette, occasionally laughing good-naturedly at her students, and once bending her own body into the desired two-point position, poised slightly forward on an imaginary mount in the center of the ring.

At length the class commenced a slow circling, hugging the rail, excluding one game if terrified candidate called forward to ride the course. I watched with empathetic nervousness and some glee as she sat back, took a deep breath, and commenced wildly kicking her horse. It was a gigantic beast, white with a shaven mane just starting to grow back, a hulking, unmotivated punk.

"Left leg! Left leg!" The instructor turned round with the rider, traversing the course with her own body as the woman, all novice determination, finally attained a slow galumphing trot towards a low crossbar, approaching it from a clearly unfortunate angle. Naturally enough the pale beast veered off completely, forcing the poor woman, all sweaty frustration, to circle him back and get him pointed in the right direction and sluggishly trotting again. Meanwhile the remaining contingent, June among them, swiveled in their saddles to watch this effort while continuing to circle the rail.

The white giant maintained his extremely uninterested gait, plainly considering a second evasion; the rider resorted to her crop and he delivered a grudging canter, approached the jump with near comical resignation, and took it without effort or interest. Then he shook his spiky head and conferred a rude snort before defiantly subsiding back into an outright walk.

"No! Keep riding him! Don't let him get away with that! Keep him going. Get him moving! He's not done yet; he has to go all the way around."

But the rider was kicking futilely at the animal and laughing with relief. "He is?"

June was approaching on an elegant bay. She was wearing a helmet and a tight knit shirt over tan breeches; the outfit narrowed her already slight body into something frankly unnatural, all gigantic eyes and little pointy chin like one of those short gray extraterrestrials that abducts rustics. The animal stuck his moist, warm nose under the bottom rail and started to chew off what green he could reach. I offered the appropriate compliments, keeping my distance; horses are less reliable than cats and a lot bigger. With the humility of a supplicant, metaphorical cap in hand, I reiterated the purpose of our meeting.

Nodding, patting her horse's broad neck, June seemed pleased to be looking down at me. She fervently pursues some mythical Greek goddess by Founding Fathers personal ideal; you can see her striving, and it's exhausting.

So even if you weren't already familiar with her position on the Landing issue you only had to look at her. Ostensibly a Democrat, June invariably identified with the business community as representing the ideals she considered the foundation of civic excellence. No need to be consistent; the priority was to get elected. She's got a bulging forehead, a ready moue of contempt for any ignorant adversary, and level gray eyes to see through unrealistic bullshit. "It's imperative we staunch the financial erosion." That's her idea of casual conversation. And she was hardly alone in censuring Philadelphia's prohibitive wage tax: precious few industries remain within the official city limits although our hospitals and universities and some major pharmaceutical firms keep the municipality afloat if dangerously exhausted. But if you ran a decent mid-sized business it was only responsible to locate to one of our many pleasant suburban industrial parks or office complexes.

June made an aborted attempt to halt her horse's gluttony, but there's probably only so much you can do about dominating a thousand-pound creature if you didn't learn as a child. Anyway he was probably a rental, a mercenary just doing his job and nothing personal. Of course June remained gracious, and she'd automatically centered herself upright in the saddle; she crossed her hands into an easy pose over the reins, presenting a reasonably effective image of cool competence. She also looked terrified; I suspect riding was some kind of test of courage, so of course thoroughly admirable. "You know, I sympathize with David. I respect his commitment to PennDesign. He's not another demagogue thinking about reelection. But those guidelines are vague on every critical

141

point, just wishful thinking playing with public expectations, and that's irresponsible."

She meant what the hell was up but preferred not to ask, what with always having to project her superior knowledge of the universe. It's the same with Ruth, that identical fearful pride acting to extinguish possibility. (People I know tend to flow into each other like that all the time.)

I said, "The mayor's pushing the Casino plan irregardless." "Ha! Persistence isn't everything; these people who think they can make something succeed just by refusing to concede. There's incredible over-saturation, you know that, all the casinos are losing money; Atlantic City is imploding! But it's like we don't see it. We want to turn the whole city into an amusement park, but how does anybody get the money to play? Do they all work for other casinos?"

"Well, but say the riverfront casino gets approval from Harrisburg – no, I'm not saying it will, don't start! Just assume it hypothetically, or something less definite but promising occurs, and then tell me what it would take to get that Landing proposal through Council?" She tried again to pull up the head of her stubborn mount; I waited as the two completed a tedious circle in place. The smell of the place was beginning to bother me, as was the powerful mound of intrusive flesh and teeth looming above me.

June came back around frowning. "Well nothing. There's nothing I can imagine; I mean, that won't happen anyway. How can the Control Board make that decision without approval for the site? Oh, it's completely ridiculous! Even under those circumstances Columbus has the votes, unless you know something different?" She didn't, that was plain. Her eyes, as they focused on me, were dancing in the bright sun, but I could see the irritation. "Of course there's that incident when van Zandt died. He might have been wavering towards the casino, it's possible, but they still wouldn't have the votes."

I'd figured the same myself. Anyway I had nothing on van Zandt, not so much as a hint of a rumor despite my best efforts; so far as I know no one's uncovered anything to this day. But still, that was interesting.

She half-turned in her saddle again, looking back into the oval: almost her turn at the course, then turned back to examine me with an expression somewhere between disappointment and real anger. "You know, Con, it's always nice to see you, whatever it is you think you're doing."

I nodded. "I'm not sure what I'm doing," I admitted. And this is a typical day for me. "You're actually certain Columbus will happen, then?"

"Oh, I think so. I think we're better people than we're given credit for." After which remarkable declaration she gave me a second in case I had anything interesting to say after all, then added an apologetic smile goodbye. She sent me yet another backward glance as she turned her mount into the ring.

Starting back to my car I heard the instructor shout: "Gallop, June! gallop!" So I walked the few steps back to watch. June was perched way too far forward on the neck of that lovely animal, her skinny legs flapping wildly. They cleared a bale of hay maybe two feet high at a less-than-sprightly trot, the horse bored but obliging, but even from my moderate distance I could tell June was elated to the toes of her polished brown boots.

I waved in congratulation. Why not? No matter how good the horse or how valiant the effort she was never going to catch up.

She was right about Columbus, though, about it's ability to mesmerize the money people with images of future renown and a resurgent river district. Mayors are temporary, Columbus would outlast the administration, and it seemed very imposing and very conventional, as close as you could get to a fiscal guarantee. I thought so, anyway, and so did that semi-circle of intently self- interested types up at the PCPC meeting, present solely to safeguard the potential of the architect's elevation at the side of the room, a Columbus of clean office towers gracefully interspersed with luxury high-rise housing, with our dilapidated Great Plaza amphitheater reborn as a state-of-the-art outdoor concert venue. The whole fantastical complex was positioned against a background of photos of the river and its two cities, as if it had a right to take proprietary pride in the soaring blue arch of the bridge.

Which miniature hypnotic vision compelled a meaty, well- groomed supporter to place his meeting binder under his chair, rise, and smile at us with one of those frank and eminently reasonable entrepreneurial smiles. Even so he had an air of urgency about him, in the set of his shoulders and in his minor frown, and there was a defensive edge, too, in the positively infatuated glance he cast at the model.

"I'm sure we all want to develop this location in a way that will prove financially as well as socially beneficial." This an admonishment to the PennDesign presenter, now thankfully restored to his own chair off towards the windows. "I would point out that the community desires outlined here automatically eliminate anything suggestive of what I shall term a Vegas manqué. Thank God, because we're all familiar with the many past attempts to develop this section of the waterfront and their truly extraordinary record of disaster, and I cannot help but feel such a downmarket move would prove yet another fiasco."

An utterly serene conversational tone with that confidant smile, a kindly pretense of equality to emphasize the overall superiority of the majority and raise the stifled indignation of the unbelievers.

Speaking of moral certainty and people who pronounce their Liberal politics the way their parents used to pronounce the word "Christian", consider Councilwoman Margery Haskell, a woman incapable of political self-doubt and according to my calculations one of the two holdouts on the committee, the other being David Cevallos. Seeking a line on the strangely unquenched optimism of the casino proponents, I caught up with Margery as she was exiting the ornate Caucus Room at City Hall in a clutch of unknowns and supernumeraries. Spivak and Murphy were in there still, standing and talking, Murphy doing his serpent smile. The Caucus Room is exactly what you'd picture for the top secret meeting room of an ancient extraterrestrial evil society scheming to conquer the planet.

Margery put a firm hand to my back, courteously but with no hesitation whatsoever, and propelled me down the corridor, through an anteroom, and into her private office. Isolating me there, virtually pinned in my chair by her informed fervor, facing her legendary wall of diplomas, a great fan of them spreading out behind her – all degrees,

145

too, not a single masquerading tribute. She sat there with her hands at ease on her desk, just waiting. "Good of you to see me," I said. I could see her shiny scalp through the tight little curls around her hairline; the rest of her was concealed inside a chocolate ensemble, a straight shift and jacket, clearly expensive stuff.

"Your nose is beautiful," she told me once. "Stop cowering." She does not get my schtick.

Margery's been married forever to a mellow mathematics professor, the kind of man you look at and know he's never experienced serious anger or frustration in his entire life but who invariably radiates a deep understanding for those less evolved. They had a couple of daughters already in college. Otherwise I still don't know much about her personally, only her official biography and some vague assertions. Probably she envisions herself a heroine, probably with some justice, but she's such an aggressively triumphant woman, stern and superior.

Another option is that we just intuitively dislike each other. For what it's worth, a number of her colleagues privately delight in disparaging her, partly from envy and partly because Margery is so fucking patronizing. That instructive hand on your arm, insisting you listen and learn. "She has to face her own ignorance," Ruth says. "It's the only thing that can possibly save her now."

The esteemed Councilwoman was fixing me with a sternly cordial expression. She returned my remark, her voice cool and pleasant. "I'm glad you can see me. So many people can't anymore."

These women who prefer the offensive edge. "Well, of course."

Regarding me with that friendly yet purposive expression, sherry-colored eyes challenging under that restrained aureole. An extremely intelligent, surely successful woman and yet this implicit belligerence. "Let's get to it; I'm delighted to have this discussion. I appreciate your diligence. But if I were you I wouldn't bother searching for any connection between our Mr. Manetti and the casino proposal. A natural enough suspicion, but I assure you unfounded, in fact absurd."

Margery was perfectly correct in that we were much too early in the process for criminal opportunity. The obvious implication was, as she said, absurd, but we were both aware of the potential.

"A Vegas on the Delaware. That's what everyone's so afraid of, though why they're terrified is mysterious when there's reason to think it would be a great success." For a moment she concentrated on the air behind me, I suppose gazing at this idyllic vision of the future. "Do you know what would happen? People would actually go there; the Landing would become a genuine destination. Or perhaps you would prefer the Gallery?" This with one of those knowing, accusatory glances at me, God knows why. I truly resent it when people insinuate like that, ascribing opinions to me that I've never even considered.

As to the Gallery, it didn't even exist anymore. It used to be a predominately diverse mall at what was then the Market East train station, in its last years degenerated into mostly discount and dollar stores and generally patronized by that loud, pushy element that rudely invades the space of people just trying to go about their business: all those undisciplined and increasingly exotic ethnicities, obstructive and child-infested and always so, I don't know, reproachful. A population providing that paranoid prick of urban danger that keeps the better sort patronizing suburban high-end retail and illegal drug centers like King of Prussia. Market East served businesspeople catching trains, the urban poor, tourists in search of the physical remnants of Philadelphia's glorious history, and anyone heading to Reading Terminal Market for quaint Amish goods or lunch. Here's something I love about that train station: there's a mural on the tunnels that depicts the four seasons in trees and shrubs, square tiles designed to flow into an image at speed, from a moving train. Unfortunately trains slow and stop at a station, so no one's ever seen this effect but only some separate, static tiles, like gigantic pixels.

Margery said, "Gambling's coming into downtown Philadelphia, however regrettable that proves. There are serious concerns but there's strong popular support, and the mayor knows if the Landing site is ultimately rejected the default will be Market East or the immediate area." She spoke with her usual depth of authority but what did it matter what the mayor felt? He could be as wrong as anyone.

And I had reason to doubt their certainty. Lower Market Street backs up to Chinatown, and Chinese community leaders sensibly fear that the proximity of a slots parlor is likely to exacerbate, if in fact wasn't deliberately designed to exploit, the gambling predilections of that populace. Some years back a nearby location, a former department store, was selected for a gaming license, and that suggestion evoked sufficient outrage to kill the plan. City Hall knew what to expect.

Margery paused for dramatic effect, taking the opportunity to examine her surroundings as if searching for a forgotten conclusion. Then she moved in closer over her desk, adopting an air of serious confidentiality: "That license has to go somewhere that satisfies the constituents, but we can agree it won't be West Philly or Kensington. It will go somewhere white folk want revitalized, therefore if it's not the river then it will be downtown Market Street. And while there's a slight chance that will succeed there's a much higher probability of catastrophe." Someone approached from the outer office, saw me, and entirely disappeared, perhaps into a random beam of sunlight. I could smell dust, air freshener, and disinfectant.

"Market East is symbolic of Center City's economic decay. Low-end gambling is not likely to stop the violence. Shiny rows of electronic slot machines will not attract suburbanites away from higher-end casino options, but you and I know that ludicrous projects do go blundering forward. I am determined to prevent that happening."

"I don't know." I didn't. The casino slightly higher up the river was doing fine despite it's inconvenient, downscale location. Although she had a point about the violence, down in those dim subterranean walkway tunnels to nowhere. (As of this writing, the Market East train station has been renamed Jefferson Station; Septa sold the naming rights to the Jefferson hospital system. I think this hilarious but no one else seems to appreciate the joke. Meanwhile the Gallery is reportedly being transformed into more of those upscale outlets, but the last time I had to walk through there the food court and most of the stores were abandoned or shuttered, the kiosks vanished, the subterranean space dim and just plain spooky.)

149

My doubt turned Margery garrulous. "The Columbus people know full well Center City already has a glut of unoccupied office space. Surely you realize that if this mayor had some better way to push fiscal revitalization anywhere in this city he wouldn't be talking about casinos?"

"Except you don't have the votes."

"Council will make the decision that best benefits city residents." All those devotees who faithfully expected her to defend their interests against the whole hostile encircling Delaware Valley, who needed to admire her and depend on her and just plain believe in an idol. We were walking back towards the elevators, past closed office doors: a doctrinaire, entrenched populist commander in the battle against urban disintegration, and a short, scruffy question mark, all hair and nose, toting a battered canvas messenger bag. At that moment imagining a Council meeting room, members sitting deaf and certain over their notepads, impatiently glancing at their phones.

"So you're expecting a miracle? Is that what you're saying?" When she was so educated, such a stern realist: it made no sense.

"I realize you think I'm somewhat dense, Con, because I don't adopt your limited version of reality. But things happen as they're meant to, the right solution tends to manifest." It was fucking inexcusable. Ruth couldn't have said it better.

"God wants a casino? Seriously?"

She picked up a plain yellow pencil and started turning it round her fingers. "I have a strong idea that this story is just unfolding. The future is determined in part through continuing to move forward with faith. In that sense belief certainly creates reality, in case you didn't know. But then, I know better than to argue matters of faith with you." The implication being that, unlike such callow ignoramuses as me, she herself knew God personally, was familiar with his methods and intentions, and found them acceptable, even laudatory. And yet I wouldn't call her religious. It's more that she has complete faith in her own beliefs.

So she nourishes them, and sometimes her certainty loses battles before they've even properly begun because there's so much she simply refuses to hear. That's how she recognizes evil: it's whatever stymies her success. Of course she supported this mayor, what choice did she have, but she supported him without denying his myriad flaws, eliciting more than one cowering confession before her magisterial throne and brushing away his promises with experienced disdain. To resolutely promote his agenda in countless conference rooms and school auditoriums, square and firm, her eyes fixed on social justice, her mind expertly determining what was really possible and what could and should be done next.

Once, not really all that long ago, East Market was a genteel avenue lined with legendary department stores one right after another: Strawbridge's, Lit Brothers, Gimbels, Wanamaker's: relicts of that even earlier era when Philadelphia was unarguably the greatest of all the many great manufacturing cities, a veritable mercantile paradise. Today only the facades of those lovely, ornate merchant palaces remain, extraordinary city blocks of them carefully restored and officially protected, magnificent and improbable, their interiors divided into downscale commercial space or offices and apartments. You walk this way on a cool, empty dusk and hear coarse laughter coming down the street from nowhere specific, mocking and somehow personal.

Today Macy's was the sole real downtown holdout although technically a carpetbagger, occupying the old Wanamaker building, cleverly maintaining the old traditions: the eagle statue and the humungous organ and the Christmas light show, childhood traditions to lure in today's nostalgic adults. Most of the better retail trade has wisely fled across Broad Street to reestablish itself west of City Hall, in with the sleek new towers, the Penn Center and Liberty Place and Comcast buildings, all that contemporary city that erupted once skyscrapers were finally permitted to look down on Billy Penn's hat. If only west of Broad Street so as not to obstruct the view from the river, so as not to allow Colonial or Federal or even Gilded Age history to vanish into the future.

No, I'm being really unfair here; downtown's so much better than it was even twenty years ago. Ask anyone. People have tried, that's the truth, and even somewhat succeeded. But that isn't to say it's what it once was. Much of East Market below Broad is safely avoided until around 7th Street, where you start to pick up the vibes from the historic district, and then it's all sunlit expanses thronged with tourists, horse-drawn carriages decked out with plastic flowers, newer museums and visitor centers, early Greek Revival banks, and chipper guides speaking from touring trolleys. Wander off Market Street and you're strolling by the brick rowhouses of Old City with its secret gardens behind wrought iron gates, sheltering trees, and doorstep urns overflowing with ivy and bright impatiens. There's a preserved complacence about those marble stoops, a nourishing goodwill that emanates from satisfied visitors and the general beneficence of people with money, an energy that supports a host of tiny galleries and better restaurants. Naturally the Independence Hall area dominates the district, that serene Georgian edifice constantly choked with gaping visitors all marveling at how terribly small and simple it is considering what it gave birth to, the rollicking, unimaginable size of that. Continue on towards the Delaware and you're passing smaller offices and retail and the newer hotels and condos nudging I-95 near the riverfront, or instead head south and you're swallowed up by the reticent brass-and-brick luxury of Society Hill, secluded streets quiet to your foot. At Front and Market Streets shuttered enterprises mingle with small functioning businesses; it's an intriguing enclave, the air deliciously infused with a bohemian twang, experimental yet exclusive. It's where you encounter stoic Tamanend, Billy Penn's Lenni-Lenape partner in peace and patron saint of America, right there at the foot of the highway overpass at the Landing, standing on a turtle.

Go south a block to one of my favorite stretches of Chestnut Street because it features pretty much every possible variety of international cuisine. Continue down the block towards the river where right between a family Mexican restaurant and an upscale Brazilian eatery stood the storefront housing Donny Mealy's reelection headquarters, its window signage shouting in your face, its very existence either blighting or completing the ambience, I'm not quite sure which.

I found Mealy in his inner sanctum, on the phone, looking as usual like the owner of a shady but flourishing used-car dealership, the kind who does his own deliberately cheesy commercials. In actual fact he'd been a successful insurance executive before taking to politics. He's shrewd, competent, has a juvenile ego and remarkably bad taste - you have to wonder who raised him – and he's a complete pile of shit who loves to advertise that fact because he really doesn't know better. He's that kind of asshole.

"Con," he said. "Con." And indicated a chair, so I sat and listened to one side of a confidential conversation regarding the legal problems of the son of a worthy constituent. Speaking a name I recognized, giving me a wink.

Finally ending the call, turning to me with a big smile that showed molars, soft cheeks dimpling, dark eyes gleaming from that pampered complexion. "Con! What are you up to today and should I worry about it?"

Although I'd superficially explained my mission, setting up this interview. "What I really want you to tell me is how you envision the waterfront a decade into the future. All of it, not just the Landing, but of course that area, too."

Laughing, smoothing that vanity hair as if deep down he knew he was only a caricature. Do these people simply not get what we think about them? Or is the charade only for the gullible and the hell with your perception, I'm in it for the win and you don't matter? "Oh, let's see, what do I picture there? That's an interesting question." I nodded in acknowledgement, doing my foreign and modest bit; I generally don't notice myself doing it anymore but that time I did. "Well! I'll tell you then. I see a new financial center with landmark buildings designed to compete with the best contemporary architecture in any major city in this country, all of it fully occupied and integrated into the heart of the city but still easily accessible to the suburbs and New

Jersey." He'd certainly collected all his words, and handed them to me with a totally unconcerned face, not even bothering to act interested.

"And you really see this happening?"

And in that instant, the words just past my teeth, I knew Columbus was doomed. Knew it as surely as I knew my own address, knew it well enough to bet the rent money, even though my conviction was utterly irrational.

"Dude," I said to myself. A word I picked up during my brief legal career and can't exorcise, although I only use it to myself.

Mealy sent a quick suspicious glance at me, probably catching something odd in my expression. "What could stop it?" With spread hands.

And I could only shrug in return.

Maybe a week later the mayor's office scheduled an announcement on this very topic. I stopped in at Thom's office, pleased to discover him ensconced behind his cluttered desk, his jacket over the back of his chair and his sleeves rolled up. He had an 18th Century map of the city directly behind his chair, symbolic or pretentious or both, and a photograph of Ruth on his desk, looking windblown and laughing out of a silver frame. I sank down on his official leather sofa and leaned forward to clasp my hands between my knees. "What's all this about?"

"A casino at the Landing, ultimately. That much I can absolutely guarantee." Delivered with the practiced satiric, rueful face. "Another move in the same tedious game. Do keep me informed."

Down in the mayor's reception room His Honor's press secretary came forth to address the city, posing before a magnificent, flag-flanked fireplace in an equally glorious

155

room brimming with gilt and crystal and marble, with a gold-patterned carpet and a coffered ceiling and its every inch of wall space papered with portraits of our former mayors, all these worthies glaring out at we few repugnant journalists sitting uneasily on our plain wooden chairs.

The press secretary, a middle-aged and unremarkable female in a dowdy gray pantsuit, informed us in that quiet but invariably rude voice common to municipal officials that the mayor was filing a complaint against Philadelphia City Council to force action on a zoning ordinance designed to facilitate the establishment of a slots parlor on Penn's Landing, as Council's refusal to act on the matter constituted, either fortuitously or by design, a deterrent to those seeking to invest in the proposed project to the benefit of opposing financial interests.

Fine. Additionally, the mayor declared himself greatly impressed with the guidelines established by PennDesign, which the mayor agreed clearly represented the best interests of the communities most affected by any improvements along the waterfront. Therefore, and despite the decision of the PCPC in favor of what was termed the Columbus project and the accompanying recommendation that the mayor send on to Council legislation designed to support that plan, the mayor would defer any further action regarding development at the Landing until revisions to all plans could be made incorporating the PennDesign guidelines.

So that was a clever piece of virtue confiscation, today's most popular game, the mayor utilizing PennDesign's ethical leverage to provide his own project some breathing room while not incidentally granting his true believers a tiny measure of confirmation, something to keep them coming to church.

CHAPTER SEVEN

Ruth liked to remark offhand how she was raised in a bar, that boast first an admission tentatively ventured late one night in an Oberlin dorm room, signifying a momentous breakthrough: such a disclosure would have been unthinkable not five years earlier. Right through high school she existed in a continual state of suppressed panic, desperate to conceal the shameful circumstances of her upbringing, guarding her fragile psyche against any accidental glimpse of the truth. Think about that, think about desperately lying to those school friends a bus ride outside the immediate neighborhood, a stratagem certain to fail and earn you a double helping of the very humiliation you dreaded, never mind the deadly humor of your relatives. Also garnering the notice of various officious, meddling idiots: teachers and counselors, all those dangerously inept assholes.

The bar in question occupied the corner of a side street off

Snyder Avenue, commanding the intersection, forthrightly ugly with its bright red, rounded cement belly jutting out over the sidewalk, all in all a pugnacious, unrepentant imposition on the sensibilities of the whole neighborhood. This minor landmark formed the terminus of two residential blocks, most still brick, some with siding or gray stucco, but long before the era of artisan chocolates and pho an area immaculately maintained, with clean friendly stoops, hopscotch games in bright chalk on the sidewalks, halved pimple balls hiding behind car tires, and cats peeping amiably from between lacy front window curtains. Windows that were worth the seeing all decorated for the holidays, with baskets of plush pastel bunnies, stenciled spider webs, or motorized Santas, and always those big old-fashioned, multi-colored light strings. People spent time and thought on those displays; those streets were about everyone's hard-won victory over the whole mean world, about being at home in a protective enclave of similar generous souls.

Dougherty's signified the major triumph of Ruth's grandfather Ted, a photo on the mantel with the kind of frank smile no one's had since World War II, a man whose ambitions were confined to his unassuming family tavern, his squat building with its wood-paneled upper façade and the family name etched in gold on the single glass door. When Ruth's dad took charge he had the two long windowless walls partially rebuilt in murky glass blocks; later again, during an unusually lucid interval, he had them restored to the original paneling. Inside it was nothing out of the ordinary, with no taint of professional décor but just the usual dim interior and that hard aromatic smack of beer and cigarette smoke and steam, with the expected shelves of jewel-toned bottles fronting a mirror with gold-etched Victorian curlicues like a real Western saloon: a mirror that reflected everything back at you in a friendly fashion, flattering to an adolescent girl. The booths had maroon leatherette seats, the bar was of battered, polished oak, and there were half a dozen small round tables towards the rear. For a declared tavern Dougherty's offered little in the way of food, mainly burgers and steak sandwiches on Italian rolls from a big plastic bag left hanging from the front door every morning. But during prime business hours it provided a pleasant refuge for mere acquaintances, people remote enough to present no real danger but welcome for purposes of mental and emotional realignment. So Dougherty's was convenient and did its job, effectively serving the immediate vicinity.

From the start half-hearted, though, and here's the reason: it was an inheritance that made Dougherty's possible, the proceeds from the sale of Ted's mother's house and not Ted's own sweat and determination. That rankled, and he held a grudge, and then he decided not to try too hard in order to demean the legacy.

Francis Dougherty, once he inherited, expended most of his attention on his vintage jukebox, his precious baby. God knows where he got it from. It held the place of honor in the very center of the long, narrow room, dominating the wall directly opposite the mirror so all its flashing and winking and gleaming chrome was gloriously magnified. Frank kept it stocked with all his favorite pop classics, the melodic essence of a sentimental era

- Elvis and Sam Cooke, Sinatra and Nat King Cole, songs with lyrics that were deeply romantic or cleanly sad or mid-century cool but essentially based on promises, lost or fulfilled but promises, those eternal foundations of all civilized life. Because Frank himself was all about promises.

If Dougherty's wasn't remarkable in any way, once Frank took command it was definitely going to be, someday. Frank was certain of that, and he could delineate grandiose schemes with the best of them. It was always just about to get underway, that transformation into a destination South Philly restaurant with class and renown. Not right now, but when the time was right. "Money, Ruth." Except Frank could never quite grasp that action on his own part was required, not even when it came to minor improvements or repairs like a loose bolt on the men's room door or a faulty freezer. Instead he simply waited for something better to happen, apparently feeling he should wait for some cosmic go-ahead, meanwhile expending immeasurable nervous energy treading water, dealing adequately enough with disasters but otherwise just managing to pay the taxes and keep the whole slapdash enterprise square with Licenses and Inspections. The relatives tended to descend a bit too often for Frank's taste, people who just couldn't take a hint yet expected infinite courtesy and mysteriously received it, too, even while they made clear their avid distaste for the family business. Or at least that's how the daughter of the enterprise saw it. But more often they eschewed the bar itself for the house a few streets over. Pat, Frank's fraternal twin, proved the most frequent unwelcome visitor, forever infuriating despite his falsely affectionate smirk, his deceptively meek wife Kate trailing obediently in his wake. Pat who consistently addressed his niece with a full formal Ruth Marie, virtually pushing her an unbending arm's length away in order to forestall any repugnant familiarity. But to Kate she was always Ruthie, because Kate could never remember how much her niece despised that particular diminutive.

Even for fraternal twins they were remarkably dissimilar, as if on purpose, for a joke. Family opinion

161

unanimously accorded Pat the more attractive appearance, upholding this opinion with religious fervor, permitting no argument for all the decision seemed ludicrous to any rational outsider. Frank was tall and lanky and not merely handsome but remarkably so, a silly movie-star handsome people noticed on the street, with a deeply cleft chin and very fine light brown hair and a constant air of conceited certainty: really a bit of the bully with his feet planted too wide apart in a mocking but defensive posture. Whereas Pat was shorter, wide if not exactly fat, with narrow shoulders and a characteristic proud curve to him, and he walked with a pouter- pigeon roll: stomach forward, nose high, lips tight, a butler in: swallow-tails, a preening Jeeves. He was some kind of high school administrator of unremarkable intelligence, his casual conversation limited to himself, his family, and conventional reactions to current events, but he remained mysteriously complacent.

By contrast, or rather through the comedic law of human attraction, Kate was exceptionally sensitive and emotional, not like other people, so you always had to be careful of her feelings. It was like she longed for your attack, this tiny, round woman, this red-cheeked hard rubber ball. Theirs was a tough marriage for others to endure, what with the subtle undermining of your every minor success, the infatuated updates on their children, the lavish show-off dinners with carefully rehearsed topics of conversation.

Never mind the public displays of deep mutual contempt. "We're making a gym out of the boys' room now it's empty." Pat making this announcement as if propounding the secret of the universe, then sitting back for the applause, forever confident in his ability to fascinate the peasants. Ruth cringed with the embarrassment of an adolescent, imagining some ideal boyfriend witnessing this pettiness. She'd recognized Pat's coldness and fearful suspicion of her way before she could articulate it. Kate, as usual, was unsuccessfully fighting back tears. "Yeah. Well, we can still wait a little." Nice little smile.

"We have to start sometime, Kate." Self-assured, even smug, with his hands outspread. The voice of reason explaining things to the people.

"I want to wait, if that's alright with you!" And then delicately sniffing, turning that vulnerable face stoically aside. Kate was a second wife; the boys were from a first marriage back in some mythical period confined to overheard remarks and hidden photo albums, another of those family events Ruth wasn't supposed to ask about. Fortunately those stepsons were in college by the time Kate entered the picture as some sort of administrative assistant admiring the boss; she was a frail parent who flapped her hands helplessly if the boys got physical or worse: argumentative, logical.

As for Frank, his Sharon disappeared in the company of a dwarfish, good-natured auto mechanic from upstate shortly before Ruth's seventh birthday, and that was the end of casual soft hugs with the scents of lotion and female flesh, balanced meals with pretty touches like napkins and salad plates, and the tiny back garden with the pungent summer marigolds and Easter hyacinths. Now they only had a meager scattering of pale crocus and daffodils and some scant grass given over to bright dandelions that Frank yanked up when the mood took him, although Ruth rather favored their stubborn sunshine. Some three years later Sharon perished for real, decimated by a female cancer that

163

simultaneously killed Ruth's burgeoning fantasy of a loving return along with something else in her young soul. I mean what can you say about a woman who goes and gets cancer? Frank informed Ruth of this life-changing event in his usual self-conscious manner almost a whole year after it occurred, making a game of it.

"You'll never guess." Mocking her, really. "You remember when I was so upset last summer?"

"No."

Her dad consulted the patient heavens: "See!"

All of which constitutes a disturbed and uncomfortable if not unique situation, nothing to serve as a real explanation. What can I say? How can I explain the cult of Pat, the demigod status accorded him for no reason except to keep the mob rule going, unless the entire perspective is Ruth's delusion? Pat's value was an integral piece of the family faith: it reflected the will of God. And since Pat took outright reverence as his due, he was obviously much too busy to spare a moment's attention on an insignificant, unattractive creature like Ruth, or a personal conversation, or even one personal phone call for that matter. But that was her fault; that was because she acted like a wild animal instead of a young lady.

Despite being destined for greatness, the world inexplicably considered Pat an average drone, not especially attractive or brilliant or even moderately interesting – an unread man of no hobbies and no conversation. Well, back in her very early youth Ruth never questioned his superiority. Wasn't he always ready to answer a rare emergency request with good- natured noblesse oblige? But by late adolescence she saw him for an uninteresting asshole. Even as an adult she automatically pictured him leaning back glass in hand with that superior smirk, expecting to have his ass kissed.

So Pat was in charge of the family opinions, a plump priest at the alter mailing out holiday missives laden with condescension, and hosting holiday dinners with too much heavy crystal and a bewildering array of wines. Welcoming them into his tiny Center City townhouse in a merely respectable neighborhood off Spruce Street where you had to admire everything but never belonged. Smiling down at them from some enormous, undeserved distance. Ruth knew she'd never win no matter how famous she got, that it didn't work like that. That she was insolent and would learn her lesson one day. When she smiled her joy was afraid to show itself and she blushed. She still does.

All this by Ruth's estimation, which means accuracy is problematic; I suspect a lot of this history is mere wishful retrospection or worse. But she insisted on reciting it, and that process was obviously painful for her at times. That was something she needed from me, that retelling, a kind of catharsis. But there has to be more to her story, or maybe less, because there's no real explanation for the barely concealed enmity in that family. And what about Ruth's own deep sense that she didn't really count?

Pat suffered greatly from childhood, his diabetes coloring everything between those brothers, but Ruth callously dismissed stories about emergencies and a sick boy's loneliness and dread. It broke the twins in two, and maybe the healthy, handsome boy bullied the stout weak one, who's to say? And if Pat was triumphant now he suffered still with decaying vision and heart issues, numbness in his feet and an unexpressed terror of amputation you could find in his eyes.

"Everybody suffers," Ruth said, refusing to care; she'd developed a real talent for not giving a shit. "He's just like all my family, looking for some weakness so he can attack. They're nothing but animals."

Kate the eternal romantic accepted Pat as her destined soul mate from their uncoordinated courtship, loving him obediently and resenting him to the depths of her unexamined soul. Kate was a contented fumbler, crippled by vast reserves of immaturity and resentment. The kind who manages to scald herself at Thanksgiving dinner and insists on being taken to the emergency room: just that pedestrian and obvious. If Pat played the affable host, Kate was the eternal young daughter of the house, always late or disorganized: you couldn't trust her with so much as a houseplant, and there she was married to a diabetic. She forgot no slight however ancient or minor, and took positively orgasmic delight in nostalgic regret. This was Ruth's self-appointed substitute mother.

All that began one Sunday afternoon in a long-ago October when suddenly there was Kate on Frank's stoop, chin high, explaining in wobbling tones how she'd separated from Pat because she couldn't go on like that, why did he have to be so cruel? Delivering a fine dramatic display of deeply wounded virtue and repressed tears but her hands shaking nevertheless, her gray marble eyes immeasurably hurt. Ruth was astonished and excited at this extraordinary display of energy, this evidence that Kate after all had some grasp on reality. Maybe things actually could change. Or so Ruth felt, listening from inside her room with the door almost closed, a concealed, watchful forest animal, a primal spirit foreign to the entire race of civilized people and only really comfortable there on the cool floor where she could lurk in her natural habitat.

Temporarily, then, through some largely tacit concession, Kate moved in on them, appropriating the small third bedroom they used for storage, dispensing implicit dissatisfaction and excessive gratitude in equal amounts. Sitting there on the twin bed of a dim, crammed space so miniscule you could touch the closet, radiator, and door without moving, she happily spilled her soul to her niece in detailed, self-laudatory marathon sessions. This while Ruth, just turned fourteen, perched obediently on the one wooden chair, flattered if already skeptical at this initiation into the family's inner workings.

Theirs was a house exactly like every other on the block, narrow and straight through, living room, dining room, and kitchen opening into each other and cement steps giving directly onto the sidewalk in front. It sat halfway down the block in the old neighborhood, the kind of place where even very small children got sent to the corner store alone for milk and hoagies and ice cream sandwiches, where you knew some Mummers personally and you shopped along the smelly confusion of the Italian Market. There was this faint lingering familiarity of ginkgo and slippery elm over backyard walls, of dark brown seedpod crescents falling along back drives. Pungent weeds ran rampant over the few abandoned lots, or just sometimes, by special grace, those dumping grounds of old tires and rocky cement chunks and crushed plastics disappeared beneath a miraculous blanket of giant sunflowers, something straight out of a movie if you had a gullible teenage imagination.

Kate religiously thought the best of everyone, to her own stubborn pride, so of course when she wasn't feeling

167

humiliated by him she unreservedly adored her husband. So when Ruth dared to call Pat even a little unread or unimaginative Kate came down on her hard, looking furiously off to the side in deaf, righteous distress and waving a dismissive hand. "Just stop it!"

Such unthinking betrayals felt all the more brutal because Kate, doting on her Ruthie, professed loyalty against all detractors. Weren't the two of them the only nice, generous ones? The ones who put feelings and kindness first? Ruth made a willing enough acolyte; anyone was better than no one, so Kate strove to impress with her sophistication, with movies and museums and real restaurants, and sometimes a few remembered lines from some famous poem. Then there were sentimental little gifts for no occasion, always elaborately wrapped: perhaps a meaningful brooch or a cute porcelain figurine to cherish forever. Only let Ruth get too self-confident and question the family creed, slightly impugn the great Pat, and that was the end of her compassion.

Anyway, in less than one full cycle of holidays Kate drifted back to her husband, offering no explanation, neither victorious nor subdued, just packing up her shopping bags and departing on a sulky sniff. Ruth attributed this happy reconciliation to Frank's unacceptable sniping, his constant frustration with her intractable, unashamed lassitude, her universal refusal. Given such a marvelous opportunity Frank was reverting to the basic family type, taking another turn at intimidation. It made Ruth ashamed, and she experienced only a grateful relief when Kate overcame her habitual inertia long enough to get herself up off their tired plaid couch and back to Center City.

Their sporadic closeness survived because of some mutual benefit and because there was, despite everything, real acceptance and love. Because Kate was after all a good woman, in fact infinitely better than Ruth on so many grounds. Occasionally she even ventured into the bar alone, marching in all cheery and unconcerned, seating herself with a proprietary air to confide more details of her placid, martyred existence to her niece in those rehearsed monologues, amusing and self- deprecating but comforting, in their way, because familiar and intimate. Until that nascent rebel, reaching age seventeen, basically ceased communicating with her altogether, or with any of her family on any but the most impersonal level. Thereby confirming everyone's opinion that she was growing up into a physically clumsy and socially uncouth young woman urgently in need of charm school (Pat's suggestion) or a therapist.

"Ruth doesn't share." Even Kate repeated it right to her face. "She doesn't listen." Even Frank, increasingly embarrassed by his ungracious daughter. "Yeah, I know she doesn't. I guess she has important secrets." With a significant look at his child, wedged into the booth opposite those two shabby bullies. When you're dealing with extreme emotional poverty you learn to hoard. Ruth endured adolescence squinting out at the world in moderate pain, because Frank was erratic at best regarding dentists or eye exams unless unavoidably prodded by some school official. So every morning Ruth pushed the pus from over a crumbling molar, and by sixteen she'd learned to appreciate the numbing effect of the whiskey her dad kept in the china cabinet, especially when combined with painkillers. Then one day for no reason she finally realized everyone in

169

authority over her was an asshole, so she walked out of class and spent five hours on a subway ride to nowhere, exhilarated with herself, and I don't think she's ever gone back.

That was hard on Frank; he was desperately lonely those years with Ruth still at home but implacably distant. Not that he deprived himself sexually, you understand; he had those amazing good looks and that deep widow's peak, the deliberate twinkle in his eye and the facile Irish charm, and sometimes if not often he cared enough to go looking. For Ruth this meant the occasional need to cover her head with her pillow to shut out the arrhythmic thumping through the bedroom wall, some woman's routine moaning and Frank's occasional satisfied grunt. "He thinks he's too small," one woman told Ruth. It made her anxious, even though her father never expressed interest in a permanent relationship. Difficult to judge how much of Frank's preference for liberty was authentic and how much an accommodation to fate: something angry or unfortunate generally intervened to spoil his neighborhood amours.

But if sex wasn't an issue, Frank was deeply frustrated in his constant hunger to be heard and appreciated by eyes that held no latent threat, for a sheltered space where he could expand into his natural gregarious self. He had a sociable soul but was cursed by an inability to attract a social circle or even maintain a reasonably close friendship through the irritations of everyday life. Not that he ever faulted his own fearful defenses or attempted to moderate his behavior. Frank kept to shallow waters; it was never any use urging him out further.

His daughter had no such limits, being quick to analyze and damn her father's psyche, intelligence, and eternal soul, and wholeheartedly reject his tastes, reasoning, and life. She noticed things, she knew life was different in those other houses down the block, she hung out and went to sleepovers, she sat around placid dinner tables fending off the usual pleasant parental queries. She watched her best friend from fifth grade get complimented on her appearance with no irony or resentment; she heard college dreams discussed without jeers and parental excuses. She existed in a state of constant anxiety, waiting for the expected explosion, the next histrionic crisis; stress enforced her alienation from the race of normal people, but isolation brought clarity. She and Frank, confined together, inevitably fell into an abusive pattern. Ruth had to share his television viewing and provide an approving audience for his clever commentary or sarcastic howls. They played tense board games together late into school nights, Scrabble or Monopoly, Frank openly gleeful if he won, preening broadly, condescendingly patting her on the head. Once, when she revolted, he broke in her bedroom door, and despite the most fervent pledges whenever he happened to need her cooperation never found the time or money to replace the skewed hinges. There was constant yelling over anything, loud imprecations that made the neighbors turn overly kind; everything was about continually having to placate and admire and agree. Even today sudden noises make her heart jump with physical terror.

Don't get the wrong idea: he was never once actually violent, never more than vaguely threatening. It was never that easy, you could never confidently point a finger.

Not with the dad who shouted at her to stop coughing when she was suffering with her usual month of untreated winter bronchitis. Or criticized her thoughtlessly, heartlessly, when Kate and Pat threatened an appearance. "Walk straight. Put your shoulders back. Try to act decent for a change." Boasting about her grades to outsiders but privately mourning, "I wish I'd had your opportunities."

Don't ask what ever prevented him from pursuing his own dreams, although given his utter lack of self-discipline how much more explanation was required? That's why he'd always been the default successor to the family business, a safe sinecure for someone of his modest abilities and drifter's personality. Better to place Frank behind the bar, dispensing his foolishness in an established small business. Anyway, Pat had a college degree to get him the hell out of the neighborhood, so after Ted's death Frank, then twenty-six, got himself a loan and bought out his twin's interest, and that was it for his life.

Except there again we have an incomplete report, not precisely inaccurate but deceptive. Converse long enough with Ruth, flatter her with attentiveness and a very different Frank walks onstage, a dad she was proud of, a man with some local success at his own destined vocation. Here was the quintessential neighborhood politician, a committeeman who put his peers to shame, master of expansive promises, peddler of minor favors, delighting in all those critical social interactions. Wonderful the evening interrupted by a tentative knock at the door, the phone call presenting a vital inquiry to be righteously pursued. How delightful to be entrusted with an urgent request to facilitate, or a favor to be brought to the door of the ward leader, that latest incumbent in the succession of worthies who rapidly appeared and disappeared, losing influence or else trudging on to greater glory or prison. Campaigns with street money handed out over the bar in discreet envelopes, and election nights at Dougherty's with the poll watchers eyeing the television and everyone bringing in the numbers hot off the machines. It was all so dramatic and unpredictable and important, even prestigious. Occasionally there were important cronies coming in to the bar to settle their mutual opinion, glass in hand. Ruth mostly detested them. On more than one occasion when she was entrained to kitchen duty turning to question her weekday presence with clumsy innuendo, unfairly refuting her wide-eyed protestations. "Oh come on, Ruth!"

"Yeah, come on!" Frank would scoff in agreement, like we all know you're really some kind of lying promiscuous truant bitch.

Those low-level Democrats, unlike their more elite brethren, were human and liable to err, and accordingly honest about themselves. In Philadelphia as elsewhere that comfortable honesty still reverberates down the neighborhood generations.

Frank himself often eyed that next step up the political ladder to ward leader, except he was continually delaying his pursuit of that prize until the right moment. He had Ruth to worry about, for one thing, and a business to run. You had to understand, there was no time as it was.

Frank was actually a fairly interesting human being in a lot of ways, and that wasn't something you could say about anyone else in the family. Not Kate, who never read books, nor Pat who considered Post-Impressionism unnatural modern stuff and implicitly discouraged too much learning unless you were talking about a business or technical degree. Nor his sons, Ruth's privileged cousins.

But Frank inspired Ruth's sporadic crazes with his own sudden enthusiasms, passions for archeology or painting or astronomy, each one abandoned at its peak with myriad excuses when he fell back into a mindset that valued safety above dreams, shrewdness above wisdom. Back to the shifty Frank of easy lies and secret shames and imprecations.

He had an unquenchable eagerness about him, a potential for living that showed in his dramatic storytelling, his willingness to embrace physical adventures, his talent for sheer silliness, games and nonsense. He appreciated Joyce and Shaw and Yeats, proud of his excellent taste but driven primarily by real delight. Getting hold of *Fanny and Zooey* somewhere and insisting Ruth listen to him read it aloud, the two of them halfway up the stairs, not because it was literature but because it was funny.

Or he was buried in one of his histories of the Holocaust, marveling aloud at such suffering. "You can't imagine what people go through." Maybe it was Elie Wiesel's *Night* he'd be holding on his lap, his face suffused with a higher purpose, and he'd raise his chin so you could see he was personally identifying with these people, sharing in their agony and terror. You had to respect him for that. "Boy, it makes you appreciate how lucky you are." Or maybe that was more of an accusation. Conversely Kate never bothered to question anything. Like Frank, she loved excuses, loved sitting Ruth down to count them out aloud with something approaching awe, her precious rosary beads. Kate who during a trip to the Art Museum when Ruth was still moving slowly after ovarian surgery kept tugging at her niece's hand and talking over her mumbled remonstrances. Sympathy was her prerogative and she didn't like people infringing, not even her Ruthie.

Although I think this incident actually belongs to a later time. It's hard to tell, because Ruth's invective is often wrapped in opportune vagueness, but I recall her once telling me this surgery came after college. And it's prudent to remember that she's describing people much admired in their various professional and social communities. Kind, reliable people always there for their families, good parents with children who love and stand up for them, normal people leading satisfying lives. People I know nothing about. People who came through for Frank whenever he needed cash, which was often. Or maybe Ruth was right but these genuinely nice people behaved negligently towards her out of spiritual thrift, because there was only so much generosity of spirit to go around. Maybe they had to keep their viewpoints narrow in order to not see.

"This is about me," Ruth said.

There were breaking points, of course. Especially once

Ruth had it worked out, once she could speak her feelings. "Parents kill their own children every day," she informed Kate, knowing nothing less melodramatic would penetrate that protective placidity.

"Just stop that." Turning her stony profile.

"Yeah look the other way so you can go on pretending to be Saint Kate of Philadelphia but never get your fucking hands dirty!" Running off in hysterics, instigating much adult fuss and conversation until finally Kate phoned Ruth to demand in a deeply hurt, preposterously adult tone: "First of all, how dare you say that to me?"

So as a relevant result of all this solitude and stress, Ruth developed very original ideas about God and her own destined place in the universe. Frank was no advocate of the church; he was terribly thin-skinned for one thing, and just educated enough to enjoy ridiculing any unlikely dogma like virgin birth and Immaculate Conception or gleefully speculate about whether Jesus was schizophrenic. Enough that he'd endured a church wedding at Sharon's insistence, not that she didn't really know better herself but she retained a superstitious loyalty to romantic Catholicism, to saints and mysteries and stigmata and all those numinous sources of power over fate, and for some reason she associated all this magic with marriage.

So naturally the child Ruth was horribly jealous of her churchgoing peers who were privy to this secure fount of glory, and developed a taste for those same romantic concepts, internalizing a reliance on myths and miracles, reading books on Bernadette and Fatima, making novenas. Gradually accumulating her own idiosyncratic canon, realigning this and that tenet or concept or ritual as emotion dictated. Discarding it all when it got too ridiculously weighty but then starting all over again.

"I found this children's book in the back of the basement closet, it must have been my Mom's: Paradise Lost or something like that where in the end God destroys the world. The Armageddon page had this drawing of a city with skyscrapers crashing down and people trying to shield their heads and fleeing in terror. Right then I absolutely rejected that whole notion. Not my city."

And she sat invoking a half-sensed presence of God on her narrow bed, begging for assistance, and thus coerced the first of her light-struck epiphanies, physical words from nowhere bearing privileged spiritual insights personally delivered to the pleading adolescent. Not visions, you understand, not hallucinations, but simply breakthroughs of comprehension that left her breathless, reassured, and certain.

Memorializing that initial experience in watercolors on pale blue construction paper and pasting the result above her crammed student's desk: Necessity = Philosophy. Meaning that reasons were secondary, the product of mostly unconscious desires or needs. And that was the crucial first step towards her great escape. So Ruth became the girl who knew God considered her worthy of special enlightenment, which changed everything. Also note: Ruth's God was male, no question, end of story. Very, very uncomfortable with the notion of a female deity, and you could see this reflected in how she defined God, all that progressive separation away from everything whole and nourishing. Yet her overall approach to that male philosophy was adamantly feminine: intuitive, emotive, illogical.

Thus set apart she entered her teen years bopping down school corridors safely laminated inside her music, moving at her characteristic disjointed tempo, endlessly reprising the cherished song collection that filled the emptiness with meaning. Superstitious tunes, some specifically dedicated to marching off in the mornings, others for homecoming, a certain few saved for a special reward or in jubilation. Incorporating words and rhythms into her physical self, connecting to her synchronized and highly sentient universe. Juvenile pop anthems transmuted into movement along filthy sidewalks past intimidating glass doors, unblinking faces, mottled tree bark, amazing handkerchief gardens, across intersections of glaring afternoon traffic.

All through those years Frank smoked trashy menthol filters, less dangerous he claimed, part of his plan to cut back. But suggest he really quit and he exploded. "I can't!" Never anything except that blank refusal, and worse after Ruth married and had little time for him. When the cancer started in his bladder his first response was a furious indictment: "I've got cancer!"

Then his lungs were involved, and almost immediately after his brain. The doctors were reassuring: the progression was perfectly normal. By this time Frank had sold the bar out of the family and retired from neighborhood politics; he wasn't exactly struggling financially, but maintained only a tenuous, mandated holiday connection with any family except for Ruth. He'd lost interest, is what happened, because he had nothing to gain, so he wrapped himself up in a plaid bathrobe and his routine, balancing out the hard emptiness, scrupulously avoiding any meeting or even phone conversation with Pat unless provided adequate warning and frequently not even then. Despite all his best impulsive efforts, life never delivered enough in return, but he remained stalwart in his shabby wool overcoat that afternoon as, diagnosis in hand, he commenced his march towards eternity. What else was there to do? And there's the planet's trash disposal system, letting the redundant self-medicate themselves out of existence.

We're up to the current era now, when seeing Ruth was a fairly rare delight for Frank, but they were both aware of a severe shift in consciousness between them, as if they'd reached some kind of tacit agreement with Ruth the virtuous victor and Frank uniformly conceding her unspoken accusations. He sat raised up by his hospital bed and Ruth pressed her forehead against his, wordless in his embrace because she could count on one hand the times he'd hugged her unless for public benefit. Now his arms were starved for her, completely loving. He'd become strangely subservient, a skeletal figure with sparse hair and flickering eyes sucking Ensure though a straw, listening raptly to her inconsequential patter, sometimes openly crying out in pain.

Once I met her there, at Jefferson; I and a few of my colleagues were trailing along a ground floor corridor in the wake of the mayor's crony, Tim Baylor, and several other self- important and vaguely recognizable people in buoyant mood. Baylor was busily lauding the achievements of a non-profit called PhillyCares; the occasion marks my first encounter with that esteemed organization.

PhillyCares was the brainchild of Mimi Norton, one of Philadelphia's most determined community angels and some kind of business or family connection of the Baylors although, sorry, clearly from a different class. That day she was clad in a regulation blue pantsuit and wire-rimmed glasses, a businesslike facade that underlined her authority but did nothing to lighten her habitually defensive expression: the tight lips, the proud shoulders.

According to its slick literature, PhillyCares aimed to provide hospital patients those things insurance or family circumstances could not, things like transportation, toys for sick children, home help and cleaning services, even wigs for cancer patients. They mentioned all that and much more, a suspiciously broad mandate, boasting that their endeavor gained acclaim and gratitude every day, acquiring ever more of those desirable corporate and individual contributors.

Ruth was in with Frank, but of course she was drawn to the media fuss. And I guess the encounter conveniently met some secret ambition because she took it as another sign from Heaven and thereafter pursued PhillyCares as if it were her destiny. I watched her pull aside a tallish organization flunky, offering him that frank hand, speaking confidentially. Norton joined their conclave after concluding an announcement about increased city funding, the obligatory congratulatory smiles, and accepting Baylor's personal commendation which included his brief reiteration of the mayor's special initiative in support of such outstanding charitable and volunteer efforts.

And whatever Ruth really thought anymore, she stopped seasoning her broadcast chatter with those scathing condemnations of easy virtue: "All this well-publicized involvement in universally applauded humanitarian activities, this cowardly method of washing souls; it's a kind of moral masturbation. Not that these proven virtues don't have to be maintained, of course, but that's just drudgework, it's nothing to do with moral courage. Not when there's absolutely no possibility of censure because everyone you know agrees you're being generous, even brave. So yeah, you have the gall to look down and blush modestly while you recite accepted opinions. Fine."

Remarkable to think of all that ensued from that purely accidental encounter! As the PhillyCares people dispersed I went over to say hello to her, and that was when I first suggested doing a profile; that was the moment I became her official biographer, her intimate companion on some obscure journey of discovery. She accepted with only a passing second's rational hesitation, fully accepting me as a fundamental component of her magnificent predestined life. Partly she was already in an exalted state that day, breathless. "It's good because as it happens I'm reviewing so much in my life right now; when you go through something like this with a parent you look at what you've done with your own life."

I asked about the conversation with Norton. "Are you turning humanitarian?"

A comically reproachful glance. "Just sharing my own very limited expertise, giving back. They need publicity and I can help them get it." And in fact she did an entire broadcast from that hospital, a modestly successful, perfectly standard affair that cemented my impression that she and Mimi Norton hated each other like poison and both of them knew it but neither had any intention of letting personal animosity overrule their purposes. You could almost hear an entirely different conversation going on, paralleling their polite compliments and sympathetic pleasantries.

Frank continued to fail. Kate dutifully tottered in unannounced to say good-by to her brother-in-law, all wrapped up in her own deep grief, leaning heavily on Ruth, staring at the patient with anguished eyes. Pat would be coming too, she promised, but the idea of such a visit threw Frank into such obvious agitation Ruth felt forced to forbid it.

"Oh honey, how am I supposed to tell him that!"

But Ruth couldn't tell him either; she'd been infected with her father's phobia and had an illogical but very real horror of her uncle's presence, an excruciating terror even of being seen by him. Which desperate abhorrence reflected their shared need to avoid the mortification of Pat's confident condescension. That kind of reversion to the old sick dynamic would surely annihilate Frank's weakened soul and profoundly undermine Ruth's fragile psyche.

So Kate was forced to act as intermediary. "I told him," Kate reported by phone, self-important. "Ruthie, he was almost crying. You don't realize how hurt he is! His own twin."

Thom was leaning in the doorway of the Askews' sunlit Chestnut Hill kitchen, listening to Ruth's half of this exchange. Her habit was to present her family as an irritating but ordinary joke, but I suspect Thom, who surely knew better, was bleeding for her.

She set down the phone and shrugged. "Oh crap! Never mind, at least I made Kate come through for once. But my God, these people! It's hard to believe!"

Just heading to lunch one early afternoon, exhausted as usual those days, she phoned Frank's room to have Pat pick up, his voice as unctuous and instructive as ever since he for one was doing the right thing.

"Your father can't talk to you right now, Ruth Marie. He's having his lunch." She could just make out Frank's low tones in the background, recognized the artificial inflection he adopted to impress important people.

"I was so outraged I just hung up. I literally couldn't believe the gall, talking to me like I was a child and he had the right to correct my manners. And never any apology because I don't have any feelings anyway, I'm an ill-mannered heathen so why should he apologize?" Relating this with a voice literally shaking with fury and humiliation. "And all chirpy, too, and oh so patient. He just loves to feel sorry for me while he makes clear he thinks I don't have any feelings or decency."

Those final days Frank's emaciated torso would arch in agony and he'd scream without restraint, watching her and pleading. Ruth found herself cosseted by various professionals eager to dispel her intermittent guilt, highly unintelligent people certain they'd reduced the final mystery to a clear set of rules. She stared into Frank's now cleanly beautiful face while he patted her hand in reassurance.

An assured young women requested her attention, ushering her into a seat in a tiny downstairs office. "Unfortunately your father's not responding well to treatment."

No shit. Ruth just waited.

"The priority now is to alleviate the pain." And there followed an explanation of sufficient morphine.

"So you believe in an afterlife?"

Confusion, but then a practiced recovery and an apologetic shake of the head. Please explain?

"Because you're saying that death is a better choice than any life, even a life of intolerable pain, and that only makes sense if you believe there's someone to experience relief. Otherwise you're just not making sense."

The woman relaxed, nodded to herself, and rose without bothering to dispute any category mistake. "I'll let you think about it."

Think about what? Later that day they transferred Frank to the hospice floor and increased his morphine, expertly engineering a painless death. Ruth took the call at work.

Bob, the usual recipient of her anecdotes about Frank the colorful neighborhood character, surprised her with an instinctive hug the day she returned from bereavement leave. "So no more stories about old Frank?"

But said with an unmistakable undertone of secret satisfaction. Maybe if she could cry, but she could never cry except for happiness. Probably Bob was disillusioned because he'd attended the funeral and she hadn't, although she'd explained how she was repelled by the idea of an embalmed Frank out on display in accordance with his stubborn Irish notions. Because how admit the physical terror she felt at the thought of meeting Pat, of being annihilated by his mere presence?

CHAPTER EIGHT

Lawyer joke: thirty-three attorneys go into a room. Except most of them aren't really lawyers yet, only law school graduates.

What happens after law school is you immediately enroll in another course designed to get you through your bar exams. Eventually you spend two or three unrelievedly horrible days sitting in front of a designated identification number in a convention hall or its ilk making educated guesses on a computer form or scribbling vaguely professional-sounding issue-spotting crap, with a break for awful coffee and crock-pot hotdogs on cold buns with those packets of neon-green relish served up by kindly volunteers. None of this is even remotely fun; it leaves you with a sick sense of impending doom, and your brain by this point is barely functioning except that it knows better than to focus on all those student loans. After that you get to stew through an unpleasant three or four months' limbo while you await the results, if you're fortunate accomplishing this in the Caribbean or Europe, if you're not working at some sort of interim law-related job. My particular circumstances involved rent and child support, which made immediate employment imperative. Happily, it was also available.

In a burst of energetic panic some months earlier I'd supplemented the usual law firm applications and sporadic interviews with resumes to every legal staffing agency in town, scoring a temporary assignment after an extremely cursory interview. Me and about forty other recent graduates out of Temple and 'Nova, Penn and Rutgers and Widener, as it turned out, and even some people from Virginia and New York. All of us gathered one morning in the expansive marbled lobby of one of those Center City office buildings, most of us naïve and perplexed. This was a job, right? Not just another interview?

We were collected and herded into elevators and up to the offices of a major firm, then into a spacious meeting room, bland like all of them but expensively appointed and nicely supplied with refreshments, salads and sandwiches and chips, all that kind of stuff. I shared a table with three vaguely familiar faces from my own law school: Eric, a nice Korean boy from Radnor, a fatalist already determined to fail in the legal profession; Josh, romantically dark, gangly, and ethnic; and Petra, an immensely ambitious young woman already slated for a smaller firm in a better suburb. She had one of those faces I saw all through law school: saintly and long, with a thin nose, shrewd eyes, narrow lips - that dedicated type. They're everywhere, winning approbation. We four immediately amalgamated into a sarcastic, defensive clique, thenceforth and for the next several months communicating primarily with each other in a desperate attempt to confirm our individual humanity. Even today we remain useful acquaintances on the social media level although far from friends. All three were significantly younger than me; the guys held libertarian in that superficial manner of so many struggling but basically self-confident young professionals I know. "Put in some decent safety nets and leave me the hell alone." Petra was of course a dedicated Liberal. The presumptive elite: they practiced subtle, unconscious linguistic games, tailoring tired political and economic terms to a contemporary fit, ignorantly reconfiguring the whole wide world in the process. It's a subtle phenomenon and I really can't speak to it except that it skewed everything as it inexorably pushed me aside.

That morning we viewed a power-point presentation about some ongoing litigation with additional commentary from a few partners and associates, followed by another slideshow with a different set of associates explaining the intricacies of the database we'd be working in. The more suggestible among us perked up like real lawyers.

At which point we were abruptly brought down from those windowed, pampered heights to a career purgatory or maybe even a genuine existential hell: a dungeon, a gigantic, dedicated basement space, strangely dim despite its fluorescent office lighting, filled with row upon row of computers receding back into infinity, a hundred monitors at least, each on its bland yellow station with a keyboard, a mouse, a plastic file holder, and a web-backed office chair. Wires and cables, bundled into thick snakes, were shoved into the interstices. Other than that, the room contained a few carts of assorted office junk, a coat rack up front, and gray industrial carpet with a chemical smell.

Thus my indoctrination into the generally disdained and discreetly closeted realm of document review, that evolving backwater of the covertly over-crowded and ultra-competitive legal profession. Edata is interesting from an abstract cutting- edge perspective if you aren't stuck doing it yourself. It's better known now, of course, this providential creation of the profession's ongoing upheaval, this new universe of digitized tedium just lucrative enough to pay the rent but never stable or rewarding enough to quiet that sickening little twinge of sick failure in your stomach, the constant sense of any real professional life slipping away.

"So what kind of law are you looking to practice?" Josh was eager like that, never still enough to be where he was, although in this situation it was a natural question.

"That's a benefit to working here; you buy time to find the right position." Petra tended to peer quietly over people's chairs issuing helpful advice, sensibly condescending. "Would you mind my showing you something?" I've rarely met a female lawyer who wasn't a bitch, forever determined to top you. Maybe all the nice ones flock to public interest law; I was mildly surprised Petra wasn't headed that way but it turned out her future firm advised non-profits. I only put up with Petra because I knew she was talking to herself, like all of us, and therefore something was pretty screwed up in her perfect world.

"Or just some job," Josh said. "Dude, just a real job I can land before someone else here beats me to it."

Now me, I liked doc review from the beginning, probably because I'd already had a real job and could appreciate the difference. Contract work, document review, is a necessary consequence of the computerized office; it involves the identification and categorization of electronic records, generally from some humongous corporate client and in response to a discovery order. Data that, collected in hardcopy, would fill the Comcast Building several times over with email and contracts and spreadsheets and miscellaneous effluvia ranging from the legally privileged to the merely confidential to the excruciatingly personal. The private chatter of obnoxious senior executives with their proud Americanism and misogynistic jokes and family photos from some church event along with inspirational words of pseudo-wisdom to be sent to twelve of your closest friends.

"Imagine when it all coalesces into the electronic noosphere, one omnipresent mind," Ruth says of the Internet. "I mean, when it becomes conscious. At least now God has the decency to stay quiet." Freely altering the definition of God, which is the history of God.

So the job was kind of cool and totally stupid at the same time. I could pretty much choose my own hours and basically I didn't do shit; it was free money. Sometimes I extended myself too much due to this problem I have with ambition and ego, but then I inevitably screwed up because my thoughts were profoundly elsewhere. I just couldn't take it seriously or convince myself it mattered. So I absently clicked the weeks away, happily overpaid for bracketing documents, complacently performing essentially mindless manual labor down in that lawyer's sweatshop while my younger colleagues grew increasingly nervous and restive.

I even enjoyed the forcibly companionable atmosphere, how when you talked to one person you were basically sharing with the room. I got drawn into these unlikely discussions about wedding plans and restaurant critiques, uncensored political opinions and the latest from the tabloids, all that trivial shit. Which at least helped keep me reasonably alert.

But I can't deny there was something ugly down there, too competitive and slightly desperate personality-driven infighting.

But that's true everywhere.

But not with the same utterly helpless desperation. Those stares when the fully employed started to filter out and we rejects understood the familiar rules weren't working for us. Then when we realized it wasn't just us, it was Armageddon. Plus I was that tiny bit older so courteously included in every discernable way but in a subtle yet absolute sense automatically discounted. All in all an extremely superficial camaraderie, no missing you when you're gone, which only added to the overall impression of living in some kind of karmic waiting room.

Our location emphasized this sense of transience. Our quarters were on Market Street about two blocks from Septa's Suburban Station; you could access the building from one of those endless station tunnels if you weren't alone or given to nerves. Have the right swipe card, slip through an unmarked entrance below the unaware pavement life and there you were at the office, directly below all the marbled lobbies and security desks and well-appointed conference rooms of all those legal and financial firms. On crappy weather days you never had to risk exposure to the drenched streets of Lawyerland, out there where good old Billy Penn was hovering directly above you leaning at his tipsy angle, his back to you but still dominating that blank sky.

Of course that's myopic nomenclature; there are obviously as many financial and commercial institutions along those particular city blocks as law firms, and conversely numerous law firms outside the immediate precinct, including some famous ones. But I experienced a particular sense of ownership in that limited area where colleagues not infrequently met by cordial accident at food carts or on train platforms, and I started to make the attorney assumption unless I actually knew different, especially with those certain types, the one with that particular avidity about them.

And there were disadvantages beyond the temporary nature of the job. There were startling, mysterious clanks and groans and random heavy thunks and metallic shrieks. There was a total absence of job security, a daily awareness that frayed the nerves: your case could settle overnight and leave you laid off without warning for days or weeks or forever. As a result you felt grateful to be assigned a project, then immediately resented your own immense relief, but you had no recourse because you didn't work for the firm, you worked for a slimeball legal staffing agency that had no clout but shared your paycheck on the basis of, they cut your paycheck. And the same or nearly at every major firm up and down the street, it was almost always about working down in some basement.

But it was a job, and jobs were scare in the law biz to pretty much everyone's surprise, even mine. God knows why, when there was plentiful literature available on that unsettling subject. Maybe the whole descent into dystopia was too much to absorb outright; somehow we'd all envisioned ourselves graduating into an earlier era, possibly the crass, lucrative eighties, inheriting those extinguished opportunities, well- prepared to meet already obsolete goals and expectations.

The insinuating chill of reality hurried Eric into his characteristic rancor; he started half-humorously threatening to sue our law school. "Dude, they pay students to do volunteer work and then count that as a job for their employment numbers? They count non-attorney jobs, too."

Petra was invariably reserved but sympathetic and prepared to minimize our qualms, more certain than we of our futures. I remember late one evening, her tote bag on her shoulder, she turned to capture the size of the room, empty except for the few guys doing seventy or eighty hour weeks, living at their computers. She was just standing there taking it in. "I'm so glad I had this experience." And you could tell she meant it.

There were vermin everywhere. I enjoyed watching Petra's morning routine: gathering up a tidy mound of mouse droppings despite the traps along the walls and under our tables, then running a disinfectant wipe over her station, under her keyboard, over her seat, always smiling at herself like a good little soldier. Once, and this is for real, one guy gave a yelp and stood up, and then the girl next to him yelped and stood, and delightfully it continued along the row with each person jumping up in sequence exactly like a cartoon until finally there was the tiny furry creature - smaller than you'd think, hardly bigger than a quarter - disappearing into the wall. Those fuzzy little rodents didn't upset me; I figured infestations were unavoidable since the basement of a posh building in the city is a basement in the city and there's not much you can do about it. It wasn't like we had the kind of large, impudent rats they had back on campus. And I appreciated the complex Rube Goldberg machinations our interlopers employed to navigate over our

192

cabinets and wire bundles to reach our microwave popcorn packs.

But the bugs got to me a little. That first day I was standing in a bathroom when I noticed the pattern of the mottled institutional linoleum shifting, rearranging itself courtesy of tiny individual elements like miniscule silverfish, neutral in tint and almost translucent. Those were the small ones; later on I met some of the fucking gigantic brown cockroaches casually loitering around. Occasionally you came upon a half-dead specimen, ineptly whacked, its little brown legs and antennae waving pathetically. The girls covered the dying ones with toilet paper and fetched some amenable guy to do the final stomp and disposal.

One afternoon Petra came rushing back white and sweating because she was just sitting on a toilet when she noticed the roach climbing out.

That same week, a roach fell from a ventilator fan onto her shoulder. She screamed really sharp and angry. But word was we had it good, in fact the best: we were treated with absolute respect whereas at some other firms they stipulated work hours and you had no Internet access. And maybe they paid better in New York but you worked out of an actual closet with water pipes. Anyway what could you expect with firms needing so many people on an uncertain basis?

Along with pretty much everyone else there I persisted in my job search, and I had no difficulty whatsoever getting interviews: I got dozens and went to all of them, suitable or not, only nothing worked out. It's possible I'm just making excuses here, but the truth is I don't make a pleasing appearance; given a choice, I wouldn't hire me either. I'm used to seeing people scramble around for some rationale for their instinctive dislike. Plus maybe I already knew better and deliberately undermined myself; God knows I flagrantly eschewed the conventional job- hunting advice. I never assumed the proper attitude of eager gratitude. I literally never sent one thank you letter or even email. I exuded disinterest if not scorn, lied outrageously and obviously, argued for the hell of it, and once almost snarled. All these offices at the smaller firms where they had metal security doors so the lawyers worked locked inside bank vaults.

What I was doing was writing and taking it seriously, one of the stupidest things you can do in this world and worrying to everyone who cared about me or had any interest in my future. I wasn't yet thinking in terms of journalism, though, not only because I had no background in it but because the inflated self- importance and paltry ethics of the news business repelled me. Plus I figured it was beneath my literary talents. They say law school changes you; what it did for me was to restore what academia and corporate finance had leached away: confidence in my own opinions, the desire to explore new ideas, and delight in my own obnoxious, insistent, attention-seeking voice even when it inspired general avoidance if not outright dislike.

I was back. I didn't give a shit. Or if I did it was still better. There was a lot of cynicism involved. I was definitely on the attack. I was suffering a resurgence of an old complaint: a sense of being used. Everyone wanted my input, but instead of acknowledging me they read my own words back to me, right to my face, obliviously taking credit for my anecdote, my explanation. So many people simply didn't realize I existed except to serve them, kind of like a dictionary. I mean, this has historically happened to me, but in that particular basement situation, where I was already an anomaly and frankly much more dour and repellent than anyone else so hardly a typical candidate for success, any slight seemed egregious, intolerable. I wanted to sue the whole world, so instead I wrote.

One initial idea was a scathing bit of satire about City Council; I came up with it watching a clip of them on television. It was weirdly entrancing, all these self-important, posturing lawmakers pushing their little pieces of possibility here and there, viciously undermining each other with silly stratagems or unconvincing bombast, practically operatic in their gravity, all furrowed brows and integrity and dedication. Who was all this melodrama for? What kind of ignorant, credulous audience did they imagine? Broad farce, and mine to harvest, and such is the human ego that even at that stage I fantasized myself a famous comedic force: an acerbic Voltaire, Philadelphia's professional gadfly.

So I set about familiarizing myself with the players, their individual idiosyncrasies and ambitions, their interactions with each other, all their usual tics and lies. An obsession I thought temporary, and I indulged myself, which was easy enough with City Hall right there down the street. Otherwise I really might have let the whole thing slide; stuff happens that way, your fate gets decided because of what you had for breakfast.

I attended my first Thursday session disguised by this scheme, peering out from behind its protection to scrutinize the chamber, members, spectators, and assorted supernumeraries. Head down over my legal pad, scribbling down every color and curve of architecture or profile. I experienced an absolutely compelling sense of coming home there in that shabby official chamber where government so blatantly diverged from the mere common good to go its own unconscionable way.

Thom noticed me that first day, my air of fresh purpose and compulsively busy pen, and came over to find out who I was and make meaningless helpful noises. Of course I immediately, pathetically confided in him, eager for interest and support, and he thought over my idea a long minute, rubbing his chin thoughtfully. "Email it to me when it's finished. I'd be fascinated to see what you make of us." And then that ugly, deliberate grin. "You strike me as someone with a happily skewed point of view." I have absolutely no idea why he got that impression, but I hoped it meant I'd aroused some genuine interest. So I sent him a careful draft and received liberal praise in return, much too florid but immensely reassuring.

I returned the next week, feeling ridiculously like a regular, and once again found myself utterly engrossed by the municipal madness, the barely discernable currents moving inside the process, hiding behind the ritual. The endless theatrics, the vital issues stripped of reason and content, transformed into voracious mutants and loosed on the city.

"Make it a letter to the editor," Thom suggested, and nodded toward a folded copy of our better daily. "They'll print it." So I pretended to think about that before racing to follow his advice, and presto my first Council piece, albeit drastically reduced, was published in our prestigious daily to a pretty agreeable reception from my immediate circle. Then subsequently two others, all a little irresponsible in retrospect, nowhere near as acute as I thought at the time but still decent. One discussed a flood of building permits for a derelict South Philly neighborhood, another City Council itself, its salaries and staff and perks. I'm positive Thom influenced this initial success although I don't know it for a fact. Next I scored an essay in the Sunday magazine, a longer and much more serious piece on a particularly vicious and crucial senate campaign. All this seemed to happen at once, leaving me exhilarated. That weekend supplement became my first regular organ, sporadically running my dissections of various political issues and antics that almost always included reports from Council, cynical but careful articles that aimed to separate the valid and possible from the dubious and self-serving.

Although I knew perfectly well newspapers were dying.

For all its redundant nonsense, Council was fascinating once you learned the rules and knew how to interpret the emotions and intent behind the tired routine and outsized dramatics. You started to follow the plot. And you immediately knew that, whatever the shifting alliances and altering perspectives and competing egos, Thom Askew indisputably owned the star turn. His almost offensively charismatic presence compelled everyone's attention, covert or outright. His angular, incorrect stance, his toothy verbal acrobatics coupled with his open delight in his own cleverness – somehow it all illogically radiated charm no matter what side of the argument you were on, and the result was a predictable surge of volatile energy whenever he took the stage, baroque emanations of resentment or infatuation.

And I found myself converted into a grudging partisan of contemporary journalism. Truth and justice, baby! Two old friends discovered in a highly unlikely quarter. Now, at that point in my meandering search for a real career the logical next step would be a job at some dreary suburban franchise newspaper or the surviving daily of a distant minor city, there to hone my nascent skills and write myself the kind of creditable resume that eventually buys you into the big time. Instead Thom, now a firm acquaintance if not an intimate, intervened a second time. I think he appreciated my variety of twisted wit because it reminded him of his own iconoclastic youth. Like me he always loved to mock assholes.

"You don't want to bury yourself in some backwater until there's nothing left of you but a short skeleton with a gigantic shnoz." And he arranged an introduction to the Editor-in-Chief of one of our two throwaway weeklies. We had them then, actual hardcopy newsprint out on the street. Carl Shurz, an immense, broad, doughy-faced individual in his forties, engulfed my hand in his own wide paw and invited me aboard on a part-time contributor basis, happily mistaking my satiric prose as complementary to his own magazine's scrupulously hipster persona. By the time I was confidently finding my way through the refigured downtown office corridors I was a staff writer, covering Council and local politics still, but now it was getting to be serious business and hard work, and there was my name on the occasional pretentious artsy-edgy cover, a photograph in grainy black-and-white in those ubiquitous corner boxes. Some

80,000 issues strong featuring my comprehensive coverage of another confounding crises for polite suburban commuters to consume along with their ethnic restaurant openings and experimental theater reviews.

During this transitional period I continued on at my doc review job, getting corporate scum out of trouble, paying the rent, paying down the student loans. Bluffing off my journalistic deficiencies while diligently widening my area of expertise to include the administration and party power brokers and other forces permitting or preventing events. I gained a hundred times better understanding of the way the city worked, of how individuals or groups navigated the creaking and corrupt system and what it demanded of them in return and what they were willing to pay in order to achieve some measure of sustainability or even a toehold on posterity. Then there were the potent loyalties rising from the wards and the unions and the community coalitions – all these elected or appointed functionaries, all those organizations, the whole top-heavy mechanism that long ago separated out from a more refined, moneyed element unwilling to soil its hands with the mundane business of city government. I acquired my first precious sources.

I was searching for America, I guess. I once read how arguably the greatest line in American literature is from Huckleberry Finn, where he says, "All right, then, I'll go to hell." That decision encapsulates a uniquely American kind of freedom, but the price is being honest about it, owning it. Few people I encountered were paying up, and that more than anything made me furious.

For my efforts I was paid, if not generously then sufficiently well enough to provide a spurious sense of security and temporarily dull my habitual cosmic angst. I was learning almost too much on a daily basis, rewriting my guts out, transforming my little universe while making myself known, and it was pretty fucking amazing.

While the weekly's offices were merely utilitarian, the personnel projected the proper urban cool; they were so hyperconscious and competitive I eventually overlooked their youthful disdain, it was so pitiful. The full-time side, the business and editorial people, were less constrained by this tension, but the occasional contributors with dead-end jobs elsewhere embodied all the latest in fashion, futility, and irony. Setting trends, to hear them tell it: responsible for that scarf worn just so on the runway, for making the reputation of that new Thai cafe. Coming in when they didn't have to, conferring over the latest New Wave revival or one-room gallery in insider pseudo- street language, wandering coffee in hand past walls painted the institutional green of a prison ward. And then there were a handful of serious journalists like me with a fundamental taste for reality, trying to produce work that mattered.

Any number of credulous if marginally influential people began making asinine assumptions about my influence; I was suddenly almost popular, cavalierly discarding daily press releases and teases and invitations, emails and tweets and naturally letters, many lacking profanity. I would say the most interesting experience from this period was the death threats I received in response to an article on our epidemic of murdered witnesses.

So as I was saying: thirty-three near attorneys go into a room, each a unique combination of lifelong virtue and intellectual ability and work ethic and simple greed and family expectations, and there they click away at documents and await the judgment of Heaven, their bar exam results. Who among this varied collection will be judged worthy?

All of them: it's a lawyer joke.

There was my own name up on the website; I felt immensely relieved although not really astonished. And that celebratory moment marked the commencement, epitome, and conclusion of my legal career. It's an interesting outcome; unlike so many of my colleagues I hadn't enrolled in law school for lack of any acceptable alternative but because law in the abstract attracted me: Rousseau and Rawls, the individual as opposed to the community, the acquired illusion of human rights. Legal procedure and the practice of the profession appealed too; I like to understand the mechanics of reality, how things eventuate in this world. The field seemed part of my natural turf, as if in confronting its torturous enigmas I was somehow unfolding my own mind. Then once I had that cheap little paper license in my wallet I was done, which I concede makes absolutely no sense.

This was some years ago now, and during the intervening years nothing much has really changed on the local political scene, but there have been repeated promises about a Philadelphia poised on the brink of a renaissance. A susceptible listener might visualize a city opening like a spring crocus, all good things not only possible but daily expected, new opportunity already in the mail. These visions arose randomly, so far as I could judge, living out their short lives without reference to any election year or resurgent popular philosophy but according to some more elemental rhythm, some recurrent natural force never anywhere near powerful enough to overthrow a destructive culture. Anyway, our current mayor, back when he was first named the party candidate, adopted a version of this optimistic vision. Hand-picked by Democratic Party Chairman Gerry Bright - Bright was an athlete gone to seed with a shark's smile and observant blue eyes, carrot-red hair, and the big bruising heart of the party itself – he'd faced the cameras one afternoon a month or so before the primary and proclaimed this latest rebirth. "There are particular ideas I've worked on for years, plans to restore the greatness of this city." Appropriate from a candidate running on jobs and education, but then he'd stubbornly refused to supply more than that until he worked it out with his new administration, anything else would be premature.

As a Democrat he was the de facto mayor-elect, nothing else was interesting about the campaign, plus he could claim Thom as a loyal if waspish supporter. So when I glimpsed Thom rushing by me one bright afternoon, a blur of unlikely plaid begging to be noticed, I shouted to intercept him and beg for specifics.

"Well, here we're past the first debate and God knows how many campaign speeches, but your candidate still hasn't clarified how he's going to initiate this glorious new age."

"I understand there's a master plan wherein we all do the best we can. Or so one devoutly hopes." Said softly, bending forward in a light laugh to show that it mattered, regarding me with that overtly shrewd look in order to conceal the insistent energy behind the obvious political smarts. He was radiating a restless joy on that beautiful day, practically bouncing on the balls of the feet. We were both just bullshitting, obviously.

Thom was looking off through one of those cold-as-death City Hall archways, perhaps pondering the municipal future. This mayor-to-be habitually neglected to pay his personal utility bills and other miscellaneous shady debts for one contentiously self-righteous reason or another, whining or truculent, which behavior elicited not one whit of public outrage except from the extremely frustrated opposition. After all, after all: he'd happily face the cameras with that ingratiating grin, explaining how his campaign required all his finances, so obviously he was doing the only reasonable thing, right? Therefore the usual type, progressing along the curve from petty criminal to incumbent.

"You should run for mayor yourself." I said. "Independent?" One eyebrow lifted.

"No, next time. After the inevitable second term." I was laughing.

Thom pretended to consider it on the spot, miming serious concentration, pushing up his lower lip like a bulldog. "I'm thinking of something a bit more prestigious." Leaning in confidentially. "Even Harrisburg is much too paltry a challenge for my talents. Let's say Capitol Hill for a proper start."

We were in the courtyard, Thom with his briefcase in both hands preparing to escape, his increasingly sparse hair lifting a bit in the breeze. I'd been heading back to my doc review job, still a necessary paycheck. We were standing on patched cement bearing a grid of the city surrounded by the signs of the zodiac, a lunatic juxtaposition. At the four corners of the courtyard official flowerbeds displayed sprightly red and yellow tulips. A clutch of teens rushed in, wary and noisy, scanning for something novel to do; we watched them safely through the archway, Thom shifting from one foot to the other, a nervous little boy.

Someone else was upon us, had been steadily moving towards us with long, firm strides that finally broke into my consciousness as I realized Thom was her target. Found you! Am I barging in? Apologies." The most local of accents, almost a parody. They kissed lightly, and I was surprised: this female was far below his usual standards, raw-boned and big overall, but at the same time too thin. Not lovely in any respect, although exuding a subtle self-importance. She offered me her hand. "Ruth Dougherty." And while performing her initial assessment she stared right at me with these acutely intelligent, huge blue eyes, so after all she did have one claim to beauty. But they were damaged, much too vulnerable eyes. She was maybe five or six inches over my five four.

"*The* Ruth Dougherty," Thom said, bestowing a slightly mocking but courtly nod.

Now that made more sense. It meant she'd be readily acceptable to the general voting public, for one thing. Interesting. She wasn't what I associated with the reputation. Ruth was a genuine local celebrity if not for any admirable reason, lacking even the gravitas of legitimate talk radio. She just opened her mouth and babbled cleverly without significance. An apparent relationship with Thom wasn't a catastrophe then, might even prove clever.

But still.

They were eating each other up. He was bewitched, flushed and embarrassed, and she was right there with him. I practically had to get between them to get their attention.

I glanced at my watch, touching on the mayor's race again in parting and she jumped right in. "This whole thing of disrespecting the law infuriates me." Her expression, I thought, inappropriately bitter, taking it personally. "I mean, half the world is struggling for rule of law."

Heavy sun beamed down into the courtyard, blinding out the gray-white stone, warming the backs of the constant passers- by in their open suit jackets and ill-fitting blouses, the middle- aged men with those status decrepit leather briefcases, the women carrying laptop bags and tote bags and designer purses all at once, and the young professionals with backpacks staring into their phones. Everyone unconsciously showing with their attempted style or make-up what they wanted to be or thought they already were. We joined the stream, drifting through a cool tunnel, emerging into the light and halting there facing west towards the business district. Ruth turned to me and grinned. "So I hear you're brilliant." "Sometimes."

"Well listen, don't you think a mayor should respect the law at least enough to lie about breaking it?"

I responded with a surprised laugh, and she launched into farewells with a small smile and finger kiss to Thom's lips. It was much too flirty and girlish a gesture for her large frame, for her whole forthright personality.

Right about that time my nascent career took one of those catastrophic turns that hit when you start to relax: my job with the weekly evaporated overnight with no warning, victim of a mind-boggling whirlwind of layoffs.

Leaving me to commiserate with those embittered cohorts still stuck on the doc review circuit, melding into old-timers, back from other assignments at Dechert or Blank Rome or down in Delaware, jobs with better quarters or worse, with different rules but the same familiar faces. Up in some slick conference room with the sweet Mary sunshines and bright boys and cautious guys and eager girls and some lawyer on the case team who doesn't quite get you're an attorney too. Permanent transients constructing a new profession, claiming unemployment to cover the empty weeks, competing with a host of fresh graduates bursting with untried ambition. I'd been undeservedly lucky, steadily employed on a single ongoing matter, but one memorable morning a veritable host of old friends filtered in on an assignment set for some months, all happily catching up on the gossip and getting their passwords refreshed, and that same afternoon the matter settled and goodbye. Resigned shrugs and slight humor, while Eric and I exchanged a quick glance and turned back to our monitors.

I stood staring at my phone in total mental shock, unable to process being bluntly denied the one outlet that justified my life, energized my soul. Newspapers everywhere were folding, of course, Philly's major dailies suffering with the rest, the entire medium stubbornly adhering to some kind of romantic, self- important self-image that overlooked chain takeovers and inadequate reportage practices harking back decades, instead pointing an accusatory, contemptuous finger at the Internet.

It happened that our sole remaining star, our great Pulitzer- bedecked glory, had just changed hands for approximately the fourth time in the last decade. This latest transition found it unloaded by a corporation who'd reappraised their ego-to-debt ratio, to be acquired by an indefatigable group of local saviors. Make that papers, plural, because that elite sheet and our feisty Philly tabloid were sisters, sharing one owner and operating out of the same building. If I hadn't been desperate I never would have tried for a job there, but I was and I tried everywhere, and miraculously they hired me for the City Hall beat. Well, what they were actually doing, during those first few months flush with hubris, was hiring selectively but terminating wholesale, gathering in the young and retiring their more senior employees, a policy of assisted retirement that dispersed experienced reporters and editors to marginally healthier papers elsewhere and instigated discrimination claims still in litigation. Additionally the paper eliminated most national and all international offices, never mind its former vaunted claims of global reach, and instead launched a daily section targeting the more prosperous suburbs. The declared idea was to cut it all down to cost-efficient, manageable size, but new hires included several virtually illiterate celebrity columnists, all of whom fortunately vanished quickly enough to spare everyone major embarrassment. It was sort of tragically hilarious when it wasn't just sadly delusional, everyone still stubbornly thinking newspapers mattered.

I was something of an exception in that I wasn't exactly young or famous, but they already knew me and I came cheap, so there I was working for the paper that printed my first letter not all that long before, and at that point I finally abandoned my doc review default job, leaving the task of realigning the legal profession in this new upside-down world to my millennial colleagues. Over the years Josh got passionate: today he's a staff attorney at a prestigious immigration non-profit, making actual law. Eric of course stayed in place, eventually rising one step to project manager, his negativity an asset in that supervisory role and anyway he was always that kind of unimaginative bright boy. But really I'm being unfair, because the innovators at that firm are developing the new electronic legal profession, meanwhile nurturing and promoting young loyalists. Meanwhile Petra went off to her associate's job, scored a quickly truncated cable television career doing brief interviews between programs, and now she's with another fairly successful suburban firm, handling estates.

And I took myself off to the foundering and just generally wrongheaded realm of newspaper journalism and became the authentic self I am today, neither wholly comedic nor hip nor excruciatingly balanced but flatly factual about everything we all know but refuse to face. I became practiced at assuming my deceptively innocent facade, presenting myself as a naïve explorer, a mere surrogate for the reader without personal stance or agenda, a modest and endearingly wild-haired caricature. Rather gleefully developing into my current persona, the eerily insightful, coldly ethical man everyone wants to impress.

During this period the paper's inevitable downward spiral gained momentum, what with insufficient financing and the unfounded faith of the new owners. Much of the editorial staff and most of the sales people vanished; meanwhile I worked like shit building myself a discerning readership while I had the chance because what else was I supposed to do? My ex-wife did not offer encouragement, an irrational reaction because the paper represented relative financial stability for her and Sophie. Here I'd improbably landed a real job with benefits, the first since my financial services days! Partly this was just her natural resentment at my obvious happiness, but in part it was about this irresponsible business of going around implying that ideas might take priority over hearth and home, about giving undue value to insidious, trickster concepts and the mysterious tyranny of reason. Who knows what words are likely to get up to?

It made a new kind of end for us, and unlike the divorce this one was openly acrimonious and still traumatic, all her repressed rage overriding anything moderately civilized. The hate had been there since our marriage, but now it was unleashed and I learned what a horrible, even emotionally abusive father I was: "Destroying everything human, crippling her with your venom for no reason except you live to destroy. She's a little girl, you fucking asshole."

Interesting.

The paper was located in a renowned white Art Deco tower just north of Center City, a magnificent, echoing marble tomb with a newsroom of windows and columns, an obsolete monument to enlightenment and impending ruin. There was something Greek about it. I was assigned a workstation at the farthest reach of the extensive open floor, from which unobtrusive corner I absorbed the quietly desperate office scene, the empty desks with cords left dangling, the piles of deserted files on the floor. There was a disbelieving, profound sadness beneath the intelligent gentility of all those editors who frequented the opera, all those clever women with honest gray hair, all those wonderful souls stoically grieving a culture. Conversation was largely about colleagues gone elsewhere; and people spent a lot of time openly job hunting.

I had the middle of three adjoining stations: one side was unoccupied, just a counter with a detached phone; the other belonged to my cohort at City Hall, Megan Shiff, who was understandably less than thrilled to have her physical and professional territory invaded. But the paper was revving up the local emphasis and there I was, ready to be loved.

Megan was somewhere in her thirties, fair and freckled. She kept her reddish hair in a rather severe short bob, wore brown loafers with plaid socks and little if any make-up despite having pale lashes; she eschewed gyms and placidly disregarded her overall thickness. And she had this slightly pugnacious look about it, like a lot of women given to natural beauty. I have no issue with that either, only beauty is not the same as attraction. A political reporter first and last, divorced and a serial dater with impossibly high standards, her feelings were a continuing mystery to her. But once past the first week she naturally began to succumb to my cold judgmental pull and commenced rolling her chair back so we could talk without barriers. Thus she provided both quality professional companionship and a pugnacious liveliness that alleviated the otherwise dismal atmosphere, and I was grateful.

We labored under the gimlet eye and competitive wit of the justly renowned Carmen Abramawitz; in her late thirties, Carmen was stout, Jewish-Hispanic, self-dramatizing, and intrinsically maternal. My first day she came bustling over for a formal welcome, picked up a photo of Megan's puppy and remarked in disapproval or maybe wonder: "My rescue greyhound Lacey has a full wardrobe." Adjusting her baggy wrap. "Okay, I know I have issues." Carmen was an anomaly in our functional realm, a kindly rebuke to the endless gray and beige and plastic, the sharp square corners and excellent lighting and general courteous restraint. She shook my hand, settling herself into the extra chair, and absently inserted a curious finger into the soil of our little jade plant, a legacy. "So it is possible to survive in here." Rummaging through the accumulated trash tossed into our extra cubicle, examining the take-out menus. "Indian. I loved India, the color, even the filth and noise. It's something everyone should experience." And finally actually looking at me, virtually impaling me with her comprehensive gaze until I felt slightly sick, like I'd forgotten to tidy up my mind before company arrived. She owned me now, this personage in a deep red peasant dress and loose black shawl, emanating energy even at apparent rest, just waiting for a chance to be clever. She would have made a good lawyer.

So there I was, settling into another precarious position at best, wondering why the hell I insisted on behaving like a self- destructive adolescent but not urgently enough to figure it out. And meanwhile Megan devoted a good third of her day to the career question, researching how to build a successful blog, sketching out book proposals, pouring her youthful energy into the quest. "Because that has to be my priority."

I was reading the comments under one of my own pieces when I fell on a photo of Thom and Ruth captured at some benefit, she in a pale green gown, a chandelier just visible above them bestowing an elegant blessing. The force of those two personalities transcended the screen to gloat at me. Even grinning for the camera they were wonderfully absorbed in each other, two complete phonies playing out their deliberately storied romance, the viewer a necessary component of the relationship. But so what?

Love is whatever love is for you. And it was sort of a touching shot, there was this innocent element to it.

But I was surprised by the longevity of this amour, which I continued to dismiss as ultimately inconsequential. Easy enough, considering Thom's deserved reputation as a rake: there was that white-blond model who broke into his townhouse and sprayed furious filth all over his abstract paintings, broke the penis off an African carving, and slashed the white leather upholstery. A radiologist from Singapore with extremist politics and hair to her waist. A cable morning newsreader who ended up in a tabloid divorce. And another exotic, Bolivian I think, a skyscraper-tall, beautifully coiffed, silk-suited beauty in four-inch heels. They all blurred together in my mind, uniformly exquisite, charming, intelligent and educated, barring an occasional underweight entertainment wannabe. ("Boring. Why don't I learn?") Women with a talent for self-preservation, enjoying a safe temporary fling, exploiting some local celebrity.

In retrospect I should have found it significant that Ruth didn't fit the mold, I should have accorded more importance to their chemistry, because it was a very palpable force. You could feel it watching them play their little word games, all that shit, even if at the same time you recognized the underlying agendas, that mutual usefulness. I made a point of tuning in the first time she had him on her program. That was just a one-time thing, a lovers' offhand gesture, but he was a natural and listeners wanted more of him. Megan turned up in time for it; she pulled her chair out and listened while she ate oatmeal with a plastic spoon.

Ruth introduced him without much fanfare, and opened the topic of an event all over the local news that week: the brutal white-on-white neighborhood beating of a suspected neighborhood rapist, a vicious attack carried out despite the police already there on the scene, pushing into the mob. There was video, so there was national coverage; you see the officers moving with that purposeful, trained tread they have, not hurrying.

"We're all wondering whether this is about a lack of faith in the justice system." And then she took one of those recent off- ramps to insanity: "Or is it possible there was some degree of self-hatred propelling that violence? Were these people actually attacking some unacknowledged part of themselves, projecting their own self-hatred onto an acceptable target? He was one of their own, one of them. And in the end you can only get angry at yourself; that's a rule, you can look it up."

Thom took this lightly. "You think they were making him a scapegoat for self-hatred?" As if perfectly serious, and incredibly I could hear his absolute delight at her outré intellect.

"Yes, just straight out trying to destroy something in themselves. Isn't that how it always works, we marginalize unacceptable parts of ourselves. Isn't that what they teach in sociology class?"

"Yes, you say that because you instinctively empathize." And with this bit of cheap flattery Thom flatly denied her true soul, cruelly fled from everything cowering in the dark pit of her psyche, crying out for notice and acceptance, and that's how he determined his fate. "You're a marvelous exception."

Megan rolled her eyes at me. I visualized Thom there next to Ruth, the hovering attention that always accompanied his exaggerated flattery. The inevitable voice of the blue-collar community, the aggressors in this scandal. "For me, I think they should have hurt him slow so he suffered. Sent him straight to hell without the right to an attorney."

"Yes. Yeah." Always eager to explain. "Punishment is about preventing certain behaviors from becoming successful. Well, and the redemption of the offender, of course. But I don't think it should have anything to do with revenge."

"These people separate themselves from the rest of humanity. They're not even human, they're monsters." From a very young woman with a chirping child in the background. "I agree they need help but it has to start earlier. By the time the crime is committed it's too late. The money is going in the wrong direction."

"But we're all monsters." Ruth said flatly. "We need to accept that. I know I have my unacceptable fantasies, really awful feelings. And I'm not going to tell you about them!" And then guided by that maddening because mostly perfect instinct for self-preservation she turned back on topic.

Megan raised her scant eyebrows. "I'm surprised. She's out there, but she definitely isn't the kind of white supremacist nut I thought."

I nodded. "She's a different variety of nut."

This public mating dance culminated in a small private wedding in the back garden of a wealthy mutual friend. It was inevitable but still mildly shocking. Lacking any other option I tolerated the situation but resolutely continued to consider it temporary. Ruth, in her adolescent fashion, truly adored Thom, but that infatuation would soon enough evaporate, leaving her free and unhurt. Only what of Thom's uxorious contentment now he'd convinced himself he was in love?

But for the moment they seemed to be reveling in their honeymoon happiness. "I feel blessed by the universe, although I suppose everyone feels this way at first," she confessed. This was at a private dinner party some months later; she was next to me, Thom across from us, and she was gazing happily at him through a low gleam of squat white candles. "It's such a holy state: holy sex, holy breakfast." Then catching my expression and reverting to her usual sardonic tone: "Probably not an experience you're familiar with." She examined me and shook her head. "You know, Con, there's no God in your face. There's no trace of anything transcendent about you at all. It's remarkable."

CHAPTER NINE

City Councilman David Cevallos posed beside the Columbus monument at Penn's Landing, his broad face radiating intelligent purpose, his substantial bulk shifting a little uncomfortably from one thick leg to the other. Here was a reassuring presence, this man who proudly flaunted his years, judiciously considered his words and actions, and naturally enough took serious offense at thoughtless interruptions.

This memorial is made of towering dark gray stone, a truncated obelisk. From my perspective a few steps below, both man and monument were lost in the glare slanting in from the usual bleached noon sky. I lowered my gaze to the Camden side with its remnants of human civilization, a blur of false promises. I find the Columbus sculpture unfortunate, those immovable sails climbing up an authoritarian phallus, the overall resemblance to some kind of covert receiving device for extraterrestrial messages. Still I like that it's there; the fact of it comforts me. A street fair surrounded us and descended towards the water, not really crowded that weekday afternoon but still lively: food vendor booths and hammocks, bocce ball, swan boats. Nobody sent much more than a curious glance our way. Temporary and intimate, the pop-up park was jammed summer nights with happy young holding hands and strolling and families eating at tables under colored lights. From our location we could see down to the Great Plaza and the broad gray river beyond. A minimal entourage: one enthusiastic aide, a handful of dutiful journalists, one photographer, and a handful of strays from the park who'd edged up as close as possible to the magic of our traveling importance machine.

"Five centuries," David said. Precious knowledge weighs heavily upon him: there's always so much to consider, it's such a difficult journey from that initial spark of certainty into speech capable of making a difference out in contemporary society. This business of being heard is an immense responsibility. "Five hundred years." His silver gargoyle's head inclined towards the memorial in acknowledgement of this honored immigrant ancestor. "Can you imagine what he would think if he arrived here today?"

David is a born educator, a man of infinite patience, exacting about details, always ready with a thoughtful compliment or encouraging comment or appropriate anecdote. Now he paused to inspect the swift Delaware below us, silver-lit and sparkling aloud, extolling its own undoubted power. A dangerously alive river although past its active years.

"Then there's our own Mr. Penn, who knew this river well. When he first set foot on this great continent he envisioned a new kind of future here on this land between these two great waterways, the Delaware river and the Schuylkill river. What is fascinating to me is that William Penn was really what we think of today as a city planner; he designed a wonderful town where houses had gardens, where streets were broad, and where there were numerous open city squares. And this was simply because he thought about people first."

Ordering his realm into neat streets for suitably allocated functions, prudently incorporating brick and open spaces as preventatives to plague and fire, and if his gentlemanly green country town was quickly claimed and reshaped by the merchant class, Penn's more humane sensibility lingers: an underlying notion, a rational, moderate Quaker predisposition evidencing real thoughtfulness and a reluctance to trust the indolent common run of humanity with their naturally arising cities. Despite a constant temptation to scoff at the utopian futility of our founder we really do know better, we value Penn's notions and accomplishments. That righteous and rebellious non-conformist pouter pigeon preening himself up there on top of City Hall, just waiting for us to realize he's been right all along. Our immensely complacent Mr. Penn. "In these confusing times we appreciate Mr. Penn and his wisdom. We're discovering him all over again, this true visionary who honored fundamental human values." Mr. Penn the futuristic pathfinder.

David motioned us into his wake, and together we descended the endless flights of steps and platforms, detouring around yellow police tape protecting repairs to the cement, crisscrossing pathways of faded, pinkish fake brick until we got down to the upper rows of the amphitheater. The utilitarian metal skeleton of the stage dominated the space, its back to the water, boxed in by billowing blue plastic printed with ads; it made a tidy enough frame for the Delaware. A few vaguely nautical pennants, blue or yellow, languidly lifted and collapsed against their poles in the mild breeze off the water. Those ran south, occasionally interspersed with American flags moving with the same nominal, insufficient enthusiasm.

Our little coterie was growing irritated and restive; we'd been with David from early morning, through too many overheated, futile hours. But that was entirely for our own reasons, not his, and certainly not to provide an audience for more empty pontification. We'd met at a North Philly elementary school near the border of his district, at the ancient kind of schoolyard with a black iron fence enclosing a cement courtyard swarming with highly alert children pretending to laughing indifference. Trailed David up the shallow entrance steps and into the usual crumbling barracks of an inner city school, another example of incomplete repairs, blocked-off classrooms, buckets and rags against water-stained walls, and the permeating smells of disinfectant, insecticide, bathrooms, and general rot. A place that wore despair like the latest cool fashion, accentuating its hopelessness with enforced gaiety and outrageous promises, with posters and visions and standard exhortations to a better existence, as if the whole point was to elicit rage. And perhaps those children will one day rise up and simultaneously reject both their actual and encouraged lives to create a third avenue of existence, maybe calamitous but at least honest and exciting. Maybe that's already happening.

The hallways we filtered through displayed patches where the plaster had been stripped from walls and ceilings and never replaced. Contrite, we followed David on into Mrs. DuBois' third-grade classroom in order to witness and document another of his holy causes, because David was a consummate nudge forever hectoring the

219

community, entreating and reprimanding the populace to its own betterment. This classroom was a shabbily disguised office with low yellow desks pushed together to form long worktables and autumn leaves cut from construction paper taped over dun-painted walls. Although there was still a discernable start-of-semester ambition clinging to it, an eagerness like fresh air mingling with the aromas of young children and duplicity. Mrs. DuBois, a thirty-something, plump African-American woman in a knee-length navy skirt and neatly- striped cotton shirt stood in front of the whiteboard, elbows out, hands clasped in front of her. But she was no star-struck provincial; she was a woman who took charge and triumphed over challenges. You could see it in her forthright gaze and firm posture.

"Who can tell me who this gentleman is?" As if those kids hadn't been thoroughly coached. Thirty-odd little countenances broke into immense grins, thirty-odd small hands shot into the air taking a few of those lithe young bodies partly up with them, while a few opportunists delivered skittish asides to their neighbors. David, an erstwhile teacher, stood in debonair silence beside Mrs. DuBois in his Italian suit, a caramel fabric with a golden shimmer accented by a quiet mauve silk tie and a pale pink shirt. It was his trademark now, all that sartorial splendor setting off the markedly suave demeanor, it was expected at any public appearance. But really it was the most outstanding, deliberate contrast imaginable, style befriending brutality – his darkly pitted complexion a broad, desolate moon, his features crude overall, his nose frankly bulbous, his stocky body too heavy for comfort. But his attire, his exaggerated masculine grace inevitably celebrated civilization and even beauty. He shone, he bowed his noble head and released an infinity of stars.

"Ah, I'm so pleased that you recognize me! We have aspiring politicians, then? Or merely very intelligent future citizens?" A pleased posture, that thick torso companionably forward, his deeply serious tones playing about that lovely Latin lilt. "Well, let us start. You, young gentleman! Pointing out an immediately abashed kid in the second row. "Please explain to us who it is you believe me to be."

The boy glanced at his teacher. "City Councilman David

Cevallos."

"Ah, I see! City Councilman David Cevallos. Yes. Well, I concede that to be correct!" Then with one hand he encircled the room; I noted the oil paint clinging to his fingernails. "Well, and who are you that I have the pleasure to address here today?"

That one was unexpected and required some rapidly interchanged glances. Finally several voices explained that they were Mrs. DuBois' class or a version thereof.

"Yes, I thank you very much for that proper introduction." Nodding, his hand rubbing a thoughtful chin. "Well then, Mrs. DuBois' class, can you tell me this, since you're all so well informed! Can you tell me what precisely that means, to be a City Councilman?"

David sat himself on the edge of Mrs. DuBois' desk, ignoring the adult chair obviously positioned for him at the front of the room, flicking an invisible piece of lint from his knee, gravely surveying the expected forest of well-prepared hands. At length he recognized an exceptionally eager girl in a middle row with sad Mediterranean eyes and a smooth olive complexion. Despite a preponderance of African-Americans the children made something of an ethnic stew, a mix of bobbing braids fastened with bright plastic barrettes, spiky-haired proto-punks, and contained or else truculent, hip Asians.

"Young lady, what is it a Councilman does?" "Make laws!"

"Make laws. That's almost exactly right. But let me say that I don't think this answer is complete." Strewing confusion over the obedient masses. "Well, let me enlighten you. Members of City Council do a thousand things, much more than merely making laws, although this is very important too." Slowly nodding, nodding. "For example, I build buildings. I pave streets. I put out fires. In fact, I even teach school."

Here suddenly struck by an interesting thought. "Did you know that long ago I attended this very school? As a child I sat in this very classroom."

"Yeah! We knew that!" It would have been impossible, they would have had to have been blind and deaf not to know all about the legendary alumnus exhibited before them in the actual flesh, one of those extraordinary, rare beasts who knew other successful people and lived inside the mysterious celebrity kingdom.

"I see you do know. That's very impressive. You are very well informed. And do you know also that Mrs. DuBois, this Mrs. DuBois standing right here today, was also my third grade teacher?"

This was met with vociferous objection.

"Oh, but I would certainly never mislead you." Then turning courteously to the teacher still standing primly at the front of the room: "Tell us then, how long have you been teaching this class, Mrs. Dubois? Wouldn't you say it's been almost a century now, give or take a decade?"

"Seems like it."

They are natural confederates, both of them the kind of people who respect social workers.

"Then with your permission let me ask you a question, if I may ask a question of the teacher. Do you think anything has genuinely changed from when you started all those years ago, what with the many changes out in the world and all the magical electronics we have today?"

She smiled politely and ignored the inquiry, knowing full well he was merely transitioning into his patented motivational harangue. Earnestly gazing out from his perch on the desk, cupping his meaty hands against his sizable pouch. That's how you always picture David: looking down at someone with paternal affection and that gravity lurking just underneath, like exhaustion. "I can tell you what has never changed, not in all that time, not with all our modern electronics, which is that every single one of you has been given a precious gift: the opportunity to choose your own future. This is incredible! In all of history you are among the few children fortunate enough to be able to choose what your life will be."

"God chooses," said an affronted little voice from the middle of the room.

"God too. You and God together, that goes without saying. I apologize if I did not make myself clear." And he let the protective blank silence, the cautious waiting continue while he carefully examined his own palms, readying himself to sow wisdom in this hostile ground, even knowing.

"Inside your own head you can dream wonderful secret fantasies but unless you obtain an education you will not achieve those things no matter what they are, no matter if those dreams are of computers and outer space or sports or music. But you see it's a kind of a test. Are you smart enough to want to be smart?"

However much they truly understood of this effort at indoctrination, an unmistakable fog of resentment was drifting up from those tiny desks now, a thick security blanket of rebellious disinterest. Their impossibly small backs were still, their posture resigned, their faces uniformly expressing a boredom nearly surpassing human endurance. No doubt twenty years from now they'll value his message, having forgotten how it was literally impossible to stop the inchoate hurt for an whole endless day without recourse to the usual methods of distraction or oblivion, to instantly acquire sufficient souls. How their particular deficiencies were as much beyond their control as cancer and equally tragic but unfortunately outside the current fashion in victims. Because if they could, then they were already somebody else, receiving another congratulatory pat on the back. But yes, eventually they'll blame themselves. That morning they simply glared back at the mockery of this enemy come to further diminish their fragile self-respect, promising rewards to the lucky, using the truth against them.

David stood then, gazing benevolently down at them. Not saying to them: "Love wisdom for its own sake. Read for joy. Learning is the greatest adventure imaginable. It will make you value humanity." Instead he said, "Let me repeat this so that you always remember: your time in school is where you decide your entire life."

Speaking with such urgency while the children mostly ignored this tedious demand to become a more convenient problem, amenable to current solutions. And all this ridiculous effort because David truly hoped, even expected mere words to shift their precarious lives that critical bit towards alignment with his truth, so that finally they would be able to hear him. It was a matter of wearing them down, accomplishing a few precious millimeters of progress with each repetition.

"I want you to watch carefully. Is everyone watching? Well then, here is what the world owes you." And he turned over both empty palms. "And this is what you can have." And he expanded both arms to embrace the universe. "And this is how you can win in this world." And he reached out and embraced the classroom, pointing to the posters and bookshelf and computer in turn, pointing finally at Mrs. DuBois who smiled back at him. And then he was waving in farewell and cleanly finding his way out.

In the Hispanic neighborhood stretching up North 5th Street into Olney, up among the flashy boutiques and cheap furniture stores and bodegas with hand-painted signboards and tiny taquerias and religious stores with resin crucifixes in the windows, that area climbing north towards the Asian gangs further up and the Russian mobs north of them, this gospel of education was generally considered fine so far as it went. But listen, I have no true knowledge of this community, all those pragmatic believers patiently climbing up the continent, but from what I could gather David was everyone's strict but important uncle who kept getting re-elected for all the profound reasons that manifest politically. His continued re-election seemed to me inevitable even though David was getting older and a little out of touch, an aging Latin king.

In his student days he learned easily, and he veritably worshipped knowledge, any knowledge, even though he had no idea what to do with it except swallow it whole like a communion wafer. It was a gift, all for free, and accepting it put him at the top of his class at Central High with a Mayor's Scholarship straight through Penn. From there he developed his social and organizational skills with additional degrees until he became an administrator in this very same disintegrating school system. Look at him now, fighting to make them see.

After the morning's heartless classroom diatribe we headed down to the Landing. It was a gray sort of day with a few scattered breakthroughs of bright sunlight reflecting off the water like brilliant afterthoughts. And it was chilly. I think a lot about weather because I generally don't like it. I don't like the cold or people who can't seem to feel it. Waiting there that day, the wind hit us unimpeded. I sighed and lifted my eyes to the blue arch of the Ben Franklin Bridge, its nearby material presence at once impressively concrete and utterly ethereal.

We formed a watchful semicircle facing away from the water, our backs to the vague squalor of Camden with that noticeable white dome of the aquarium in its midst and the impressive ghost-gray battleship New Jersey lingering at the shore. Here on the Pennsylvania side, below the Seaport Museum, there's another retired battleship: Commodore Dewey's former command the USS Olympia. Her final official act was to convey the body of the Unknown Soldier to Arlington; now she sits as a reminder of a former ethos, her hull painted a sickly pink at the water line, then white, and then a horrible tan above, so that she resembles a gigantic serving of Neapolitan ice cream dished up, for some reason, next to an urban pleasure marina with piers marked out with little translucent pinwheels. You viewed her in disbelief because she evaded the expected categories, until eventually you noticed the submarine lurking in her shadow. The Becuna's a Vietnam vet so black and low she virtually disappears within her own dark aura. Both vessels float stationary at this uncertain destination, still reeking of death and blood and fear, two uncomfortable veterans refusing to amalgamate into this half-hearted recreational venue.

Also there's the Moshulu, a different matter entirely, a huge black-and-white sailing ship now converted into a decent restaurant, eminently suitable for professional or special occasions. From her decks and dining rooms you sense that she likes it here, you feel her wood expand happily while she rocks at her ease.

There's not much else: the ferry station, sometimes a motorboat or two on the water, on rare occasions a cruise ship. Few people as well; unless there's some concert or ethnic festival on it's mostly joggers or random tourists trying to read the ruptured historic markers lining the pier. Otherwise the emptiness is noticeable; even the seagulls don't much congregate here, there's no point. And except for our summer festivals and those few major holidays where there are fireworks over the bridge the greater public either ignores this site or holds it in abeyance. But I need to be clear for the benefit of anyone not from around here: Penn's Landing isn't a complete wasteland, it's just an underutilized venue, obviously shabby and crumbling around the amphitheatre. A lot of people like it well enough the way it is, the Great Plaza and the lights on the bridge, a tall ship or battleship to tour and another one to have dinner on, even the casual lack of coherence, the human perspective reflected in that friendly hodgepodge. And I don't want to disparage those summer concerts and movies, or even the lackluster festival weekends let alone Freedom Week with its proud celebrations. Also there's the newer Festival Pier a little north, but I don't count that although maybe I should. The River Rink is fine too, especially at Christmas. But as a general rule it's only shuttered concession booths, and it takes you much too long to walk the nothingness from the ferry landing to the stage. There's just not enough there to overcome the inconvenience.

Look west at Philadelphia and there are the newer hotels and the clean white spire of old Independence Hall, then further up there's Billy Penn and further west of him our sparse handful of actual skyscrapers glaring from the constant haze, irradiated by an invisible sun. Then really look, examine it carefully and without preconceptions, and you start to notice the dilapidation, the collapsed infrastructure of our obsolete factory town, the brick walls bearing painted traces of ancient painted advertisements. Remnants of that former vital mercantile city are plentiful here along this river, that old living Philadelphia that was once so vigorous and callous and dangerous.

But David was looking away from the city confusion and gesturing instead at the narrow property isolated between the river and I-95. "I want you to imagine what we can create here. I want you to dare to envision something created with the people of Philadelphia in mind." Staring south towards a few skeletal cranes and one slowly approaching freighter. The confluence of the Delaware and Schuylkill was somewhere way down there, past the old Navy Yard to where the great Delaware Bay opened out into the Atlantic. Moving ponderously as usual, David turned north to face the looming blue span of the bridge pulling the gray sheen of the river around with him, wrapping himself in the idea of it. "We have been blessed with incredible potential here."

Unfortunately all that potential is exactly what's killing the Landing. It's a history so elaborately improbable, so magnificently preposterous you start to wonder if there really is some species of curse at work. How else explain the supernatural antipathy to success, the almost mystical ability to forestall progress; it's a force so elegantly malicious eventually you find yourself secretly rooting for that evil imp no doubt hiding under the pier.

It starts with the initial, determinative clearing of the riverside slums, the fill brought in to build the Landing, the Society Hill renaissance and the reclamation of the lower city. All that was well before my arrival in Philadelphia, of course, and a potent enough victory for any comparative metropolis, except thus far and no farther because then everything starts to fall apart. Certainly by the time of the Bicentennial, when there was extensive restoration around the historic district and they put in all this miserable pink brick composite that immediately started to decompose. When everyone started seeing the value and trying too hard. There was NewMarket, that strange, vaguely nautical mall with wooden stairs to higher levels of struggling or failed shops and restaurants, its superfluous banner left hanging over the river for approximately forever.

Mike Miller

There followed numerous developers armed with familiar hype: it made for a hilarious sequence of newspaper extracts (even funnier read in reverse chronology), a dependable succession of confidence and catastrophe. The excerpts below offer a typical recounting of one typical attempt, and if you think I'm exaggerating look it up yourself:

May 1997 - Largest developer in nation – entertainment complex with 11-screen movie - mayor acknowledges mayors have been making similar promises of development at site for decades

August 1998 - 17 movie screens - progress being made - demolish existing Great Plaza - two ice rinks - still hostage to rent and construction costs October 1998 - Step forward with lease agreement – developer not legally committed until board of directors votes and construction commitment given - start locking in leases

January 1999 - Board okays deal

April 1999 – Children's Museum to occupy part of complex – the mayor pledges five million in city funds

September 1999 - Art Commission approves location for

Children's Museum

October 1999 - construction delayed - opening spring

2002 - state approval needed to remove ramps connecting Columbus Boulevard to Market and Chestnut Sts. - current RiverRink stays put for now

October 1999 – many retailers sign on - project skewing upscale

February 2000 - developer seeks additional public aid money from Port Authority for enhancements - delays taking legal control of site

230

March 2000 - new worries over Riverfront complex as start of construction is put off again

May 2000 - done deal - construction to start in August

September 2000 - later start, demolition will begin in October – City Commerce Director states opening is set for 2002

October 2000 - opening pushed back six months - Commerce Director skeptical

October 2000 – developer: there's no way we'll stop now April 2001 - developer still not ready to start

May 2001 - naming rights deal near - significant step in closing funding gap

October 2001 - Penn's Landing Corp. tells developer to put up optionpayments or retreat

October 2001 - project in doubt

Once in town I adjusted to the pace of local development, the way it happened while you weren't exactly paying attention instead of with a string band and fireworks. With the Landing, I perversely started to enjoy feeling like an accurate prophet of doom. During this same time discreet sections of the waterfront to the south and north towards Northern Liberties were successfully exploited in a reasonable, effortless manner. Only a mile north of Center City, in the Fishtown section, they opened what's still a successful casino.

David was reiterating those idealistic community demands, describing multiple points of entry over the highway, each with its own anchor enterprise. There was no mistaking his quiet satisfaction over the mayor's sudden backing despite the blatant strategizing behind that move.

231

Why couldn't they all work together? It wasn't impossible. Hands spread, appealing to our reason.

Okay, so that was the point of this little field trip: getting out to the public his willingness to work with the mayor, incorporating that riverfront casino into the otherwise intact PennDesign proposal, the good guys joining forces in the name of the citizenry. Why not?

"But as the mayor has correctly pointed out, the way the Columbus plans stand now it would be impossible to integrate that proposal with the community requirements. Not with Columbus remaining anything remotely like what's envisioned now. If that can be remedied, then certainly I'll look at it again." Of course, he would, and of course Columbus was being hurriedly revised to meet the new standards, and of course David would welcome their cooperation but meanwhile why not collect some free public approval?

He stood there silently, almost smiling at us, waiting.

This coltish, eager young woman from our tabloid sister, all long brown braid and an undergraduate's uncouth body language, jumped into the silence. They like them scrappy and competitive over there; it's pure over-compensation. "Can we talk a little about your recent exhibit?"

Because our presence, believe it or not, was largely due to some of David's paintings of mediocre merit stupidly loosed on the populace. When suddenly certain people had something to say about it and tried to develop an issue where there wasn't one, stirring up bile, wasting my and the public's attention.

"Of course, we can. I completely understand your interest but frankly I don't know what else you think I can tell you? That is the point of art, you see? It speaks for itself." That grave nod again, validating our necessary inquiry but delivering his response in exactly the same patient, instructive tone he'd used with the children.

And he turned to lead us back up to the parking area, attempting to direct the conversation onto the Landing and other generalities, but we all knew that wasn't going to happen. Not when his opening for that particular exhibit featured a premier party stuffed with celebrities and the media hype typical of a Hollywood scandal. Made us look.

When this all started Megan and Carmen indulged in a kind of ecstatic frenzy, delighting to question our moral mentor, heaping on the scorn. I found their behavior infinitely more objectionable than David's silly amateurish art but equally embarrassing. Not that the paintings in question were technically worse than his usual merely competent output, just confusing: a white goat, bathed in brilliant sunlight climbing our famous Art Museum steps, a pile of droppings steaming it his wake; a stout motherly type dangling (dropping?) an infant off a roof, into jungle; Christ on his cross, fully naked, thoughtfully smoking a joint. The oil colors were muted and dreamy, the figures cut sharp against their backgrounds, often outlined in black. What the hell was any of it supposed to mean? Nothing very original, if you ask me, but at the same time what was the problem? I mean, so what? Then there was a photo of one painting on the tabloid's front page: a circle of Caucasian children holding hands while sitting in the middle of traffic, cars speeding by to either side and one heading directly for them. Questions were raised but at its worst it was pretty half-hearted, I think because whatever the symbolic

233

meaning there remained something sanctified about art and most people didn't want to trespass. Isn't art supposed to be offensive? But David's mysterious images really were felt as a betrayal, a subversive slap to his largely traditional constituents. His district preferred that he stick to painting naïve cultural clichés, Hispanic children or exuberant neighborhood scenes in primitive colors applied with broad strokes of the palette knife. This wasn't overt, you understand; outwardly everyone was supportive, loudly so. But one opponent in particular, another Democrat, gave out with some low opportunistic mutterings about David being out of sync with his public or even senile. I mean for about five minutes this was being discussed in the city although as I say, it never developed any real momentum.

The Askews were at the opening, of course; it was at a tiny gallery on Pine Street, a place you wouldn't look at twice walking by. Ruth has this conflicted relationship with David: sometimes she writhes under his notice like Crystal, but I can tell she respects his opinions and his experience. It's like she's a little girl safe hiding behind her father but darting out to stick her tongue out and get his attention. She and Thom were staring at a painting of an abstract sculpture, and she was basically reaming him out, deriding his opinion of the painting and conceptual art in general in that arch, instructional tone you use with cultural inferiors.

"Whatever the medium, a statement is just that - a statement. Art requires more." The taunting was mitigated by obvious fondness but still uncomfortably acerbic. She might be furious.

There followed a lengthy pause, but Thom must have tacitly, graciously encouraged a renewed assault, because she resumed her argument with that same condescending, outsized patience. She was wearing a very unfortunate shade of bright blue. "Art has a purpose: it's about making things beautiful so they can be grasped, incorporated, and left behind. That's what beauty means. You can't just appoint something art if it doesn't work. You do not have that prerogative."

"Alas poor Koons, he'll be totally shattered; Hirst will wail. All these many decades chasing a tragic delusion." His manner gently reaching out to me there off to his side, inviting me in, but I ignored him, feigning interest in a nearby portrait. Ruth's superior, practiced flow was making my temples throb.

"Writing but music and poetry too, all the arts are pioneers clearing the way for reason. Poesis means to create, not to instruct. And yes, alas." I'd heard the speech before, and I was seething with quiet fury for him. She almost never mocked his affectations in public like that.

"Which is why that thing is just junk." Indicating the statue depicted on the canvas, a mildly unconventional but mostly boring conglomeration of random curves of polished steel atop a rather frumpy pebbled stone base; it looked like a giant had smashed a pitcher on the patio. Never mind the confusing aspect of it being painted into a canvas.

"Outside the scope of the argument because hideous by anyone's criteria."

"Well, yeah, that's true. And not that conceptual art is necessarily bad, either. Some of it's truly transcendent, not at all sterile, not requiring some ironic, despairing explanation. But that's only when it's escaped."

I saw David wandering around being courteous, seeing to the wine and hors d'oeuvres but generally keeping a watchful distance and a supportive eye on his handsome, anxious wife. He was also plainly a little drunk; when I acknowledged him across the main gallery he smiled broadly, apparently much pleased with himself. I watched him address Margery, leaning in affectionately while she gently inched back, looking grim. Later when he came over to me he confided without prompting: "I can remember much of my infancy. This is unusual, I know. But I remember my mother holding me on her shoulder and burping me, and I even remember shitting myself and having my mother come change me! I remember how I felt then, how I was a wholly integrated person. And that's what this is about. That's where it comes from, that wholeness." Making a wide gesture to the walls of canvases.

Tragic that someone can be, fundamentally, an artist, without ever being a good artist. The pundits, both political and aesthetic, were not appreciative, but he ignored all of it. I mean he genuinely thought his derivative crap mattered, which I thought kind of terrific in an understated, suicidal way.

"He was trying to be controversial and he nearly succeeded. Look, there are clear messages in his stuff and they aren't especially nice." Carmen was in our vacant cubicle, swiveling with her short legs peeping out from under her flowered caftan, catching a sunbath. "Lucky he's not up for reelection, otherwise he'd have had issues with the Democratic Committee pronto." So ostensibly neutral yet purely radiating venom,

"That's ridiculous!" Which it was and she knew it. They made me tired. All this about a man's evolving ideas of beauty, and whose business was it?

Megan looked over, lip-gloss in hand; all these women put on lip gloss in public now. "If nothing else, it shows a serious lack of judgment."

art!"

"What the hell's the matter with you, anyway? It's just bad

But they were both through with me; I got defensive jeers,

I was abandoned. That's how badly they needed to attack the man; it went that deep and personal.

One unexpected consequence of David's artistic contretemps was June giving up her riding lessons because, she told me, she overheard the stable's owner, a decent, dowdy Virginian, denigrating David's whole Hispanic culture as crude and superstitious. Or so June claimed, but later she told someone else she actually overheard a nasty remark about herself. Whatever happened, she felt compelled to sacrifice her passion for horseflesh.

David meanwhile moved forward with no more than a nod to his concerned constituents, over time restoring that fraction of his reputation undermined by the longing to make beauty.

One evening at this Cuban place on Walnut Street he indirectly touched on his paintings. Resettling his bulk in a low, square leather armchair, his crude features illuminated by one of those tiny restaurant candles: you mostly saw the deep cleft dividing his nose and the spongy, pitted landscape of his complexion. He was slouched at an elegant angle, both wary and at his ease. It was noisy with girls' shrill voices but he seemed to consider it a suitable venue for conversation. "Now listen," he said, shifting his torso towards me. "It's channeling, I would say. The spirit leads and it creates what I need to create. Sometimes it's things I don't quite understand myself, except I know how they feel. Often it's the same thing over and over. Often my own face!"

It all blew over quickly, of course, and today if you mention it everyone seems surprised, as if it all happened decades ago and possibly to someone else entirely. But he's been given notice; he's being watched.

It was all still fresh that afternoon at the Landing, and I thought he seemed not so much defiant as irritated with mankind in general, and I sympathized. Of course, the politician understood our business perfectly well, and eventually he nodded, acknowledging the implied quid pro quo. Pausing in his ascent with the river below and behind him and the city looming ahead, presenting an unintentional image of progress, a muscular evocation of tankers and earth-moving machines. "My paintings reflect my god-given soul. That's why it's not for me to justify them. But I think," and he paused, searching out words. "I think I was trying to surprise my old ideas." And then he waved a dismissive hand back at us and continued his climb.

I own one of David's canvases; it's from several years earlier and if it's not great art it's still affective. A tall, very thin man in a simple gray business suit much too big on him is walking out of the canvas towards you; behind him a street of shabby rowhouses retreats into a translucent smudge of horizon. This man has great determination in his mouth and chin, but his posture and his eyes reveal an expectation of defeat. I don't really know what dignity's supposed to mean - I suspect it's something we made up, like human rights - but that painting is all about heartbreaking dignity.

CHAPTER TEN

This young woman bearing down on us seemed vaguely familiar but it took me a minute to place her, so during that interregnum I employed the old self-denigrating grin and modest shrug. Then I remembered: Manetti's table that night at Luigi's, barely identifiable now because she'd dressed herself up like a good Catholic girl, complete to a discreet but clearly visible gold crucifix at her throat. I was with Ruth, getting the story on her involvement with PhillyCares, and we were crossing the hospital lobby towards an exit when here was this person determined to intercept us. Ruth for her part was physically assuming her own distancing celebrity demeanor but I couldn't tell if she'd recognized the girl or if it was an automatic response.

Halting directly in our way, a tentative hand reaching out to Ruth. "Marlene Angeli. I'm so happy to run into you again." As it was already late evening I found that statement slightly ominous. Marlene took an obligatory glance round. "I don't mean to hold you up," she said, making it clear she fully intended to be very inconsiderate.

"We weren't in any special hurry." Ruth said, still professionally distant, and then she just waited until of course Marlene rushed into the silence, babbling girlishly. It was my own damn fault. It was because Ruth had cemented herself to PhillyCares, was veritably obsessed with that outfit, and I was fascinated by this dangerous determination and curious to follow the event. I'd monitored one of her remotes and a television appearance promoting the charity, and I suspected she was unwelcome presence basically forcing herself into the ranks of experienced year-round soldiers, a poseur demanding to be accorded undeserved respect. You'll think I'm projecting but I knew her and she wasn't concerned in the least with the beneficiaries of all this energetic effort. And what about all those remarks about the cheapness of obviously virtuous works?

"Everyone misunderstands me. And you should know better because I've told you before that it's about the sanctimony when there's no moral courage required. I'm doing necessary drudge work, that's all. Someone has to, always."

They'd been at the hospital to make an announcement in the children's atrium, a half-dozen physicians and organization people with Ruth central, positioning themselves against that backdrop of crayon and light to declare a major initiative, a series of neighborhood fundraisers and broadcasts hop-scotching the city from the dilapidated west to the boring northeast, with personal appearances by various local entertainment and sports figures, the whole effort scheduled to wrap up with a sentimental, self-congratulatory children's Christmas party and final remote. I understood them to mean this as the start of a tradition, PhillyCares asserting its arrival.

And Ruth was going in with full support from the station, express approval even from Stanley, and why not? You wouldn't turn down such a well-connected public

241

campaign. Plus she'd calculated every minute and penny of her involvement in interminable meetings with Jimmy Blue, their chunky, blond promotions manager, shut up in his tiny closet of an office. PHA and PhillyCares between them brought the initial project down to reasonable proportions: a firehouse Halloween party, a popular South Philly diner on Thanksgiving, that sort of venue, which was clever. When I asked Ruth why the charity wasn't doing online fundraising she seemed surprised and stood considering it furiously for a moment before finally shrugging the question away. "I don't know. Why is there even still music on the radio?"

I watched a news crew from a local network affiliate cross the lobby at a controlled trot, probably fleeing Mimi Norton and her intimidating cohort of devoted community activists. Lane and Tim Baylor emerged in their wake, crossing from the elevators with a polite smile, lingering in the light outside the entrance a moment before disappearing into a taxi. They had an aura about them, not exactly of glamour, more of implicit intent: they were people heading off to make something happen.

And this Marlene was clearly very determined, but compared to Norton she was a mere amateur, relatively easy to dislodge. I looked at Ruth, wondering whether or not she was likely to commit another convenient if embarrassing public gaffe now I needed one, but she was listening to Marlene with a patient, patronizing expression, obviously flattered by this lesser daughter of South Philly.

The girl was talking across me in a perfectly considerate voice with a South Philly twang lurking in it, a sort of dormant brutality. "I've heard you talk about the work you do with PhillyCares and I really admire you."

Biting with cute uncertainty into a lower lip clean of make-up. "Listen, I realize I'm imposing but would you mind meeting someone, a patient? I mean, I know it's late but she's like a really huge fan and I know she'd never forgive me if I didn't ask."

"Of course, but I only have a few minutes." And Ruth immediately adopted this flagging posture and an appropriate frown, the kind that implies a mild headache but no big deal.

"Oh, that's wonderful of you!" So we headed towards the elevators with Marlene practically prancing, but once in the car she faced us with an open, serious expression. "I know what you're wondering, and just to get it out of the way, Jimmy really is my uncle, my mother's brother."

I held up both hands in protest. "Okay."

"Well, it's true so it should be okay." And she shepherded us along the well-lit corridor, past all the doors into misery - a moan here, an inappropriately intimate glimpse there – then around the well-lit nurses' station and abruptly into a standard double room. The window side was vacant; the nearer bed held an incredibly old and emaciated woman, a shrunken hunched dwarf, advanced age now her predominant physical feature. Her tiny body was swaddled in a hideous crocheted afghan, that kind with squares of lime green and pink and baby blue. Small, coffee-colored eyes peered up out of this cocoon. I could see a sallow countenance, a broad and stupid peasant face, but she remained unaware of us, focused on the suspended television currently blasting out something youthful and melodramatic. I deduced she was at least partially deaf.

Marlene moved to dominate the woman's vision and spoke to her very clearly. "This is my great-aunt Lina. Aunt Lina, this is Ruth Askew from the radio!"

The eyes located and grasped us, her head and body following along reluctantly; a serious undertaking, this shifting of so much unwieldy flesh and liquid. She set about examining Ruth up and down, her mind sluggishly processing this apparition, until eventually there came a visible, almost electric start of recognition, the papery cheeks divided into something resembling a smile, and Lina reverted into an obedient hostess: straightening her back and neck, insistently indicating the plastic visitor's chair until Ruth gave in and sat herself down, me loitering superfluously behind her, increasingly annoyed.

"Very pretty." Lina made this outrageous if kindly pronouncement from between scary dentures, then struggled for something else to say while we all grew increasingly uncomfortable. Finally: "I like your husband."

"Yes, all the women like my husband."

That elicited a splutter of wet laughter. Then Lina set about extracting a wad of tissue from some hiding place and pressed it against her lips, and that took a while.

"Unfortunately he's a very busy husband lately." In fact City Council was prominent on the local news that day: just yesterday the Pennsylvania Gaming Control Board had set a date for public hearings on the slots license to be held not in Harrisburg but right downtown at the Convention Center, although Council had yet to decide on development at the Landing.

Lina answered forcefully and to the point, demonstrating an unexpected awareness "Gambling is not good. It's a sin." The narrow voice invested the final word with unexpectedly crude venom, but she immediately, almost comically reverted to her harmless, kindly aspect. "I like you because you say anything, always crazy."

"Well, that doesn't seem like much of a compliment!"

"And now you come to say hello to me." She managed to shift her cocoon and I noticed a supermarket tabloid behind her on the thin hospital blanket. "I know about you! I hear your program." A finger wag; Lina clearly knew what was expected of her. "You care about people in here." Marlene was in a chair over on the window side, her ankles demurely crossed, her eyes avid; meanwhile I kept to the doorway, still hoping to expedite a getaway.

"I never do anything important myself; I just talk about it." This was outright rejected. "No, no, no! Don't tell me, I know!"

But Ruth rose, stretching her arms rather lazily, radiating unconcern. "I sometimes fantasize about really being of service, providing material things, you know? Shelter, food, medical treatment. Or else jobs, education, legal aid, so everyone's as lucky as me. But for that you have to start at the bottom and put in the time. You have to be dedicated. Charity's very competitive, you know, and very clubby; it's tough to break in. Me, I'm just a poseur, a hanger-on pretending to be a professional. And I'm incredibly impatient. Sometimes I'm deliberately obstructive just because I resent the people who do matter, the real people." The real people.

"But I'll tell you what, nobody should be so sure of themselves. I mean, suppose you do save a life, stop a war, feed the people, cure a disease, but you've inadvertently rescued the person or created the situation that results in a suitcase bomb. If Germany had won World War One, would there have been a Holocaust? If there hadn't been a plague, would there have been breathing room for the Renaissance? I mean, history's nothing but irony?"

Then she shook her head, scanning our carefully neutral expressions. "But at least I know I'm ignorant. That's the main thing. At least I don't take myself so seriously I can't see anything or anyone except my own importance."

I heard the resentment under that one, so once extricated from the Manetti connections and again crossing the bright lobby I proffered a sympathetic cue: "How's it going, anyway, working with Mimi?"

"Oh, I was just being petty." That said with a self-deprecating little shrug. We pushed out to a breezy city-lit evening, excited young voices just offstage, the air cool enough to stimulate but not chill. "It's just, you really can't imagine how incompetently the whole thing is run. Mimi says so herself; it's not like it's some kind of secret." We stood there letting taxis pass while we waited for Ruth to formulate whatever it was she intended to spill. "For example, she'll hire someone for administrative work, then literally just throw them behind a desk and totally ignore them, but when they screw up and don't get to their calls or log things in right they're just let go. And then it repeats. In the last year there's been something like five assistants. Mimi says their accountant, the guy who's treasurer, keeps screaming at her about the books, but she just says she's not about the money, the people are her priority." Turning to me so I could see her intelligent concern. "She pushes away reasonable solutions like using college volunteers. Says we can't manage them yet even though we need the help and they could do time-consuming things like shopping and transportation. I don't know, maybe this is a normal part of setting up this kind of organization, all this creative chaos. Or maybe my evil suspicions are right and it's all about her ego and everything she does is so important there's no place for criticism or even help."

"Maybe." Or maybe Ruth was exploiting an actual issue to win some pathetic little contest, bolster her own humanitarian ego.

According to its website, PhillyCares was a registered 501(c)(3) with a touching and praiseworthy if somewhat short history and three board members: Mimi Norton as president, Tim Baylor, and another man whose name I didn't recognize as the concerned treasurer. I considered the Baylors personable but otherwise very typical of successful people anywhere, that is to say, tediously exceptional and lacking any unexpected quirk or deficit. He was a hefty football-player type with a tidy mustache who reminded me of the long-suffering middle-class father on any sitcom. I knew him to be an accountant as well as an attorney. His relationship with the mayor went back to Temple Law and continued through their big firm experience and that transitional period when the mayor first entered local politics and Baylor was establishing his private practice. Lane Baylor struck me as upright, brilliant, and self-respecting, nothing more. Both stood up to scrutiny, presenting as an effective partnership with credible adolescent offspring and decent real estate holdings that included a small apartment building, a beach house in Margate, and a tract mansion in a gated Bucks County development. Their connection to Mimi Norton was obscure although there seemed to be some long-standing family relationship involved, and I found that very vagueness more credible than a ready explanation. Like so many married couples the Baylors displayed a similar public attitude: considerate but slightly authoritarian, resonant of deep community connections and long-term political pull. Both advocated for high-profile good works involving the more obvious variety of social benefit, the kind espoused by complacent schoolchildren: food and houses and jobs for all. PhillyCares occupied modest enough offices in an undistinguished rowhouse in Fairmount, a regulation narrow brick structure smack in the middle of a slightly gentrified street of identical buildings. I was met there by a well-groomed and stylishly clad young Asian woman who permitted me to enter and sat me opposite her desk in the tiny front room, probably a converted porch. I thought about Ruth's summary and wondered about the girl's job security. This receptionist or whatever tactfully refrained from commenting on my lack of appointment, merely seating me on a vinyl couch under a photo of our esteemed mayor. But Mimi herself, when she emerged some twenty minutes later, evinced barely-suppressed irritation and openly consulted her watch. "You're a big Askew supporter, a personal friend, right?"

"I think it would be presumptuous of me to claim friendship. And I never discuss my personal politics." I handed her some additional spiel and she led me into a smallish conference room, obviously a refitted dining room, with one narrow window giving on a back drive and little decoration beyond a tasteless arrangement of silk flowers: pink, orange, and yellow roses in a green glass bowl sitting beneath one of those bland inspirational posters with an eagle soaring through an expanse of cerulean sky.

She pulled out a chair and motioned me into another across the table, setting down a plastic accordion file and a mug of tea with the tag hanging over the side. The cup handle and rim were deeply grimy, so I excused her not offering me refreshment. By contrast the table was clean and polished, and the chairs, part of an ordinary Mediterranean dining room set, were aligned to rigid perfection. In fact now I looked even the corners of the carpet, the windowsills, and the curtains were spotless, punished by a definite aroma of disinfectant or insecticide or both. Nothing was casual or welcoming, there was none of the friendly, overburdened clutter of most small non-profits. In fact, this was not a nice place; it was more the refuge of a woman who expected censure because that was how the world always treated her. Take me for example.

"So what is it you want here?" This is how she welcomed the press? She lapsed into interior thought for a brief minute, then emerged suspiciously. "I don't know what you know about us?"

A lot more than I'd known even fifteen minutes ago. I examined her, the ordinary business attire, cherry red plastic nails and clumped mascara. Up close, in her native habitat, she was a recognizable type: a woman with a decent enough but commonplace brain who'd been afforded sufficient opportunity to advance her native abilities, who'd found success because she fit the rules and now basked in her own triumphs while constantly looking over her shoulder for the police or God or whatever. A fervent acolyte of the system in a designer business suit one size too small.

I summarized Ruth's comments without identifying the source, and she nodded, not grudgingly but as one on

249

familiar terrain. "Okay. We're not perfect. I'm assuming you know I'm the first to admit there's a lot that needs to be fixed on the administrative end. The point is, we're fixing it. We're doing that. But let me tell you something." Here she leaned forward, deliberately pinning me in my chair with this satisfied certainty. "We fill a need. Little things, you'll say, but they count. That someone is there caring, that counts. We hold hands and ease burdens other people don't think about or realize matter, things like money for carfare or hotels or television, minor things we can afford and arrange. Help with laundry and providing the right kind of nutrition and just buying stamps to pay bills and getting the mail out. You ask at Penn and Jefferson and Temple and all the other hospitals and hospices and rehabs, they all know about us."

Another quick inward glance, as if for consultation, as if on a deep sigh of the soul, her troubled but compassionate posture indicating a Christian desire to count even me on the side of the angels. Allowing me to glimpse the vulnerability beneath the regrettable belligerence. "You have to understand the need, the pain we see every day. There's an immense hunger for these personal services many people either can't afford, or if they can they always need more. Sometimes just having to take the bus can make things that much more difficult if not impossible." She shifted her comfortably round bottom in her chair the better to scrutinize me.

I nodded gravely. "Sure. I did note that some of your services overlap already available programs. Wigs for cancer patients, for example, and transportation. But I admit I don't have a good enough grasp of how all this works with insurance coverage and so on. I suppose there are gaps and that's where you come in?"

"You suppose correctly, but it differs widely. You may explore all that at your leisure. If you really are interested in writing about us, then I'm perfectly willing to show you what we're all about, every day. And it's an important story, it should be told in depth. But this is difficult work, not an exercise in self- aggrandizement or an opportunity to gain personal recognition. Do you understand what I'm saying here?"

Well, it was explicit enough. I examined her obdurate if polite expression. She had the tight mouth and determined chin of an exhausted crusader, and wary hazel eyes behind purple- tinted glasses fastened to a thin gold chain. Her earrings and necklace were studded with colored glass, more of that purple accented with jade and pink. I would never have trusted her with anyone I cared about, not even for five minutes. I gave her the old tilted head with inquisitive glance, and waited.

"We do have a real need to get our message out to the public and that is obviously why I agreed to see you today. We have achieved some degree of name recognition but that does not necessarily equate to increased financial support. We want money, Mr. Manos. We want more small donors and naturally we want more large corporate and individual donations as well. That said, I have no intention of allowing this organization, which I have personally created and nurtured, to be undermined by anybody's ambitious grandstanding. I don't care who they think they are."

Back in my own blessedly straightforward cubicle I considered the animus and opportunism binding Ruth and

Mimi Norton. Then I thought briefly about Marlene Angeli with her notorious uncle and her ancient great-aunt and her demure disguise. Disparate situations with a similarly shoddy, deceptive feel to them, but after a moment's thought I dismissed Marlene as irrelevant to anything I was interested in, and I still maintain that opinion although you may disagree. PhillyCares was a different story, and there were political implications, so I focused there. I did some superficial research, accessing what I could online and checking with a few beneficiaries, but everything seemed kosher, and why not? The phone rang, and I heard the matronly voice of one of my reliable City Hall sources sounding sorry for herself, which is how she always sounds. We agreed life was nothing but unappreciated drudgery and she got to the point: "Something happened with the FBI."

I rearranged it: "You mean the FBI is investigating something at City Hall? Or someone in the administration?" She'd be more likely to know if it involved the administration.

I'd insulted her, and she was pissed at me. "Like I said, they were right up here. What else is that supposed to mean?"

CHAPTER ELEVEN

Ruth gestured to the fragile young trees lining Market Street, waist level in their huge stone planters but currently despoiled by ugly plastic stars and twinkling yellow-white lights so cheap and garish I cringed for my city. "There's immense significance behind the myth. Something radical and enormous actually happened."

Christianity at Christmastime from the ultimate insider's viewpoint, delivered effusively and with absolute assurance. She was genuinely aglow, as if the tacky decorations made her legitimately beautiful, as if the season itself temporarily synchronized her soul to the celebration. Ruth was joining in the Black Friday frenzy as tradition required, tasting the holiday, out shopping for her personal Christmas miracle the way normal people shop for sweaters or toys. Joyfully inhaling the reasonable chilliness of the city, the clarity of the cement and the emptiness of the air. The Philadelphia season, as usual lately, lacked the cruel impact of real winter, bringing more of an absence, as if the turning of the year created a beneficent interval before the advent of bitter cold.

Confiding in me, eagerly rehashing an earlier search for something she was already sure existed, that same surety of Michelangelo and the forms already present in his block of marble waiting to be revealed. That's a singular creative certainty, an almost physical faith. Couple it with an unfaltering ability to succeed right from childhood, the intelligence and character to easily achieve whatever you try for and you have the unconscious, visceral basis for belief in God.

So being Ruth, she was filling me in on her unique state of grace. Because once she'd accorded me sole legitimate authority over her public reputation, mine was the only last judgment that really counted.

Philadelphia gives bad Christmas these days; it's just a half-hearted imitation of what was once truly both magical and festive. Now it's a lot like those deadly nostalgic rituals families insist on even when they're reduced to a few doddering remainders who probably couldn't stand each other to begin with. If you're officially a good person you can't avoid the command to rejoice.

But why try, if your purpose is to reinvest the old naïve celebration, cutting through Macy's main floor with its dimly lit rococo brass and marble excess and the scents of cologne and leather. A feminine quest, with the seeker inexorably drawn to our one legitimate downtown department store, its extravagant displays and luxurious visions of an ideal future. With above you the same old adorably quaint lights and fountains playing to children sprawled on the floor by the old Wanamaker's eagle statue, that retail totem long ago captured by the enemy. Lifting your shopping bags past toddlers on laps and more sophisticated children leaning back on their palms obediently imitating awe at the trite images of locomotive and Santa and Christmas trees punctuated by ancient tunes and the truly embarrassing narration of the light and fountain show. Updated recently, I know, but not enough.

Ruth meandered critically through these retail marvels, aping enchantment, graciously scanning the colorful counters, the silks and jewelry cases, the palace ballroom décor, crystal on pink cushioning, oversized red and green wreaths, silver and gold trees. She was honoring her outsider adolescent self, or maybe trying to find her: the young Ruth who absorbed this season with the sharpened appreciation of the excluded, who through this encounter with universal rejoicing first discovered her own value. One holy, exquisite Christmastime in a Center City even then past its time, no longer given to marvelous articulated windows but still a place of unexpected solemnity, pregnant with the potential of the New Year. Catholicism was only a romantic mystery to her then, Christ a great if increasingly urgent possibility, and she had no words, merely the inchoate emotions incident to being just thirteen with your private world in chaos. And then you suddenly discover that you're integral to this extraordinary, eternally unfolding promise, with everywhere songs celebrating your own extraordinary life yet to be.

Given which experience, it naturally becomes your responsibility to explore and maintain the faith, especially when that's exactly the kind of exegesis you love, when you have a real genius for clarifying universals, clearing off the sentimentality and dogmatism and unearthing the simple truths, the useful stuff. "Because I never really understood the sacrificial aspect that everyone is supposed to just accept, the "Christ died for our sins" part. It makes no sense. It's just an excuse, like how they used to try to explain people inventing dragons before they realized it was from finding dinosaur bones."

Settled in another coffee shop but by appointment this time, for a formal colloquy between spiritual heroine and faithful biographer. Only months after our summer encounter and I'd been pulled into her game after all. This was the second of our three interviews; the first and most exhaustive was at PHA - about the station, about her family. For the third we returned to PHA and environs, and she ended it by describing a nonsensical Atlantic City event.

So anyway a couple of years back Ruth, baptized in infancy but thereafter separated from any faith, finally collected the nerve to join her church. But you see this was questionable to begin with or just too late, after so many years devoted to intent contemplation of Christian philosophy guided only by her internal sense of truth. Her instincts had by then led her to construct a fairly baroque, certainly idiosyncratic, and above all highly heretical theological edifice: not today's lazy nonsense of an understanding, all-forgiving deity eschewing both insistence and punishment, although not absolutely not that, either. Ruth embarked on her journey back to the fold weighted down with fatal originality. Blundering in, fully expecting the experts to examine her soul but for some reason unafraid. "I felt God wanted me to return to the Church and obviously He knew what I thought."

She basically she lied.

She rendezvoused with her church-appointed spiritual guide at the double glass doors of the parish elementary school; the Askews had recently and reluctantly abandoned Center City for a commodious, fifties-era fieldstone place in Chestnut Hill. Now as she reached the bottom of the few cement steps a man loomed out of the October dusk, a big, broad man past retirement age wearing a lightweight blue windbreaker, exuding decency, booming affably.

"Hello there!" Patting her back as if this were an accepted form of special attention and Ruth, familiar with the social practices of ward politics, recognized a neighborhood player. His hair was sparse and colorless, his bland features enlarged with age and bonhomie, his bulk comforting.

"I'm Lou." And taking her elbow he guided her into the vestibule, dimmed at evening. Saint Pat's Elementary was a newer building and lacked the anticipated redolence of chalk and disinfectant; designed low to the ground, it was as contemporary and unsubstantial as a small dentist's or Realtor's office in a strip mall, and this impersonal ambience was emphasized by the décor of low, bright blue couches against off-white walls, and beige drapes backed by artificial plants. It was so unremarkable it felt defensive, like someone was running a scam or there was anyway something modestly disreputable going on.

"Foll-ee me, my dear." And Lou directed her through the neutral lobby and into a corridor bearing evidence of the structure's purpose: Halloween themed crayon drawings taped just below eye level down the hall, doors with glass on top giving onto shadowed rows of tiny desks. They traveled a fairly convoluted trail along dim, tiled hallways, Ruth of course feigning interest in the art works. Eventually descending a flight of metal stairs to an over-heated basement and almost immediately turning into a brightly lit room.

An aggressively welcoming space, casually furnished with deep armchairs and a visibly luxurious old sofa upholstered in some durable beige plush material. There was a tiny kitchen area with a microwave and an apartment-sized refrigerator right inside the door. A small round table held a coffee maker, paper plates and cups, and an open tin of Danish butter cookies. A half dozen people were sitting around, some with refreshments, most openly nervous.

Ruth assessed the group and settled herself on the sofa next to a lovely young Hispanic girl with a supermodel smile, clad for her introduction to the faith in a tight, low-cut knit top, an equally snug black skirt, and plentiful make-up, her mass of gleaming sable hair reaching to her tiny waist. "I'm Angie." And she lightly touched the thigh of the young man on her other side. "This is Peter." Then indicating the nearer armchair: "And that's Loretta."

"Loretta Frank." This was a decidedly more mature young woman, maybe in her early thirties, visible years deeply etched around her mouth and lurking in her eyes. Rising, she shook hands with a nice grip and an inappropriately meaningful expression, as if something of great moment had just passed between them. Loretta was fully as tall and sturdy as Ruth, with light brown hair in a flattering pixie cut and dark-lashed hazel eyes; she was dressed in a pearl sweater, good wool pants, and polished loafers. Sitting again, her shoes inadvertently brushed Ruth's booted feet; both women hastily withdrew their extremities.

"Evening." That from Peter, wedged down in the soft depths of the sofa. He looked like an habitually courteous young man, not that you can really tell, but he was neat and unremarkable in his shirt and slacks and unbuttoned cardigan. He had a frame that seemed a bit too fragile, sweetly affectionate features, and an overall attitude that struck Ruth as inappropriately trusting, almost to that disquieting degree where you have to be careful to maintain your distance.

Three more people sat around the tiny kitchen table: a thin, jittery blond in her thirties, an Asian woman of about the same age in a flowered cotton housedress, and an older woman of the determinedly nice breed in a peach blazer. Ruth rose, collected herself a Styrofoam cup of instant coffee doctored with enough chemicals to make it passably drinkable, considered the cookie tin but bypassed it for appearances' sake, and settled back into the soft embrace of the sofa with an inadvertent sigh of general relief. Lou saw everyone settled, then positioned himself in a plain wood chair next to the kindly peach woman and looped a heavy arm over her shoulders. "This is Betty; her job is to keep me in line and make sure I get it right. She's been working at that job for forty-two years, with what success you'll be able to judge for yourselves the next few months."

Only months then, not years - reassuring to Ruth, the religious secret agent.

"Well." Lou put his hands flat on the table. "Think it's time to talk about God?" That was Betty's cue to assume command. She said, "Let's all introduce ourselves, and each please explain why you made the decision to come tonight."

Angie was engaged and really wanted to be married in Saint Pat's. "I've seen a few weddings in this church and it's the most elegant setting you can imagine

259

when it's all decorated." Peter was fulfilling a promise to his new Catholic fiancée and future stepson, so he wasn't Angie's intended. Loretta was a serial seeker: Eternal Word television, serious Buddhism, a dalliance with Judaism – nothing seemed to suit her soul. The high-strung blond woman was repaying a secret debt to God but declined to go into particulars.

Their accepting eyes turning to Ruth, really interested to learn about this celebrity. "I've studied religion and specifically Catholicism in some depth. Religion matters to me, I take it seriously, it's the most important thing in my life, and I've come to realize that the Church has consistently anticipated my own discoveries about God. I feel now as though I can maintain my faith through those times when I don't agree with the Church."

"Well said, young lady." Lou nodded gravely while examining his own clasped hands. "That's exactly what faith means." And Ruth sank back into the sofa cushions with a surreptitious little glance at Loretta and gulped sweet coffee as a kind of reward. Truth can be so useful.

This isn't my interpretation, obviously, but Ruth's own retelling that Black Friday, reflecting on her experience. "I think I'm a pretty good interpreter of Church policy; I see layers of meaning behind strictures that, taken on their face, seem archaic or legalistic. You have to understand the Church as the literal body of Christ, organic and evolving. Maybe sometimes it's not ready to accept change because the old ways have something to finish, but that's why there's a process of absolution or reconciliation: in order to give everyone time to catch up."

They toured Saint Pat's to establish familiarity, a devout little clutch staring up into the usual shadowy, vaulted interior, running their appreciative hands along the polished pews, examining the amateurish plaster plaques depicting the stations of the cross and the unremarkable stained glass windows displaying, in that light, the dark purples and greens of bruising. Lou opened a closet to show them the huge plastic bags of communion wafers, a thousand little Styrofoam discs, and took them into the vestry to explain the ordered rows of vestments, specific costumes for each phase of the calendar.

Back at the main church they deposed themselves on both sides of the central aisle, Lou facing them from further towards the alter, his meaty hands on the pews to either side. "When we use the term "ritual" we're saying that everything that happens in the church has a very particular meaning and history. It's being done to remind us of what we believe and to reinforce us in our everyday faith. When we say the *Apostle's Creed* we're stating what, as Catholics, we affirm. When we pray the *Glory be to the Father* we're saying that the Father, Son, and Holy Ghost are one God. In this church we believe that Mary, Jesus' mother, was herself born free from corruption. We believe in the resurrection of Jesus Christ. As devout Catholics we believe that the consecrated Host is the physical body of Christ."

He leaned his backside against a pew while they reveled in the mysterious dust motes and evocative trace of incense, the tired gentility of the rose velvet kneelers and dark patterned carpet, the golden wood and racks of misaligned missals and hymnals.

"These beliefs are mysteries; they are revealed to us, but they're never explained to us. This is because God wants us to approach Him only through our faith."

261

Ruth shifted, although not merely at the tyranny; she could never tolerate a mystery. "I tend to think of the Holy Spirit as a kind of universal synchronicity. And grace as the measure of how our life circumstances match reality, what we want versus what's possible."

Later on everything got substantially more intense, in fact almost too intimate for Ruth, who felt the drama artificial, a travesty of passion. Was authentic fervor even possible under those circumstances, God lurking so close, or only some desperate performance designed to placate the hovering deity?

Now they were required to utilize their familiar basement haven as a confessional, to share deeply. This brought silence and tilted heads poised to jump or swiftly evade, everyone rehearsing their portion. Angie looked downright terrified; Peter sat up very straight and polite in his armchair, listening with widened eyes, while Betty nodded serious encouragement.

Loretta spoke up impulsively, wanting it over, her eyes half closed and her hands on both chair arms to hold herself up. "I'm a cliché: no particular father, mother with a series of abusive boyfriends. When I was fourteen I took off with this guy; he did heroin so I did too. He hit me, we broke up, and for a long time I did nothing but try to survive, which means exactly what you think."

And she grimaced in a studied, wry manner. "Well, anyway, I was lucky: I began to have visions." Ruth was entirely drowning in envy. "So I started to read, which I'd avoided up till then." She used both palms to smooth down her boyish hair. "This whole experience was terrifying; I think it changed me physically, like altered my brain chemistry. I literally became someone else." She paused a moment on this pronouncement. "My family didn't have any idea of religion, so I started doing research, I guess. Something about Jesus always attracted me, and when I turned to Christianity and I felt this sense of welcome. That's the best way I can describe it."

A respectful silence.

"I don't actually relate to Jesus." Ruth offered this conversationally, as if it didn't much matter. "Or I only relate to the idea of Him, but not the meek Jesus but the one who brings a sword. Not as Jesus, either, but as the Christ. The whole sickly- sweet Jesus embarrasses me; and then so many of the people who love that image are plain unintelligent about it, and I'm a social coward." She sat forward and clasped her hands in front of her knees. "That kind of Christianity is too nice, and I'm not nice. I prefer God the Father, the remote, severe God. That's how I feel, anyway." Cautiously looking round for their reaction. (Anyway, that's what she claims she said, but I wonder; Ruth really is a social coward and that was awfully brave and concise.) The class twitched and wondered how best to respond, but

Lou merely nodded emphatically. "We all come to Him in our own way. He'll take it from there."

Lily, the agitated blond, made her confession at the following session, sitting stiffly from beside Ruth on the sofa, speaking from within Ruth's protection you might say, her pale hair making a sharp angle against her cheeks, her expression brittle but resolved. "You should know I didn't come here for what you'd call religious reasons like the rest of you. I'm not convinced of any of this." This delivered in a rapid alto, practically a low hum. "My daughter got a really bad cancer; she was three. I made a promise to God that I'd join the church if He'd help her like she wanted me to help her, but I couldn't. It was almost hopeless, her prognosis, but then out of nowhere, like one morning she was in remission. So I'm keeping my promise." "Oh my goodness," Betty said, seeming neither troubled nor especially surprised. "Well, then we know that God wants you here for His own reasons, and that's all we need to know. And we are so glad that your little girl better and that you are here with us."

Which startled Ruth into viewing ordinary, overweight Betty in the divine light of pure good will made manifest. And there was Peter catching her glance for a moment, so they nodded to each other in mutual understanding. Ruth briefly considered hugging him but didn't.

"But that was a very real moment." Ruth was staring down into the dregs of her coffee, explaining all this to me. "I accept that I'll always disagree with the Church on certain things but it doesn't really matter. It really doesn't, though." That last to my skeptical expression. "If there's one thing I know for an absolute fact, it's that God wants me to think on my own."

"Really. And have you figured out how there's a heaven without time and context? What about ultimate kindness and the victory of virtue?" But she just shrugged, unfazed. "Betty and Lou, they're worth something. You and I both know I just bullshit and wait for the applause."

"You're maybe a little facile."

So now after confirmation she's drifted from the church's more stringent rules and expectations to become a holiday Catholic at best, and she's pretty much lost touch with her classmates. And forget about skipping the

Eucharist because of not having made your confession. And forget about confession.

She was smiling to herself that Christmastime afternoon, a little flushed from all the self-exposure, meanwhile carefully examining the tinsel garlands across the café windows, the pink wreath at the cash register and the cardboard reminders to be joyful. "Another absolutely true thing is Christmas Eve, that universal hushed expectancy. Something important happening."

But despite her defense of Catholicism, by then Ruth was more into New Age stuff, seeking support in the wisdom of the ages, hooked on Internet and magazine horoscopes. When did that start, that digression into sentimental, undemanding spiritualism? I don't know because she was wisely shy about this stuff. I think she just needed specifics, certainty: what would happen, and where and when. I only found out about it at all when I happened to catch her reading this crap on her phone; being a garrulous Gemini, she launched into explanations. "I know it seems crazy but you can't ignore the history or dismiss the coincidences. Only first you have to forget the popular misconceptions, the idea that the stars control us. It's nothing like that. It's that everything is naturally synchronized. I mean, theoretically you could tell the future of the universe from a study of bathroom towels or restaurant menus. The difference is astrology has been charted for millennia; it's an accessible map of the Holy Spirit. It's about grace; it's about moving through time accurately, with wisdom. That's what real miracles are, they're raising your hand and commanding the waters to part exactly when the waters are going to part anyway, except of course they wouldn't unless you were there commanding them, because it's always a hundred percent on each side of every event. That's another thing people don't really get yet, how responsibility isn't divisible and one hundred percent on one side actually means there's also one hundred percent on the other."

Even at work, even though she had sense enough to keep deleting her browsing history, continually drawn to those encouraging website truths straight from the angels and the nurturing universe, the supportive warnings and opportunistic hints delivered on a daily, weekly, monthly basis: Reject negativity, because a positive attitude attracts opportunity. Reject toxic people. You don't exist in order to meet everyone else's needs; your first responsibility is to live your own life. "I know! You get all that vague clichéd crap, too! You just have to learn who's who."

I shrugged, because what else was there to do? "I would argue with you, but just because you're wrong doesn't mean you're not right. Isn't that how it goes?"

She just stared at me like I was the crazy one, and I remembered how she only thought in terms of sin and virtue.

Also she was visiting psychics. "That's an entirely different thing, a talent that has to be developed. Real ones, I mean, not the scam artists." I suppose this went back to that restaurant experience fortuitously whetting an appetite for security and release from anxiety. Suddenly she noticed that real answers were available everywhere, at least according to all those crude pavement signboards on side streets with arrows pointing up narrow flights of stairs. "Of course these women are basically phonies, but even so they have this shrewdness that comes from practice, this developed intuition." When succumbing, she would casually check for lurking witnesses, then rapidly climb another of those steep staircases while assuming an exaggerated air of impulsive fun. On into some tiny, dim apartment containing a dark-skinned young woman and a quiet baby, several scuttling cats, and too much cheap, flashy furniture: red plush and small mirrors, exotic occult figures and mysterious framed images. Tarot or palm? Full deck or partial?

"You're a good person. You will live a long life. You have an enemy who is jealous of you, a woman with short dark hair? You're worried about an older woman, a relative perhaps? No, no, you don't have to worry about your job. You are very intelligent and you will always make a good living. Don't be afraid of this, of your own success! But your heart! So much negativity!" "They're all exactly the same," Ruth said. "I mean, to the letter! It's like they're members of some secret sisterhood because they all deliver this identical crap." But like Diogenes she kept seeking that one honest psychic. "And the idea of dead relatives hovering around when you're in the bathroom – talk about creepy!

And again: "It makes my skin crawl, my dead relatives knowing what I really think, watching what I do. I don't want them anywhere near me."

"What about the telephone ones?"

"Oh, like I would trust them! That's just pouring money away! And then after a while they cut you off. Or that's what the Internet articles say. They don't want trouble. You can tell it's just a business, like any call center." Hands waving. "Here's the thing. I turn to these people because I don't have enough faith. I've never had real faith, not the kind that jumps into the future and creates the world. But that's what truly living is, that kind of dumb faith."

But it was Christmas, fraught with background music from decades and even centuries ago, and she was aching to explain another momentous adolescent insight, to share yet another glorious if burdensome secret.

"I realized that the real reason for Christ's death was to protect the people, the Jewish community and by extension the community of mankind. Think about it: crucifying Him was the right sin, so Christ returned from the dead to demonstrate His forgiveness. That's the real meaning of redemption. It meant we could evolve without the increasingly unbearable weight of original sin, all that agony piling on us more and more. It's the only way it makes sense." All this pronounced with that familiar air of patronizing patience and restrained glee.

Waltzing through Christmas in time to her internal orchestra, celestial light breaking with a stupendous fanfare from gleaming brass trumpets, joyful music descending on the world in great arcs, reverberating to the depths of the earth and sea. And everywhere bright angels standing near to deliver the good news, even in the mean doorways and empty offices and subways tunnels of our gray city.

CHAPTER TWELVE

Out in Lancaster County you get Amish men with beards driving black buggies, retail outlets, mushrooming cookie-cutter townhouse developments, modest theme entertainments, silos on sloppy-looking dairy farms, corn fields, and the usual run of unimpressive strip malls and general highway effluvia. It's unattractive to me because it never coalesces into a conceptual whole but insists on remaining a bunch of scattered ideas trying to attract families desperate for wholesome entertainment. Also it's not a great milieu for driving your moody girlfriend and cranky teenage daughter through a freezing downpour, more sleet than rain, past huddling bovines, the occasional horse kicking up water, and dreary family-style restaurants with bus parking.

We found a parking space at one of those ubiquitous outlet malls and pushed through the downpour towards some trendy clothing emporium. A half a minute crossing the parking lot and I was drenched, the wet seeping into my socks and my fingers were numb inside my gloves. I could tell Sophie was really angry, which is how she reacts to life's aggravations these days: everything's a personal betrayals. Then we were swallowed up inside the welcoming light, surrounded by everything current in the correct colors, at the mercy of the usual blandly intrusive background music. A handful of avid fellow shoppers were rifling through piles of expensive crap.

Crystal scoped out the scene and moved off on her own, and I drifted off a little myself in order to observe my daughter. Her universal snit had been partially eclipsed by greed, but there was enough of it left to keep her occupied. She stalked over to a display case of tiny evening bags, crystal and sequins and exciting promise, and lingered there absorbing it, her eyes glittering but her face carefully neutral.

Crystal reappeared by my side, rather sedate, as if the rain had penetrated her brain and dampened her usual expectant shrewdness. She had a handful of garments on hangers and gestured me towards the fitting rooms, so I nodded and squished over that way and waited too long for her to reappear. When finally she called my attention from a rack of discards I discovered her in a brilliant sapphire silk shift, almost beautiful except for her minor deviations from real perfection and her expression, which was contentious.

"Wonderful. Really." But she tilted her head, questioning me. I noticed Sophie watching us, then heading over.

Crystal turned to examine her reflection. "So you can actually see me?" Her face was pushed forward with a child's defiance. "Because you know how you always say I don't really exist? I wanted to find something really noticeable to make it easy for you."

For a second I wondered if the weather really had pushed her to the brink, but no, she was breaking up with me. "What I said is that's what I admire most about you."

As well she knew. She was standing in front of a wall painted in cream enamel, much smudged and marked, as anomalous and adorable as a princess at a bus stop. Sophie was just behind me; she caught my response and I saw a definite smack of approval in her eyes. Why I adore this kid.

"Well I'm tired of being invisible."

I shrugged, realizing argument was futile. Why further indulge her? But here's the thing: Crystal's instincts were nothing short of prodigious. It took me a few days but finally I realized this was indisputable confirmation of what I myself already vaguely sensed but hadn't dared articulate: a familiar dissatisfaction, a growing restlessness. Or was it more that life was perpetually dissatisfied with me? I was getting myself ready to reorganize my life into God knew what; I was feeling seriously reckless. I was actively looking to find a tall building somewhere in order to jump off and see if I could fly.

So while I was deeply shocked I wasn't really surprised, if you know what I mean. For one thing, I knew I'd exploited and betrayed Crystal's naïve assessment of my local celebrity, and she owed me no loyalty. It was an ingenious strategy, too, because we'd been over it often enough, my absolute rejection of the whole hypocritical mating dance. Play the game if you're playing, don't try to cheat and then act all superior about it. Don't try to pretend you're growing up instead of the exact opposite, fleeing from reality. Not that she meant it anyway, not really.

CHAPTER THIRTEEN

At PHA they awaited the worst with almost dispassionate impatience, but that delicate veneer of neutrality did little to mitigate the visceral shock of the next purge. It was the sheer illogical mendacity that floored you, the lack of any meaning, a chaos before words. Numbness became normal, everyone just floating along in it, observant and even curious but essentially anesthetized.

But Stanley continued to schedule regular airchecks with Ruth, leaning back in his executive chair and staring at his own crossed legs, listening intently and at least pretending to analyze every pause and stutter of her morning program. "This isn't about causing you embarrassment. It's about making you better." But she felt the personal threat, the vines encircling her ankles, felt paralyzed by layers of terror and distrust and accepted that her immediate working environment had degenerated into a pile of viscous shit. Despite his public protestations of innocence Stanley consistently managed to underline her tentative status, letting her see him glance at other options, blandly intimating the unthinkable. And could someone else do better? Someone younger, maybe still provocative but less of a loose cannon? A team player and overall better investment? Were they evaluating potential replacements during those mysterious off-site executive tête-à-têtes, listening to the best of Stanley's selected candidates?

But everything was unaccountable. Suddenly it was not only okay, it was apparently policy to mock Stanley's silly rockets and stars as a naïve failure. Real life was too baffling for soul examinations and positive attitudes. Only the signs themselves remained: maybe no one had the energy to waste, taking them down. Was that a mark against him or was he relieved? Ruth couldn't tell, but Stanley was still with them, at least for the moment.

So the two of them, their heads cordially leaning near from either side of his extravagant desk, replayed her unobtrusively expert formatics, her practiced smooth deliveries, her unflagging if slightly cynical cheer, the call letters and time checks for that listener just tuning in, the heartfelt personal endorsement of a suburban sponsor, her brief but invariably informed comments to Leslie over the news. Now Stanley slyly insulted her by applauding her chemistry with Bob, how that experienced soul reined her in, balancing out her more undisciplined flights with a typically dry comment or affable laughter.

"My job is to go over the top." But for how much longer in this strangely foreign and adversarial situation, reaching out to devoted but ultimately powerless listeners who'd certainly be upset or even momentarily furious at her absence but probably not enough to bother turning the dial.

"You think so?" Turning towards her with bland courtesy, his khakis and logo knit shirt an impeccable armor. "Well, maybe so." Interesting and dreadful that despite all this constant examination of minutia there was never any correction provided, no comment offered except that snide recommendation to rely on Bob. So it was generally a matter of endlessly listening to oneself under his pointed gaze, those eyes of his that never seemed to waver in their ceaseless search for any lapse from perfection.

"How about you? Everything going okay? No problems or concerns? Need anything?" So mildly said, with an ostensibly innocuous expression.

"No, I'm going great."

After one such session, impelled by God knows what devil to respond to the accumulated frustration and fury, Ruth decided to poke her head around the door of Sara's's closet of an office. "Is Jenny available for a minute, or is she too busy for mere peons?" "You know, you really do need to be more careful what you say." Sara delivered this constant admonishment nicely as always, without exceptional interest. "I'm not kidding. You never know who hears you in this place." She was cautiously watering the waxy pink African violet on her filing cabinet, edging the narrow spout of a plastic watering can under its furry leaves. Once seated, she grinned up at Ruth with easy complicity across the photos and paperweights and assorted knick-knacks blanketing her desk and automatically adjusted her designer eyewear. "It isn't professional behavior."

"I don't see why. It's intelligent behavior."

And a few minutes later Ruth was across the hall, venting to a stiff, bemused Jenny with apparent candor. "Because I need to vent!" Waving both hands in aggravation. "I really worry that people here think I've become cynical or just mean. Or else unbearably superior, entitled?" This with a quizzical smile at that perfectly expressionless, ladylike countenance resting thoughtfully against the back of a sofa, nestled in silk cushions patterned with full-blown blossoms, peonies or roses, ladylike and absurd in that official context. "It's because I never judge, you see. I don't think in terms of judgment; I only describe, and that frees me to say what I think."

"I don't think I follow." Jenny reached to take and unwrap a hard candy from a bowl on the coffee table, sounding genuinely intrigued. "I mean that everyone is equally awful so pointing out faults is interesting but not derogatory. Just analysis, not judgment." Biting into her lip, trying to get all her random assumptions into some kind of logical order. There was a framed photograph on the table, a dark man in his sixties, notably handsome in his hiker's outfit, posing in front of a forest waterfall.

"Take Hitler," Ruth continued, and Jenny blinked at her. "We talk about him like he was literally a monster instead of human. We refuse to acknowledge that we're like him, but if we can't then everything's hopeless. I'm not explaining this well." She shrugged in irritation. "The thing is, I recognize all that's shameful in myself; I claim it."

Between them on that boudoir sofa: the awareness of twenty-four recent terminations carried out despite the promises issued from this same ostentatiously comfortable office. Jenny conceding her deep disappointment while surveying them methodically, the full station staff sprawled out before her sitting on other people's desks or leaning against the fabric cubicle walls. "It was the promise we made to ourselves at that time. Unfortunately we weren't able to meet our primary goal."

Well then.

"I knew they'd already decided about me, so why not?" And later to Stanley in front of the observant cubicles: "I admit I'm glad to be spared the cosmic philosophy." "I think that makes sense. We have larger problems to address at the moment, but don't confuse that with the program itself not working."

"I don't exactly agree with that logic." Laughing to the audience.

"Ruth, come with me." And he led her to a storeroom and shut the door on them and he was right there in her face. "Do you even realize how inappropriate and plain weird you are? Half the time I wonder if you're actually crazy and I'm fucking sick of it." He took a breath, shook his head, turned and left her there, shaking.

I encountered both Askews late one Thursday afternoon. I was incautiously heading towards the light from Thom's inner office, hoping to discuss the revised Columbus plan with all those required community guidelines clumsily tacked on, and the probable responses from the mayor and Council. They were both on the couch, slightly apart, obviously embroiled in some personal drama. Ruth was talking, ranting actually, in this low, incessant voice; she glanced up when I came in but continued irregardless, ignoring my presence to the extent she even registered it. "The presumption being that I've failed in my life by not following her miserable advice." Kate, that oblivious matron given to issuing lengthy handwritten missives to her niece, self-laudatory biographical fantasies in her tiny perfect script intended for Ruth's spiritual betterment, so that Ruth might open her heart, forgive her loving family, and find true happiness. Struggling to maintain her version of the past against Ruth's angry corrections.

"And if I say anything about myself, such as where we've been on vacation, or someone famous I've met, then she starts talking really loud right over me. And mysteriously can never remember anything I tell her about myself, or makes it clear she doesn't trust my judgment about money or politics or even movies or restaurants. Just listens and gives me this phony smile and says well, I'll ask Pat or one of the boys."

Thom had a hand on the sofa near to her but not touching. He caught my eye for a second and turned away.

"Sitting there with this expression like the fucking Virgin Mary saying how she's so proud of my accomplishments when none of them ever really gave a damn about me and all anyone ever did was look the other way. They gave me infinitely more to overcome by making everything unanimous, that's what. Sitting on her ass and criticizing my dad who at least had a life. How dare she? Passive aggressive emotional cripple."

I looked a question at Thom but he was still sitting back, paying judicious attention to all these details.

"If she does care about me, I've never seen any evidence of it. I don't think she realizes I exist except how it affects her. If I died, she'd feel really sorry for what she had to go through." That infinite, mutual resentment Ruth was somehow unable to express to Kate now her aunt was too inclined to overestimate her own resiliency when taking another strategic fall, although not old at all by modern standards but only in her late fifties. Then when the two were together all the rage evaporated, vanishing as if unimportant or even unjustified.

Thom responded with a kind of compassionate irritation. "You know this is obsessive; you're literally going to make yourself sick."

I visualized the Kate Ruth had described to me, watchful and given to ladylike pastels, sitting quietly apart from a husband increasingly sarcastic and judgmental, tormented by his disease. Smiling nicely with her hands folded over each other in her lap, profoundly insulting her niece from the heights of sentimental self-congratulation.

"So it's okay that she's still patronizing me and treating me like shit, like it's okay to take her resentment out on me? And then sometimes, I swear she looks at me with this cold look, like underneath it all she hates me."

But I knew this was merely sporadic; aunt and niece would be fine again soon. Meanwhile it was impossible for me to say anything or leave. Thom had one foot up on his other leg and was absently brushing at his shoe, meanwhile looking at Ruth in this very sharp manner, like he was trying to solve a difficult equation. I'm sure he was aware of my discomfort. "And now all this nonsense to make me crazy." They were turning against each other, Pat and Kate. Sick suspicion taking firm root because he was pushing her to move to a senior living community and she didn't want to be told what to eat and have to listen to old ladies talking about their health or see vacant, drooling old men all day although there she was on the phone to Ruth at every new crisis, Pat back in rehab: "I deserve some time to myself, don't I?" Then he insisted she go sort out her own family documents and photos and what business was it of his if she kept her private things, her precious context? Why couldn't he leave her in peace instead of always trying to control everybody? It wasn't his decision except they both knew it was. They'd had a physical fight! Kate threw rolls of toilet paper at him! Now she was dangerously depressed, or so Pat reported with kindly self-importance on Ruth's voicemail. It was hilarious and tragic but what was Ruth supposed to do?

Thom said, "She isn't going to change at this point, is she?" Looking at me as he put the question, and finally Ruth acknowledged me too.

She rose, and we all automatically got into our coats and got ourselves out onto Chestnut Street, relishing the cold air. "It makes me furious, the way she never has to acknowledge how she's treated me. How they've all treated me. Like an illegitimate, deformed fetus." A final great epiphany as unburdened to me: "I understood by the time I was nineteen, I think, and then everything changed for me. It wasn't that I practiced meditation, it was much more casual, but I had to fight through to the answers." In her bedroom with the twin bed and sheer white curtains and windows giving onto the back drive.

There on consecutive nights sweating over urgent, slippery concepts until ultimately grasping a satisfying solution whole from the living air. "I knew I'd had this experience, that's all. It was sort of pink, tinged with pink. Everything crystallized; and it was so childishly obvious it was almost silly." Ruth folded into a chair by a student desk in a rowhouse in South Philly, neighbors' cars and voices in the drive outside and her radio playing.

We were walking along South Street when she confided this, a vicious wind throwing stinging sleet pellets at us, Ruth wrapped inside this huge olive-drab down coat. This was our third and final real interview; she'd been catching me up on work and Stanley, meanwhile dawdling along despite the cold, feigning interest in the tattoo parlors and the boutiques stocked with cheap exotic crap and hipster apparel. We had no excuse for being there except we were bored with her office.

"I realized that because our thoughts are identical with our physical brains, we're completely integrated with the material world. Biologically we desire to be exactly what we are and what we will be. Only we need to be ignorant of that truth to make it work."

Of course she knew it was outrageous; a sideways glance admitted as much, and then she was walking a little ahead of me. An apotheosis of sorts: getting that out, adding it to our narrative. I admired the logic: obviously you can't fully experience terror and agony and despair if you know you yourself created the situation. No railing against God then, no pity for the slaughtered millions. And what of the eternal soul? "It's determinism, but we remain entirely in control because like everything else it's always one hundred percent on both sides." This while looking off to some romantic distance above the blank Philadelphia skyline, eyes shining with certainty and a little trepidation.

"Sometimes I look away from people on the street, but not because they're ugly or disabled or anything, but because I'm embarrassed for them. It's about absolute respect for every person's ultimate decision to be themselves."

With a noticeable halt and correction, and I bet you a month's salary she meant to say "black" or possibly "homeless" instead of "ugly" or "disabled." Knowing who she came from and how deep that shit runs.

"Anyway the important thing about total physical responsibility is that it really doesn't change anything. Not when you actually think it through." Early in the new year Stanley asked her to compose a formal call policy, asked her to discuss the recall contest yet again, asked that she make notes with Leslie regarding the newsbreaks each morning immediately after the show and email them to him for consideration during their next meeting. All this although her numbers remained strong while the rest of the day trended marginally downwards, including the intimate syndicated show running evenings. He mildly objected to her liner readings, as if trite advertising copy could be materially empowered by sheer volume, as if her listeners would abandon their trust just because her pitch lacked resonance. "We talked before about enthusiasm. I asked you to make it bigger." Not said critically, but more as an observation. Also untrue, at least so far as her excellent memory served.

"Bigger than that? Okay, I'll try." Intimating her contained, incredulous laughter. And in response, Ruth widely flaunted this ability to excel while putting in as little actual effort as possible. "Believe me, I know this job is a sinecure! I know how lucky I am!" she gloated to the receptionist, a nice motherly type who smiled back without comment.

So Ruth filled her superfluous office hours checking out horoscopes, comparing forecasts about eclipses and conjunctions between outer planets and other celestial events, double-checking all communications if Mercury was retrograde, pinning fresh hope to each new moon while respecting the dictates of stern Saturn and welcoming the beneficence of smiling Jupiter. "You see they all agree on the main points, so even taking my enormous gullibility into account there's obviously an underlying validity."

And frequently on those sites that identical cruel reiteration: we all choose our own lives before we're born. Ruth found that sentimental, childish notion hilarious but indicative, too. "You see how that basic truth keeps resurfacing."

Then one morning her ubiquitous yellow legal pad was missing from its place beside her keyboard, and that initiated a frantic search that eventually led in unacknowledged certainty to Stanley's office. And remarkably he was already in at that early hour, his door wide, her pad clearly visible on his otherwise empty desk. She entered on a brief knock and indicated her property. "Did you need to see something in particular?"

"I walked over to see you and found this left out on your desk. I think we've been clear about company policy on leaving documents exposed like this."

Okay, maybe that really was the new protocol for the office at large, but it was never anyone's practice. "It's just my own notes." That was stupid of her; he pulled out the office memos she'd stuck between the pages and spread them out on his desk, one by one.

Naturally she left the same pad out again, if only over her lunch break. That time Bob came in from his own nearby cubicle. "He came by twice. First was before you left; he caught me staring and stopped by my desk, said he wanted to sneak a chocolate." There was a crystal bowl of those miniature Hershey bars on another desk in Ruth's shared office. "Then again while you were out, same reason." The Case of the Coveted Candy.

That time she found Stanley in Jenny's office, the two of them seated behind the coffee table contemplating the damning evidence. Catching sight of her in the doorway, Jenny said, "Ruth, come take this." She held out the pad, not rising. Then as Ruth lingered, waiting for their next move. "No, we'll talk about it later."

"It's the blatancy of it. The open evil. I truly don't understand how people explain that kind of behavior to themselves."

Ultimately she was called to a formal conference in Stanley's office, Jenny and Valerie Zhang in chairs pulled up to his desk, signifying a second and final written warning, the three of them reading out unlikely expectations and deadlines. "I asked you to create a caller report and bring it to me this morning, which you failed to do." Stanley read that from his own notes.

"Actually we already have that report; I email it to you each week. But I sent you an additional copy this morning since you requested it."

"That doesn't matter. I asked you to bring it to me yourself." Shifting his thin frame, looking at Valerie. "We also have the issue of the amount of time off you've taken this past year."

"No, I still have loads of PTO left."

He handed her his list of corrective measures and a pen for her signature. "That doesn't matter."

CHAPTER FOURTEEN

The stupid young woman was actually arguing with Ruth, her paying customer, as if her tawdry predictions were God's own truth instead of the usual practiced crap. And this attitude from a garish, immature immigrant in a closet of a storefront business virtually open to the frigid Atlantic City boardwalk. As if the crescent moons decorating the chalk-pink walls, the luminescent white hand outlined on the purple signboard represented some actual body of arcane wisdom and she were a learned disciple who commanded powerful prophetic forces. Basically, as if her customer was a complete idiot.

Ruth huddled in a tiny gilt chair beside an equally miniscule table, bending in against the miserable chill and critically scrutinizing the cards as they were revealed in turn, familiar Rider-Waite designs rapidly turned into significance by slender dark-skinned fingers. Flashing out from beneath ornate gold-toned rings weighted with semiprecious stones in pink and lavender and milky opal. The entire array of gems, cards, and the woman's half-hearted costume, peacock and ruby gauze under an unbuttoned navy wool coat, faded into an old-fashioned exotic postcard in the gloom of the overcast day and the scant lighting. The reader's dark hair was pushed back from

284

a narrow face; she had shrewd brown eyes thickly circled in brown pencil and spoke with an assured East Asian cadence.

"You must listen. You know you can be a very difficult woman sometimes." Neutralizing this with a slight grin.

It hadn't started out as overtly adversarial, just as more of the same, with an amateur signboard beckoning from without and the occupant offering a restrained welcome, courteous but with that delicious hint of exclusivity, as if she wasn't the kind to perform for just anybody. The real prices were naturally much higher than those advertised outside, at least if you wanted anything substantial, and then came the introductory rigmarole, the choice of deck and secret wish, the shuffle and cut. And all this time, that sharp professional assessment.

Ruth tolerated the initial nonsense, impatient but not seriously irritated by the tired ceremony. "I see you are a good person. You are going to have a long life with no big sickness. I see that you've had to overcome a great deal in your life. There was a lot of sadness in your early life." All the usual, and those clever eyes constantly searching Ruth's carefully blank expression, her deliberately unrevealing clothing and accessories, the restrained jewelry and nice but hardly exclusive handbag.

So fine, they were done with the preliminary moves. Ruth straightened and fingered the plain silver chain at her neckline. She was wearing a fairly inexpensive black cashmere sweater and plain blue jeans under that dingy down coat, and felt confident of presenting an overall uninteresting appearance, what with her fair hair dangling in damp strings, her cheeks splotched with red from the cold and rain, and her distinctly moist nose.

"Your heart is not happy. There's an imbalance. Your chakras are out of balance." One long finger pointed out the Queen of Swords simpering on her throne against a pale blue sky, except the card was reversed, the weapon pointing down from the cottony clouds to penetrate the heavens. Not a very good position for that particular card. "This has to do with how you open yourself up to love. You have a restlessness and a deep dissatisfaction. This is because your heart is alone, maybe?" This inquiry with what her customer viewed as an offensively impertinent sideways glance, any spiritual compassion already moderating into a sales device. Ruth sighed inwardly.

"My heart is fine. I'm actually only interested in my career right now; that's why I came in. My job is definitely not fine."

This was received with increased sternness, and an imitation of great wisdom blatant enough to be amusing if it weren't for the sheer duplicity, the heartless avarice. "No, no, your career is fine. You are always safe and you will always make enough, in this you are very fortunate, you will never have to worry about this part of your life." The smarmy condescension exacerbating Ruth's frustration.

"Trust me, I have to worry. And I don't know why I can't get an answer to one simple question, the thing uppermost in my mind but apparently, I'm not supposed to be worried about it, it doesn't exist. The whole universe insists I can't see what's happening in my own life."

"Because this darkness in your aura is making you unhappy and you don't see so clearly. All your problems are to do with your intimate relations, with your family, with the people who are next to you."

Ruth was shaking her head, not merely impervious to such suggestions but now perfectly furious. "I have no family. My family is all dead." Not even troubling to conceal her wedding band.

This tantrum, too, was ignored. "But I see you were meant to marry and have children, more than one. I see an older woman, maybe one with bad health? No? I see this, for some reason. Maybe not here in the body anymore, but family doesn't go away just like that, poof! They stay with us in spirit." She underlined this with a neat flap of one hypnotic, dominating hand. "This imbalance, this is a fact and you will stay dissatisfied unless you heal this. I don't understand." Looking up comically. "Why don't you want help? Don't you want to be happy?" And she shrugged her narrow shoulders.

"Well, I don't have children. Why do you people keep saying that, like I got careless and missed out on my own destiny? That's stupid. And the fact is I believe dissatisfaction to be the highest state of being. You could say it's my religion. Life is dissatisfaction. God is dissatisfaction. Life is an aberration by definition, so trying to live in peace and balance means running away from life."

Still the girl remained utterly unfazed, no piece of Ruth's rant remotely denting her professional confidence. "So then why are you here?" Clear mockery now, although she must have realized she was forfeiting any tip. "Look at these." And she gestured at a narrow credenza in the corner behind her where a bronze goddess figurine, surrounded by an array of dull crystals, simpered from atop a light blue doily. "These are special crystals for healing. You need a special prayer and a crystal to lift this darkness from around you."

"No thanks." Ruth, having heard this spiel before, put down two twenties and a ten and walked out into what was by then merely a drizzle, momentarily grateful for the drops against her cheeks.

It had to be Atlantic City despite the seasonal closings, not Harrah's or Parx or anywhere else nearer home because the ritual, the buildup, was a necessary part of the process. Part of how you invoked the truth. The boards were slippery beneath her boots, but despite the cold, sloppy weather they hadn't been totally abandoned by the usual winter crowd, overweight and ill dressed and fairly desperate, or else merely elderly and of modest means and expectations. People who came down almost every day in their natty warm-up suits or sporty blazers, women with multiple tote bags, men in baseball caps. Gulls were everywhere, one instant mere black or gray silhouettes vanishing into the low clouds and the next unexpectedly close, emitting raucous screams from open yellow beaks, hovering competitively for a potential meal or squabbling meanly over scraps down on the rain-pocked sand while the waves came boiling in, sliding over the sand like hissing glass. Nevertheless, some stalwarts, bored or romantic, bent under the wind down at the shoreline or sat hunched into sweatshirts and blankets atop the litter of seaweed and the sharp shards of clam and mussel shells. Further out fat gray humps heaved into the low heavens as if in continual discomfort, and close above them, separated by one band of unlikely light, a wooly blanket of cloud moved north urgently, practically fleeing.

Ruth covered ground with her characteristic easy strides, observing herself in her mind's eye, tall and slim and defiant, sometimes glimpsing herself in storefronts where she seemed amorphous and puzzled, a mildly inappropriate figure examining closed-up souvenir shops and T-shirt emporiums and eateries and arcades and costume jewelers. On past Fralinger's, its windows piled with boxes of salt-water taffy and ribboned bags of macaroons, past the bright-painted Western-themed façade of Bally's Wild West. Past the descent to a through street leading back to the outlets and the new Convention Center before it lost itself in the slums that comprised the genuine Atlantic City beyond this shallow, unconvincing stage set by the sea.

She'd been swinging her arms while walking and her fingers were numb from the cold. She flexed them, then pulled down her glove to check her watch, its face misty beneath the crystal. Just past noon. And then, maybe pretending the hour carried some significance, she abruptly reversed direction, resuming her spuriously purposeful march but now heading northward, back past the familiar landmarks, past the discouraged scattering of rattling jitneys and pleading rickshaw pullers and the couples clinging to each other for shelter. Past Resorts and the garish turrets and arches and general gilded excess of the Taj Mahal, past the old Steel Pier, a legend reduced to whirling carnival attractions and dispirited displays of stuffed animal prizes, deserted then anyway. Continuing north past the modest city museum and a tiny art gallery.

The clouds were breaking apart, allowing vagrant patches of sunlight to warm her back. The beaches this far up, posted for lack of lifeguards, were mounded with uneven dunes and resembled deserted construction sites. She passed a row of small private homes, a few fastidiously kept up and jauntily painted in Caribbean blues and greens and yellows but others in between them unabashedly deteriorating. That stretch gave way to newer condominiums, unimaginative edifices of terraced concrete, until eventually the sad casino city fell behind and the boardwalk gradually rose higher above the water, transforming itself into a bridge over a bottle-green ocean.

Still moving briskly, Ruth made her way through a very different population, largely although not exclusively African- American: lone bulky men in sporting vests or content families out fishing despite the weather surrounded by the appropriate webbed lawn chairs and umbrellas and coolers, an anomalous enough scene in the January gray. The sun was managing to maintain a thin, filmy presence, occasionally brilliant where it touched the wet boards or gently breaking waves. Children leaned against the rail and spoke confidingly to each other while their parents tended to business, looking after their lines, searching their coolers.

Ruth checked her watch once again to find she'd been walking for over an hour; she stood still, hands thrust deep into her coat pockets, earning stares from the others out that way. Right there internally reiterating her simple, perfectly reasonable request of God, specifying yet again exactly the kind of clear answer she expected, an answer without any preposterous uninvited advice or mean Delphic ambiguity. So, she was actually going to do this. Reversing direction, a second time, this crazy woman striding determinedly nowhere, she started back energetically enough but observant now, feeling out the atmosphere, not exactly thinking except to appreciate the faint sunshine and tolerable wind. Passing by the same fishing families and unkempt hazardous beaches and recent construction, past the querulous gulls and the few tiny scudding sailboats cutting the horizon.

Once back at the boardwalk proper she slowed and commenced a fresh search. So many of these places were shut for the winter months. And then it was difficult to remember who you'd been to before, even recently, because the women were as weirdly identical as their storefronts, they all had the same middle-Eastern complexions and hand-painted windows and pseudo-spiritual knick-knacks and practically the same names. A better alternative was to peer up the short cross streets, back towards the decaying municipality behind the tourist facade. And there protruding from a doorway halfway down one such street, across from a massive casino parking garage and next to a tiny Mexican restaurant, stood another of those hand-painted sidewalk boards advertising "Tina – Special Ten Dollars" with the outline of a palm in bright purple and the familiar list of prices: full deck, partial, palm, or crystal ball.

Ruth answered this shoddy appeal with her practiced pantomime, a woman struck by a sudden novel whim. She pushed through a heavy glass door crisscrossed with a string of jingle bells; their noise effectively covered her automatic self- deprecating laugh.

The expected cramped space, crammed with white resin patio furniture, dominated by a middle-aged, exceptionally stout woman with the usual dusky skin, wearing a pleated gauze skirt that spilled over her knees in a river of rich claret. A central round table, draped with a cloth of gold, bore a pedestal in the shape of a woman's hand, the tapered bronze fingers caressing a cloudy glass globe, the object surprisingly small, about the size of a baseball.

"You like a reading?"

"Sure." Ruth said, playfully humoring this person, bent on indulging in a mild adventure. Together they scrutinized the posted prices. "Let's try the full deck." Full deck was fifty dollars here, too.

"Full deck, okay." The psychic, presumably Tina, extracted the deck from somewhere on her person; the cards were edged in gold and well worn, soft to Ruth's hand as she obediently shuffled and cut them into three somehow inadequate piles.

"Think of one thing you wish for."

Complying, Ruth envisioned her wish and demand as one with an excited intensity, as if truly poised on the brink of the unfathomable. That familiar flick of the cards, intricate ancient images unveiling their symbolic messages. "I see you are a good person."

"You bet."

The important thing was not to succumb to frustration, not to let her justified irritation obstruct that precious answer.

"You're going to live a long life. No big health troubles." Flip, tap. "You've had sadness recently about an older person, a relative maybe? You are very intelligent. You should work with children; this is what you were meant to do with your life, you know this?" Looking up at her client with approval, one woman to another.

Betray nothing.

The cards expertly overlapping into a crescent; a full deck reading was no simple Celtic cross but a generous peacock display with every card in the deck claiming a position, and that meant you could never interpret the spread for yourself. But probably there wasn't any meaning, probably it was all guessing and intuition with the cards just a prop, handy to point to and make it all your client's fault, claim professional distance. Heavy black eyes rose from the reading, prominent and shrewd. "You have a darkness around you, a negative aspect. You know this? This is a very strong cloud, like a weight holding you down to something from a long time ago, in your family maybe?" A swift gaze for any reaction, searching Ruth's inexpressive countenance. "Your chakas are ourof balance. I think this is maybe why you came to see me?"

"Well, I've been worried about my job. That's what I was thinking about. I want to know whether I should just leave and avoid being fired, because otherwise I'm going to be terminated, or if I should stay because I'm in the right, because it's not fair. If there will be a miracle, I guess."

"I think you are worrying for nothing. Your career looks good; you have no real difficulties in this area." The dark eyes intrusive and insistent, just like all of them. "This is not where your darkness is; this shadow is in your heart, not your wallet." The surprisingly thin lips slipping into that generic smirk.

"I wish that were true. Anyway, tell me something? Is there some kind of school where you all learn this? Or a guild, or what?"

Tina actually did look a little startled at that. "No nono. You must find a teacher and this takes many years to learn. And for you, you have to concentrate on this imbalance, because this is why you think about the wrong problem, you think about anything else in order to run away from the real trouble."

"No sale." Once again Ruth simply dropped the cash, rose, and exited. One hundred bucks, but it was over; there would be no more psychics for her ever. "Come on!" Frustrated, insistent, she almost said it aloud. Well, no more intermediaries; Ruth would directly confront her God. She regained the boardwalk and immediately entered Caesar's, dim inside with one of those bleary, busily patterned hotel carpets, a few lackadaisical couples and the occasional lone addict sparsely populating the gaming tables. As usual, bar the Asian enthusiasts, most of the daytime players were at the slots, most of them past retirement age; they all had that typical glazed and obsessed expression, living automatons. Everything material on the casino floor – clientele, machines, tables, lights – blended into an elusive confusion, virtually disappearing into the garish ambience itself, into the whirling and winking and scrolling of six-figure progressive jackpots and that unmistakable sound of a thousand xylophones striking at random.

Ruth strolled the floor with a critical eye, feeling her way, awaiting enlightenment. Not a theme machine, Star Wars or Vampires or any other idiocy to confuse the issue with contrary concepts, and certainly not a Wheel of Fortune with those dull rows of sevens and bars and cherries that chimed as if they were actually worth something when they weren't. Anyway the money part was irrelevant to her at the moment, and luck not at issue because luck discounts merit or meaning. This was strictly about the clear voice of God.

Although once you really looked at the faces focused on those revolving symbols, saw the concentration directed towards that infinitesimal chance, you realized these players were actually supplicants immersed in desperate prayer, that it was all about personal redemption, about getting one's ultimate due. Especially those with no hope left barring the miraculous. So that was the exciting, deceptive hope blowing through this place, the fantastic idea that here your life could be revalued, justified; you could receive that heavenly confirmation you always knew you deserved, show them all, make it come out right while after all.

Ruth paused near a likely machine of simple celestial signs, positioning herself behind the shoulder of a tiny fragile woman with white poodle curls, and watched as the woman rhythmically depressed the Play Max button. This particular machine took five quarters, so if you failed to bet all five lines you could get cheated out of a jackpot. It was one of the newer machines without so much as a vestigial lever. Ruth lingered, watching carefully as the computerized rolls spun and the illustrated heavens blurred together, the victorious golden stars, full-faced suns, and creamy crescent moons gradually slowing into promising versions of Stanley's silly cartoons. That idea made Ruth smile. The elderly woman at the machine waited with a tiny, patient frown as the lines fell into place one after the other, the last and determinative row with a reluctant mechanical jerk. And there really was a perfect row of three crescent moons shining across the center line. Fake money fell in a lovely electronic cascade of sound, colored lights played while the automatic display racked up a decent few hundred credits. So Ruth searched the vicinity for an identical machine, and right on cue a wizened man in a natty brown jacket – an angel? - rose and courteously held the low back of the swiveling stool steady as she seated herself. Ruth nodded rather numbly and smiled at him.

"Good luck." And he drifted away.

She fed in a twenty out of habit, scanning the prize list. You needed three triple stars for the biggest payout, plus there was a wild card, a comet. Ruth connected to her God again, imploring Him for that honest answer, just the truth, and bet the maximum. One chance, no do-overs. The heavens spun, merging briefly back into the primordial chaos before separating out into identifiable cosmic components, each one sliding obediently into its righteous place in the slots universe.

A full sun and another, and then a third. Of course a third. The blessed shock of an actual, indisputable response. The sun would shine, everything would be okay, and so have faith.

CHAPTER FIFTEEN

Now everything starts to accelerate and then it shatters. I was just through the door of Thom's outer office one evening, barging in as usual because I never learn, when I saw Donny Mealy in with Thom. Saw rather than heard, because no one was speaking, and maybe that was what made me hesitate and then instinctively back up to the threshold. Even with the lights off in the outer office I was visible but even so I froze because the significance in Mealy's posture was unmistakable, a suspicious intensity in his back and shoulders and the tilt of his head, and then because he was just standing there too long.

"It's me giving you advance notice, that's all. Charity starting at home and all." Startling me, Mealy's voice unctuous and bullying but most of all plain silly, almost a little embarrassed.

Thom's response was immediate and thoroughly exasperated. "I have absolutely no idea what it is you're trying to say." I couldn't see him but I could imagine his expression of polite, even amused annoyance, those eyebrows reaching for enlightenment. I stayed there stupidly blocking the exit. Winter dark concealed the freezing city outside, deepening our unconscious intimacy.

"I'm saying sometimes things get exposed unexpectedly so it's not a good idea to be associated with the wrong people even if you're completely innocent." Mealy remained rooted to his spot on the carpet, framed by a far window that faced the identical window of the identical office opposite. The two rooms were connected by a stone frieze of toddlers at play fully visible only from those two private chambers, a fitting metaphor for the City Hall culture of secret immaturity. "Especially when you've got family to protect. And even say you just cut all ties, even then immediate public exposure is going to do some damage."

"Right. And?" Purely furious.

"And again I'm just speculating here but if I'm guessing right, then say Columbus goes ahead, then there's an element of mutual consideration. It's a natural human response. You see what I mean?"

Columbus?

A minor pause. "Not even remotely."

"In that case I recommend you give it some thought." Mealy started towards the outer office and I turned and fled down the corridor more silently and rapidly than I would have guessed possible. Past the open door of Mealy's own offices where a slight blond woman waiting there looked up at me, startled. She had an expensive-looking briefcase on her lap and a confident but impatient expression. I continued at a less remarkable pace, placing her. Yet another seat at Manetti's table, which made three, and her being there was no coincidence. I hurried straight down and out onto Market Street, welcoming the fresh night, excited to fit it together.

So what did we have? That threat had to reference Ruth's involvement in PhillyCares, beyond doubt then a dubious enterprise. But at this point even Thom probably couldn't dampen her passion, what with the organization's vulnerability and her delusional intention to remodel the whole questionable enterprise into some kind of personal throne of glory.

So okay, Manetti probably had something on the charity; that was reasonable, and it didn't bode well for Ruth's humanitarian ambitions.

So Manetti and Mealy – what was the connection there? And Manetti apparently had an interest in seeing Columbus succeed. But - Columbus? And anyway, Columbus was already succeeding, so why risk this stupid crap with Thom, especially when he was known to be in favor of it anyway.

That didn't make any sense.

Thom was back at City Hall agonizing over this shit, no doubt slouched down in his chair, chewing his knuckles. Making light of it even to himself, but thinking, plotting. Facing one of those situations where doing nothing constitutes a dangerous decision in itself, all because he'd married a self-important idiot.

The FBI was investigating something at City Hall but probably that concerned the administration and was otherwise irrelevant.

Okay, let me digress wildly and consider a symbol not only of the city but also of redemption and renewal. I've always cherished this minor obsession with the Ben Franklin Bridge: its lovely blue span, simultaneously familiar and remote, like all bridges promises a clean rebirth in another place, the weight of the past abandoned.

With the American dream, first you have to run away. Sometimes, says the bridge, it's the only way; otherwise you'll never figure it out in time through so much obstruction and confusion. Move through space instead, that's why it's there.

About fifteen years ago they commemorated the seventy- fifth anniversary of the bridge by opening the traffic lanes to pedestrians, the entire length taken over with the expected accoutrements of municipal celebration stretching across the Delaware: podiums and folding chairs, souvenir and refreshment stands, a plethora of honking classic cars, horrible alleged works of art, an Uncle Sam on stilts, face painters and balloon artists and fiddlers and all that sort of tedious diversion. One lane was assigned to buses for shuttling the footsore back to their respective home states. I thought it all generally disappointing, but then my sense of occasion is often out of proportion to reality. When I want to celebrate, I want unrestrained joy, not obligation; when I grieve, I want ashes and wailing, not casseroles and platitudes.

But I took proprietary pride in the size of the crowd flowing in through the various Center City arteries; at Arch Street, everyone was funneled into one pleased, compact mob, pressed through narrow wooden barricades guarded by mounted police to be ultimately released at the foot of the bridge itself. Here you had a choice: take the narrow, elevated pedestrian lane or walk the thronged roadway with the masses? I peered up against the sun at the raised walkway; it seemed to be floating in the empty heavens, terrifyingly remote and perilous, a world away from the familiar bricks and trash of the river slums. I can bear heights but I don't love them; I opted for the crowded street- level alternative.

That walk to New Jersey proved unexpectedly strenuous but I plodded with determination, anticipating a return trip on one of those convenient, air-conditioned shuttle buses. The crowds made it difficult to navigate the limited pedestrian space between all the vans and vendor tables and snaking cables and miscellaneous crap lining the route. I ignored as much of that as possible, instead peering out through the ironwork at the blank sides of old factories and warehouses, smudged rectangles of brown and black, pocked brick walls marked with soiled white. The river, once I was over it, seemed sedate that afternoon but as powerful as ever, its color a silvery-gray that shifted to brown after you stared at it a while. A tubby ferry was chugging its way over to New Jersey for some reason, and another was heading back towards civilization. Of course, there I was marching to Camden myself, trapped by my own stubborn intention. Amiably pondering brilliant, practical old Mr. Franklin himself, how he would have approved lending his moniker to a bridge; likewise, Walt Whitman, whose namesake span I could just make out to the south. Literature and liberty create each other, together they create civilization, and all three are bridges.

That afternoon, standing right over the middle of the Delaware, I felt at home, so although I was only a couple of years out of school, for the first time I seriously wondered if I'd ever find a permanent place anywhere or never reach Ithaca. But wasn't that the point? Wasn't that better? Maybe I needed to stay in sync with the zeitgeist, always speaking from this very minute. Of course, that was romantic youth. What eventually happens is that the everyday hypnotizes me and I forget my rootless nature until something makes me realize I've been carefully undermining my own foundations all along. Forgetting is my version of lying.

This time, Crystal had made me remember. Another of Ruth's dictums: "America is a country founded on an appreciation of human ignorance. That's the real American motto: But I Might Be Wrong. That's our greatness; that's all that really matters. Anyone who's never realized he might be wrong about something fundamental is an idiot. Anyone who's never questioned his own politics shouldn't be allowed to vote."

It was evening, and I was sitting in my cubicle staring at my monitor and thinking about bridges and liberty and ignorance and endless transience, and wondering what I wasn't seeing and what was going to become of me.

The paper was in bankruptcy, hundreds of millions of dollars in debt and about to be auctioned off like some suburban split-level in foreclosure. The city desk was clean to the bone, there was only a faint vestige of the advertising department, and editorial was being serially discarded like used paper towels. There were maybe three hundred employees overall. Plus we were still facing litigation with the union over the staff reductions.

All this was outlined for us late one afternoon with some briefly introduced nonentity from the Newspaper Guild in hilarious required attendance. I was enormously outraged even though I wasn't directly affected at the moment: that was displaced fury at myself for setting off on another wayward escapade down yet another futile career path. You tell yourself you're part of a veritable horde of resentful white collars, part of the great global reorganization, but I can assure you the knowledge does nothing to mitigate the personal humiliation. Not when there were still so many successes everywhere, smug and sleek with their designer briefcases and healthy college funds for their children.

I needed to find a real job.

Carmen was removed to something like New Jersey obituaries, some deliberately offensive assignment; she took the hint without undue fuss and found a position with local public television. Thereafter we lost touch except for one text a month or so later thanking me for an ecard: "Love the sharp funny FYI interviewed real movie star believes in karma profound." She's still there, so I presume she's learned proper respect. It's not like we were ever friends. Once during my performance review she told me, as a compliment: "I don't know why everyone says you're so difficult to work with."

The paper merely intensified its same strategy, still hoping to bring us into the contemporary world by giving priority to the website and featuring even more of the local stuff the reader really desired and less of all that tiresome in-depth national and international news. Our sister tabloid again proved amenable to the program, but it was meeting with increased resistance in my newsroom, our ivy-league editors suffering for their journalistic ideals. You saw it in their posture, in their defiant sincerity. They were so correctly outraged with the whole heedless world. So just like the real nightmare reporters - and we had plenty of those self-destructive clichés, eternally on the scent - I grasped at my little municipal scandals, Manetti and Mealy and Columbus plus whatever was going on over at

PhillyCares and then the FBI investigation, even though I knew it was nothing but the usual kind of malodorous human mulch, what else? Hoping against my own common sense to eke out a measure of acclaim and with it some temporary security, because underneath I was frantic.

About ten days later we had one of those unseasonably temperate March afternoons, and I walked all the way over to Rittenhouse Square, eventually settling on a bench near Walnut Street where I could watch the bustling office drones eating lunch and the idiots already in shorts and the observant, disreputable loiterers and the college kids using their sweatshirts as blankets. Probably everyone meeting some implicit obligation but surely some taking real enjoyment from the ritual. I was betting she would show, and of course she did, right on schedule, that literal fat lady taking her customary position off the path. She was wearing a gleaming red-gold faux fox jacket and her hair, dyed jet black, was piled on top of her head in a fantastical jeweled tower. I was being deliberately ridiculous but I wanted either inspiration or a clear failure – something decisive anyway. I wanted her to sing down the curtain on the whole disjointed, lunatic carnival of color and noise so I wasn't involved anymore. Because think it all through:

Even after a thorough effort I couldn't find anything on PhillyCares financially or even anecdotally. Mimi Norton was Santa Claus. "The story there will break on its own before you can do it," my grumpy bureau chief pointed out succinctly, and I could only nod, knowing he shared my frustration.

I went and talked to the FBI about Mealy and incidentally van Zandt, garnering a perfunctory word of thanks and the distinct impression I was annoying them. No one seemed very concerned about my story blowing an official investigation, which was hardly flattering. (In retrospect, I could have thought that one through better, not that it matters now.)

Mealy's blond office visitor, easily identified from published photos with Manetti, was Frances Wilenski, an attorney in a respectable enough New Jersey firm. So she represented Manetti and she was waiting to see Mealy, so what? She'd seen me too, and must know I'd overheard Mealy with Thom, but again, so what? So Mealy delivered a friendly word of caution to a colleague, rumors picked up somewhere, why bend it all out of context? And Mealy had plenty of disposable funds only not the inexplicable kind, nothing to raise suspicions you didn't already have.

And what in the world could connect Manetti to Columbus? Both the developers and the financial people were utterly reputable; it was ludicrous to imagine them scheming with the mob. Why would they? Now maybe if it were the casino project, but it wasn't.

We conferred that long morning, my bureau chief and our eminently reasonable political editor. We examined what we had and admitted to virtual certainty, substantial ignorance, and utter impotence. All we could do was keep scrounging around and wait.

Meanwhile Ruth was still touting PhillyCares despite whatever Thom shared about his encounter with Mealy, but that didn't surprise me; as Mealy himself explained, leaving would only expedite exposure. Her obstinacy and ego were responsible for her own looming disgrace. She'd look the fool, but Thom would be fine, the city was completely infatuated with him.

So, I sat and studied all the other crazies at the park, conceding that whatever I'd involved myself with would continue to happen until it finished and there was nothing I could do about it anymore.

I was at a dinner that night, a retirement party for a gentlemanly sports columnist at the Pen & Pencil Club. As bars go the place is less than impressive, with a mediocre menu and ditto beer list. It's famous mainly for dishing up crock-pot hotdogs into the early hours, plus it's a convenient venue for the mayor to drop by for scheduled casual intercourse with the chummy relaxed press. There's this frankly irritating ambience, a forced companionability and determined lack of affectation that exemplifies inverted snobbery. To be fair it's the same at MacIlhenny's, my preferred bar, with its mix of downtown residents, history professors, and novelist wannabes, and where even the junkies act ostentatiously at their ease. That night I was floating in a state of grudging acceptance, slightly drunk but not detached, when just before ten o'clock there commenced the disjointed chiming and buzzing of multiple cell phones and the movement of heads and bodies towards the mounted television. This attenuated film critic standing near me told to the room: "Askew died."

CHAPTER SIXTEEN

The story: Alan Johansson, a junior majoring in business management at Temple, and his girlfriend Sheila Urbano, a cosmetologist, spent the early part of that evening just driving around doing nothing in particular until for reasons unknown but without being under the influence of any foreign substance Johansson sent his 2012 Honda Civic screeching straight down Montgomery Avenue towards the heavy Broad Street traffic and flat into Thom, jaywalking the diagonal from the Liacouras Center to his parking garage. Crossing with an uncharacteristic, egregious disregard for his personal safety on a dark street, somehow ignorant of the immediate roar and light. Thom who was always so attentive to his least paper cut and sniffle, moving blindly towards an utterly stupid death.

I admit, at first I didn't know what to think.

I waited at the district police headquarters with everyone else. We were told Johansson had been given a processed cheese sandwich. A lawyer from the suburbs showed up armed with concern and described his client as distraught and confused at being involved in all this when he was just fooling around.

Entirely predictable comments from the mayor, a minor and unexpected insult. More emotion from the expected Councilpersons: David expressing shock and devastation, June looking perplexed. And Margery for once seemed vulnerable, as if she'd just experienced what the world was like for other people. "He was a gentleman in the true sense of the word," she parroted. They were all saying it while they ran those required composite profiles on the news, old clips in disjointed time pulled as background for effusive biographical sketches that captured nothing essential of the man himself, his drive and humor, his intelligence and charm, his neurotic tics and compulsive understated insistence on decency and common sense and his vaunted, controlling ambition.

For me this was another reminder that life is profoundly uninterested in people. What's hilarious is the way everyone manages to forget, how everyone's cowering psyche goes running back into some safe fantasy world and then they pretend they're brave little soldiers carrying on when the truth is they simply can't face an indifferent universe and normal life is pure escapism.

Even I was guilty, because my own first impulse was to try to make sense of it. I entertained some muddled suspicion involving Mealy and Manetti panicking because they'd exposed themselves, deciding to clean it up, something like that, even while I knew that was stupid. Well, there was no video for once, and that was a little odd. But what could it show, anyway, other than lights and movement. It was entirely random, there was no other rational possibility. Except initially I didn't grasp how much of Thom's true legacy, his essential human dignity, depended on that unsettling truth.

Two days later I got some surprising news courtesy of my favorite City Hall source, her voice babbling excitedly in my ear. There'd been some kind of early-hours scuffle outside Thom's offices. Other people repeated the same rumor, adding details about illegal access and then some kind of shoving match out in the corridor. Then the local news was citing an anonymous police source regarding a federal investigation and the bungled removal of listening devices.

I was open-mouthed.

Next morning it went official, a pert FBI spokeswoman issuing a brief confirmation that bugs had indeed been removed from Thom's offices but shutting down insinuations regarding a federal investigation of the deceased. "Councilman Askew was not a target nor was he in any way implicated in any wrongdoing." That was all, with no hint as to whether other Council offices were similarly accessorized. The U.S. attorney's office refused comment. The mayor's office expressed concern and outrage.

This was a Friday. Monday morning I was present for a press conference at the FBI offices on Arch Street presided over by someone in actual authority standing behind a podium in front of a nothingness of beige paneling to explain our city to us.

"We're today announcing the conclusion of a wide-ranging corruption probe targeting the offices of the mayor and directly involving some twenty individuals closely connected to him, although I must strongly emphasize that the mayor himself was not a target. However the investigation was aimed at the dealings of the mayor's personal friend and supporter, attorney Timothy Baylor, and has today resulted in thirty-three counts of fraud and corruption and additional charges against Mr. Baylor and persons involved with him. We are dealing with a systematic pay-to-play practice of extortion under which those hoping to do business with the administration were expected to contribute to organizations controlled by influential friends of this administration." She transitioned into dismissal mode. "We are continuing to unravel what can best be described as a web of corruption connecting various offices in City Hall."

I went back to my office where there was Megan, twirling a little in her chair, frowning to enhance her concentration. "So the wife. Baylor closely connected to Norton and PhillyCares, and the wife all of a sudden so big on them." Of course, she was right.

An accidental convergence of entirely separate but concurrent scandals, Mealy slithering into Thom's office with his pathetic effort to clinch the Columbus deal for God knows what reason, meanwhile broadcasting directly to the FBI. No wonder the feds weren't excited by my precious revelations.

Well, figuring the Councilman to be in full panic mode I headed over to City Hall. We were back to winter temperatures and the general populace was acting like that was an affront, sheltering in their jackets and practically cursing the gray clouds. The steam from the sidewalk grates was suddenly as thick as dragons' breath and you completely vanished walking through it. Everything was emphasized and sharpened, the invigorating city environment infecting the pedestrians with a phantom sense of purpose, then draining the energy right back out of them with myriad minor frustrations.

Mealy's secretary, an attractive Latina in her thirties, reported him in a meeting, but I handed her a murmur and ingratiating grin and barged along in, assuming the assembled company would be eager to talk to me. Then I sat my ass on the arm of the requisite leather sofa, all casual concern.

Automatic raised eyebrows all round, look at the humorously arrogant little insect. One thing I'll say for Mealy, he didn't look ruffled but just as usual, flourishing in hair and body and wallet, lush but never fat and with that constant unctuous sheen. The others I knew by sight but not by name: an overstuffed younger man with an habitual squint standing behind his superior's shoulder, and a thin woman in her thirties at the far end of the couch with that self-righteous minor politico look, wearing a dark pencil skirt and expensive heels.

In contrast to his spartan neighborhood storefront this was a refined interior, with a Queen Anne reproduction desk and tables, and shimmering royal blue draperies pooling onto an antique carpet.

"You want to tell us what this is all about?" Mealy was evincing petulance more than concern, which for some reason I found a little touching.

"Yes, well, I want you to correct me if I'm misinformed here, but I understand the FBI is about to connect Jimmy Manetti, the Columbus project, and this office in an extortion scheme."

Everything in the room abruptly stopped for about one satisfying heartbeat, then smoothly resumed as if oblivious of that little blip.

"You hear from who?" That was the younger guy; Mealy was carefully seating himself behind his elegant desk, loosening his shoulders. "Because I can tell you, they're leading you down an incorrect path. They're making unsubstantiated assumptions and that can be dangerous." The nameless one strode around to stand behind his superior, the better to glare at me. The female remained jammed into her far corner of the couch, mouth shut.

I shrugged.

Mealy spread his hands as if mirroring my wonderment. "So what can I say to you?" That shoulder roll again, as if the expensive blue suit didn't fit so well. "Sure, I know these people, they're my constituents, I meet people here and there in passing, socially. Is that a federal case? I have no business or other kind of connection to Manetti. Same with Columbus; I know the people involved because right now they're important people to this city. We're talking about my district, what do you think? Anyway, what's Manetti to them?"

That was a really good question; I wished I knew the answer. You thought instinctively about unions and construction, but that was crazy. I mean sure the union bosses look out for mob interests, that's only to be expected, but today only the Democrats have any real influence with labor.

I eased myself out, confident Mealy would continue riding those protestations straight to an extended stay up at Allenwood, the favored mountain retreat of Philly officials. Riding my nervous energy, I spent most of that night putting together my first Columbus piece. Most of it was questions and filler, background stuff. The next day my bureau chief, political editor, and I met with the paper's attorney so she could tear it all apart again. But the prophetic substance survived: something's rotten, here are the players, wait and see. My great journalistic achievement.

Obviously too early for backslaps and handshakes, but I accrued a few enjoyable encounters, attempts to stem the text. First came Marlene Angeli, her lithe figure draped in modest charm, exiting the elevators and inquiring for me, scanning the newsroom anxiously. I went to meet her halfway. She was all dressed up in a proper little black suit with a short skirt, subdued make-up, and a strand of pearls; she looked like she was coming in for a job interview.

I pulled the extra chair over to my cubicle and she moved it even closer to mine, possibly distrusting the newsroom's casual assumption of privacy. Looking down and smoothing her skirt but not apologizing for her intrusion.

"Mr. Manos, I'm really worried so please tell me what's going on."

"Well, if you're concerned for your uncle, you probably should be."

"But none of these accusations is true! He told me and I can always tell when he's lying." Vulnerable eyes upward at me, imploring in what would have been a laughable cliché except for the genuine concern compelling the charade, weighing down her troubled little self. A deep frown of anxiety and dark circles under those melting brown eyes. "So who's telling you these things anyway?" she asked. "Because I know it has to be somebody who's against us for their own reasons, so I think I have the right to know. Then maybe I'll tell you some truth about whoever that is." Now that was a pretty businesslike proposition and presented as such, neither a plea nor a demand but offered with a poker player's neutral caution.

"I happened to get advance notice of what everyone will learn soon enough from official sources. That's the truth, Marlene."

She gave me a further shrewd look and either believed me or not, I have no idea.

Next I was virtually ambushed by Mimi Norton; she marched into my building as I was finally heading home, a righteous gold bar in a camel coat, studded leather boots, and a glittery designer bag. Standing formidable in the middle of the airlock, blocking me by force of character. I went debonair and asked if she'd like to go across the street for coffee but she glared that offer into oblivion, too full of indignation to leave room for refreshment.

"I have nothing to do with mobsters, Mr. Manos." I expressed surprise. "I believe you!"

"That's not what you've been claiming. You have been stating in print that I'm mixed up with the mob, which is legal libel. You listen to me." And she came towards me in a decidedly unladylike fashion. "I have certainly made errors in judgment, and maybe was led astray and handed the wrong idea about how these things work. But the fact is I help people when no one else does. If I make money too that's my private business."

A woman pushed through from the lobby, giving us a curious stare in passing; a slim, well-toned professional in a trench coat carrying a soft leather briefcase that matched her beautifully cut chestnut hair. Mimi used that breathing space to readjust her costume and perhaps recover from her initial explosion. As a matter of fact, she looked better, comfortable. Much of the terror was gone; she was on familiar ground now, fighting in the open. "And I do help people, not just in hospitals but in the projects and in houses that are practically falling down on their heads, seeing that they get treated like human beings. So I don't need some holier-than-thou intimating that I'm conspiring with criminals."

"I think you're the victim of a misapprehension. I never intended to imply that you knew or were in any way connected to Mr. Manetti. On the contrary, I've attempted to make clear that there's only a coincidental connection between the city corruption scandal in which you're possibly involved and a separate pending blackmail scandal involving the Columbus proposal and Mr. Manetti."

Stepping back, she scrutinized me from out of the protection of her outrage, reminding me of a suspicious turtle; I could see her anger diminishing like the daylight still lingering there on the horizon. After a moment, she gave a decisive nod and simply decamped.

And even Crystal manifested at MacIlhenny's one evening, incidentally a place she liked to hang out despite the addicts and intellectuals. Go figure. She came in dressed down in jeans and minor makeup, dragging in this fresh-faced, hulking dude and sitting cozy at the end of the bar. "A real attorney," she said.

He engulfed my hand in a careless giant's grip. "I hear you wanted to be a lawyer yourself."

"I learned better."

"Ha!" He gulped his beer and gave me a professional once- over. "So what's the real story on Askew, anyway? You must have some idea."

I just shrugged, tired and troubled. They seemed tolerably content but I judged them both too superficial to

315

tolerate each other for long. Soon enough he'll stop being manageable and she'll get anxious because underneath it all she's empty. Later he'll try to remember her but not be able to recall anyone in particular so he'll make something up.

She looked up at me and asked about the story, so of course I expanded on it and on my future plans, but she listened with a distracted version of her usual flattering attention so I could tell she wasn't that impressed, and anyway I was still insulted by her lack of faith. The public was likewise treated to a succession of necessary encounters, explanations to the city. One such obviously from Tim Baylor, firmly facing the cameras lurking outside his recently ravished offices to explicitly refute every scurrilous allegation and welcome a full investigation. Yes, he certainly handled any number of lucrative legal matters on behalf of the city and yes, he also encouraged potential business associates to contribute as generously as possible to certain political action committees supporting the aims of the incumbent. So what? Moreover, he'd heard truly despicable rumors concerning a wonderful charitable organization, PhillyCares, simply due to his involvement. That concern must under no circumstances become collateral damage, a victim of confusion. He would not permit innocent people already facing tough circumstances to be further harmed by media or political opportunism.

He seemed as blandly self-assured as usual, not that I expected less, standing there broad-shouldered and stalwart in front of the double glass doors to his personal suite, the gold etching partially visible behind him. "Yes, I firmly believe, and I know that others targeted by this particular investigation believe, that there are strong indications of political shenanigans, that there are political factors behind these allegations involving Harrisburg and even Washington. And we will not rest until we make clear to this community exactly what's really going on here. We will, quite simply, prevail. We will refuse to let this happen."

So nothing but the usual unimaginative corruption, the kind you've forgotten next month.

Meanwhile Ruth punctiliously fulfilled her own public responsibilities, stifling real strain and bewilderment, sheltering behind the empty rituals of traditional bravery. I called her as a duty, although to be honest I just wanted to talk about him.

"Dear Con." That distinctive, vibrant voice hungrily consuming my concern, sliding right back into our false confidentially. "Everything is so horrible." And I mumbled a meaningless response but she was determined to continue right over me, overriding her own discretion with sheer speed. "No, you don't understand. Right before he left I was literally screaming at him. The last words we ever had."

"Screaming?"

"Because he was insisting again about PhillyCares and Mealy, that I separate myself immediately, all that crap, and he just would not let it go. And I told him it was exactly the excuse the station needed, dragging them into that, and I wasn't going to cut my own throat." She paused there and I waited her out. "You know what I've been going through, the deceit and hidden agendas and all the corporate shit. They would have thrown me out like a piece of garbage. They probably will now anyway." With a painful throat, suppressed tears starting to hurt. "Well, I'm sure he realized that?" I didn't really know what to say.

"Not enough. You know how I can never admit failure. I never really let him see how bad it's been." And then I suppose the strain overwhelmed her because she apologized crying and hung up.

"He must have been worried out of his mind," I said to no one. And it was so simply, terribly sad. Thom imprisoned himself in his own ideal of romantic love, and Ruth expanded under his effusive adoration even more than she did from my own stupidly flattering attentions. His idealization whetted rather than satisfied her starved soul.

CHAPTER SEVENTEEN

Finally, we were treated to the full Manetti-Columbus revelation, including Ruth's own accidental role, making her look a fool. This all proved a satisfying comedic interlude, the innumerable fraud, conspiracy, and extortion charges coming down against the various players. The pay-to-play scandal fell below the fold not merely because of the Landing and the coincidence of Thom's involvement but because the whole Columbus affair was so unbelievably fucking stupid, a veritable testament to mind- boggling idiocy, in fact too stupid for a sane person to imagine which is why no one had. In a perfectly straightforward, preposterously optimistic scheme Manetti outright demanded a flat million from the potential Columbus developers as a prerequisite to facilitating passage of the necessary approvals, guaranteeing results. I simply he figured Columbus had the deepest pockets. Megan literally sputtered in disbelief: "That's it? That was their whole plan?" She made me laugh, and she swiveled to look at me like I was responsible.

"The whole world runs on stupidity," I explained, but the truth is I was pretty shocked myself. I always am, but I'm not surprised at the same time. Maybe it's common, but how can any rational person grasp the amazing depth of ignorance loose in the world at any one time? It turned out the Columbus developers themselves had tipped off the feds because of course they had, why wouldn't they? It made for a universally depressing situation.

Even today I don't know exactly what Manetti had on PhillyCares, but that organization, when examined under the spotlight of the Baylor investigation, proved to be a hotbed of tax evasion and ghost employees, all entirely Mimi Norton's doing. No wonder she was reluctant to let Ruth drag her further into the limelight. No wonder she risked it, in the end. So Baylor was right, PhillyCares was collateral damage.

And then people started intimating that Thom Askew was murdered because that was the obvious conclusion unless you were naïve or protecting your own interests.

So Margery promptly stepped forward to answer the public clamor for justice, her authoritative voice confronting the issue in heartfelt, resonant syllables "I want to address this publicly." She'd just emerged from an emergency meeting of the Commerce Committee and was staring, I thought, directly at me, although admittedly there were only a few of us present. She stood unflinching as ever, demanding our respect, both hands holding a huge purse against her black pencil skirt.

"Suspicion is not unreasonable given the circumstances." That evoked an interested murmur and a satisfactory flurry of questions, all welcomed with a determined nod. Isn't it wonderful how absolute transparency absolves you of responsibility? We could tell it was going to turn out exactly the way everyone wanted, plus now we were allowed to discuss it.

"Thom Askew fought for reform; he fought for an ethics bill that addresses the very abuses our papers are full of today. Through no fault of his own he was caught up in the investigation into corruption in City Hall. He was key to the Penn's Landing decision and incidentally connected to the criminal machinations surrounding the Columbus project. It's imperative that the current uncertainty be addressed."

I'd forgotten about the ethics bill, but it was irrelevant anyway now she was utilizing her God-given right to throw reason overboard whenever it suited. Can't let facts impede the great design. I mean, what do proof or reasons have to do with her kind of visceral truth? "My own opinion? I think there's more to this story. That's what my experience tells me, but I don't yet know any more than any of you. I am not rushing to judgment nor should anyone else."

I pushed after her down the corridor to cut off her retreat and tried to shove myself in front of her but she kept moving, a determined general, so I had to yell at her from the side. "What is the matter with you?" My voice was squeaking, I was so furious. "Do you realize what you've done?"

I suppose I looked borderline insane, frenzied hair and feral snarl. Margery stopped then and stared down at me with a kind of exasperation, gathering her doctrine. "I'm not about to permit this matter to slide under the rug. I am not that person." All lit up inside, her spiritual self tremendously, even sexually excited over this new hold on the future. "And you can stop glaring at me. And please spare me another of your endless condescending explanations. I'm in no mood for more of your self-serving shit."

So I backed up and then turned aside from that broad, burnished face carved in absolute conviction. I've never patronized her: if I offended it was out of ignorance. I know myself what it's like to be invisible or else humored, the deadliest insult of all, so I suppose it's inevitable I return the favor when I can, but it won't happen again with Margery now I realize how resentful she is. I started to retreat but she came behind me to address the back of my head: "I've talked to the witnesses, the ones who saw the other man. Have you? No, because you know everything already, except how things work in this world. You have no clue about what really goes on."

Sure. In her alternate reality.

The following week she busied herself conferring intently with assorted peers, the goal being the belated passage of the aforementioned ethics bill in tribute to Thom. Johnny Spivak joined in, and Harry Ciccarelli made the appropriate executive noises. June Dupre likewise automatically threw in her support along with a little crude opportunism. "I know I speak for all of us in expressing my deep personal grief." In fact she looked mildly stunned but resolute and oddly luminous. "Today I acknowledge a personal obligation to carry on the legacy of Councilman Askew, his generosity of spirit and his belief in the future of our city."

So she was looking to usurp the mantle. Good luck to her, because she makes a poor wannabe idol. Anyway now we have the Ethics Board and various other safeguards to prevent any such scandal recurring so in that sense we've finally entered a new political era.

David's performance was muted compared to his colleagues', more a solemn acquiescence to an obvious city imperative. But he stepped up to that responsibility oh so eagerly, giddy like all of them from the sense of fresh opportunity brightening City Hall, not a fading don after all but a man expanding his personal power. I knew I wasn't imagining it then, and now you see I was right.

"We all need to be patient." This was up in the hallway outside Council, David pausing beside a smallish statue of some minor foreign patriot. Unusually resolute, as was due the urgent situation, and as always emanating that measured solidity. "First, I myself promise that the people of this city will achieve the honest administration they deserve; I am making this promise. Regarding the heartbreaking loss of my friend and colleague, of course we all understand that the circumstances require clarification, and I'm confident our various law enforcement agencies will successfully unearth the complete truth.

In retrospect, I'm amazed how completely blind I was to David's enormous ambition. He literally couldn't resist, that's all it was, not with the incumbent badly damaged by innuendo. So there he was shifting over into an entirely different psychic landscape, marching towards oblivion with his customary grave aplomb.

One way or another the barbarians always win, don't they? Futile to reiterate the results of the thorough police investigation with the feds right at their shoulder, already completed for God's sake with nothing suspicious discovered, the kid in the car not connected to anybody, no student loans magically disappearing, no credible evidence of anything else. Only nobody's fool enough to trust official information these days. Why bother to point out how Thom had nothing on Baylor or Manetti or even Mealy, how his death served nobody, that there wasn't a single coherent motive and the conspiracy shit was the result of dim- witted self-indulgence coupled with that new refusal to admit that facts can even exist. Post-truth truth is a public prerogative, the ignorant rabble is in control and they know it, and what they wanted, what Philadelphia wanted was a great municipal martyr, a city saint, a fucking people's hero.

I understood all this but I tried anyway, although the suspicions were already so certain, entrenched in all the media. The most popular had someone with Thom to push him into the path of the car; there were even witnesses who saw the two men together that night. Several times I was accused of being part of the cover-up, identified with evil as personified by Manetti or Baylor or the mayor, or that anonymous enemy of everything that benefits ordinary people, or the dark matter warping the cosmos.

But then, Thom himself deliberately lied to us, flattered us mercilessly in his own interest, unfairly appropriated every glittering ideal to reflect his own ambitions. It was utterly fucking irresponsible, and now we've lost our lodestone, we have no one to perform for or impress. I don't say it's necessarily wrong to represent wonderful ideals, only now we're left with these lovely imposed imperatives we can never achieve, splendid self-images we can never equal, so instead we cherish the hidden enemies that keep us brave failures.

We caught Mealy posturing along a downtown side street one morning, surrounded by the requisite grim phalanx of attorneys and flunkies but supported by a distant light of redemption beckoning from beyond this undeserved ordeal. Automatically smoothing his mane for the cameras, smiling but for once not too broadly because understandably furious at these outrageous deliberate distortions. The wife, essentially plastic in a neighborhood brunette way, hung onto his elbow and precisely mirrored his expressions, staring into his face devotedly while dutifully aping outrage or determination.

Manetti made a far better impression traversing a similar back street, wifeless, ordinary, and businesslike, saluting us without rancor if without much interest. Why not? He'd be back soon enough; no one gets too stressed over non-violent mob activity these days. He stopped just long enough to deliver a final statement to the city. "In so far as any rumors going around that I had a hand in the death of Councilman Askew, let me say this is bullshit. For me, this was an upstanding gentleman and I personally never had any argument with him."

The Columbus developers exited the stage as if eagerly awaiting their cue, while the backers virtually vanished in place. As for a Center City casino, despite Margery's dire prediction that final license was awarded to the sports complex area in South Philly, pretty much where it was first meant to go some eons ago. And that actually makes sense, doesn't it? As for the Landing, there's been some talk about a walkway under the highway but I don't see how that's much of an improvement since you can already walk over it.

And Ruth, that favorite of immoral providence, floated above these tumultuous currents, always at her best in times of chaos, mysteriously immaculate and for an extended sympathetic interregnum utterly untouchable. At PHA the flowers and tweets and email condolences from caring or dutiful souls blessed her office and spread out over the general premises until they were carted off to some hospital. Meanwhile Ruth moved with the requisite quiet dignity around the cubicles and down the bland corridors, past the half-opened doors, sometimes distracted but always essentially competent, always a professional.

Stanley faced her full on one early morning to deliver the required compassion. "You should take a break, go take some time for yourself. We would have no problem under the circumstances." It was just short of an order. Only she hadn't really wanted even her legal bereavement leave, there was just no real choice. "It's like being made to feel like a fraud because you don't grieve the right way. Fuck them." You had to remember that she'd only just lost her father as well, that her earth was moving. Bob offered a supportive neutrality; even Jenny was vaguely warm. Clearly some cosmic consciousness was monitoring them, compelling this simulation of concern. "But it's right," Ruth said. "It's about respect for our common humanity. And it buys me time, because I absolutely can't stay here. I'm just waiting for the right door to open. I know it'll happen."

Perhaps she was right, because although Stanley was let go not many months later I think Jenny's still at PHA. And there were signs Ruth was recovering that perilous snarky edge. For example, an on-air call from a young woman, probably in her thirties and nearly sobbing in empathy: "It's so inspiring that you still believe in God. I don't think I could."

That silence went on so dangerously long it made me look towards the radio, until finally: "Maybe you should get a better grasp of life on this planet."

Even so, there was noticeably less of that outlandish wildness and defiance and originality: she was too busy scrambling around for some idea of who she was supposed to be now.

And she was obviously still a fortunate woman with plentiful options and connections. She accepted an email invitation to a dinner for supporters of Children's Hospital, another institution where she'd extolled the munificence of PhillyCares. This was up at the Crystal Tea Room at the Wanamaker Building, a lovely venue, all chandeliers and pink and gilding, although with trashed odds and ends stashed in convenient unlovely corners and a bit of wearing on the chairs. The shabby-genteel ambience adds a comforting element, so it's a popular site for ladies' lunches and moderately high-profile non-profit events.

Ruth picked up her folded name card from the maitre d's podium, scouting the tables for a friendly face, wandering critically through the seated scattering of quiet but influential supporters and pragmatic physicians and realistic administrators. No familiar face looked up at her, no welcoming glance invited her to join any table she lingered near. Probably these stalwarts identified her with the PhillyCares fiasco, or maybe they intuitively recognized the ignorant, untried soul beneath the shoddy braggadocio, the personality never satisfied to be one among equals but forever aiming to surpass. Maybe coming was a stupid mistake. She identified an elderly female with untidy gray hair and an agreeable demeanor, an oncologist she'd worked with on several occasions; memory evoked the face of a hairless teenager infused with that infinitely optimistic expression they all have, his nearly translucent fingers unwrapping the present they'd brought for a boy his age.

So she insinuated herself into the woman's party, bestowing slight indiscriminate smiles and nods to the company, reaching out to gently stroke one of the silky leaves in the centerpiece. One bearded middle-aged man gave her a fleeting and mistakenly familiar smile before abruptly turning back to his conversation. No recognition anywhere despite all the recent press; these people had better things to do.

Ruth tapped her card around to make her name visible and fixed the older woman with a meaningful gaze, forcing the poor woman to give an obviously spurious start of surprise and wrap her in a brief, belated hug. To Ruth, always overly sensitive, it felt like a slap.

Certainly she evoked no real interest from this congregation of the truly experienced and proficient, these clubby casuists making Ruth's irrelevance clear. Or so she felt, stuck there swallowing indifferent house chardonnay for courage, barely masticating course after course of unremarkable food, enviously monitoring the spoken and tacit praise being passed among these estimable individuals. Seventy dollars worth of mortification.

She said, "People rejoicing in their ability to help others. I was jealous and humiliated. Sometimes I'm so ashamed of myself it's like a sickness of the soul."

This was during one of our final real conversations, Ruth purporting to view this unfortunate dinner as a gift, a shove along the road to greater authenticity. Today I know her next move was already well underway, the critical decisions made. Also from this conversation, another troubling dream or vision: "I saw Kate dancing. She was about twenty, and she was radiant with this wonderful open smile, and she was dancing sort of side to side like a marionette. And I was scared to death. I can't lose her yet. I can't." Even while she dreaded being with her aunt, with having to endure the endless, vicious praise of Pat the Perfect and his wondrous offspring, those recipients of all the Dougherty energy and hugs and support as opposed to Ruth, so justly discounted and ignored. Everything was moving away though, and taking her outrage with it. The problem with the dead is they're so easy to forgive, but to forgive and let go is to confer absolution, demonstrate that they never hurt you all that much too begin with. You lose your righteous edge.

When there we were in Center City one beautiful Fourth of July morning: Ruth, most members of Council, sufficient press, and the mayor along with the surviving remnants of his administration. Representatives of the Mural Arts Program sat up front with the other dignitaries, accompanied by a covey of proud volunteers from the immediate neighborhood, everyone facing the side of an art house movie theatre a short walk up from Penn's Landing at Walnut Street. The mural itself was still shrouded beneath two stories of blue tarp crisscrossed with a nylon line of diminutive American flags that flattened and flipped in an incessant breeze, and the tarp likewise billowed and fell, everything intricately alive, the invitees constantly pushing their hair out of their faces and holding tight to their programs. Usually the Fourth brings us scorching heat with the threat of thunderstorms, but that day was temperate, and the interfering wind - an insistent horsefly, an uninvited ghost – made the light unreliable, shifting everything erratically from industrial gray to a bright glare and back again to reproachful shadow.

They'd arranged the audience in a semicircle that completely blocked the sidewalk, with a flimsy podium sprouting multiple microphones the focal point. Curious pedestrians, forced to walk in the street, kept rudely close to the protective municipal sawhorses, some lingering to become spectators themselves, curious to see what kind of memorable experience they'd lucked into.

Ruth was in an off-white silk suit; with a nice bouquet it would have made a fine mature wedding costume. A modest bride, she was sitting remarkably still, her hands crossed neatly over the tiny purse in her lap. And she gazed straight forward, betraying neither expectation nor agitation, merely occupying the moment.

Our mayor looked around at all of us, bestowing his prim smile. "We are here to celebrate a life." He settled into a lecturer's quiet authority, ignoring conversing passers-by and the staccato midtown traffic. "A life worthy of this great city." Margery sat squarely in front of the podium, serious and sure. June's bowed head was just visible far off to my right, near the street, that cap of golden brown hair politely tilted. And David sat skewed sideways in his chair in the second row, critically alert.

"I know we often disparage this city and we have reason too, in fact we must redeem our shameful history of unchecked greed and ingrained corruption and deliberate callousness towards our fellow citizens. But I do not despair," the mayor continued in that soft voice, standing there with both hands on the podium. "Indeed, I take heart every time I look out at a gathering such as this one and see so many individuals who work to make things better. Selflessly and consistently, year after year, exhibiting a truly humbling dedication. But out of even that incredibly impressive group, some extraordinary individuals rise far above the rest."

Ruth was seriously listening to this crap; a random remark in the audience caught her ear and she turned, affronted, where I knew Thom would have relished decimating this show. From my position leaning against a protruding corner of the wall I saw her lean over to exchange a word with Gerry Bright, sitting next to her; Bright responded with a bland, avuncular smile, a politician's smile, practically patting her knee.

"These are people who are intrinsically fine. We all recognize them. We all treasure them. We all secretly wish we were them, born with their great grace and their wisdom and their charm. Their inherent nobility. They demand our attention and our respect. In today's world where the media creates instant but temporary fame, we who have the trust of the people must remember and honor those we recognize as great." Here he paused to scan the assembled members of the press in a rather accusatory manner. And finally he turned to the covered wall.

June had her jaw thrust forward to show devotion. We'd met earlier; actually she'd practically pounced on me as I arrived, her hand immediately at my sleeve. Moving up close, meeting my automatic smile with unwarranted intimacy. "How're you doing?" Not waiting for a reply. "I still can't really deal with this."

It took me a minute to unravel her expression, and then I was startled into a rude laugh. She shook her head and then placed her other hand on my other arm as if we were about to dance.

"You didn't know? Seriously, you never suspected?" And she certainly seemed surprised. "Well, you see what it is, guilt all mixed up with grief."

With those anxious eyes emanating wary tragedy, anxious to appropriate the widow's privilege. I broke away, muttering something or other, shocking her a little with my churlish behavior.

And the worst of that is, even though it's crazy and it turns the whole world upside down, I still have to wonder. So, she wins. "I don't have to tell you about the wonderful work done by the Mural Arts Program. Wherever they place one of their magnificent works, they incorporate members of the neighborhood into their designs, and they insure that the themes they depict have significance to the people who will see them every day. They utilize the willing hands of the community to manifest those paintings, those visions of hope and mutual support that everywhere redeem the otherwise blank or graffiti- infested walls of our city. I don't have to point out to you how appropriate the choice of subject matter is in the particular example of their art we are met to unveil today, this holiday of all days, in this city of all cities."

Margery, still apparently delighted to be through with me, had Harry Ciccarelli up front next to her, with Spivak and Murphy right behind, all four leaning confidentially towards each other but not speaking. There was some kind of energy around them. They were up to something. Shit.

The workmen up on the scaffolding were waiting, as were the two on the sidewalk, one at each side of the shroud. At the mayor's signal, they gave a couple of surprisingly gentle tugs, expertly allowing the cloth to collapse into a blue puddle on the cement.

And there was Thom, huge and irrepressible, all fulsome ugly grin, slouching just as usual behind a desk that skewed out towards the viewer. Both the immediate foreground and panoramic background surrounded him with images lauding his public concerns - street vendors and capped university graduates, the elderly in wheelchairs, construction workers, police and firefighters, businessmen with briefcases - all this colorful array painted in varied disproportion against the idea of an active office or the milky Philadelphia sky. And there was City Hall in the background, too, with Billy Penn peering over Thom's shoulder. When unexpectedly if discreetly I started to cry.

CHAPTER EIGHTEEN

Back in my real life, an existence entirely unrelated to most of this narrative, I went and bought my first house. Invested in a false image of stability, and me a forty-year-old with a teenager and no future. It was a single in an established neighborhood in East Falls, which is a decent kind of place despite being technically in the city, with just enough grass and sidewalk trees and flower beds and squirrels to make it feel like a happy cliché. Obviously, this was partly about Sophie, but it was equally about my search for permanence. Or maybe I was nesting, pregnant with whatever new self I was turning into for the next time being. There was an outside, a tiny front patio with a wrought iron railing, and a narrow backyard for some patio furniture and a barbecue. The kitchen has sufficient space for a table to sit around and converse like a suppressed intellectual, and I bought a new television to properly consecrate the family hearth. The neighborhood isn't exactly city or suburb; it's more like an idealized small town with porches and bicycles and front doors with lace curtains. Residents care about their gardens: their flowering magnolias and cherry trees, their summer tomatoes and herbs. They care about their neighborhood, their world, their pets, their climate, their schools, and their bowels. It's fairly pleasant, and I think I'll be reasonably content.

Now that we'd actually selected one of those tiny Realtor's offerings my daughter found it way too modest and common; that's her age, but I had to agree, it was anyone's unremarkable house as opposed to our reputedly hip city digs. That was kind of the point, but normalcy is an insult to her these days. She's morphing into a surface radical, all clothes and attitude, which I guess is inevitable. I don't mind because we both know her sensible inner compass keeps her pointing towards the conventional. She is no dreamer. When I suggested she use her excellent math skills for aviation, even space exploration, she said, "Fuck you, Dad," and turned back to her phone. I can see her becoming a corporate executive or some other dull success like that.

The paper moved too, fatalistically abandoning its venerable tower, its spiritual as well as material body. What remained of its tattered soul flitted to offices in an old department store building on lower Market Street, a regulation cubicle farm with happy designer touches in primary colors, kind of a cross between temporary garage quarters and clown college.

I knew I wouldn't linger, not that this is entirely by choice. Our newsroom was merged with that of our sister tabloid, and there were cutbacks, lots of them, including Megan. We hugged; she cried a little, and now I have a new, competitive cohort. I miss Megan's grudging support.

And then, unbelievably, the entire business was simply gifted away to a non-profit created solely for the purpose of preserving a traditional newspaper for the city.

We've become an admitted artifact, a museum exhibit. So I've decided to deal more directly with the universe. Truth and justice! Because what choice do I have? So this book first of all, not to be obvious, and I think I'll be free of all this extra weight once it's finished and out there. Arguably I've been tending this way my whole life. Plus my truth actually is better than yours. And wouldn't it be wonderfully ironic if I ended up in radio? Again, seriously, what's the alternative? Trusting in something else? What did you have in mind? The world is splitting into irreconcilable pieces and reforming in some unimaginable way. People think they've got it figured out but they're wrong, it's a cataclysm, even the rules of change are changing.

My conversations with Ruth, always sporadic, died out completely at that time; neither of us had any more interest in that misbegotten profile. But I recall one last phone call where she shared an anecdote from before her marriage. She's riding in a car with another woman when her friend started talking about angels, claiming she once narrowly avoided being hit by a swerving truck only because of this young man in a brown coat who came out of nowhere. Ruth said, "I knew it was true because I've known angels wear brown coats since I was little. Once one came and sat on our front steps." I have no idea what that was about, but she wanted to share it with me.

And then with no discernable break: "You know I only stopped being afraid once I realized I was a victim s there was nothing wrong with me, it was them. That was the most valuable insight I've ever experienced in my life, that vindication. It dissolved all my confusion. I can't even remember what I thought about myself before then. Even my dad totally agreed in the end; it was in his eyes. It was how I won.

Which brings us around to August again with fall edging in, a swallowtail butterfly slitting over skittering brown leaves. I'd been to the Askew house in Chestnut Hill a few times for formal holiday gatherings, nothing personal. The vicinity mimics an upscale suburb but it's actually located within city limits, making it a convenient situation for those affluent officials required to maintain a primary residence within Philadelphia. There's some rather attractive architecture, venerable landscaping, and a lot of quaint retail and faux Colonial crap. Chestnut Hill was incorporated into the city in the mid-

18th century after the Nativist Riots, an anti-Catholic movement reacting to complaints about Catholic children having to read from the Protestant bible in school. Rumors spread, churches and homes were burned, people died.

Back in 1844, if you needed law enforcement in an outlying area you asked a constable to get the county sheriff to collect a posse, so it wasn't easy keeping the peace. Rioting exploded again around July 4th that year, and somebody got hold of a cannon and fired it. The clear need for adequate peacekeeping culminated in the Act of 1854, which made the city and county coterminous and incidentally condemned the Philadelphia County Sheriff's Office to such vestigial duties as shuttling prisoners to court and auctioning off foreclosed property. Any number of regional small towns with their own industries and ethnicities were abruptly combined in name but nothing approximating fact, evolving over the decades into our current city of distinct neighborhoods. So if colonial

Philadelphia was born of Quaker tolerance, today's larger city is the legacy of religious bigotry.

Anyway, Chestnut Hill is on the whole a lovely place, with gray fieldstone houses shining silver, much wrought iron, generous shade trees, and gardens bordered with humungous azalea hedges, a springtime explosion of pink and white. The precious pseudo-Colonial shopping blocks gleam with the plate glass of familiar chain emporiums, trendy eateries, and that upscale cutesy element of gift shops, boutiques, and art galleries.

The Askew place was another square gray pile set back on a standard lawn with one young sugar maple, a white wrought iron bench next to the front door, and two balanced oval flower beds planted with an explosive array of orange marigolds, crimson salvia, and something taller and feathery in silver, a vibrant professional tableau with no redeeming idiosyncrasy. Very young firs in a strict row formed a palisade along one side of the property, and the windows had shutters painted what was no doubt an historically authentic shade of dull green.

A small crescent of bricks marked the doorway, and on that sunny afternoon it featured a semicircle of microphones: Ruth was going to make some kind of statement. She'd called to invite me, in fact insisted I be there, so I anticipated a charitable endeavor in Thom's name, heartfelt and fairly high profile, a providential career path and fount of personal respect. An ideal solution, a personal victory.

Of course I should have known better. And then the unexpectedly healthy crowd, the news vans at the curb, and that sense of something actually going on I should have known about.

Even so my immediate reaction, seeing them in the open doorway, was utter stupefaction. There was Harry Ciccarelli with Ruth, and Gerry Bright just visible behind them. And then I wondered how the hell I could be so dumb. Of course they'd suggest it. Of course she'd agree.

Bright spoke first, sketching out the background, coming across as properly honored but deeply satisfied. "As you all know, Council currently faces the difficult task of filling a vacant seat." An unremarkable loyalist was already in van Zandt's chair, designated a permanent replacement, and that wasn't the Democrats' concern anyway. They were busy pressuring Mealy to resign, eager to replace him with a younger, uncontaminated union lawyer.

And Ruth Askew would replace her late husband as Councilperson-At-Large, pending the almost certain result of a special election in November. Rising on his exalted reputation rather than her own clouded name, acquiring the remaining three years of his term and potentially additional terms.

"As a Democrat?"

I wasn't the one asking, but she found me in the assemblage and gave me a little grin. "Not actually a surprise, is it?" And that was true, considering she'd inherited Thom's huge moral legacy, and also because somehow it wasn't a surprise. Only there was still the issue of all that year's outrageous, gleeful extremism.

"This is about ideals I've always supported with my whole heart." She sent another smile to Bright, deliberately impish, like a proper cute puppet, then turned back and continued with increased conviction. "What's important is that everyone knows the kind of person I am. But I will say that the Democratic Party was my first political home; it was my father's party and it gave me my ideals about what government could accomplish. My husband represented those ideals better than anyone else I've ever met, and I'm proud to be able to carry on his work."

Plus they asked; they wanted her. Don't overlook the importance of that conciliatory move towards the bitter prodigal daughter.

The two men were moving apart, both emanating an exhausted gratification that spoke of an unpleasant task expertly completed. Ruth continued on for a bit but nothing else pertinent was said, everything was perfectly clear.

While we were milling around in departure she came over to me. "Stay a few minutes." So I trailed inside after her, into that studied display of intimate comfort.

Books everywhere, a self-congratulatory show of erudition - or more than a show, it was sheer exhibitionism. Books casually stacked on the coffee table with their titles every which way, built-in shelves with paperbacks in front of hardcovers, books in half-cases on the balcony overlooking the great room. Mysteries and history and popular science, politics and law and religion, contemporary literary novels from every prestigious short list and classics in matching covers: Dickens and Austen, Lawrence and Hemingway, Salinger and Twain and two Durrells. Various sections dedicated to momentary enthusiasms: Jack the Ripper, the Knights Templar, Colonial-era Africa. Jean Kerr and Dave Barry with a volume of Perelman pieces. Heinlein and Asimov, histories from Tuchman and Ambrose and Boorstin. Best-sellers by political pundits of every stripe, biographies galore, works of French literature both modern and ancient with the balance in French (did either Askew read French?), obscure British satire from the middle of the last century, Kerouac and Ginsberg and Ferlinghetti. Books to impress, compulsively acquired and clearly considered holy.

They had only original art, running the style spectrum but all rather pleasant and some actually good although nothing outstanding, nothing that soared. Otherwise the furniture was contemporary, beige and bland, accented with unfashionable brass lamps, blue and yellow ceramics, and a tattered quilt draped over a chair back like pretentious sunshine.

I reached down a framed photograph from the white marble mantle. "This is your father?" A thin man with a strong nose, Ruth's nose, and hazel eyes that challenged you in order to conceal; he posed with a narcissist's ease, confident of his good looks. I wouldn't have trusted him much, myself; he struck me as a superficial type, the kind of guy who prefers shrewdness to intellect, who loves a clever angle.

Ruth perched herself on one corner of the sofa, legs crossed at the knee as was proper for her skirted suit, and gestured me to the easy chair opposite. "I've decided to sell this house. It's hard but I think it'll be better if I make a fresh start."

There was a dog, which I never knew and wouldn't have suspected; a feathered Irish Setter with tags dangling at its neck suddenly bustling about the coffee table being friendly and inquisitive. He tried to inspect my crotch with an intrusive nose and Ruth took him by his collar and stroked his head.

341

"He was a Christmas present from Thom, as if I were a little girl. It was wonderful." Then she sat up and adopted that familiar earnest expression and got to the point.

"It's a way to make sense of things." In fact it was brilliant, an impeccable professional escape.

"Except your husband's death was senseless."

She tilted her head and got a bit fervent. "Everything has meaning. What it turns out to be is for me to determine."

"That's crap." I said. "It's cheap. You know better."

"I know you blame me. You think he was upset and distracted, hurrying home."

"So do you."

"Maybe. Probably I guess."

How brave. I'll tell you something else I think: I think a certain kind of man might find himself in a situation where the only possible resolution is a fatal mistake. In the end, every man constructs his own death. She was waiting, I suppose automatically expecting my admiration or sympathy. But eventually she sighed and straightened, resuming that pleasant but businesslike demeanor. "May I have your professional opinion? Will I crash and burn?"

"Maybe" I couldn't begin to grasp the possibilities. "I don't know. Or maybe not." She could be so competent, so easily successful. Or would the crazy kick in again, if it ever left? "Or maybe you'll learn something."

"Well, I'll be giving it all I have. But you know, I think politics is where I belong; it feels right. It fits." That with finality, and she stood in dismissal; even the dog was on its feet, favoring me with that typical befuddled dog stare. I rose obediently and stood there across from her, not wanting to think yet.

She was looking at me from those huge blue eyes with their familiar intensity. "I want you to understand this isn't just about ambition or even about having a purpose in life. It's so much more. It's a reclamation."

visit Mike Miller at www.asmikemiller.com
or on Twitter at @asmikemiller

Made in the USA
Middletown, DE
14 May 2017